TABULA RASA

BY THE SAME AUTHOR

Medicus
Terra Incognita
Persona Non Grata
Caveat Emptor
Semper Fidelis

TABULA RASA

A Crime Novel of the Roman Empire

RUTH DOWNIE

BLOOMSBURY

NEW YORK · LONDON · NEW DELHI · SYDNEY

Published by Bloomsbury USA, New York
Bloomsbury is a trademark of Bloomsbury Publishing, Plc

All papers used by Bloomsbury USA are natural, recyclable products made
from wood grown in well-managed forests. The manufacturing processes
conform to the environmental regulations of the country of origin.

LIBRARY OF CONGRESS CATALOGING-IN-PUBLICATION DATA HAS BEEN APPLIED FOR.

ISBN: 978-1-60819-708-8

First U.S. Edition 2014

1   3   5   7   9   10   8   6   4   2

Typeset by Hewer Text UK Ltd, Edinburgh
Printed and bound in the U.S.A. by Thomson-Shore Inc., Dexter, Michigan

Bloomsbury books may be purchased for business or promotional use.
For information on bulk purchases please contact Macmillan Corporate
and Premium Sales Department at specialmarkets@macmillan.com.

To those who wait, not knowing whether news will ever come.
With respect.

Nescis quid vesper vehat.

You do not know what the evening will bring.

—Macrobius, *Saturnalia*, Book II, 8.2

TABULA RASA

A NOVEL

IN WHICH our hero, Gaius Petreius Ruso, will be . . .

watched by
> Aedic, a boy who sees something amazing

motivated by
> Albanus, his old friend and former clerk
> . . . and by embarrassment

worried by
> Candidus, a young clerk, nephew of Albanus

exasperated by
> Fabius, the local centurion

puzzled by
> Nisus, a pharmacist
> Regulus, a victim of attack by natives
> Grata, the absent girlfriend of Albanus

assisted by
> Virana, a pregnant girl whom nobody else wants
> Gallus, his baby-faced deputy
> Valens, an old friend and colleague
> Mallius, a quarryman with a hen

A lucky charm

led into trouble by
> Tilla, his wife, formerly known as Darlughdacha
> Daminius, a junior officer

surprised by
> Gracilis, a clerk
> Mara, Tilla's mother, long deceased

reassessed by
> Pertinax, formerly the second spear, now promoted to prefect of the camp

informed by
> Olennius, a builder
> Silvanus, Candidus's centurion
> Larentia, a girl with a mole in the right place

misinformed by
> Lupus, a slave dealer
> Piso, Lupus's agent

welcomed by
> Senecio, the head of a native family
> Branan, youngest son of Senecio
> Susanna, an old friend in Coria

not welcomed by
> Conn, an older son of Senecio
> A group of fur traders

fed by
> Enica, wife of Senecio
> Ria, landlady and part owner of the local snack bar
> A kitchen maid

commanded by
> Accius, tribune with the Twentieth Legion

insulted by
> Serena, wife of Valens, and daughter of Pertinax

ignored by
> Rianorix, husband of Tilla's cousin Aemilia

set upon by
> Various Britons, mostly for the best of reasons

And his fate will be influenced—from a distance—by
> Cata, a long-suffering girlfriend
> Dubnus, another son of Senecio (deceased)
> Inam, young neighbor and friend of Branan
> Matto, a bully
> Lucano, elder brother of Matto and a bigger bully
> Petta, stepmother of Aedic
> Pandora, legendary owner of a box (or jar, depending upon who you believe) full of bad things and best never opened.

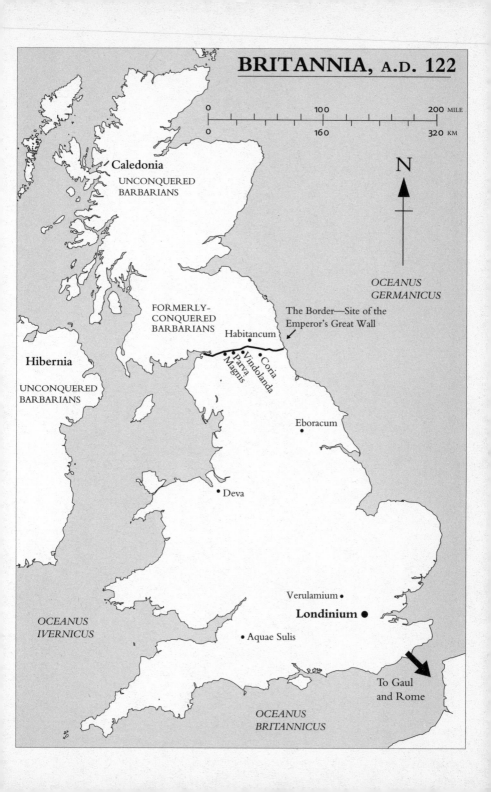

1

IT WAS EASY to believe that the rain threw itself at you personally; hard not to feel persecuted and aggrieved when it found its way into your boots no matter how much grease you slathered on them. It blew in veils across the sides of the hills, whipped along the crests, and cascaded in streams down the valleys. The river had burst its banks, and the meadows beside it mirrored the gray sky. Turf squelched underfoot and supply carts sank into the mud, so that whole gangs who should have been building spent the short daylight hours sloshing about, clearing drains and filling potholes. Men pulled hoods over their heads to stop the wet from going down their necks and then had to keep pushing them back to see properly. Inevitably, there were accidents.

Up at the wall, the rain made earth heavier to shift and washed white streaks of fresh mortar out of the day's build. In the quarry, hammers skidded off the heads of chisels. In the camp, tools and armor went rusty overnight. Doors stuck, leather was clammy, firewood was hard to light, and bedding smelled of damp wool and mold.

And then, after another long night in chilly beds, serenaded by a ragged chorus of coughing and snoring, the builders woke to an innocent morning full of birdsong. The sun rose in a sky that had been rinsed clean. Crisp views stretched for miles across hills that rolled like waves toward the north. Men nodded greetings to each other as they lifted the sides of tents and hung everything out to dry.

Some even dared to hope that the worst was over. Most knew it wouldn't be. This was October, and the weather was only going to get worse. Already a strategic retreat was planned for the end of the month: The legions would march south to hunker down in their winter quarters, leaving the permanent garrison to tough it out here along the line of the emperor's Great Wall until the next building season. If the garrison troops were bored or cold up here, there were—as the legionaries were happy to remind them—plenty of ditches to be dug.

And then it happened.

It was a tearing, gut-wrenching roar, like a thunderbolt crashing into the depths of the underworld and shaking the ground beneath their feet. Medical Officer Gaius Petreius Ruso ducked and clamped his hands over his ears, but the cry of "Earthquake!" died in his throat. The noise wasn't how he remembered it. Besides, this was Britannia, not known for earthquakes, and whatever it was had stopped.

Ruso and his assistant straightened up, glancing at one another as if to confirm they had not imagined it. Beyond the stone wall, a panicked flock of sheep was racing across the hillside. Dogs had begun to bark, sounding the alarm in the surrounding scatter of native farms.

Ruso bent to retrieve his medical case, wiping off the mud on the grass at the side of the track. Several loose pack ponies bolted past him, narrowly avoiding men who were sprinting down from the camp while grimy and breathless figures were hurrying up to meet them. Somewhere over the chaos, a trumpeter was sounding the call to assemble.

Ruso was already heading downhill when a wild-eyed man in a rough work tunic grabbed him by the arm. "Sir, they need a medic in the quarry!"

The quarry, even when it was full of legionaries cutting stone for the emperor's Great Wall, had always seemed relatively peaceful. The *tink-tink* of hammers on wedges rang out like the pecking of metal birds above the gurgling of a stream that was swollen by summer rain. Everything brought in by the army—men, tools, work sheds, lines of plodding ponies, lifting gear, wagons—was dwarfed by the raw cliff face that loomed above them.

But now, as Ruso followed the quarryman down the track to the foot of the cliff, he could see that the far end of the rock face had collapsed into a steep chaos of mud and boulders. He winced, reminded of the devastation caused by the Antioch earthquake. Hundreds of collapsed buildings. Voices calling for help from beneath wreckage too heavy to shift.

The quarrymen were lucky: They had only just retreated to eat their midday bread and cheese in the rare sunshine when the land slipped. Another head count was being conducted, just in case; but as far as anyone knew, the quarry was now empty apart from himself, the half-dozen men of the rescue team, and one unfortunate officer. Ruso's assistant was already hurrying back up to the camp to fetch two sensible orderlies, a light stretcher, straps, and warm blankets.

While the rescuers were checking their ropes and ladders, Ruso eyed the full extent of the slide. At the top, a couple of trees hung over the edge as if they were looking down to see where the ground had gone. Below them, torn branches and splintered wooden scaffolding poles lay on the surface or stuck out at odd angles. Several huge rocks had come to rest partway down the slide, as if they were waiting for some fool to free them with a careless movement so they could tumble down and smash into the others at the bottom.

Daminius, the optio in charge, rubbed his forehead with his fist, adding another streak of grime. Then he raised the arm to point. "See that big boulder there, sir, just past the fallen tree?"

Ruso gulped. He had naïvely assumed that the trapped officer would be lying at ground level. Instead, the limp and muddy shape that he now saw to be a human being was lying head-down on the slope, out of reach. His left leg was scraped and bloody. The right vanished under a massive lump of rock that teetered directly above him.

"Are you sure he's alive?" Ruso murmured, clutching at the hope that they might be too late.

The optio called, "It's all right, sir, hold on! The medic's here."

"I don't n-need a bloody medic," said a voice that Ruso had never heard waver before. "Give me a knife."

Ruso stared. "Pertinax?"

"*Prefect Pertinax* . . . to you, Ruso." He might be seriously injured, but he was still the man who had terrified Ruso ever since one of them had been a very new medic with the Twentieth Legion and the other had already reached the exalted post of second spear.

"Sorry, sir."

"Don't worry, sir," called Daminius. "The lads'll get you down. Just hold on a moment and we'll get them organized."

"I don't want . . ." Pertinax's voice cracked. He tried again, weaker this time. "Can't risk . . . more men. My leg's gone." One bloodstained and filthy hand grasped vainly at the air. "Give me a knife."

Daminius nodded to a man who was approaching with a dripping waterskin tied to a scaffolding pole. Ruso recognized the grubby bandage around a minor sprain of the left wrist, and noted that its owner had abandoned the vanity of being blond since stumbling into the fort hospital a while ago with one eye full of vinegary hair coloring.

Daminius called up, "We're going to get some water to you now, sir. Try not to move about too much."

"A knife." Pertinax repeated. "That's a . . ." He stopped, as if he could not remember the word. "That's an order."

Daminius instructed his man in a voice too low for the prefect to hear, "Gently, eh? If anything moves, drop it and run."

The no-longer-blond man nodded and adjusted his grip on the pole.

"The water's just coming up now, sir."

Pertinax groped toward the skin. Water cascaded down his face before he managed to clamp the opening against his mouth.

Daminius drew Ruso aside. "You see the problem, Doctor?"

"How long has he been asking for a knife?"

"Ever since he realized how things stand."

Ruso said, "If he's up there much longer, he'll die anyway."

"We wondered about getting a rope on and pulling him up . . ."

"Not if the leg's still attached."

Daminius nodded, as if he had already thought of that. "Besides, the movement could bring the whole lot down on top of him."

"Can you stabilize the boulder?"

"It's too high to prop, and too heavy for ropes. And we're not going to dig underneath to get him out."

With a feeling that he was not going to like what came next, Ruso prompted, "So?"

The optio looked at him. "Could you cut the leg free, sir?"

Ruso swallowed. "How am I going to get up there?" Let alone, *how am I going to perform surgery at that angle and in all that filth? And what about that huge boulder teetering over my head?*

Surprisingly white teeth showed as Daminius's filthy face spread into a grin. "That's the spirit, sir. We reckoned if we put you on a rope, you could work your way down and across. Then, once you've got him freed, my lads will come up and get him."

Despite the absence of his centurion—or more likely because of it—Daminius was managing the situation with impressive calm. No wonder they said he would not be hacking rocks out of the ground for long.

Just as this thought crossed Ruso's mind, an imperious voice called, "It's all right, I'm here!" and the rescue party had to stop to salute Centurion Fabius's approach along the track beside the stream. Fabius's horse was being led by his personal slave. His carefully curled hair was in disarray and he was swaying in the saddle. Ruso could smell the drink on his breath as he proceeded to apologize for being delayed, demanded a full update on the situation, and then expressed his shock and dismay. Pertinax, meanwhile, remained trapped.

"We need to make a decision," put in Ruso, who thanked the gods every morning that he had been excused from sharing quarters with Fabius and wished he had not yielded to this morning's request for medicinal wine.

"We need to make a decision," agreed Fabius, lurching to the left and grabbing at the saddle for balance. He frowned at Ruso. "I don't know what's in your medicine, Doctor, but it's making me feel very odd."

"It's up to you, sirs," said Daminius, looking from one officer to the other. "We could do as he asks and give the poor sod a knife."

The waterskin fell from Pertinax's hand, bounced down the rubble, and came to rest just out of reach. The no-longer-blond man poked at it with the pole, and the movement set a couple of stones tumbling down the slope. A loose trickle of earth and more stones slithered to fill the gap, then something shifted above them and a miniature landslide skittered downward. Everyone except Fabius stepped hastily back. It was a moment before anybody spoke again.

"Try not to move, sir," the foreman called, stepping forward to retrieve the empty skin.

There was no reply.

"Sir?" tried Ruso, then, "Pertinax!"

A vague movement of the hand that might have been a wave.

"Oh, dear!" observed Fabius. "He's not looking very good, is he?"

"Prefect Pertinax!" called Ruso, "Are you sleeping on duty?"

"Cold up here," came the mumbled reply.

"A brave man," said Fabius. "Remarkable. Do you think cutting his wrists will work if he's upside down? Or would he have to stab himself in the heart?"

"Won't be long now, sir!" called Ruso, kneeling to check the contents of his medical case and trying not to think about the loose debris above him. "Keep him talking, Daminius."

"If anybody goes up there," observed Fabius, gazing up at the loose slope of debris, "it should be me." But the only action following this noble thought was a hiccup.

Ruso turned to Daminius. "Have someone send an urgent message to the hospital at Magnis for Doctor Valens. He needs to know his father-in-law's been seriously injured."

Ruso felt a hand on his shoulder. Fabius's watery blue eyes looked deep into his own. "Good luck, Doctor. You're the only one—the only one who understands."

"Go back to the fort and lie down," Ruso told him. "And no more reading. It's bad for you."

Fabius nodded gravely, and with, "Carry on, Optio!" he allowed his slave to lead him back toward the very small fort of which he was, to the misfortune of its garrison, commanding officer.

Above them, Pertinax seemed to be groping in vain for a dagger that was not there. Daminius called, "We'll soon have you down from there, sir!"

After they knotted the loop of rope around Ruso's chest, Daminius reached toward him and hung something around his neck. "My lucky charm, sir. Never fails. If you're in trouble, just shout, and the lads'll pull you out."

It was kindly meant, although Ruso could not see how he would escape a further landslip unless he suddenly discovered how to fly. Glancing down at Daminius's charm lying beside his identity tag, he saw that the little bronze phallus did indeed sport a pair of wings. He hoped it was an omen. As he tied a borrowed helmet under his chin he said, "My wife's lodging over Ria's snack bar. If I make a hash of this, you'll have to send somebody up there to tell her."

2

RUSO HAD PICKED his way crablike across several feet of debris
when he put his weight on a stone that slid away under his foot. For
a heart-stopping moment there was nothing beneath him; then the rope
jerked taut around his chest. Now he was suspended, helpless, one side of
his face pressed against cold rock. He forced himself not to claw against
the sides and bring down more debris as he heard the stone skitter on
down the slope. Praying that the men holding his rope would stand firm,
he hung like a creature playing dead, feeling the cut of the rope and the
thud of his heart. Somewhere miles away, voices were asking if he was all
right.

Was he? He didn't know. In what way could a man who might be about
to bring tons of rock down upon himself—as well as his patient—be said
to be all right?

He lifted his head and glanced across to where Pertinax was lying head-
down, eyes closed, just out of reach. The face was gray even under the
grime.

It was not too late to grant the mercy of an honorable suicide. The man
had already enjoyed a long life and reached the pinnacle of his career.
Now that he had assessed the situation from close quarters, Ruso could
decide that Pertinax could not be saved. With opened wrists, the prefect

would have a much quicker and cleaner death than he might have to suffer in the aftermath of dirty wounds. And everyone would say Ruso had done the right thing.

Daminius was calling, "Are you all right, Doctor?"

"Wait a moment!"

If only he had been given time to prepare for this. If only he had not wasted the morning dealing with trivia: trying to find reasons not to eat supper with his wife's dubious acquaintances; complaining about the odd disappearance of his new hospital clerk; hearing a long trail of petty grievances from men who imagined he could do something about them.

He muttered a prayer to Aesculapius for the surgery and one to Fortuna for a lucky escape, and took another look. The trapped leg was visible just above the ankle. There seemed to be a second boulder beneath it, pinning it in place. The foot was probably crushed beyond repair.

Only a few more inches and Pertinax might have tumbled down the slope to safety. Now if he were to be rescued, Ruso would have to work his way up under the overhang of rock and crouch there, slicing flesh, carefully sealing off delicate blood vessels and wielding a bone saw while he tried not to think about the weight precariously balanced above his head. Even the patient thought it was not worth the risk. As for what Tilla would say . . .

It was usually best not to think about what Tilla would say.

He thought instead about Valens's wife, and their boys, and how he would no longer be an honorary uncle but the man who had helped their grandfather to die rather than try to save him.

"I'm all right!" he called. Stretching up to the left, he managed to get a grip on the root of a tree that was buried in the mound of debris. "It's Ruso, sir. Nearly there now."

He hauled himself up and across, feeling the muscles burning in his arm and shoulder, and tried a tentative foothold on a broken scaffolding pole.

When he got there, Pertinax's eyes opened for a moment and then closed again. His face was oddly striped where trickles of water had washed the mud away.

"It's Ruso, sir," he repeated, scanning for other injuries. "Can you tell me where it hurts?" He could see nothing else apart from scrapes and bruises, but then he could see very little under the muck, and he wasn't about to start cutting clothing off. "Let's get you out." He untied the rolled cloak from around his waist and draped it over the prefect's body. "I expect you're a bit cold?"

Faintly, without opening his eyes, Pertinax mumbled, "Go away."

The prefect's skin was clammy. The man was deteriorating fast. Ruso looped the spare end of rope around the handle of his case before balancing it on the slope. He felt as clumsy as a child's dancing doll suspended on the end of a wire. "Sir," he said, opening the case and grabbing the probe that always slipped out of its clip, "your foot's trapped between two rocks. I'm going to get you free now and then we can go back to the fort."

"Uh. Too late."

"No, sir. If we do this, there's a very good chance—"

"Kill me."

It was possible Ruso was about to do exactly that, but not in the way his patient wanted. "I can't do that, sir."

"Bloody useless. All of you."

"Yes, sir." Ruso blew away some loose grit from the skin of the unfashionably hairy leg. Searching for a topic to distract the patient, he discarded the weather as too trivial, the landslide as too frightening, and any mention of supervising the hospital as more likely to depress than inspire him. What Pertinax thrived on was challenge. "Sir, if you die, your daughter and your grandsons will be left in the care of your son-in-law."

"What?"

"Valens will be looking after the family, sir."

"Man's an idiot."

Ruso grinned. "You're absolutely right, sir." He glanced up, inadvertently clunking the borrowed helmet against the rock above him. He held his breath. Nothing happened. He let the breath out again.

As if the gods were being deliberately perverse, the light changed. The sun went behind a cloud, making it even harder to see what he was doing down here under the gloom of the overhang.

The foot would be safely clamped in one place while he worked, even though it was at a difficult angle and he couldn't get underneath it properly. But if Pertinax thrashed about, he could set the whole slide in motion again. Ruso scooped away some of the muck from beneath the man's calf, then swabbed the skin with diluted vinegar. He needed an assistant up here to hold the patient. He didn't have one. He set the dirty cloth aside, wiped his hands on a clean one, and reached for the scalpel.

"Keep absolutely still for me now, sir. This might sting a bit."

It was even more of a lie than usual, but what else could he say?

Pertinax gasped and cried out.

"Sorry, sir. Well done." He must keep him talking. "You can't go kill-ing yourself, sir. You can't leave Valens in charge."

"Unreliable."

"Exactly, sir. Here we go. Keep still now." *Because if you don't, I can't tie this off and you'll bleed to death as soon as you're the right way up.* "Nearly done."

"Dunno what she—agh!"

"Well done, sir. Not long now. Have you seen your grandsons lately?"

He wiped the blood again, trying not to get mud in the wound. Trying to see exactly what he was doing.

A voice called, "Shall we come up, sir?" The stretcher had arrived.

"No, keep clear."

He took out the bone saw, swore under his breath, and wrenched off the helmet that had tipped forward over his eyes. He flung it as far behind him as he could manage, safely away from the slide. "Nearly done now, sir. You'll be free in a moment."

Pertinax was rigid. His body was shaking with the effort of keeping unnaturally still when his every instinct must be to struggle and scream. Ruso felt the saw bite against the bone, and prayed.

3

IT WAS LUCKY the leaves were still on the trees or the soldiers would have seen him by now. They had been so busy running around and shouting orders that nobody had noticed a boy creeping along beside the stream until he could get near enough to see the whole of the amazing thing that had happened in the quarry.

The one tied to the rope had made it across to the one who was stuck under the rock now. He moved very slowly, as if he were frightened. Aedic had never seen a soldier frightened before.

The one on the rope was . . . Aedic stretched out and parted the leaves with the tip of his finger. The one on the rope was hunched up right underneath the big rock, trying to do something to the other one's . . . What was that in his hand? Surely he wasn't going to cut the other one's leg off? Aedic felt his mouth fall open, closed it again, and swallowed.

First the dead body, and today a Roman having his leg sawn off. It was the most exciting week he could remember since the day the soldiers turned up and threw everything out of the house and called it "helping." This made up for not being able to tell the others about the body. Almost.

He still wasn't sure he believed in the body himself.

He had been hiding in the tunnels his family's sheep had made through the thick clump of bushes. In the middle the ground still smelled faintly of sheep, even though the flock was long gone, but around the edges was the sharp stink of wee. He didn't like it, but you got used to it after a bit and at least it meant the soldiers who were building the wall had left these bushes here to use as a latrine instead of chopping them down along with everything else. Farther down the hill, the bramble berries were finished; everyone said you mustn't pick them past the end of September and it was true—they were dull and shriveled—so he was even hungrier than usual. He had eaten all the cheese he had taken when Petta wasn't looking, sucking it slowly to make the taste last longer, just like Mam used to tell him. It was nearly dark now, and it was starting to rain again, and still nobody had come to look for him. The patrol had gone past and wouldn't be back for ages. He supposed he should get up and go home before Petta gave his share of supper to the dog.

He was rubbing his foot to get rid of the pins and needles when he heard . . . a gasp? A grunt? At the time he wasn't sure what it was, but it wasn't the wind in the leaves, and it was much too close.

So he had shifted carefully to one side, trying to get a better view out between the tangle of rough stems. The thing grunted again. A shape was moving up the hill away from him. If it had picked up his scent, it wasn't interested. It wasn't afraid, either. Too big to be a man; too upright to be a pony or a cow. He lost sight of it, and then it reappeared up by the black line of the wall. He could see its shape against the remaining light in the sky. Two legs. A man, then. But he was not tramping along, carrying a shield like the men on patrol. He was carrying something big and heavy on his back—something that he now let fall onto the ground.

Over and over again since then, Aedic had closed his eyes and pictured that moment, trying to decide if he really could have seen a human head and an arm that flopped down as it fell. Whatever it was, it blended into the ground. The man stretched up into the rain, loosening his muscles after the strain of the carrying. Then he bent down over the new length of wall and lifted off the covers.

How could he be inspecting the work in the dark?

Perhaps he had lost something.

He must be a soldier, because nobody else . . .

But Aedic wasn't a soldier, and he was there, so perhaps the man wasn't a soldier either.

If it had been daylight, he might have run up and offered to help. It was all right to go near the troops as long as you were careful. Some of them wanted messages delivered in exchange for an apple or a taste of honeycomb, or they asked which way to go or who could sell them things. Some of them were even glad to see the local boys because they missed their own sons at home, wherever that was. Sometimes when nobody was looking they let people travel in the ox wagons. If you said you had a big sister, you might get offered a ride home on one of the pack ponies, but Aedic kept quiet about the girls at his cousins' house. He wouldn't have dared to let Da see him with the soldiers. Not after they had turned the family off the farm and dug great trenches across the grazing. They had set fire to the houses and hacked most of the trees down for scaffolding and firewood. When one of Grandfather's tottery old friends came to sing a song to the dying trees, the soldiers shouted and threw clods of earth at him until their centurion told them to stop.

Sometimes, when Aedic saw the soldiers tearing the land apart, he thought that was what was happening to him too.

The man up by the wall seemed to move about as if he were working in daylight. He was bending to pick up filling stones from the pile.

Usually the soldiers built up both sides of the wall with rows of the big square stones that they had cut out of the hillside, and then they filled the gap in the middle with things nobody would see: rough stones and clay and sand and sometimes, when the officers weren't looking, lumps of turf. But that day the rain had got worse. When it rained like that, it washed the wet mortar out and left white streaks down the outsides of the stones, so the centurion had come and told them to stop before they filled the middle in. Aedic had watched them pack up their tools and heard the centurion telling them to make sure they covered the sides up properly before they marched back to the camp. Then he had stayed up there and seen the man carrying the thing that looked very much like a body, and when the wind dropped he could hear the familiar thump and clunk of stones being thrown onto a pile. Up there in the dark and the drizzle, all on his own, the man was filling in the middle of the wall.

The filling-in seemed to go on for a long time, and Aedic's thoughts had drifted to his dinner and the dog when he realized the man wasn't there anymore. This time he heard the footfalls. He held his breath as they came down the hill toward his hiding place. Then a cry and a curse and all the bushes shuddered and spattered raindrops. There was the pale shape of a hand, so close that he could have reached out and touched it. Aedic narrowed his eyes and kept as still as a hunter.

The hand lifted, the bushes shook again, and the man was back on his feet and away much too quickly for anyone carrying anything heavy. Whatever it was, he had left it up there.

Even after days of thinking about it, Aedic did not understand what he had seen. But when he thought about telling anyone, the squirming in his stomach told him not to.

This was the first time in days that he had managed to sneak away from his chores for another look, but he was not even sure where the body was now. The soldiers had built up lots more rows of stones and filled in the gap between them. This stretch of wall was too high to see over. He had been about to run back to the cousins' house before anybody started to wonder why he was taking so long to find firewood, but then came the terrible noise from somewhere down in the valley, beyond the soldiers' road. And now here he was, seeing the rock all tumbled down and a bloodstained and muddy old man struggling and crying out as the other one was trying to cut his leg off while all the others watched.

"Hey!"

Aedic jumped at the sound, and grabbed the branch to steady himself.

"Yes, you!" the voice shouted in Latin. "What are you doing up there?"

But by the time the soldier got there, Aedic was down the tree and gone.

4

THE PATIENT'S FAMILY had given Tilla two hard-boiled eggs, fresh bread, and a cup of warm milk with the usual warning about not drinking the water from the stream. It was kindly meant, but she had been here for most of the summer and heard it a dozen times before. *If you wait long enough, the muck from the building work all sinks to the bottom, but no matter what the soldiers tell you, everyone knows they piss in it.*

That was the trouble with soldiers, Tilla thought, stepping aside onto the grass verge to let a couple of carts rumble past, and glancing up to where small figures were moving around on the scarred hillside. You couldn't trust them.

Her anger rose again as she remembered the plump girl's anxious insistence that her injuries were nothing: She had tripped and banged her head on the doorpost, and then fallen awkwardly. She did not need a healer. She just needed to rest for a while. She was sorry for all the fuss.

Tilla had done her best to be gentle as she set the broken fingers straight, but Cata still cried out in pain.

"Your mother tells me this sort of thing has happened before."

Cata sniffed. "I am very clumsy."

Tilla laid the compress over the grazed and swollen cheek. "You are lucky none of the bones of your face are broken."

The girl kept her eyes closed, like a child who wanted to be invisible.

"You may not be so lucky next time."

No reply.

"You must stay close to your family," Tilla told her. "And they must put in a complaint to his centurion."

Still no reply.

"Do not go near him," Tilla continued. "Do not waste a single moment hearing how sorry he is, because it will mean no more this time than it did the last."

Just when she thought she might as well have been speaking to a deaf woman, Cata said, "You don't know him."

"No," Tilla agreed, "but I am older than you and I have met men like him."

The girl's swollen lips trembled. "I thought you would understand."

"My husband does not beat me." Did she imagine this was what all soldiers' women had to put up with? "If he did, I would leave him."

"Sometimes he is very kind."

"I am sure he is. Drink this." Tilla handed her the cup. "I am sure he is fond of you, in his own way. And after he has killed you, he will be sorry he did it, and he will miss you very much."

But the girl showed no sign of having heard.

Tilla did her best to be patient with these girls. It was not so easy to leave when your man knew where your family lived, and he had friends who could have people arrested and searched. Only last week a soldier had come to her demanding to know where his woman was and blaming Tilla for encouraging her to run off. Tilla, who had seen how cowed the girl had become, was secretly delighted. Her family did not know where she was, either, but a small boy had arrived with a message to say that she was safe. Tilla had to go back and tell the soldier that it was no good pestering the family for information: They knew no more about where the girl was hiding than he did.

So much of being a trainee medicus, she now saw, was not about medicine at all but about the complications of people's lives.

She passed the south wall of the little fort and turned the corner into the huddle of civilian buildings. For once there were no off-duty soldiers lounging about and ogling girls, or carrying their children on their shoulders down the street, or haggling with the shopkeepers. They must have been kept in. It happened sometimes, usually for reasons that were not interesting enough to be worth the bother of finding them out.

The change in the weather had lifted everyone's spirits. The cobbler was whistling a tune, hammering nails into a sole in time to the rhythm. The baker called to her across the counter as she passed. He grinned and held up a raisin pastry. It was a way of saying he hadn't forgotten.

She thanked him, slipping the pastry into her bag.

"Don't tell Ria," he said. "She'd have sold you one."

"I shall sneak it past her." The baker and Tilla's landlady were brother and sister, but business was business. "How is your little girl?"

"No more trouble so far." His tone was still wary. "It's been near enough six weeks."

"I am sure it was just the fever," she assured him, wondering if he and his wife ever used the word *fit* in private or whether they were afraid that speaking the name would somehow bring one on. A family who had lost two babies at birth had no illusions about how easily a surviving child could be snatched away into the next world.

He began to pile the loaves from one half-full basket into another. "I hear your man's busy, eh?"

"He is always busy," she agreed.

His hands stilled. "Did you not hear? Where have you been?"

She hurried back to the lodgings feeling faintly ashamed. A woman who had just been told that her husband was taking part in a tricky rescue should be fearful for him, or proud of him, or probably both. Instead, she was cross with him for taking such a risk.

On any other day she might have been proud and worried, but today was different. He had promised.

One night was not much to ask. She had put up with his relatives for a whole summer. Apart from meeting her cousin and her uncle a few years ago, she had asked nothing of him—except for tonight. And he had given his word, even though he was plainly uneasy about it. But now he had found some sort of crisis, and as usual it seemed nobody else could deal with it. He would be late, if he turned up at all, and she would have to explain why her Roman was not there, and how was she to know whether they would understand? She hardly knew them herself. They were not real relatives.

They might have been, though.

It was a peculiar thought that she might have been the old man's daughter. If Mam had not broken her promise and run away with her father instead, Tilla might have spent her whole life here, milking cows and growing vegetables, grumbling about the Romans and refusing to speak Latin. Thinking a trip to market was exciting, a journey to the seaside a once-in-a-lifetime adventure. Knowing and being known by all the neighbors and never wanting to leave. Or maybe desperate to get out? Neighbors were not always kind.

Instead here she was, trailing about after a foreign husband. Living in temporary lodgings, having to eat meals from snack bars, while half their possessions were stored miles away in Deva. Soon she would leave behind most of the people she had grown to know here over the summer. Probably she would never see them again, because you never knew where a soldier would be sent next, and if you wanted any sort of marriage, you had to go with him.

The shutters that formed the entrance of the snack bar had been opened up to let in what was left of the autumn sun. A group of dark-skinned men dressed in rich colors were seated outside, chatting over the remains of a meal in a tongue Tilla did not recognize. She wondered what they made of the drab décor of the only bar in town. Ria looked up from stacking cups behind the counter. "I hear your man's a hero."

"I will tell him you said so," Tilla promised, feeling guilty. At least he did not beat her, and he was not a maid chaser like the centurion at the fort, whose kitchen girl had come to her in tears begging for some charm or potion to keep her from falling pregnant.

Ria leaned across the counter, jabbed a bony finger toward the men outside, and whispered, "From Palmyra. If you want any silk, let me know."

"Not really."

"Pity," she observed. "I could have got you a good deal."

Someone in the back room was humming a tune Tilla had heard the soldiers singing on the march.

Ria observed, "Your girl's in a good mood."

"She doesn't like silence."

"She'll be glad enough of it after the baby comes. What can I get you?"

"I'll put my bag away first." Tilla made her way past the empty tables and into the dimly lit storeroom where Virana slept, and where a sturdy ladder provided access to the privacy of the loft room she and her husband were renting.

"Mistress!" Virana's large form was precariously balanced on a stool in front of a high shelf.

"If you're going to do that," Tilla told her, "find something safe to stand on."

"Oh, I've finished now." Virana clambered down clutching a honey pot. "How is Cata? Is it true her boyfriend broke her jaw?"

Tilla delved into her bag. "Share a pastry?" She would have died rather than reveal anything about her patients to Virana, but sometimes she wondered why she bothered to keep her mouth shut. Nobody else around here did.

Virana picked out a raisin and popped it into her mouth. "Is the master back yet?"

"No."

"He is very brave. Did his clerk come back?"

"Yes. And no."

"Shall I take your bag up?"

"Virana, you're supposed to be . . ." Tilla paused. She could hardly say *resting*, since the arrangement for Virana to work in Ria's snack bar suited everyone very nicely, including Virana, who saw it as a chance to meet the legionary of her dreams. "I'll take it," she said. "You're supposed to be careful. And don't drop crumbs or you'll be sleeping with mice."

By the time she came back down, Ria had left the bar and was clattering about in the kitchen. The outside table had now been taken over by a group of local women. The loaded baskets suggested they had been shopping over at Vindolanda; the fact that they were here suggested they were in no hurry to go home, but not daft enough to pay Vindolanda prices for drinks.

She had not intended to eavesdrop, but as she carried her beer across to the last patch of sunshine slanting in through the doorway and across a table, she realized she was in an ideal position to listen: hidden from view but able to hear every word.

"So she said to them," declared a voice with a familiar lisp, "'Why d'you have to march straight through my cabbages?' So the one in charge pointed up the hill, and he said, 'We've got orders to go up there.' So she said, 'Well, you should go around! Can't you see I've got things growing here?' and he said—this is what he said, without a word of a lie—'The Twentieth Legion do not go around.'"

"The Twentieth Legion do not go around!" repeated the others, rolling this new outrage about on their tongues as if they were enjoying the flavor.

"So I said to her," continued the woman with the lisp, "you want to do what my cousin did when they kept letting his sheep out."

Tilla took a sip of beer and waited, an invisible member of the audience. The woman was local: She remembered the thick brows and the eager front teeth. "He moved the sheep up to the common," the woman said, "and he put the bull in there instead."

Her audience seemed to like that.

"I was there when the next lot came. You should have seen them run! Tripping over each other and everything falling out of their packs."

There was general laughter, and Tilla could not resist a smile.

"See? The Twentieth Legion do go around after all."

The talk drifted to people she did not know. Across the road, a cat was picking its way delicately along the roof of the leatherworker's shop, untroubled by the puddle that covered half the street below.

Had she done the right thing about Cata? The mother had plainly been hoping she would use her influence with the Medicus to have the man disciplined. That was the problem with being honest about having married an officer: People wanted her to pass messages to the Legion. But at least this way she could not be accused of betraying anybody. Everyone knew from the start not to tell her things that the Romans were not supposed to know. And if there were times when that made her lonely, well, that was how life was. One of her mother's favorite sayings was *Nobody likes a girl who feels sorry for herself.* Which was very annoying but true.

Virana passed by her with a tray of drinks and then returned to the back room. Outside, the woman with the lisp said, "You know about that one, do you?"

Tilla held her breath. They had been offered a room here after Virana had given a sob story about her baby's father being dead. "Well, he might be," Virana had insisted when Tilla challenged her about it later. On the other hand, there were plenty of candidates for fatherhood still very much alive and serving with the Twentieth Legion, and Tilla had known she could not keep it quiet for long.

"They all live together over the bar here, you know."

"No! Really? I thought he lived in the fort."

Tilla frowned into her beer and wondered if she should walk away. Or perhaps stand up and let herself be seen. She did neither, despite another of her mother's favorites: *No good comes of listening to gossip.*

Someone asked a question she could not catch. "Enica says the wife is barren," said the woman with the lisp. "But she says he's had more luck with the slave, as you see."

Tilla struggled to stifle her spluttering as the beer went the wrong way. Enica was a member of the family she would be introducing to her husband tonight—if he managed to turn up. She had explained when they first met that Virana's child was nothing to do with her husband, who was not a maid chaser. And Virana had said so too, and Enica had said . . . It did not matter what Enica had said, because it was clear now that she had not believed either of them.

Somebody said, "I heard they picked that one up in Eboracum and she isn't really a slave at all."

"Hmph. I'm surprised the wife puts up with it."

"The wife's probably grateful to be taken in," said another voice. "I heard he rescued her from the Northerners."

"That is just what she says," said someone else. "Did you not know? He bought her. She was in a brothel down in Deva."

"That can't be right. Isn't she a Roman citizen?"

Tilla wanted to shout, *I was only lodging in the brothel! Why didn't you just ask me?* Instead she took a large gulp of beer.

Somebody said, "And the old boy's really invited them?"

"That's what Enica said. Because she looks like her mother. You can imagine what Enica thinks about that. Conn too."

"Ah, but Conn is a miserable offering these days, don't you think? Not a bit like his father. Or his brother, may he walk in peace."

"They all end up that way, girl. Look at mine."

"What? Dead?"

"No, he just looks it. Bad-tempered."

"Mine too," chimed in another voice. "Never happy unless he's complaining."

"Still, it's a bad sign if he's like that already at his age. You want something better at the start, no?"

And they were off into discussing the reasons why the son of the man whose hearth she would be sharing tonight had slumped from being a fine young man to a miserable offering.

She could not argue: The one time she had seen him, Conn had certainly worn the face of a man who had found a dead rat in his dinner. Perhaps it really was because his once-betrothed had been raped by a soldier during the troubles and refused to get rid of the soldier's baby, and perhaps it wasn't, because these women would believe any scandalous nonsense they were told. They deserved to be shamed. To be set straight. To be made to say they were sorry for being so spiteful. To be made to *feel* sorry.

The trouble was, anything she said now would leave them with even more to gossip about than before. And nothing would make this evening any easier.

She drained her beer, clapped the cup down on the table, and strode across the bar toward the back door. It would have been better if she had not knocked over a bench on the way, but she was not going to turn around and pick it up. Nobody was going to see how pink her face was.

5

"NOT BAD, CONSIDERING." Medical Officer Valens finished his examination of Ruso's handiwork, moved the lamp away, and let the damp cloth fall back into place over the wound. He surveyed his sleeping father-in-law for a moment, then turned to the orderly. "I'll be here all night. Call me if there's any change or if he wakes up." Standing in the gloom of the hospital corridor, he murmured, "What do you think?"

"He was already weak when I got to him."

Valens said, "Anyone else would be dead by now."

"Has Serena been sent for?"

"Of course."

For a moment Ruso felt bad for doubting it. But the way Valens added, "He *is* her father," suggested he too had considered leaving his wife in ignorance back in Deva. "It's strange. I always imagined the old boy was indestructible."

Ruso said, "You don't have to cover for me tonight if you don't want to."

"I don't mind," Valens assured him. "This way I can tell the wife I did something useful."

The room by the hospital entrance was just the right size to be an office, a pharmacy, or an overflow storage space—but not, unfortunately, all three at once. It was certainly not big enough to store anything that was not supposed to be there, and Ruso felt firmly that a dead hen fell into the latter category. It lay in the deflated way that dead hens did, with its head flopped over the side of the desk that should have been occupied by Ruso's clerk.

Valens said, "Has somebody brought you a present?"

"Not that I know of." Grateful patients sometimes offered gifts, but he had no idea where this had come from. He hoped it did not have lice.

Valens pulled a thin wooden writing tablet out of his belt. "One of the centurions asked me to give you this."

Ruso took it across to the lamp and flipped the leaves apart. A Centurion Silvanus from Magnis, the next fort along the line, wished him to know that Legionary Candidus was no longer stationed there. He had left there a week ago and was now working as a clerk in the hospital at Parva.

The fact that it was Ruso—now standing in that very hospital at Parva— who had raised the query in the first place, did not seem to spark any curiosity. The whereabouts of a man who was no longer his responsibility was clearly not at the top of Centurion Silvanus's worry list. Ruso noted bitterly that the message was written in one hand and hastily signed in another. It seemed Silvanus had a clerk of his own—one who had turned up and done his job as expected.

Valens had seated himself on the pharmacist's table. Fortunately the pharmacist was on leave and so unable to object. Valens extended one leg, hooked a stool, and pulled it over for a footrest. "Bad news?"

"My clerk hasn't reported for duty for three days. Nobody seems to know where he is."

"Ask for another one."

"It took me two months to get this one. Now he's vanished."

Valens surveyed the teetering piles of writing tablets stacked on every available surface. "He seems to have been very productive while he was here."

"He was supposed to be sorting all this mess out. But he didn't seem to know where to start."

The table swayed as Valens leaned sideways to peer over the top of splayed wooden doors that were held together by only a taut length of twine around the handles. "There's more in here."

"Don't touch that. The staff have taken to calling it Pandora's cupboard. Open it and we'll all be sorry."

Valens said, "Perhaps he's fallen on his sword."

"I hope not. He's Albanus's nephew. I promised I'd keep an eye on him."

"Not the one with the pungent bath oil?"

"That's the one. Candidus." They had both been introduced to Candidus some years ago, but the youth had—understandably—been more interested in watching passing girls than in meeting old army friends of his uncle. "Albanus wrote and said the boy was having problems settling in at Magnis," he explained. "I asked for him here hoping he might have taken after his uncle."

"And had he?"

"Well, he looks very much like him, but he's not what you'd call a natural administrator."

Candidus had followed Ruso on his ward rounds, dutifully scrawling on a wax tablet, never once asking him to repeat or spell anything and replying cheerfully, "Yes sir!" every time he was asked, "Did you get that?" It was an insouciance that Ruso had only briefly mistaken for competence.

"There's only one Albanus," Valens told him. "You were spoiled. Neither of my clerks is a patch on him."

Ruso looked up. "You've got two clerks?"

"I know. It's hopeless, really. For the number of beds, it should be at least three if not four."

Ruso said nothing. Several months ago, when Valens was short of work and out of favor, Ruso had petitioned the Legion to take him back. Now Valens, who was no more skilled or experienced than he was himself, was in charge of a hospital with deputies and departments and flunkeys and rows of porters who lined the corridors and saluted as he passed. Or perhaps that only happened in Ruso's imagination. But there was no escaping the fact that Valens had a comfortable post in a base at a major road junction while he himself was stationed at a makeshift unit in the toy-sized fort of Parva, with the added joy of a clinic in a tented camp that was slowly sinking into the mud.

Another man might have demanded of the gods what he had done to deserve this state of affairs, but Ruso already knew. This was what happened to upstarts who were known to be acquainted with the Emperor. Now that Hadrian had gone back across the sea to Gaul, Ruso was suffering the fate of teacher's pet when Teacher had left the room. He supposed he was lucky his fellow officers hadn't stripped his clothes off, tied him to a tree, and made him eat his homework.

Valens said, "I'll ask around at Magnis, see if somebody knows where he's gone. From the sound of it I can't imagine anyone will have poached him."

Ruso glanced past Valens at Pandora's cupboard, and pictured again the words *He is rather a sensitive boy* in Albanus's neat handwriting. It was hard to imagine how a sensitive boy could have lasted beyond the first week of basic training. Indeed, unless the bitten fingernails betrayed a nervous disposition, Candidus had shown no sign of sensitivity to anything except the dangers of hard work. At every opportunity, he had abandoned his duties and wandered around the hospital, chatting to people. Several of them seemed to have been given the impression that he was in charge. Ruso might have been almost glad to lose him, except that he had then done something unexpected.

Immediately after an exasperated Ruso had ordered him to get his back-side on that stool and not move or speak until he had sorted out the orders for blankets and buckets and updated the repairs list, Candidus stood to attention behind his desk and said, "May I speak, sir?"

"Briefly."

"I've made a bit of a mess of things so far, haven't I, sir?"

"Yes," said Ruso, surprised by the young man's frankness.

"I'm sorry, sir. I've never been a clerk before, sir. I was hoping you wouldn't notice and I'd just pick it up as I went along."

"Then you should have stayed at your desk and listened to what you were told."

Candidus swallowed. "Are you going to get rid of me, sir?"

Ruso sighed and leaned against Pandora's cupboard. If the lad hadn't had the same skinny build and innocent eyes and floppy black hair as his uncle, it might have been easier to be angry with him. "Just get those orders done. We'll talk about it tomorrow."

"Thank you, sir. I'll do them straightaway."

"Good," Ruso said, not sure if he was being taken for a ride. "If there's anything you don't understand, ask. Don't guess."

"Yes, sir. I will. And I won't. And I'll do better from now on, sir."

But the next day Candidus did not turn up, and nobody had seen him since.

It was a moment before Ruso registered what Valens was pointing at. "Is there something underneath that chicken?"

Ruso reached underneath the soft feathers and drew out the thin slivers of another writing tablet. As he did so he felt a stab of guilt. He was already late. Tilla would be waiting, and the hen would still be dead when he got back tomorrow. On the other hand, he needed to check that it belonged to him, especially since he might run across the donor by

accident and fail to thank them because he had not paused a few short
moments to open a—

"Oh, hell."

"From somebody you don't like?"

"It's from Albanus."

"Albanus sent a dead bird all the way from Verulamium?"

Ruso scanned the letter. There was no mention of a hen, which he
assumed must have come from somewhere else.

To Doctor Ruso, greetings.

*I am happy to say that I hope to see you soon. Fortune has granted me a post
as tutor to the children of a prefect who is currently stationed at Arbeia.*

*I shall try to call upon both yourself and Candidus, who I hope is settling in
well. I cannot repeat too often how grateful I am to you for taking him in.*

*Thank you for your good wishes to Grata, which I regret I have been unable to
convey to her. Believe me, sir, if you knew her as well as I now do, you would not
have sent them.*

*I hope you are enjoying the best of fortune, along with your wife and Officer
Valens and his family.*

Farewell.

Valens said, "What do you think he's found out about Grata?"

But Ruso was not interested in why Albanus had fallen out with his
woman. What he wanted to know was where Candidus was, and he
wanted to know it before the lad's uncle arrived and asked the same question. The letter was dated two weeks ago. Albanus could be here at any
moment.

"He'll turn up," said Valens. "If he doesn't, Albanus can look for him.
And I'll see to Pertinax. You're having a night out tonight."

"I know."

"You don't seem very keen."

"I'm not."

"Stay here, then. We'll get the food brought in. Invite the lovely Tilla
and your, ah . . ." Valens paused. "I've never quite known what to call
her."

"Virana," Ruso reminded him, although as to what she was . . . *Ah* was
probably as good a word as any. Virana was neither a slave nor a freed-
woman. She was most definitely not a concubine. Nor, at this rate, was
she ever going to persuade some hapless legionary to call her his spouse.

There was no word for *a pregnant stray whom my wife took in without consulting me*, and if there was a word for *and she is worryingly attractive, which is why I try to avoid being alone with her*, he was certainly not going to speak it out loud.

"Well, we can invite her if you like."

"We can't," said Ruso, well able to imagine Virana's excitement at an invitation to dine inside the fort. "I have to go and meet some of Tilla's people. And I'm late," he added, knowing he could not put it off any longer.

Valens shook his head. "No good comes of mixing with the wife's friends and relations."

"I know."

"If you're eating somewhere decent, can you have some sent in for me? I can't leave the father-in-law."

Ruso cleared his throat. "Actually I'm going to the house."

Valens's eyes widened. "A native house? At this hour?"

"I'll have Tilla as protection," Ruso assured him. "We're staying overnight."

Having demonstrated his nonchalance, he paused with one hand on the door latch. A man on a dangerous mission should leave details of his plan with someone back at base. Just in case. "It's only about half a mile. West on the main road, over the stream, up the hill, and turn left before you get to the camp."

Valens looked even more surprised. "I thought the lovely Tilla had barely a soul in this world, and one of them lives just down the road?"

"I know," Ruso confessed. "It struck me as a remarkable coincidence too. The old man's a friend of the family. He saw her at market and mistook her for her mother."

"Ah."

He had begun now; he might as well edge toward the part that was really worrying him. "Have you heard about the old man who sings to trees?" The moment he had said it, he wished he had not.

"The crazy man?" Valens was going to be no help at all. He was enjoying this.

"Tilla says he's not crazy. He's just very traditional."

"What does *that* mean?"

"That's what I asked. She said, 'You'll see.'" He paused in the doorway. He could not tell Valens, any more than he could tell Tilla, about his discreet enquiries with Security. The old man was deemed to be harmless, as were two of his sons—one because he had been killed in the troubles a couple of years ago, and the other because he was only nine years old. But the name of Conn, the eldest, turned up in watch lists all over the place. He said, "I'm just not sure why he's bothering to make such a fuss of her now when they never really knew each other."

"Because she's turned up practically on his doorstep?"

"Or because he thinks she'll be useful to him in some way. You're sure you don't want to go back to Magnis tonight? I'll stay here and see to Pertinax."

"Absolutely not," Valens assured him. "I want to hear what happens."

6

RUSO PULLED HIS hood down over his eyes and strode on, perhaps the only man on the wall who was glad that it was nearly dark and starting to rain yet again. The patrol who had just passed would not know that the figure turning down a track leading only to native farmsteads was one of their own officers.

He had so nearly escaped. In a few more days, the Legion would be on the march back to Deva. If the wall had run a couple of hundred paces farther south, the family would have been turfed off their land and ended up somewhere miles away. The old man might never have seen Tilla at the market and seized her by the hand, begging to know if she was Mara come back to him. Unfortunately, the wall was where it was, and the military zone had only sliced off a few of the family's fields. They had stayed to eke out a living on their shrunken farm, hidden away down a slithery track that was almost impossible to make out under the gloom of the dripping trees. Ruso pulled his cloak tighter around him and trod carefully.

That was what he would have to do, metaphorically speaking, when he arrived there. Unable to explain his misgivings to Tilla, he would have to stay alert for any hint of suspicious activity or attempts to compromise either of them. If these people thought they could persuade him to become their tame Roman, they were very much mistaken.

Reaching what must be the fork in the pathways that Tilla had told him about, he followed the curve of the right-hand route, and eventually the shape of a gate loomed ahead. He paused. The locals let their dogs loose at night to repel thieving soldiers.

There was no barking, just the sighing of the breeze in the trees and a spatter of raindrops. He took a deep breath and called, "Is anyone there?" in the language his wife had taught him.

"I am," said a young voice. For a worrying moment it seemed to belong to the large dog that was sniffing at his hand.

"Hello," said Ruso, leaving the hand where it was and edging the rest of himself farther away.

"Are you the doctor?" asked the voice.

"Yes," said Ruso, just able to make out the shape of a boy attached to the dog. This must be the youngest son.

"I'm Branan."

"Ruso. Sorry I'm late."

"Now I can go in out of the rain." Leading him across the uneven cobbles, Branan shouted, "He's here!" and moments later a glimmer of light appeared. A shadowy figure standing in the shelter of the porch handed the lamp to the boy and greeted Ruso with one word in British: "Weapons."

Ruso had expected the request to be couched in politer terms. "Who are you?"

"Conn. Do not pretend you have never heard of me. Give me your weapons."

The boy pushed back his hood. From behind a curtain of wet curls, dark eyes glanced from one man to the other.

"Is my wife here?"

"She is."

Ruso raised his arms, not wanting to pick a fight before he was even through the door. He felt himself being searched, and the boy's fingers tugging at the fastenings of the scabbard. Conn said something to the boy in their own tongue about not taking the blade out.

The familiar weight of the sword lifted and was gone, borne away by a native into the darkness. Ruso tried to ask, "Where's he taking it?" but if Conn understood, he chose not to reply.

Walking out of the fort without his armor on had been a matter of choice. Handing over an eighteen-inch slice of razor-sharp iron to a hostile local was definitely against regulations and against common sense too. He hoped his wife really was here.

Tilla had assured him several times that her own family had never collected enemy heads, nor predicted the future from the entrails and death throes of murdered prisoners, nor crammed people they did not much like into giant men made of wicker and burned them alive. But he had seen some of the things natives had done to stray soldiers. When pressed to admit that such things happened, Tilla changed the subject, choosing instead to remind him of the evils she had seen in the amphitheater. Usually in a tone that suggested he was personally responsible for them. So it was a relief when Conn pushed the door open to reveal several figures seated around a central fire, and one of them rose and hurried across to him. "Husband!"

She reached up to unfasten the clasp of his sodden cloak. "I was afraid you might not come."

"Of course I came," he said, trying to sound as though he had been looking forward to it all day. When Conn walked away he murmured, "Watch out for that one."

She put a hand over his. "These are my people. We have to trust them."

We. As it struck him that she did not sound sure of them herself, she prodded him in the small of the back. He stepped forward into the firelight and she announced, "My man is here!"

The creature who exclaimed "Ah!" from the depths of the carved chair probably looked less alarming when he was not seated beside a steaming cauldron with his wild white hair and deep-set eyes lit from below by orange flames. At least he looked welcoming. The hand clutching the walking stick shook with the effort as he hauled himself up to stand. A young woman with broad shoulders, capable hands, and a serious expression stepped forward from behind his chair to help him. Ruso guessed she must be Conn's wife. He had tried to stay awake while Tilla explained all this, but he had only been listening for the gaps so that he could grunt in the right places.

There was movement in the dark spaces behind the wicker partitions, which were hung with furs and painted shields. Above them, over shelves filled with what looked like apples, he caught the glint of metal slung under the thatch. Not his own sword but curved blades. Farm tools with sharp edges.

Figures emerged from the hidden parts of the house and padded across the bracken-strewn floor to gather around the fire. Ruso blinked, feeling his eyes beginning to smart. The smoke from the hearth was making a poor job of finding its way out through the thatch. He counted four more adults and several children. All staring directly at him. Finally another figure emerged. He was happier than usual to see that pregnant belly and welcoming bosom below a smiling face. Try as he might, it was impossible to note Virana's features in any other order.

"Grandfather Senecio," announced Tilla in her own language, stepping forward to address the figure leaning on the stick. "This is Gaius Ruso of the Petreius family from southern Gaul. He is a healer in the pay of the emperor's Twentieth Legion."

Ruso bowed.

"He is a man of honor, and I have chosen him to be mine," added Tilla, as if she were challenging anyone to argue.

The strength of the voice that replied, "Good evening, Roman," took him by surprise. Perhaps the man was not as ancient as he looked. "I am Senecio of the Corionotatae."

The introductions that followed seemed oddly formal in the murk of a round house smelling of smoke and sheep and whatever was in the pot, but the man betrayed no obvious sign of craziness. Conn was now standing by his father's chair. He had the same strong features and curly hair as his father, but although he was not gray, the sour downturn of his mouth made him look almost as old. His young wife, still unsmiling, was called Enica. Branan grinned at Ruso through the wet snakes of hair, revealing dimples and a gap between his front teeth. Ruso decided he liked Branan.

The names of the rest—the man with one eye, the tall thin man, the woman with the thick brows who lisped when she spoke, the one with nothing remarkable about her, the gaggle of wide-eyed children—were swept out of his memory by the thought that the adults only had to reach up to seize scythes and pitchforks and . . .

. . . And he must pull himself together. They probably always looked fierce. Who wouldn't in a place like this? Besides, it was surely bad etiquette to murder guests, even in Britannia.

After the introductions there was a lot of shuffling about as everyone settled themselves around the hearth. Conn's wife, still giving the impression that she was not enjoying this, placed him next to Tilla. The animal pelt covering the bench tickled the backs of his legs. The bench rocked as Virana lowered herself down onto the other end of it.

Senecio said, "We hear you rescued a man from the fallen rocks."

"Yes."

"First the sky is against you with the rain, and now the earth."

Ruso hoped the old man wasn't going to veer off into craziness. Or religion. There were stories of him yelling at thunderstorms as well as singing to trees. "It is good of you to invite us."

"Darlughdacha is very much like her mother," said Senecio, reaching for a cup made of turned wood. "We have been recalling good friends long gone. Her mother and I were very close at one time."

It felt strange to hear Tilla called by her native name. As though this man had some sort of ancient claim upon her. Meanwhile Enica scowled at Tilla as if looking like one's mother were some sort of crime.

The man continued. "Friends are always welcome at my hearth."

"And at ours, Grandfather," put in Tilla. "When we have one."

"Yes," said Ruso again, putting an arm around his wife in a gesture that he hoped looked protective, and not as if he were clinging to her for support.

"Soldiers have no homes," Conn said, looking round at the household as if he were explaining something new. "This is why they do not understand what it is to turn people off their land."

Tilla said, "My husband's family has a farm in the south of Gaul. His brother looks after it."

"The south of Gaul?" Senecio raised one white eyebrow. "I hear the land there is very dry in the summer."

"There is not much rain," Ruso agreed.

"How many cows do you have?"

"Just the one." Aware that the Britons would think he was a pauper, he added, "We have a lot of vines and olives. Some . . ." He turned to Tilla for the native word, then realized there wasn't one. "Some peaches," he said, "and a little wheat."

"Wine and oil," Senecio mused. "You can feed a family on these things?"

"We sell them." Not very profitably.

"Ah." It was Senecio's turn to explain to his audience. "The Romans have to use coins," he explained, "because they cannot feed themselves on what they grow."

Conn said, "This is why they come here wanting our good land to grow real food on."

Ruso felt Tilla's thigh press up against his own. He wanted to tell her not to worry. If they wanted to score points at his expense, he would put up with it. It was only one evening, and if these people were gullible enough to believe that he had been lured away from the sunny vineyards of southern Gaul by windswept grass and reedy bogs, nothing he said would change their minds.

He waited for the next challenge, but instead Senecio said, "You have a good understanding of our tongue, healer. This is not usual in a foreigner."

Ruso put a hand on Tilla's knee. Perhaps they really were clinging to each other for support. "I have a good teacher."

"That is as well. We do not speak Latin in this house."

"Never mind!" put in a cheery voice from the other end of the bench. "Now my mistress is here, she can teach you!"

Tilla hissed, "Sh!" and Virana subsided with, "But I was only saying—"

"Sh!"

Ruso was fairly sure that there was a difference in British between *We do not speak Latin* and *We cannot speak Latin*. Perhaps Senecio too wanted to lay down some boundaries.

Senecio handed his cup to Enica. As she poured the beer, he reached back and squeezed her thigh.

This was unexpected. Either Ruso had made the wrong assumption about Enica and Conn, or he had at last found evidence of Julius Caesar's assertion that the Britons shared their wives. Was that what *very traditional* meant? He hoped he wasn't expected to share his own wife. Or, indeed, anyone else's.

Senecio took a gulp and held the cup out. Enica, whom Ruso no longer knew how to place, took it and brought it across to him. Ruso nodded his thanks. As he drank he could hear Virana whispering, "Why don't they want to learn Latin?"

Tilla murmured, "I think they already know some."

"Then why will they not speak it to the master?"

It was Tilla's turn with the beer. When the cup had gone back to the old man, Ruso heard, "Because they want to stay Corionotatae."

"But they are Corionotatae."

"They don't want the children to forget where they come from."

"But how will they get by without—"

Tilla's "Sh!" almost covered the sound of Senecio's announcement that it was time to eat and that their guest should be served first.

Enica stepped forward again.

Virana hauled herself up from the bench. "I'll do it!"

Enica paused, ladle in hand, and looked to the old man for instruction.

Tilla seized Virana by the wrist. "Sit down!"

"But you said I was to help!"

"Enica will do it."

Virana pushed her hair out of her eyes and slumped back down. "I never know what helping I'm supposed to do and what other people are there for."

Moments later Enica had done her duty and Ruso had realized that she must be the old man's wife, and Branan's mother, and that was perhaps why she was less than thrilled at her husband inviting the daughter of his old flame to eat with them. By the time he had worked this out he found himself with his own beer and nursing a thick wooden bowl filled with stew at the temperature of molten lava.

He had assumed the woman would go on to serve everyone else, but instead she served only Senecio and then stepped back. Senecio gestured to him to begin. Evidently the foreign guest was expected to eat first.

Ruso glanced around. He had attended all manner of dinner parties, most of them reluctantly, but never before had he been expected to put on a display of eating for the rest of the diners. Tentatively, he licked the bottom of the spoon.

A child's voice declared, "He doesn't like it."

Someone said, "Sh!"

"Give him a chance!" hissed Branan.

He glanced at Tilla. She made a small scooping motion with one hand. Was this some sort of a test? Tilla had urged him to eat. He must not let her down. He lifted the spoon again.

There was a soft shuffle of feet and fabric as his audience shifted to get a better view, and he was struck by the thought that they might be trying to poison him.

The edge of the spoon seemed cooler now.

There was a brief moment between the tasting and the burning, a further brief moment in which he thought that a gulp of air would help, and then the pain in his mouth was gnawing its way down his throat and into his chest.

"It's very good!" he gasped. "Very—" He must have snatched at his beer, because much of it seemed to miss his mouth and course down his chin.

"Very good!" he repeated, wondering if the Britons knew the story of the Roman prisoner who had died after being force-fed with molten gold.

"He likes it!" declared someone.

He saw smiling faces at last. The child who said, "He made a mess!" was ignored, and Enica busied herself serving everyone else. So he probably hadn't been poisoned, then. But if he thought the difficult part was over, he was wrong. Senecio had been softening him up.

"We hear, healer, that you are a friend of the emperor."

Gods above, how had that rumor reached the ears of an old man in a mud hut? It was the last thing Tilla would have told anyone, even if it were true. And it was the last thing he wanted these people to believe. Ruso emerged from another swig of beer and said, "Not exactly, sir. We have met."

"I have another fine and handsome son waiting for me in the next world, sent there by the emperor's men during the troubles."

"I am sorry to hear that, sir," said Ruso, who was not supposed to have seen the security report.

"My family and I would like to know," said Senecio, "why the emperor wants to build a wall across our land."

A list of possible answers scurried around Ruso's mind and were chased away by the burning in his throat. The official reason, to separate the Romans from the barbarians, made no sense. There were barbarians on both sides, and army posts too. To collect customs tolls? To defend the land? To fix the limits of the empire? To give the troops something to do? To mark Hadrian's footsteps in a province where a new city—his usual legacy—would be as useful as a straw spear? None of it sounded convincing in the face of a man who had lost a son and half his farm, and he certainly wasn't going to repeat the common view amongst the men, who believed the wall was an admission that Britannia would never be fully brought under Roman control.

"It is the fault of the Northerners," put in Tilla. "If they stayed at home and kept their hands off other people and their property, there would be no need for a wall."

Senecio nodded. "Your family was a great loss to us all, child." He turned to Ruso. "And you, do you think the great Emperor of Rome was troubled by the Northerners killing our people and stealing our cattle?"

Ruso doubted that Hadrian was in the least bit troubled, but he was not going to say so. "If it stops the raiding, it will be a useful thing for everyone."

"Oh, it'll stop that all right," put in Conn. "It'll stop farmers getting their animals to pasture, and families from visiting, and traders from going to market."

Ruso took another long swallow of beer while somebody said something he did not catch.

"Gateways?" sneered Conn. "They're miles apart!"

Everyone wanted to join in now. The conversation shifted around the hearth, and Ruso had a few moments to finish his own drink and most of

Tilla's while trying to convince himself that his throat was not swelling shut. Around him there were complaints about the stream, which as far as he could make out had turned undrinkable lower down since the landslide and . . . something about the soldiers buying up all the food and damaging field walls and leaving gates open. Tilla was looking uncomfortable, and he wondered if they grumbled like this every evening or whether it was for his benefit. If it was, they needed to enunciate more clearly.

The one-eyed man was complaining about a cart that the soldiers had borrowed and damaged.

"You told us they paid for that," put in someone else.

The one-eyed man said that was not the point. Ruso, struggling to maneuver a chunk of vegetable onto his spoon, was fairly certain he heard, "You said it was falling apart anyway."

Senecio stepped in. "As you see, my people are not slow to join an argument."

Ruso said, "I didn't mean to start one."

The old man gave a dramatic sigh. "It is the tragedy of these islands. Our tribes saw Rome coming and, instead of uniting, the leaders fell to quarreling amongst themselves."

Ruso tried to form a facial expression that showed he was paying attention. He felt slightly detached from what was going on, but he was not drunk enough to offer opinions on the Britons.

"So now," Senecio said, "your people and ours must live side by side until Rome decides to go away again."

"Yes." The old man must have been disappointed when the building started; it was clearer than ever now that his people were in for a long wait.

Senecio said, "There should be no more killing."

"I agree." Ruso raised his beer cup in approval, but the old man had not finished.

"Marriages between our women and your men are not always successful."

Not sure how this was connected with killing, Ruso said, "My wife and I have known each other a long time." He was still just about sober enough to censor *whereas you only met her last week.*

Senecio raised his own cup. "Mara's daughter has made her choice. Until your people leave our land, healer, we will look for ways to live together."

Ruso drank, relieved that he was safe here but hoping the old man did not imagine he was talking to someone with any power to agree to

anything. Even the blankets and buckets that he had made the absent
Candidus order had failed to turn up. He realized now how unimportant
that was. The Legion seemed a long way away and curiously irrelevant.
He could not remember why the emperor had bothered coming here in
the first place. He understood completely why the Britons were baffled
and irritated by the army's interference. They should all stop quarreling. It
was all remarkably simple. There was no need for fighting. They should
respect each other. If they all gathered together around warm hearths to
share peace and beer, there would be no need for a wall.

As the murmur of conversation rose around him again, Tilla said, "You
did well. He likes you."

"Good." He wondered how long it would be before he could eat
comfortably again.

She scooped up a spoonful and drew back as it touched her lips. "Ach!
This is still hot! Is this why you spilled the drink?"

He said, "I didn't want to spit it out."

"They would have thought you were rude," she agreed. "Now they
just think you are a man who is desperate for beer."

7

THE MEAL HAD ended. People were moving about the house: men going out to fetch firewood and check the animals; women throwing down bedrolls in the shadows beyond the partitions and urging children to have one last drink, one last wee, and be sure to wash dirty hands and feet. At last Virana had the chance to get up and help, and had come back with the news that these people knew Cata, who was lucky her jaw was not broken, and that another girl had run away some time ago and nobody knew where she had gone.

"That is what happens when you choose the wrong man," Tilla told her. From behind one of the partitions she could hear the repeated *whuf* of someone punching a feather pillow into shape. The evening had gone better than she had feared. Her husband was on the far side of the fire listening to Senecio with the slightly cross look on his face that meant he was tired and having to concentrate to understand.

Then Senecio was beckoning her over to join them, and that was when she spotted the Thing for the first time, and forgot all about long-suffering girlfriends.

"I have been speaking with your man," Senecio told her.

"I am glad of it." Tilla tried to not to stare at the Thing. It was stark and

obvious now that it had slipped outside the cream wool of her husband's
best tunic.

"He tells me you have not had your marriage blessed after the custom of
our people."

"We were married in Gaul," she explained. Perhaps the old man's sky-
blue eyes were dim. Perhaps he would think it was a bird. Then she
remembered that he had recognized her across a crowded market.

"And so far," he was saying, "you have no children."

"There is plenty of time," put in her husband. As if either of them
believed that time would make a difference.

She caught his eye and glanced down at the Thing, then back up again.
A faint expression of puzzlement flitted across his face, but Senecio was
speaking again and he turned back to pay attention.

"I have been thinking," Senecio continued, "that as an old friend of
your mother and one who can remember your family, it would be a duty
and an honor to offer that blessing."

Her husband took her hand and bowed. The wretched Thing dangled
forward as if it were in flight, then landed back against his chest. "We are
the ones who are honored, sir. Thank you."

If her hand had not been trapped in his, she might have reached up and
dropped the Thing back inside his tunic. He could have worn something
like that around the army base, but what sort of man arrived to meet his
wife's family friends for the first time with a model of a flying penis strung
around his neck? She could imagine what fun Enica and the one with the
lisp would have passing that on. She tried squeezing his hand, but he
merely squeezed it back, his warm grip showing how pleased he was with
the way he thought things were going.

Senecio was speaking again. Something about the Samain festival and
how many guests would be there to share the feast and the bonfires. "And
there will be a full moon, which will bring you good fortune."

Her husband seemed confused. She explained again in slower British,
hoping she had got it right. "He is offering to give us the blessing at the
Samain feast, on the fourth night after this one."

Only afterward, when Senecio had limped off to his bed, did she find
out why her husband had said, "Ah!" as if this was a surprise, and not an
entirely pleasant one.

"I thought that was it," he said. "I thought that was the blessing. I didn't
realize he meant a whole ceremony."

How could he have imagined that was it? His understanding must be worse than she thought. "There will be singing and dancing and lots of food, and if we are lucky Senecio will make us a special poem, and there will be big bonfires because it is Samain."

"I'm not sure I want our marriage blessed on the night when the dead walk."

"When the walls between the living and the dead melt away," she corrected him. "And you will enjoy it when you get there. Now, tell me. Where did you get *that*?"

He glanced down in the direction of her accusing stare. "Oh, that! Somebody lent it to me."

He was wearing it specially. A winged penis. To meet his wife's people. She would never understand Romans.

"It's supposed to bring good luck," he said, as if that excused it. "That reminds me. There's bad news about Valens's father-in-law."

8

RUSO SURVIVED A night in a native bed, although without his native wife. It was something Tilla might have warned him about, but didn't. She seemed to be annoyed about something. Instead he had been offered a bracken-stuffed mattress and some blankets behind the wicker partition that denoted the men's area. Senecio did not join them.

He had lain awake for what seemed like hours listening to sounds that might be rodents or might be Conn creeping across from one of the other beds to knife him where he lay.

Where was his sword? What would he do if they didn't give it back?

He finally dropped off to sleep only to be woken by whispering from behind some other partition. This was followed by giggling and the unmistakeable sounds of sex. In a house with no proper rooms, everybody could hear everything that went on.

And on.

He hoped the sounds were nothing to do with Virana. The sooner that wretched girl was handed back to her family, the happier he would be. Meanwhile he would be obliged to put up with the embarrassment of some enthusiastic native ceremony with the old man making up poems about them and everyone singing those interminable ancestor songs that Tilla used to sing in the kitchen at Deva to frighten the mice away. He rolled over on the lumpy bed and tried to go back to sleep, but the gasping and grunting was annoyingly out of time with the rhythm of Conn snoring, and then almost as soon as it was over a child started to cough.

He considered getting up to find Tilla, but it was dark, he had no idea where she was, and besides, he suspected he was not entirely sober. He could hardly stumble around the house waking up sleeping bodies to find out which one he was married to, and it seemed Tilla had no plans to come and fetch him. Valens was right: No good came of mixing with the wife's friends and relations.

He woke feeling bleary and foolish. Nobody had attacked him in the night. Conn returned his sword as he left. Ruso dismissed the murmur of "I am no happier with this friendship than you are, Roman," as an attempt to salvage some British pride. Whatever the son thought, he had the old man's approval.

Had he been feeling brighter on his walk back to the fort, he would have enjoyed the sound of the birds celebrating another sunny morning. He would have savored the smell of fresh bread from the ovens over in the ramparts. Unfortunately he felt more like the dead hen that was still lying on the desk.

Pertinax was still alive. "No hemorrhage, no excessive swelling, no unexpected pain," reported Valens. He was annoyingly cheerful, having persuaded the deputy to stay awake at the bedside while he himself just dropped in a couple of times to check that nothing more needed to be done. "He's taken some poppy but he's lucid enough to insult me."

"That's good news."

"Hm." Valens settled himself on the pharmacist's table. "You look done in. Good night, then?"

"Absolutely," Ruso lied, hoping he did not smell of stale beer and farmyard. He pointed at the hen. "Why is this thing still here?"

"Ah!" Valens looked pleased with himself. "I found out about that. I think your clerk should be returning very soon. He's on cook duty tonight so he arranged to buy a decent dinner from some chap with local contacts. A man called Mallius turned up half an hour ago wanting to be paid."

"When did Candidus arrange this?"

"Some time ago, I think," said Valens, unhelpfully vague. "So tell me, exactly how mad and manipulative are these people of Tilla's?"

"I'm not sure," said Ruso, who was not going to breathe a word to Valens about the wedding blessing. "The eldest son's a nasty piece of work but the old man means well enough. I think he's genuinely concerned about Tilla. Do you mind?" He pointed at his friend's footwear, restraining the urge to cry, "Boots!" in the outraged tone adopted by Serena on the rare occasions when she and Valens were in the same room and speaking to each other.

"Sorry." Valens swung his feet down from the stool and made a half-hearted attempt to brush off the clumps of dried mud. "Apart from Pertinax it's been pretty quiet. Your centurion dropped in to ask what I thought of an invisible rash on his neck, and there was one admission in first watch with chest pains. Probably indigestion. He's in Room Five." Valens glanced at Pandora's cupboard. "I wasn't sure what to do about notes."

Ruso sighed. "Nobody is."

"Perhaps Albanus will give you a hand when he turns up."

"If he's not too busy trying to find his nephew." Ruso's brief nostalgia for the days when he had enjoyed Albanus's willing and intelligent assistance was interrupted by the sound of approaching voices. Rising above them, the scurrying of feet culminated in a thump on the door before it burst open to reveal the rumpled fair hair and pink cheeks of his deputy, Gallus, who declared, "Sirs, it's the legate!"

Valens leapt up. "I'll be off, then."

"If you run into my clerk—"

"I'll slap his wrists and send him over." With that, Valens slipped out of the room and moments later the outside door slammed.

Ruso thrust a myrrh pastille under his tongue in an attempt to sweeten his breath, and pulled his tunic straight. Then he shut the door to hide the chicken and went to head off the new arrivals before they all decided to visit Pertinax at once.

To his relief the legate decided to go in with only Ruso for company, leaving his trail of followers to wait outside.

Pertinax made an effort for his senior officer but Ruso could see he was struggling. The great man had the sense to leave after wishing the patient well, telling him he would send his personal physician, and assuring him that everything was under control. When he was gone Pertinax sank back on his pillow and closed his eyes with obvious relief.

Ruso watched the legate stride off down the street to rejoin his entourage, and decided to view the offer of the personal physician as a compliment to Pertinax rather than an insult to himself. If the next few days did not bring fever or hemorrhage or gangrene or any of the other horrors that could undermine a surgeon's best efforts, the prefect would be fit to be sent across to Magnis. Valens could deal with him and with the legate's physician too.

He was about to start his delayed ward round when a figure detached itself from the group. For a brief and unrealistic moment he thought it might be a sobered-up Fabius come to thank him for his efforts yesterday, but instead it was Fabius's deputy, looking very different without the coating of mud.

Ruso unslung the lucky charm and handed it back. "Thank you."

Daminius grinned. "I knew you'd be all right, sir. It's never let me down yet."

"Perhaps you should lend it to Pertinax. Is the quarry still closed?"

The grin faded. "The chief engineer's inspecting it this morning, sir. Meantime the lads aren't sorry to be out of it."

"Nor am I," Ruso assured him.

"We appreciate what you did, sir. If you ever need a favor, you know where we are."

Ruso was not going to let the offer lie. "If you happen to hear of the whereabouts of a clerk called Candidus, just transferred over here from Magnis . . ."

"I met him when he arrived, sir. I'll get the lads to keep an eye out. They'll be spread around till we get back to work, so somebody might know something." Daminius glanced at the legate's party retreating down the street. "Mind you, there's talk of shoring up and getting going again at the other end."

It was clear from his tone what he thought of that. Ruso had already heard the suggestion that the accident had been caused by working saturated ground with haste rather than care, perhaps spurred on by the rumors that the Sixth were ahead of their building schedule and the Second Augusta were already finished and packing to march south to Isca for the winter.

An alarming thought slipped into Ruso's mind: the thought that Candidus might have been making his way along the lip of the quarry just as Pertinax had been. That his missing clerk might even now be lying a few hundred paces south of the main road, buried under tons of rubble, while his feathered dinner lay slowly decomposing on his desk.

Moments later he left Pertinax's room reassured that the prefect had been alone up there. Thinking rationally, he could see the utter improbability of Candidus vanishing for a couple of days and then returning to wander around in the sight of any senior officer, let alone one as fearsome as Pertinax. He was worrying about nothing. The lad had probably decided that the challenge of sorting out Pandora's cupboard was too much for him and slipped away to Coria for a few days' unofficial leave. He would stroll in one morning full of innocence and excuses, trusting that Ruso would pretend to believe him because his uncle was a friend. With luck, he would turn up before Albanus did.

Meanwhile, Ruso needed to get the kitchen to do something with that hen. Then there was a ward round to be done, and over at the camp a queue would already be forming outside the medical tent.

9

MARKET DAYS IN the autumn meant a chilly start in the dark, but by the time they got there the sun had chased away the nip of frost and everyone had cheered up. His da went off with the other men, which meant he would stumble back in a good mood—or a very bad one. His stepmother went to catch the early bargains. Aedic was left in charge of Petta's son, who was not yet old enough to notice that Aedic called him "the unbrother" when Petta wasn't listening.

He took the unbrother down to the river and made him take his clothes off because Petta said if he came back with his clean tunic messed up again, there would be trouble. Everyone who wasn't being made to help his parents was down there, and as Aedic had hoped, everyone wanted to hear the story of the soldier having his leg sawn off.

Everyone except Matto, who pointed out that he hadn't actually seen the sawing happen. "Anyway," Matto said, "am I showing you how to catch trout or not?"

The one-legged soldier was forgotten. Instead there was a lot of peering into the water and stumbling about on feet numb with cold. Nobody managed to find a trout, let alone tickle one. Matto said it was Aedic's fault for bringing the unbrother. The unbrother couldn't stay still or keep quiet. He had frightened the fish away.

"There weren't any fish anyway," Aedic told him, not seeing why he should get the blame just because Matto had bragged about something and then couldn't do it. "I never saw one."

"You don't *see* them under there," said Matto. "You *feel* them."

"You have to see the tail."

Matto said, "Don't."

"Yes you do. My da says."

"What does your da know?" said Matto. "He's a drunk."

He was not going to get dragged into that. "My da's caught hundreds of trout," he said. "How many have you caught?"

"Liar!" said Matto, so quickly that Aedic knew he didn't want to answer.

"Go on, how many?"

"Loads," said Matto. "Anyway, you're lucky we let you join in. After what everybody says about you."

"*You're* the liar!" was not much of an answer, but he didn't know what Matto was talking about. What *did* they say about him?

"Ha!" said Matto, making sure everyone was listening, "Everybody knows you're a soldiers' bumboy!"

There were shouts of laughter as Aedic yelled, "I am not!"

The unbrother, excited by the argument, waved his arms about. "Bumboy! Bum-bum-bum—"

"Shut up!" he shouted. It was all the unbrother's fault for squealing and splashing in the first place. "I am not!"

He was facing Matto now, each standing on a rock with the water gurgling in between. Matto was at least a handspan taller, and heavier, and his rock was higher. Everyone else had gathered round to watch the fight. "I am not!"

"Not what?"

"Not what you said. You take that back."

"Everybody's seen you. Hanging around, trying to talk to them."

"I just do jobs for them!" Aedic wished he hadn't stayed to try and catch the stupid trout. Matto's family had been turned off their land too. The army had given them a farm miles away that the soldiers had stolen from its owners, but it was mostly rock and bog, and the family had nothing good to say about people who dealt with Romans. "Lots of people do jobs for them!"

"Ha! I bet you love the soldiers. I bet when nobody's looking you *kiss* them!"

His shouts of "No I don't!" were lost under shrieks of laughter and howls of "Kissy-kissy!" from the other boys. His face was hot. Matto's "Look at him going red! It's true!" just made it worse.

"Anyway," he shouted, desperate to stop them before the whole world thought he kissed the soldiers, "I know something you don't!"

Matto said, "Who cares?"

But for a happy moment the shouting died away. They wanted to know.

Matto said, "What is it, then? Another thing you didn't see happen?"

Aedic swallowed. Why had he said that? What was he thinking? He might have got it all wrong. It could be one of those times where you said what you thought was true and all the grown-ups laughed at you and then repeated what you'd said to each other while you tried to smile as if you'd made a joke on purpose. "Not telling."

Matto had a smirk on his face, as if he'd finally proved how stupid Aedic was. The son of a drunk. The soldier-kisser. "Liar," he breathed. Then he moved his mouth slowly round the words, "Bumboy."

Aedic squared his shoulders. "It's about the emperor's wall."

"What about it?"

"There's a dead body inside it."

For a moment nobody spoke. There was a look on Matto's face that said he wasn't expecting *that* and he didn't know how to answer. Aedic stood taller as the others crowded round his rock.

"Where?"

"Who is it?"

"Who put it there?"

"Was it dead when it went in?"

"Was it buried alive?"

Matto narrowed his eyes. "How do you know?"

Trust Matto to ask something like that. "I know . . . somebody who saw them put it in there."

"Who's that, then?"

"He's making it up."

"I am not!"

"Tell us who saw it, then!"

"Tell us where it is!"

"Is it one of us or one of them?"

"He's lying. Look at him! Liar!"

"It's true," Aedic insisted.

"Tell us who saw it," said Matto, "else we'll know you're lying."

He took a deep breath. "I swore not to tell."

"We won't let on!"

"But I made an oath—"

He couldn't say the rest because Matto jumped on him. His knee smashed against hard rock and cold water rushed up his nose and into his throat. Then there were fingers jammed up his nostrils, wrenching his head back and pulling his mouth out into the air. He managed to stop coughing long enough to splutter, "Lemme go!"

"Who saw it?"

"Let go!"

"Tell us who saw it."

"You got to swear not to tell! Ow!"

"Who was it?"

Aedic's nose was being torn off his face. The pain was unbearable. He cast about inside his mind for the name of somebody no one saw very often. "Swear!"

Matto was shouting, "I swear!"

"Hope to die?"

"May the sky fall on me!"

Aedic gasped, feeling the pain ease as he named a boy who lived with a family on the other side of the wall. It wouldn't matter. Da said they wouldn't be seeing much of anybody over there from now on because the army were going to make everyone pay to go through special gates to get across, and they would search all the vehicles, so nobody would bother. He repeated the name, running his fingers gently across his face to check that his nose was still attached. "He saw it."

"Saw what?" Matto pushed him away. "What did he see?"

They were all quiet now, wanting more. Aedic could hardly believe he had started this. The body was real now, even if it hadn't been before.

He got up very slowly. He rubbed his nose again, sniffed, and spat. "He was hiding up there one night," he said. "It was nearly dark and the patrol had gone past, and he saw a man carry a dead body up the hill and drop it in the middle of the wall. Then the man covered it up with stones and the next day the soldiers came and carried on building over the top of it."

"What man? Who was it? What did he look like?"

"He didn't say," he said, thinking fast. "He said if he tells, the man'll come and get him too."

Matto scowled, as if he wasn't sure whether to believe it.

One of the smaller boys said, "Will the man come and get us too now?"

"Don't be stupid," put in someone else. "We don't know who he is."

"We don't know anything," added somebody else.

"That's why you mustn't tell anyone about the body," Aedic reminded them. "If you tell, he'll know that you know."

Would they keep their word? Or would they go chasing after the boy he had named next time they saw him, wanting to know whether it was really true about the dead body inside the Great Wall? That was what Aedic would have done.

"Hah!" Matto cried. "You're in more trouble now. You broke an oath. You'll die a horrible death and crows will eat your eyes and worms will go up your nose."

"Back to you!" Aedic told him, but before it could all start again the unbrother slipped and landed in the water. The dead body was forgotten in the race to pull him out. After that, Aedic had a new problem: how to explain to Petta why the unbrother's clothes weren't wet and dirty but the rest of him was.

10

R USO'S ENTRY TO the big camp above the quarry was delayed by a troop of cavalry streaming out of the north gate toward the road. Then a full century of infantry marched past him. He knew better than to ask the guards where they were going. There were easier ways to find out.

He picked his way past banners and laundry that fluttered bravely above mud that wouldn't dry out until next April, and arrived at the medical tent.

The landslide was yesterday's news. The morning queue was buzzing with tales of a man from the Twentieth who had been kidnapped by the natives. Opinions differed on how it had happened—he had been collecting firewood, he had gone to a farm to buy a dog, or retrieve stolen property, or ask directions, or had been lured with promises of a woman—but one way or another, all were agreed that the unlucky legionary had been held captive overnight and only rescued at dawn when a passing road patrol heard his calls for help.

Everyone knew what those barbarians would get up to if they had the chance. Whatever had been done to him was so gruesome that it was being kept secret. The men Ruso had seen were going out to deal with the culprits.

"Do we know who it is?" Ruso asked, hoping it wasn't Candidus.

The queue consulted itself for a few minutes before agreeing that no name had been mentioned, although, come to think of it, wasn't there a clerk who had gone missing? Nobody could remember what he was called, but several were certain he was the victim. "They could have had him for days, then," observed one glum soul.

"Poor sod."

"Don't bear thinking about." There was a general grunt of agreement, and then silence while the queue thought about it anyway.

"We'll find out more before long," Ruso told them. "Until then, forget it. This sort of attack is designed to rattle us. Don't give them the satisfaction."

There was a dutiful chorus of "Yes, sir."

For the next hour Ruso forced himself to follow his own advice and concentrate on minor injuries and ailments. The victim had been rescued. The hospital staff would send word from the fort if he was needed.

As soon as he had prescribed the last stomach pill and lanced an abscess for an ungrateful carpenter, he hurried across to the gates in search of the watch captain.

"It's not your missing clerk, sir. I have it from a reliable source that he's a plumber." Perhaps sensing his anxiety, the man added, "I can show you where your man's supposed to be, if you like."

Together they picked their way down between the rows, past a sign that read, NO FIRES IN TENTS, because apparently a man intelligent enough to read might still be cold enough to suffocate himself or burn his tent down. In places the duckboards were only marginally less slippery than the mud beneath them. Someone unacquainted with the British climate had thought it would be a good idea to site a camp across the line of a stream, and despite Pertinax's past efforts to see that the trackways were kept clear and the latrines under control, large areas that had started out as a gently sloping field in the spring had been reduced to stinking quagmire. In other circumstances Ruso would have complained about the effect of the conditions on the men's health, but there was no point: Any other rain-sodden field would be almost as bad in a few days, and they were going home soon.

The shadowy interior of Tent V, Row VII contained a lone human form under a blanket: head at one end, feet—one sporting a fat linen bandage—poking out from the other. Beside him, bedding was stacked on top of a large wooden box that was in turn resting on two logs above the damp. A couple of shields in leather cases were propped against the upright at the far end. A limp and mildewed straw sun hat dangled from the ridgepole.

"Shift yourself, sunshine," said the watch captain, applying a boot to the sleeper. "Got an officer here looking for a man called Candidus."

The sleeper blinked, then scrambled hastily out of bed and attempted a salute. "I'm recuperating, sir," he explained. "Doctor's orders. Burned foot." There was a moment of mutual recognition. "You remember me, sir. I trod in a bucket of lime."

"I do," agreed Ruso, remembering the sufferer's foot better than his face. "How is it?"

"Not too bad, sir, thanks. I can manage on crutches. Or I could, if it wasn't for—" He gestured toward the treacherous pathway outside the tent.

"Candidus," the watch captain repeated. "Where is he?"

"Haven't seen him, sir."

"Not ever," suggested the watch captain, "or just not lately?"

The man scratched his head, as if this were too subtle a question for one who had only just woken up.

"He arrived several days ago," Ruso prompted. "He was assigned to this tent."

"Ah," said the man, apparently enlightened. "Him." He pointed toward a leather bag resting on a shield by the goatskin wall that separated indoors from outdoors. On top of the bag sat a helmet speckled with rust. Next to it, shoved halfway out under the flap and onto the grass, lay an untidy roll of bedding. "That's his kit, sir."

Ruso leaned across and lifted the equipment out to where he could examine it. "Did you see him arrive?"

The man was looking apprehensive. "I've never seen him, sir. He turned up while I was in the sick bay."

Ruso understood the soldier's nervousness when he examined the contents of the bag: some musty undergarments, a crumpled tunic, three odd socks with holes in them, and a pen with a broken nib. He turned it upside down over the empty bed and shook it. Two dice tumbled out. He rolled them around on his palm for a moment, then threw everything back in.

An empty waterskin was tied to the strap on the shield cover. The shield itself turned out to have CANDCSILXXVV painted in uneven white letters at the base, covering the name of a previous owner. *Candidus in the century of Silvanus, Twentieth Legion Valeria Victrix.* He definitely had the right man. Or rather, he didn't have him, and he had no idea who did.

Eyeing the meager collection of possessions, he said, "Where's the rest?" The man opened his mouth, but nothing came out.

"Food pan, cup, spoon?" Ruso prompted. "Weapons, armor?" Without the owner, he had no way of knowing what else was missing.

The man swallowed. Petty theft caused such disruption amongst men who had to live closely together that punishments ranged from flogging to dismissal. Small wonder, then, that he looked relieved when Ruso said, "If somebody else is looking after them for him, tell us now. I don't want to waste time searching the tent."

A scrabble in the box and the unraveling of bedrolls produced a bronze cooking pan with a folding handle, another pen in better condition, and a pottery inkwell. As Ruso expected, CAND had been scraped or burned into each item by a soldier who was keen to guard against this very eventuality. These were followed by two tunics, two pairs of socks, and a neckerchief, none of which were labeled but would have been easily identified by their owner.

The man seemed confident that no spoon or eating implements of any kind had been removed for alleged safekeeping, nor had any weapons or armor. Since Candidus had taken the precaution of marking everything else, Ruso assumed he was telling the truth and that none had been found when the tentmates raided the absent newcomer's belongings.

"Money?" he suggested, without much hope.

"No, sir," said the man, knowing as well as he did that any coins that had vanished into someone else's purse would be safely anonymous.

Ruso gathered up what he had managed to salvage of Candidus's possessions. "If he turns up, tell him his kit is up at the fort hospital. Meanwhile I need to talk to anyone who might have seen him."

When Ruso confirmed that he had no more questions, the watch captain eyed the invalid. "Aren't you on cooking duty?"

"I was just about to start, sir."

Outside, the watch captain shook his head. "Looks like your man's deserted, sir."

"In his armor?"

"You'd be surprised, sir. He'd look less suspicious that way. And he could always sell it later."

Ruso sighed. "I promised his uncle I'd keep an eye on him."

"I wouldn't worry, sir," the watch captain assured him cheerily. "A lot of the lone wanderers come back. It's no fun out there on your own with the natives, as our plumber's just found out."

"What happens to the ones who don't come back?"

The watch captain had no more idea than anyone else. "I'll let you know straightaway when he turns up, sir."

"In the meantime if you can find anyone who's seen him—anyone at all—I want to talk to them."

Ruso lashed Candidus's possessions together, slung them over his shoulder, and squelched his way back toward the gates. Candidus's new accommodation was a definite step down from the permanent quarters over at Magnis. Perhaps the tent—or its occupants—had frightened him off. He had not seemed the toughest of individuals, and Albanus had described him as not only sensitive but—and this was more believable—"rather easily led." But where, in this land of wide rolling hills, wooded valleys, native huts, and building sites, could anyone have led him? And what if he had not been led but forced?

A stronger-than-usual smell of burning hung in the air as he made his way back to the comparative comfort of the fort. Glancing around, he saw thick columns of black smoke billowing up into the clouds on the western skyline. Even at this distance, he could make out glimmers of orange flame inside them. A cluster of four or five things that shouldn't be burning were fiercely ablaze, and it was not difficult to guess what they were. The locals who had attacked the plumber would be long gone, but the stink of their homes going up in smoke would linger in the nostrils for days. It would be a lesson. Or another wrong to feel aggrieved about, depending on which side of the divide you were born. He could understand why Senecio, having lost one son and with another clearly spoiling for a fight, was doing his best to prevent any repeat of the vicious battles that had taken place around this border only a few seasons ago. It was a pity more of his countrymen did not feel the same way.

A squad of legionaries carrying shovels and picks were tramping past him. Their salutes were exemplary, but their gazes lingered a little too long. He glanced down at himself. Was there something unusual about him? Tunic caught up in his belt? Dirt on his nose? Something stuck in his hair? Then he realized. They were enjoying the sight of an officer carrying his own kit.

They would have been even more surprised if they had known it was somebody else's.

11

Ruso was barely through the door of the hospital at Parva when he heard raised voices. He left the door open, dumped Candidus's kit in front of Pandora's cupboard, and followed the sound. A cluster of legionaries were blocking the far end of the corridor.

The cries of "No visitors!" from Gallus, Ruso's baby-faced deputy, were barely audible above the various voices demanding to be let in on the grounds that they were his mates, he would want to see them, they would cheer him up, and yells of "You all right in there, old son?" and "Chin up, mate!"

The shape of the group shifted. They were trying to drag the protesting Gallus out of the way.

Doors opened. Several staff hurried down to join the fray, and a couple of patients stumbled out to see what the commotion was.

"Out!" ordered Ruso, pointing toward the exit. The noise of protest died down.

"But, sir—"

"You," said Ruso, choosing one and looking him in the eye. The others fell silent. "Name?"

The man straightened. "Peregrinus, sir. Century of Fabius."

"Why are you causing a commotion in my hospital?"

"Regulus is in there, sir. The natives have been at him and we want to make sure he's all right."

Gallus, breathing heavily, was still stationed between the outside world and the door latch. His whole face was now as pink as his cheeks. "It's the kidnap victim, sir," he explained. "The tribune says no visitors and no passing on information."

An orderly approached to announce that Prefect Pertinax wanted to know what all the din was and when he was going to get some crutches.

"Tell him it's under control," said Ruso, ushering the reluctant gang of legionaries toward the street door with a promise to send on news when there was any.

Back in the corridor, inquisitive heads disappeared and doors closed.

"And the crutches, sir?"

"Absolutely not!" Seeing the expression on the orderly's face, Ruso added, "Just be brave and tell him I said no. He can't catch you. He's only got one foot."

Another figure still loitered in the doorway. Ruso recognized the once-blond soldier who had passed up the waterskin to the trapped Pertinax. The bandage on his wrist was even grimier than before. He was poking at the loose end with his forefinger, trying to tuck it back in.

"You're not one of his friends too?"

"No, sir. Mallius."

"From the quarry."

"Yes, sir. I was wanting a word with your clerk."

"Is it about a hen?"

It was. The deal had been struck the day before Candidus disappeared and the delivery had been made on time. The payment had not.

"He was definitely expecting it yesterday?"

"Yes, sir. He said it was his turn on cook duty and he wanted something tasty."

It was not Ruso's business to wonder how a quarryman might have obtained a hen. He paid up to get rid of him, then turned to Gallus. Did you say there's a tribune here?" This morning the legate, this afternoon one of his tribunes. More important guests in one day than they usually welcomed in a month.

"Tribune Accius brought the patient in, sir. But he's gone now."

It was a pity. He might have gleaned some sense about the kidnap from Accius, with whom he had worked before. He dismissed the rest of the staff and said quietly to Gallus, "How is he?"

The medic scratched his head. "I'm not really sure, sir. But he's well enough to tell you himself."

Regulus the plumber, alone in Room IX, was a sorry sight. This was hardly surprising, since he had, by his own account, been jumped by a gang of natives the night before, stripped naked, bound, and then strung up on a branch by his feet and dangled head-first over a woodland stream. If the road patrol had not heard his faint cries for help this morning, he would be hanging there still.

"Starving and freezing, sir," he added, scratching his ribs with one blotchy hand and reaching with the other for the cup on the table beside his bed. "And being eaten alive. Even in October. The whole bloody place was swarming with things that bite and sting. And that was before the rats."

Ruso said, "You were bitten by rats?"

He shook his head. "I kept moving and shouting to frighten them off, sir."

Given last night's rain and nighttime temperatures on the border in October, the man was lucky to have survived.

"I wondered if they put him over the stream deliberately because of the insects, sir," put in Gallus. "They smeared dog dung on his face and honey on his privates."

The victim squirmed, either at the memory of the smell or the humiliation, while Ruso deliberately avoided catching his deputy's eye. It would be interesting to see whether the official attempt to keep this story quiet had any effect. He said, "As far as you know, were you the only victim?"

"I was all alone, sir. Just me and all them barbarians jabbering away in their own language." Regulus looked up. "They didn't get somebody else, did they?"

"Not as far as I know," said Ruso, hoping they had not, and catching a waft of wine that was presumably medicinal. "Finish your drink and let's take a look at you."

Beneath the linen sheet Regulus was indeed covered in red lumpy insect bites. He did not seem to have been beaten, but there were abrasions around his wrists and ankles. The ankles were slightly swollen and he winced when they were examined. He tried and failed to bend his ankles or wiggle his toes when instructed. Ruso pressed on the nail of each hairy big toe. The pink color returned immediately. "Stand up for me, will you?"

A pained expression passed over the blotchy face. "Just give it a try," Ruso suggested.

Regulus swung his legs over the side of the bed, placed his feet gingerly on the rush mat, and gasped. "I'm sorry, sir."

"That'll do," Ruso conceded, crouching down to look again. "How does it feel when you put weight on them?"

"Like . . . like somebody's sticking knives in my ankles, sir." Regulus's voice was weak with the pain.

"All right," said Ruso, "you can get back into bed now." He added, "Try not to scratch," although he knew he might as well have told the man to hover three feet above the bed all afternoon.

"Thank you, sir." Legs limp in front of him, Regulus bottom-shuffled his way back up the bed toward the pillow. He closed his eyes, exhausted. Then he lifted one knee and raked at the opposite calf with his toenails.

Ruso pulled up the sheet. There was much here that he did not understand, but there was no doubt that the lad had been set upon. "Have you any idea why they did it?"

"Not a clue, sir." Regulus shook his head sadly. "They just went for me. Like a pack of wolves."

"So where were you when this happened?"

Regulus reached under the sheet to scratch, caught Ruso's eye, and rocked from side to side as he tucked both hands under his buttocks. "I was lured onto native property, sir. They had a terrier bitch with pups ready to go. I'd got one reserved, see? So I went inside to collect him and that's when they jumped me." Unable to scratch, he writhed against the bedding. "You can't trust them, sir."

"So these were people you'd met before?"

"That's the thing, sir. They was all right when I went to see the pups the first time. Then they turned nasty. I told them, 'Keep the money.' I said, 'I don't want no trouble,' but they didn't listen. I tried to put up a bit of a fight, sir, but there was lots of them." He gazed down at his feet. "Will I walk again, sir?"

"I don't see why not," Ruso assured him.

Regulus retrieved one hand and rubbed his wet eyes with his fist.

Ruso handed him a cloth from the shelf by the window.

"Thank you, sir." He blew his nose into the cloth. "Sorry, sir. I'm just glad to be alive, really."

"I'll tell your friends you're doing well," Ruso told him.

"Thanks for keeping them out, sir."

"Tribune's orders," Ruso explained. "It's a pity. We could have charged admission."

12

FABIUS LEANED BACK, winced, and readjusted his cushions before patting his hair back into place. "I'm definitely not well, Doctor. I feel extraordinarily tired, and I have pains all over."

"I'm sorry to hear that." Ruso helped himself to a seat and indulged his regular fantasy of ransacking Fabius's house for medical textbooks and burning them. He kept his own scrolls well hidden from patients with a tendency to diagnose themselves, but since the visit of a traveling medicine-seller Fabius had found himself warding off an alarming variety of diseases. For some reason he thought Ruso might be interested.

This was in sharp contrast to Tilla, who had dismissed the only Latin medical text Ruso possessed as useless. Her patients could not indulge themselves with special diets eaten at particular hours of the day, arranged round gentle walks and set rest periods. Most of them were lucky to have food at all.

Unfortunately there was no one in the fort who had the authority to tell Fabius to be ill on his own time and not the Legion's. Ruso's assertions that there seemed to be nothing wrong with him had been met with surprise: Surely a modern doctor like himself was aware that looking healthy could be a sign of impending sickness? Did he not realize that Fabius had already cheated death several times by taking to his bed and giving up work, food, and sex at the first sign of symptoms?

Faced with this unassailable evidence, and suspecting the kitchen maid would be glad of the rest, Ruso had given up arguing and done his best to avoid him. But today there was no choice. While Fabius settled on his day couch, Ruso gave him the news that Regulus was as comfortable as could be expected.

"I would have gone to visit him," said Fabius, looking almost genuinely sorry, "But the tribune doesn't want him disturbed."

"I don't think he meant you," Ruso said, but Fabius was too busy thinking up a better excuse to notice the tone. Not optimistic, Ruso explained about Candidus: "I thought he must have just gone absent without leave, but I've been through his kit and he hasn't taken the things you'd expect. Plus, he'd made commitments." In the shape of a chicken.

"Perhaps he left on impulse."

"Your man was kidnapped. It's possible mine is also being held somewhere against his will."

Fabius leaned sideways and straightened the fringe on his rug. "Surely the quarry camp should be looking for him?"

"They can't find him. And he's supposed to be working for me, here."

Fabius ordered his clerk to make a note of the name, but instead of writing, the point of the stylus remained poised half an inch above the wax. "Candidus," Ruso reminded him.

"Full name, sir?" enquired the clerk.

"No idea."

Fabius frowned. "We do want to be looking for the right man, Doctor."

It was commonly assumed that the Sixth had offered Fabius's services to the undermanned Twentieth in order to get rid of him. Possibly his family had felt the same way, since he seemed to have been lowered into the centurionate from a great social height, rather than battling his way up to it through the ranks. With luck he would soon be given a medical discharge from the Legion. Unfortunately *soon* did not mean this morning.

"Since he's my man," Ruso pointed out, "he's technically under the command of Prefect Pertinax. So I'll be keeping the prefect informed about the inquiry while he's in the hospital."

Even lying gravely injured in a hospital bed, Pertinax had the power to impress. Fabius said, "Ah," as if he were seeing the situation in a new light. He examined his interlaced fingers for a moment, then looked up. "What do you think we should do?"

"Make urgent inquiries of our local informers," Ruso told him, wondering why Fabius's fellow centurions had not arranged for him to be transferred to the lead mines. "And have the kidnappers questioned, assuming we've got them. If you send a request to HQ, they can start this afternoon."

"Yes. Yes, I suppose they could."

Ruso had intended to ask only for official notices to be sent to the other forts, but Fabius's attitude so annoyed him that he added, "And if the quarry work is on hold until the landslide's sorted out, there must be spare men who could go out to search."

"Ah." Fabius turned to his clerk again. "I should think you could draft a suitable sort of letter to HQ, couldn't you? Tell them we've lost somebody."

Wishing he had the authority to order it himself, Ruso said, "What about a search?"

Fabius pondered that for a moment, then seemed to find inspiration. "Daminius!" he said. "He's your man. Daminius will have nothing to do while the quarry's closed. Why don't I ask him to see to it?"

"Yes," agreed Ruso, finding himself mimicking the tone. "Why don't you?"

Fabius turned to his clerk. "Could you find out where Daminius is, do you think?"

"He's doing something for the chief engineer in the quarry, sir. Then he's due to report to you afterward."

Fabius's face brightened even further. "Excellent! When he gets here, tell him to go straight to the doctor instead. They can all go and look for this missing man."

13

TILLA LEFT HER patient's house feeling at peace with her world. Last night's meeting had not been as bad as she had feared. Conn had been rude and Enica cold, but old Senecio had made them welcome and her husband had agreed to his blessing. Perhaps it would do some good: Who knew? Besides, it would be a change to have something cheerful at Samain. It was a time when she missed her family. Every year she slipped away to gaze out into the night in the hope of seeing her own dead walking toward her, but they never came.

Meanwhile the sun was shining, the trees were turning golden, the hedge was dotted with red rose hips and pale green globes of ivy blossom, and the mother and week-old baby she had just visited were doing well. When she got back to Ria's she would have some privacy to practice her reading: Virana would be busy serving downstairs, continuing her last-ditch attempt to snare the man of her dreams before she had to carry a fatherless baby home to face the disapproval of her family.

Tilla pursed her lips. She was not going to feel guilty about saying good-bye to Virana. That had always been the arrangement. *You can stay until you have the baby. Then you must go home.* Her husband would have sent the girl back straightaway, but Tilla had won him over, as she knew she would. So he confined his complaining to insisting that this must not happen again. *We are not taking in any others. After this we'll buy a slave and live like a normal family.* She had been tempted to say, *A normal family plants in spring and is still there to harvest in summer. A normal family has children.* But she had chosen a soldier, and neither of them had chosen the emptiness where children should have been, so there was nothing to gain by pouring vinegar into the wound.

A robin flew up from the side of the track as she approached, and sat watching her from the safety of a hawthorn. She stopped, then moved slowly forward, obliged to skirt round a puddle to keep her distance. It crossed her mind that a Roman would probably try to throw a net over it and roast it for supper. She was almost level with it now. Perhaps she could pass without frightening it.

Too late. It fluttered up, over the hedge and—

Tilla stopped again and felt her heart quicken. Felt the dread tightening her stomach. How long had that been there? How could she have failed to notice it? Over toward the fort, the perfect sky was marred by soaring billows of thick black smoke.

She ran down to the road, her skirts gathered up in her fists and her bag clamped under one elbow to stop it swinging about. By the time she was halfway back she could see it was not the fort, nor the camp. It was too far away to be Senecio's house, but it was definitely someone's farm dying below the writhing smoke, and the separate columns said it must be deliberate.

She barely heard the mule cart over the rasp of her own breath, but the local voice shouting, "Want a lift, missus?" caught her attention. Soon she was seated behind a weaver and his wife, listening to them arguing about which of their neighbors' houses was on fire. They did nothing to calm her rising fear that it was the home of one of her patients.

She jumped down from the cart at the turn to Senecio's house and started running again. She was almost at the gate when she saw the soldier standing guard.

For a moment they stared at each other in surprise, then he lifted the loop of rope and held the gate open for her, stretching out his other arm to guide her as if she were a sheep being ushered into a pen. She said in Latin, "What is happening?"

"Go on in, miss. Just routine. Nothing to worry about."

"Why are you here? Where is the family?"

"Just go on in, miss."

She heard voices. Stepping forward, she could see past the oak tree to where some of the family seemed to be lined up in the yard, facing a couple more soldiers.

Behind her the guard shouted, "Adult female coming in!"

Senecio's chair had been brought out, but he was standing, supported on one side by Enica and on the other by the small form of Branan. Conn was nowhere to be seen. Nor was the one-eyed man or the tall, skinny one. A couple of the children were crying.

One of the soldiers facing the family motioned her to join them. She heard men's voices inside the house as she crossed the yard.

The woman with the lisp moved to make space. As she passed in front of her, Tilla murmured, "Where are the men?"

"Safe," came the soft reply. Tilla took her place in the line next to Branan. The soldier in charge pointed at her and looked as though he were waiting for something.

She had seen that face beneath the helmet before. He sometimes ate in Ria's bar. He was a junior officer of some kind. For once, she wished Virana were here. Virana knew what all the soldiers were called.

"Tell them your name," Branan whispered.

She told him her local name. The other one made some attempt to write it down.

"We here," the officer announced in very bad British, "to look for man. Soldier man. Him lost. You tell."

The family showed not a trace of understanding or amusement. She knew most of them would have understood him if he had spoken his own tongue, but it was a small form of revenge to make him struggle like that: perhaps the only one they could exact without getting themselves into trouble. *We do not speak Latin in this house.* Perhaps they would share the joke later. *Him one ugly man. Him think we as stupid as he is.* Meanwhile she spoke up in the forbidden but very useful language of Rome: "If you describe him, sir, perhaps we can help."

His relief showed on his face. "We don't want trouble," he told her. "We want a missing soldier. Name of Candidus. Five feet three inches tall, thin, dark hair. Been gone three days. You tell me if you've seen him or know anything about him." He jerked his thumb toward the smoke. "That's what happens if I think you're lying."

Tilla had begun to translate when there was a metallic crash inside the house and someone swore. It sounded as if the fire irons had been tipped over. "Careful, mate," called a voice. "Yeah," put in someone else. "That could have landed on your toe."

She said, "If there is damage, I will speak to my husband and we will make a complaint."

The soldier squinted at her. "Don't I know you?"

"I am the wife of Medical Officer Ruso of your own legion."

The face brightened for a moment. "Ah! I thought so." He broke off to yell, "Steady on, lads! Officer's wife present!" then returned his attention to Tilla. "You can tell your husband all about it when you get home, miss. He's the one who ordered the search."

14

SOMEBODY NEEDED TO grease those hinges. They sounded like two flocks of seagulls having a fight. Or like a set of hefty gates in the charge of some very sloppy soldiers. They shouldn't be closed before curfew, either.

Ruso, returning from afternoon rounds at the camp, was about to shout when two shawled figures seemed to detach themselves from the fort wall and hurried toward him. Behind them, the screech of iron on stone died away.

"There you are!" cried the slimmer of the two women in a cloud of frosted breath. Ruso stared at them. "What are you two doing here?"

His wife stabbed a finger toward the gates. "I am here because those men will not let me in!"

"And I am here because the mistress is very upset," said Virana, taking Tilla's arm as if she needed physical as well as moral support. "The people at the farm were nasty to her."

The guards saluted from beneath the archway, but they were taking no chances. "Password, sir!"

Stepping forward, he murmured, "Morning star," to the guards and then returned to his wife. "There's a security alert," he explained, secretly relieved that Tilla's short friendship with the local family seemed to be over. "They won't let anyone in. You should have left a message."

"This is too important for writing down!" Tilla insisted. "I am shamed! Why are you sending soldiers to Senecio's house?"

"I haven't . . ." Even as he denied it, light dawned.

Tilla said, "They are looking for your clerk and taking names and burning people's farms down!"

"They're *what*?"

"They are burning houses!" insisted Virana. "Did you not see the smoke in the sky?"

"They searched the houses and the cow barn," said Tilla. "They knocked over the loom and the fire irons and licked the honey spoon and drank the beer and broke some eggs. They said they might set fire to everything. If I had not told them I was your wife, who knows what they would have done? And then they told everybody that you had ordered them to do it!"

"Are you sure it wasn't Daminius and the boys from the quarry? They're—"

"You see! You *do* know about it! What were you thinking? You eat at their hearth, the old man offers the honor of a blessing, and now you send soldiers to insult him!"

"The mistress is very upset!" Virana seemed to have run out of new things to say.

The trumpet finally wailed the curfew from beyond the ramparts. The guards, too far away to hear the conversation, were enjoying the sight of their medical officer being harangued by two outraged women. "There's been some trouble," he explained. "One of our plumbers has been kidnapped and knocked about by the locals. Albanus's nephew is still missing and I'm worried the same thing's happened to him. I need to be sure he isn't—"

"Albanus's nephew is not in Senecio's house!"

"No," he agreed, scratching one ear and wondering whether he ought to go over there and apologize. "But the burning was nothing to do with me. That was punishment for the kidnappers."

"But it *is* to do with you, husband! It was the house of Senecio's sister and they were invited to our wedding blessing and the daughter is one of my patients!"

"Oh, gods above!" He felt his shoulders drop. "Wife, why did you get yourself involved with these people?"

"Conn went over to try and help. The houses are gone. All their winter stores are burned or stolen and the land has been salted. Conn found no bodies, but in the burning, who knows?"

Recalling the size of the force leaving the camp this morning, he said, "They probably saw our men coming and ran away."

"And if they are not dead, how will they live through the winter with no stores?"

He was not going to attempt to answer that one.

"And then Senecio's house is full of soldiers, and when I ask them to stop making a mess, they say you sent them!"

"I came with the mistress to find you," put in Virana. "We came but you were not here!" Evidently she felt this compounded his guilt.

He hoped that at least their potential wedding guests had been the real culprits. It was entirely possible that the centurion in charge, having failed to find the guilty natives, had allowed his men to wreak revenge on the nearest ones instead. But he could not say that in front of either of these women. "We didn't start this," he said. "One of our men was attacked."

Tilla said, "What did they do to him?"

"I can't discuss it." He was still puzzled by the nature of Regulus's injuries, but leaving a naked man hanging upside down in a tree was an insult that could not be ignored.

She said, "What is his name?"

"His *name*? What's that got to do with anything?"

"Do you know it?"

"Regulus."

To his surprise, his wife bowed her head and covered her face with her hands. "No, no!" she was saying. "I told them to wait; I told them—"

A wave of guilty relief swept over him. "You knew they were planning this?"

She looked up. "Of course not! But I know of this man. His woman is my patient. They argued. He knocked her down—this is not the first time—and kicked her and stamped on her fingers. I told her to leave him. I told the family to put in an official complaint to his centurion."

"And did they?" He very much hoped not, because he could not imagine Fabius doing anything useful about it. Already he was seeing Regulus's injuries from a new perspective.

"I do not know."

"I don't remember you telling me about this patient."

Tilla pulled her shawl tighter around her shoulders. "I did not tell you."

That was good. He was afraid it might have been another of those times where he wasn't really listening.

"I did not tell you because when I tried to help that family who had their goat stolen, you told me you are not a messenger boy for disgruntled natives."

He took a long breath. Valens was right: Women's memories really did have a special place for storing up phrases they might want to fling back at you later. He said, "Well, you did the right thing."

"I have told Senecio you will apologize."

"I see."

"It is a great insult, master!" repeated Virana. "If you do not make things right, there might be no wedding blessing!"

It was a tempting prospect. "Aren't you supposed to be at work?"

Virana, as usual, had an answer. "Everybody has gone home early. Because of the curfew."

Reminded, he said, "You should both get inside. I'll walk you back to the bar."

Tilla turned her back on him. "We can find our own way. It is only a hundred paces."

He was not going to leave it like that. He called to the guards that he would be back in a moment. As he said it a late delivery cart rolled up, so the men had something more useful to do than grumble behind his back about officers who couldn't make their minds up.

Meanwhile, Tilla's frosty silence made the hundred paces seem more like a thousand. He made an unwise effort to break it with, "What was I supposed to do, tell them not to go to that particular farm because I've eaten there?" But if she knew the answer to that, she chose not to divulge it.

15

RUSO LIFTED HIS medical case to shield the lamp flame from the draft as he carried it down the corridor. He wished Valens were here. It was always easier to frighten a patient when there were two of you.

After this he would have to tackle Fabius, which put him in mind of trying to stand a jellyfish up on end. As Fabius would no doubt point out, the search for the missing man had achieved nothing except to annoy the locals. Tomorrow he was going to have to go and apologize to Senecio and his family. That was going to be even trickier than he had expected, because not only had a curfew been imposed but an order had been issued forbidding any man to venture onto native property alone.

When young Candidus finally turned up after all this fuss—as he surely must—Ruso was going to make him one very sorry clerk.

He placed the extra lamp on the side table in Regulus's room, next to the open medical case. The reflection of the flame glittered on the polished rows of scalpels and probes and clamps, and threw a shadow from the pleasing curve of the bronze catheter. Satisfied with the effect, he picked out a medium-sized hook. Then he sat down on the end of the bed, positioning himself so that whenever Regulus looked at him, the instrument case would be visible just beyond. He raised the hook into view between them and eyed his patient while casually rolling the bronze instrument between finger and thumb. "Ready?"

Regulus paused with his spoon halfway to his mouth.

"We had the mythical version earlier. Now tell me what really happened."

"Sir?"

"Don't pretend you don't understand. You've wasted enough of my time already. One of my men is missing, so I'm not in a good mood."

Regulus glanced toward the door, as if he hoped someone might come in and rescue him. He put his spoon down in his bowl.

Ruso examined the hook, rubbing off a speck of imaginary dirt with one finger and then polishing the instrument on his tunic. The bed squeaked in protest as Regulus burrowed back against the wall. Ruso looked up. "Don't worry, I know how not to kill you. I'm a doctor."

Regulus said, "You're supposed to help me!"

"Exactly," said Ruso. "So if you scream, nobody will take any notice."

"Please, sir, I don't—"

"Feel well?" Ruso finished for him. "Too much dinner." He gestured toward the bowl. "How did you get hold of that, Regulus? It was left out of your reach on the window ledge."

Regulus gulped. "I'm feeling a little bit better now, sir."

"Excellent!" said Ruso. "Soon you'll be well enough to start beating up your girlfriend again."

"Sir, I never—"

"What did I say about wasting my time?"

"It's not my fault, sir!"

How Ruso missed Valens. He would have turned to Valens and explained, *It wasn't his fault, it was hers,* and Valens would have given a suitably dramatic sigh, shaken his head, and said, *Women, eh?*

But Regulus was keen to talk even without being outnumbered. "They wanted money, sir! They were all in on it. Her parents and her brothers and sisters and all the other hangers-on. That's what they're like round here. The natives. They all just want to see what they can get out of you." He paused as if expecting sympathy.

"Carry on."

"She wanted it all right, sir. She never said she didn't. Then they started saying I had to pay them money and marry her." He squared his shoulders as if he had committed an act of bravery. "I told them it was against regulations for a man of my rank, sir."

"So when you hit her," said Ruso, recognizing the curious British expectation that a man should pay for his bride, "was that before they asked for money, or after?"

Regulus stuck out his chin. "She was already my girl! We had an agreement! And then she acted like she didn't want to know me."

"So you thought if you kicked her and broke her fingers, that would help."

"A man's got to be master in his own house, sir!"

"Absolutely," said Ruso, who agreed with the principle but had never found out how this happy state of affairs could be achieved in practice. "Remind me again: Whose house was it?"

"I know I went a bit too far, sir." Regulus scratched one hand with the other. "But I told her I was sorry. I promised I won't do it again. She said it was all right."

According to Tilla's account, there had been more than one beating. Ruso let it pass, strangely fascinated by this tale of self-justification.

"But they still went and put in a complaint," Regulus continued, "and I got hauled up in front of Fab—" He caught Ruso's look. "Centurion Fabius," he corrected. "And he told me to pay compensation to the family, and that's not fair, is it? I wasn't even on duty when it happened!"

"And were you ordered to stay away from her?" Ruso asked, glad that Fabius had at least attempted some discipline.

"He never said that, sir. He just said I had to pay them five denarii." Regulus was indignant. "I don't suppose five denarii means a lot to you, sir, but to an ordinary man like me with a poor old widowed mother back home, it's a fortune."

Ruso was not going to be drawn into a competition to see whose family back home was the more demanding. His stepmother and sisters and innumerable nephews and nieces would leave Regulus's widowed mother in the dust. "And then what happened? Don't tell me you were left hanging upside down all night, because you weren't."

That was what had struck Ruso as odd earlier. Hanging from his feet all night might well have done enough damage to prevent Regulus walking, but the foot had moved perfectly when he had used it to scratch his opposite leg.

Regulus was busy scraping at a red lump on his neck. "Perhaps not all night exactly, sir." He looked up. "But it was a long time."

"And before that?"

"They said they were sorry for causing me trouble, sir. They said never mind about the money and to stay for a beer. So I said all right, just a drop. It would have been rude to say no, wouldn't it? But I reckon they put something in it. I went to sleep in the cowshed and I woke up freezing cold with this stink in my nose and my feet hurting and everything upside down."

Ruso sighed. The alleged kidnap was more of a drunken prank than a serious attempt to do damage, but the situation was beyond salvaging now. Even though Fabius had been too slow-witted to ban Regulus from visiting the girl, and must have known that he had provoked the assault, it had not tempered the reprisals. Doubtless, an example had to be made. No Briton could be allowed to think that he could humiliate the military and escape unpunished.

"So you see, sir," Regulus continued, scratching furiously at his groin, "it wasn't my fault. You can't trust the Brits."

"Stay away from their women, then," said Ruso.

Regulus looked aggrieved. "There aren't any other women round here, sir. Only raddled old tarts."

Not all the prostitutes offering their services in the area were raddled or old, although he was not going to say so. According to Tilla, some of them were as young as eleven or twelve. But, like the stupidity of Regulus, it was a problem he could do nothing about.

Fabius's door was sticking with the damp. It was finally wrenched open by a petite and pretty girl whom Ruso recognized as the kitchen maid. She was sorry that the centurion was unavailable this evening. He was very unwell and had gone to bed early.

"I'm his doctor."

"He's asleep, sir."

"Yes," said Ruso, turning away in disgust. "That's the problem."

Lying in the cramped on-call bed after the evening ward round, Ruso was definitely not sleeping. Instead he was holding Albanus's original letter up to the lamp and rereading:

I hope you know that I would not ask this of you, sir, if I had any other means of fulfilling my promise to my late sister. However, since my present duties do not allow me time to travel, I find I am obliged to rely upon the goodwill of others to guide her son now that he is so far away. Candidus has always been a sensitive and intelligent boy, but rather easily led. However, I am sure that with the right encouragement, he will do well. If you would consider recommending him for a position where he could settle, I would be extremely grateful to you.

He put the letter down on the shelf beside the dice he had found in Candidus's bag. Somewhere down the corridor, someone was calling out. He heard the feet of the night staff hurry past, then the click of a door opening and closing. He pinched out the lamp. There was no sense in lying awake: They might not need him, and then he would have wasted precious sleeping time.

He had confronted Regulus. One task off the list. Tomorrow he was going to have to think what more he could do about finding Candidus. And apologize to Tilla's people. And demand to know why Fabius had allowed him to instigate a major search for a missing man when he must already have known that Regulus had brought trouble on himself—and if he didn't, he should have. And deal with a visit from the legate's physician. And—he realized he had deliberately left this until last—face Tilla, who had understood more about young Regulus than most of the Legion.

16

"LET'S GET THIS straight." Tribune Accius's manicured hand demonstrated an invisible straightness between Ruso and Centurion Fabius. As his weight shifted against Pandora's cupboard, the stacks of writing tablets piled on top swayed sideways. "Yesterday you wanted a search for this clerk. This morning you don't."

"I'm still looking for him, sir," Ruso explained, wishing more than ever that he had not pushed Fabius into authorizing that search. One of them was going to be in trouble here. Possibly both. "But I don't think his disappearance had anything to do with the kidnapping, because it turns out the victim of the kidnapping wasn't just a random soldier. So there's no reason to suppose my man is being held by the natives."

"Indeed," said Accius drily. "As several of those natives have pointed out in their complaints this morning."

The silence that followed was not a cue to speak. It was simply Accius leaving a space for him to consider the error of his ways. Ruso let his vision drift out of focus. It was the adult equivalent of the child closing his eyes to make himself invisible.

Accius said, "I'm told the kidnap victim was already in dispute with the family."

No doubt the outraged natives had pointed that out too.

"Did anyone know this before we burned their houses down?"

Fabius swallowed noisily. "There was a complaint, sir. The man was disciplined."

If he thought that was going to excuse him, he was wrong. "Why wasn't the legate made aware of this when he was asked to authorize reprisals?"

Fabius made a sound as though he had something stuck in his throat. Ruso, even more glad than before that he had not been involved in the reprisals, was relieved to be out of the line of fire. The silence went on until Fabius ventured, "I wasn't aware of the request, sir."

Accius moved again, and the stacks swayed in the opposite direction. "Who received the original complaint?"

"I did, sir," Fabius answered.

"Who disciplined the man?"

"I did, sir."

"Who requested the authorization for reprisals?"

"Optio Daminius, sir."

"He's your optio, man! What sort of an outfit are you running here?"

"I wasn't aware—"

"Well, you should have been. And as if that weren't bad enough, the doctor here had the bright idea of annoying the natives even further by sending men out to shake them down for someone who wasn't there!" Accius left another pause for remorse before continuing, "Obviously the legate's ordered us to stand by the actions that were taken. No apologies. An assault on one of our men can't be allowed to pass no matter how justified the natives thought it might be. How badly hurt is he?"

"He's more humiliated than hurt, sir," put in Ruso. "This all started because he mistreated a girl. I think the family just intended it as a message."

"Well, now they've had their reply," said Accius. "Centurion, you will discipline the man involved, and do it more successfully than last time. Then have him transferred somewhere out of reach. Thanks to him and you two, we've successfully managed to enrage every local within a five-mile radius. As a result, we have movement restrictions and a curfew we didn't want to have to police. Any man out there on his own will be in trouble now, if he wasn't before."

Ruso said, "I'm sorry, sir. But I'm still concerned about my clerk, and with Prefect Pertinax out of action—"

"If he weren't, he'd have told you to stop interfering and leave the deserter to his own devices."

"Yes, sir." It was true. Ruso could see now how badly skewed his judgment had been. If Candidus had been a stranger instead of a young man commended into his care by an old friend, he would have behaved very differently. Still, perhaps there was something to be salvaged from the situation. "Sir, I know one of the native families in the area. They're connected to my wife. It might help if I go and explain about the search."

"Don't say anything that could be construed as an apology."

"It'll be difficult to pacify them if I don't, sir." And even harder to pacify Tilla.

"Then get your wife to explain if you can't, man. And tell her we'd like to know where the kidnappers are. By the time we got there, they'd cleared out."

Fortunately there was no reason for Accius ever to know that the kidnappers had been potential guests at his marriage blessing. He said, "The locals don't trust my wife, either, sir. They think she's one of us now."

"I'm not surprised, if you sent men to raid her people's farm."

"I didn't think, sir."

"I hope you wouldn't have treated them any differently if you had thought?"

Ruso looked him in the eye. "Absolutely not, sir."

For a moment the stare was like a challenge. Accius was no fool, and he had had dealings with Tilla before. Ruso had an uncomfortable feeling that the tribune thought he was lying. He was not too sure himself.

"You got yourself into this, Ruso. This is precisely why senior officers aren't allowed to marry while abroad on duty."

Accius did not want to be reminded that Ruso was not a senior officer, nor that he had married in Gaul when he was in between medical contracts with the Legion. He wanted to hear what Ruso now said, which was a meek "Yes, sir."

This was met with an exasperated "Agh!" Evidently the stupidity that the tribune was forced to deal with this morning was beyond words.

Fabius cleared his throat. "Perhaps we could invite some of the local leaders to dinner, sir."

The words *to dinner* were repeated with such contempt that Fabius lapsed back into silence.

"And now it seems we have another problem," Accius continued. "Have either of you heard this ridiculous tale about a body?"

Suddenly Ruso stopped longing for the conversation to be over. "A body, sir?"

"The gods alone know who it's supposed to be," said Accius. "Or where. The point is, it's slowing us down."

"Sir?" Ruso was now completely lost. Fabius looked equally blank.

"You don't know anything about a body buried inside the wall?"

"Inside the wall, sir?" Ruso asked.

"Don't repeat the question. Do you or don't you?"

"No, sir. Is there any chance it's my clerk?"

"Of course not," said Accius. "The body doesn't exist. The patrols would have noticed. It's just a malicious rumor. We've denied it, of course, but the chief engineer's had two native transport contractors fail to turn up this morning and he thinks that's why. We had patrols not wanting to go up there last night for fear of ghosts, and if it spreads further I expect we'll have men trying to get themselves off the building crews."

"I'll tell my staff to look out for malingerers, sir."

Fabius chipped in with an enthusiastic "Any man not reporting promptly for work will be flogged, sir!"

Ruso reflected on the irony of soldiers who were frightened of their own defenses. "Do we know where all this started, sir?"

Accius shrugged. The stacks of documents shifted a little more. "We're making inquiries," he said. "We have plenty of names to work through, but they may just be people the informers don't like much."

Realistically, they might as well hunt for the source of the wind. Any minute now Accius would ask the inevitable question. Ruso decided to anticipate it. "I doubt my wife can shed any light, sir. But I'll ask."

"Don't tell her anything she doesn't already know. Or anyone else. No loose talk."

Ruso wondered how anyone could trace the source of a rumor without divulging what it was. "Sir, do you think it's just possible that—"

"No, I don't," said Accius. "And you don't, either."

"No, sir."

"There is no body, Ruso, because the wall is regularly patrolled, and besides, if there were, how would we find it?"

"Dogs, sir?" Ruso suggested, aware that *regularly* did not mean frequently.

"We've had men take a stroll up there with dogs, but it's raining and it's windy, and they can't tell the dog what to sniff for. Besides, we've got whole stretches up to twelve or sixteen courses high now. We're not going to start hacking the wall apart just because a fox has pissed on it."

"Yes, sir." The tribune had a point. Conducting an obvious search for a body would only suggest that the officers believed in it too. Besides, how far would they go? Demolish one side to examine the core? Knock it all flat? Dig the foundations out? Defenses had been rising across the land from sea to sea since the spring: vast barriers of turf and stone in which, when you thought about it, dozens of bodies could be concealed. And now, of course, Ruso was. Thinking about it.

This was not the place to say so, but the rumor was a masterly piece of sabotage. It was already slowing down progress, and there would be people who wanted to believe it. There was never any shortage of missing persons. Apart from the regular flow of deserters, there were ordinary civilians who simply went out one day and never came back. Some of them wouldn't want to be found. Others must have been expecting to return home, but never made it. Most, like the girl who had run away from her violent boyfriend, would leave families behind who were desperate for any scrap of news. As this wretched rumor spread, more and more people would be wondering if the emperor's wall was a prison for the unquiet spirit of a relative whom it was their duty to find and lay to rest with a proper burial.

While everyone would to know who it was, one thing was for certain: Nobody would want to be up there the day after tomorrow when the sun went down to mark the start of Samain, the night when the— what was it? *When the walls between the living and the dead melt away.*

Accius reached for his cloak, which he had hung to drip on the back of the door. The stacks now teetered perilously close to the edge of Pandora's cupboard. "Anyway," he said, "if there is anything in this tale, it's more likely to have happened miles away over on the turf section."

"Yes, sir," said Ruso, noting that Accius had just undermined his former denial. "Sir, about my clerk . . ."

"Let me know when he turns up." Accius flung his cloak around his shoulders. A pile of writing tablets cascaded off the cupboard and clattered across the floorboards.

Ruso lunged across the room to stop a second landslide. Accius glared at the cupboard and then at Ruso, who seized the opportunity to say, "We need someone to sort this out, sir."

"At least you could put things away," Accius observed. "This is sheer laziness. You can't even get in there with all this rubbish cluttering the place up. You shouldn't have kit stored in here." He shoved Candidus's bag aside with one foot and reached for the twine holding the cupboard handles together. "What's in—"

"Sir, no!"

But it was too late. The doors swung wide, and the tribune's feet were buried in an avalanche of wooden writing tablets, crushed scrolls, old inkpots, and tangles of twine.

17

R USO WAS BARELY aware of his steady pace along the road or of the cold rain trickling down his neck. He was concentrating on rehearsing what to say. Every time he came up with a sentence that was not an apology, he heard the voice of Senecio dismissing it.

"We had to treat everyone the same."

You ate at our hearth.

"If word gets around that we didn't search you, you could have trouble with your own people."

It is not up to a Roman to save us from our own people. And besides, it was a lie. He had not considered them at all.

"I am sorry you feel insulted."

But you are not sorry for the insult itself?

"I cannot apologize for the Legion. I apologize for my judgment."

So you think you should not have sent those men?

"I should have come with them. I should have explained. But I was on duty at the hospital."

The reply to that came in his own voice: "You were only discharging Regulus for transfer and talking to Pertinax. Things that could have waited. You should have thought to go with them."

And then there was *You have come wearing armor and a helmet this time,* to which he would reply, "We've been ordered to wear it when not on army property." But of course Senecio would not comment: He would merely observe this further insult, and Ruso would have no chance to explain.

Nor would he be able to ask the question the Legion would like answered, which was: *Why are people saying there is a body in the wall?*

Approaching the turn to the farm track, he pushed distracting thoughts aside and took stock of his surroundings. A carriage approaching from the east: a squad of infantry marching off toward the brighter sky in the west.

The russet shape of a squirrel ran out into the middle of the track. It caught sight of him, and scampered off into the woodland on the other side. Probably nobody lurking in the trees, then, but the danger would not lie here, in sight of the main road. If Conn and his friends wanted some fun, they would be waiting farther along, where the track disappeared around a bend to the right. There, they could be seen from neither road nor farm.

He moved ahead steadily, alert to the sound of water dripping off leaves and the squelch and crunch of his own boots, and pushing aside the voice in his mind that said, *You should never have come alone.*

Rounding the corner, he thought he glimpsed the figure of a legionary amongst the trees on his left, but then it was gone. Wishful thinking. He moved faster. Another forty paces. Thirty. Almost there . . .

As he approached the gate, Conn and the one-eyed man stepped out from behind the main house. The big black dog trotted along behind them. They ignored Ruso's greeting and marched up to block the gate, farm implements casually laid over their shoulders. Conn might conceivably have been working under shelter with that pitchfork, but there was no call for a scythe in weather like this.

Ruso was wondering whether Branan would appear when the boy dropped out of the tree by the gate and ran across to join his older brother. He was not looking friendly now. He had picked up an axe that was half as tall as he was.

When the boy had taken his place, Conn said, "There is nothing for you in this place, soldier."

The other man's one eye and empty socket glared at Ruso. "Perhaps he's come to see for himself."

"I would like to speak with your father."

Conn said, "My father does not want to hear you."

"That is for him to decide. My wife promised him I would come."

They stood facing each other. Rain trickled down Conn's face and dripped off the end of his nose. Ruso knew that if he flinched now, he had lost.

Branan looked from one to the other of them. "Shall I ask Da, Conn?"

"I'll do it. You watch him." Conn strode away into the house. Branan shifted his grip on the axe handle and lifted his chin, then spoiled the effect by taking one hand off the axe to wipe the rain off his nose and shove his wet curls out of his eyes.

Ruso, still behind the flimsy protection of the gate, glanced around the yard. He had barely noticed when he was here before, but he saw now that the main house, the biggest of the buildings, had so many logs stacked under the broad eaves that the walls were almost hidden. A fat hayrick sat on a raised platform under its own thatched roof. He remembered the apples on the shelf indoors. This was what the family had worked through the summer and autumn to build up: the supplies that would, if their gods were kind, keep them and their animals from freezing and starving through the long, barren months of winter. This would be what the army had destroyed over at the house of Senecio's sister.

A few hens and a cockerel with a shimmering blue-green tail were pecking amongst the cobbles. Ruso guessed that the sister's livestock had made some very tasty suppers in military quarters last night.

Conn reappeared. "Let him in."

The one-eyed man gestured toward Ruso's sword and held out a hand to receive it across the top of the gate. His other hand retained its grasp on the scythe.

Ruso would have felt more at ease if he had been allowed to keep the sword and walk in naked.

After the daylight the house seemed even gloomier than it had at night. Senecio was seated in his carved chair again. As far as Ruso could make out, there was nobody else there. But he knew now about all those dark sleeping spaces hidden away behind the wicker partitions.

He bowed his head. Senecio made no attempt to rise or to acknowledge him. Ruso thought he heard movement somewhere behind one of the screens.

Finally he heard, "Are you aware of what has happened here, and at the house of my sister?"

"I am, sir."

"I am told that this began when one of your men mistreated my niece."

"He should not have done that, sir."

"True."

From somewhere in the darkness came a thud, then a whisper and "Sh!"

If he heard, Senecio ignored it. "Your people need to learn a little respect."

"Yes, sir." They needed to learn a great deal of respect, but since they were usually the ones with the swords, it wasn't likely.

"It seems you learned nothing from the falling of the rocks."

Ruso did not reply. He was not going to get into a debate about whose gods were the more powerful.

"The man you have lost is not here, and we know nothing about him."

"Yes, sir."

"If you had asked, we would have told you. We would also have asked our neighbors."

"Yes, sir."

"I had hoped," the old man continued, "that we could work together."

"I would have liked that," said Ruso truthfully.

"It is a pity you did not trust us."

On the far side of the hearth, where orange glowed through ash, the sky-blue eyes were gazing into his own. This time it was harder to fight the urge to look away. Two nights ago Ruso had been offered the kind of tentative friendship that might have helped in the search for Candidus. But the moment there was a dispute, he had forgotten all about Senecio's *We must find ways of working together* and lapsed into the old suspicions. He had, in short, acted like a fool.

Searching for some sort of concession if he could not offer apology, he said, "Sir, if anything was broken or stolen here by the soldiers, I will personally make compensation." He could probably get a loan against his pay to cover what they had lost. There was no point in pretending he would go to the Legion. The army always assumed compensation claims were exaggerated—which they probably were, since the victims expected to be shortchanged—so that even if money was paid, it was rare for both sides to be satisfied.

"Will you be compensating my neighbors?"

"I can't do it for everyone."

"Then you will do it for no one."

He was not going to insult the man by trying to change his mind. "I respect your decision, sir."

Senecio inclined his head.

Ruso bowed. "Sir, my wife is very embarrassed. She had nothing to do with what happened."

"She is your wife. She has made her choice. Do you have anything else to say?"

"No, sir."

"We will see that you are safe as far as the road. Do not come back."

18

SOMEBODY HAD GATHERED up the mess of records and writing materials and crammed most of them back into the cupboard. The surplus was piled into a wooden crate that had been shoved under the desk so there was no room for anyone's knees underneath. This hardly mattered, since there was still no sign of the man whose job it was to sit there.

Ruso had removed Candidus's kit to his own lodgings, but the chaos, like a fungus, now seemed to have spread to the stores. Gallus was standing in front of the shelves, pulling down a succession of boxes and rooting through them in search of linen suture thread. He interrupted the hunt to draw Ruso's attention to an unopened message addressed CANDIDUS, CLERK.

It was from Supplies. They could not understand why the hospital had sent urgent requests for buckets and blankets and bedstead repairs when the repairs were already in hand, six buckets had been delivered only last week, and all orders for woven materials had to be submitted a month in advance of the delivery date, by which time the Legion would be back in winter quarters at Deva. The orders had therefore been cancelled.

Ruso dropped the missive into the crate. "The idiots over in Supplies have thrown out all our orders. They say we've got buckets already."

Gallus glanced up from the latest box. "Somebody did find some buckets at the gatehouse this morning, sir. But there were only two left by the time he tracked them down."

"And has anyone come to start on the repairs?"

"Not yet, sir."

Ruso sighed. "Tell me some good news."

"The legate's physician was here to see Prefect Pertinax earlier. He seemed quite satisfied."

"Good," said Ruso, not sorry he had missed the legate's physician, a haughty Greek with a reputation for seeing his colleagues as competitors.

"He said no bathing until the stitches are out, only gentle massage, and don't let him get up."

"I'll cancel the dancing lessons, then. Did you tell him we've no bath suite and the masseur only comes twice a week if we're lucky?"

Gallus's baby face looked even younger when he smiled. "No, sir. There were some instructions about diet that I've written down for you—ah!" He retrieved a spool of thread. "And Doctor Valens is here, sir. And, er . . ." He hesitated, passing the spool from one hand to the other. "Sir, I've been wondering whether I should mention something. It's about the clerk. I hope I'm not wasting your time."

Ruso waited.

"I wasn't trying to listen, sir."

"I see."

"I'm sure it's nothing, but I couldn't help overhearing."

"Now you *are* wasting my time."

"Sorry, sir." Gallus's neck was turning pink to match his cheeks. "Sir, when the new clerk was here, I heard a conversation he had with Nisus."

Nisus was the pharmacist who usually sat opposite the clerk's desk. "And?"

"Candidus was rattling on about something—about freed slaves being allowed to join the army or something—and Nisus interrupted and said, 'If you don't stop talking, somebody around here is going to get killed.'"

Ruso stared at him. "Nisus?"

"Yes, sir."

"And did Candidus stop talking?"

"I think he went to chat to somebody else, sir."

Ruso scratched one ear with his forefinger.

"I'd have mentioned it before, sir, but you had men searching houses for Candidus, so I thought you must have had word that he was out there with the natives."

"I see," Ruso said, not wanting to dwell on the embarrassment of his mistake. "Well, I'm glad you've told me now. Don't tell anyone else." Conscious of the irony, he added, "We don't want people jumping to wild conclusions."

"I'll keep it quiet, sir. I just thought you should know."

"Do you think it was a serious threat?"

Gallus clutched the thread to his chest. "Honestly, sir?"

"Preferably."

"Candidus was annoying, but I don't really think anybody would kill him for talking too much."

"Hm," said Ruso, who had known men to be gravely injured in fights over a borrowed spoon, a habit of cracking the knuckles, and a stolen coin that had later turned up in the owner's own pack. "I have to admit," he said, "it's hard to imagine Nisus getting seriously worked up over anything." The pharmacist, a legionary of mature years and few words, seemed to have no ambition beyond weighing and measuring, drying and distilling.

"Perhaps I misheard, sir."

"I think it's more likely Nisus was telling him to shut up in words that he couldn't fail to understand. When's he due back from leave? I can't remember how long I signed for."

Gallus cast a glance at Pandora's cupboard. "I could ask someone to look for it, sir."

Ruso shook his head. "Don't bother. He'll be back before they—"

He broke off as the door opened. Valens strolled in, nodded to Gallus, and seated himself on the table of the absent pharmacist before announcing, "Prefect Pertinax is feeling very much better this morning."

"He is?" Ruso asked.

"Oh, yes. He managed quite a long string of invective before he told me to get out."

Gallus, stifling a grin, retreated.

Ruso said, "How long until Serena gets here?"

"Anytime from tomorrow." Valens sighed. "You really know how to cheer a man up, Ruso."

"I practice on my patients." Ruso gestured toward the crate under the desk. "Supplies have just thrown out all our orders. How am I supposed to run a hospital when I end up chasing around for blankets and buckets?"

"Surely it can't be that difficult?"

"You'd be amazed. We order basic items from the stores two hours away and they take a week to turn up. If they get here at all."

"Well, it's no good complaining to me," said Valens. "I'm on your side. I don't have the faintest idea how these things work. But good luck sorting it out."

"I need a clerk."

"That reminds me," said Valens. "I had a chat with your man's centurion. That chap called Silvanus."

"The one who wrote and told me Candidus was here."

"Yes. Before he would say anything else, he wanted to know if Candidus was dead."

Ruso looked up in alarm. "Why would he think that?"

"Because if he is, he was a bright, friendly lad and a sad loss."

"Ah," said Ruso, guessing what was coming.

"Otherwise he's lazy, he talks too much, he's fond of gambling, and he thinks he's a comedian. Probably why the lads at Magnis called him Perky."

"I see." Ruso pulled open his purse and tipped the contents into his palm. Half a dozen small coins, a boot stud, a scattering of fluff, and two identical dice with the numbers carved as concentric rings in the bone.

"Silvanus said he couldn't see why he would desert. As he put it, it's not as if you were asking the lad to do any work. All he had to do was park his arse behind a desk all day."

Ruso rolled the dice across the worn surface of Candidus's desk. He rolled them a second time. Then he picked them up, examined each of them, and rolled them one by one before handing them to Valens. "You try."

The legs of the table creaked as Valens shifted sideways to make space. The dice rattled across the ink-stained wood several times. Finally he selected one and tipped it back and forth in his palm. "This one's weighted," he said. "Six nearly every time."

Ruso said, "He could have made enemies."

"Silvanus says he was in debt to couple of people. Nothing major, but they didn't expect to see their money back."

"Anyone who owed money to him?"

"Nobody who would admit to it."

Which was not the same thing at all. "Thanks anyway. You'd better get back to Magnis."

"I'll keep my ears open. Oh, and I'd steer clear of Pertinax for a while. He's not impressed with having visits from three doctors in one morning.

Especially when none of them will give him any crutches. And now somebody's told him there's a dead body in the emperor's wall."

"Oh, gods above. Who told him that?"

"I've no idea. You've heard it too?"

Ruso shook his head. "Unbelievable," he said. The tale had reached a patient who had not left his bed for days. If this was sabotage, it was even more effective than its perpetrator could have hoped.

"You don't think it might belong to your clerk?"

"I don't think it exists," said Ruso. He had once been in trouble for failing to obey Accius's orders back in Eboracum and he was not going to make the same mistake again. Especially after the fiasco of the search. "I'm going to write to Albanus today and tell him his nephew's deserted."

"I thought you'd decided his disappearance was highly suspicious and he ought to be here collecting hens?"

"He probably acted on impulse," said Ruso. "He'd already managed to seriously annoy people here, including me."

Valens looked disappointed. "I was hoping this might turn into one of your escapades. Finding a body and going around accusing people of murdering it."

"I haven't found a body. Nobody has."

Valens scrutinized him for a moment. "Pity," he said. "You've been so much more entertaining since you met Tilla and adopted the native tendency to overdramatize."

"I'm not the one who's overdramatizing," Ruso pointed out. "You are. Candidus is absent without leave. I'd imagine he's either lazing in the baths at Coria, or he's bought himself a trip south on an empty supply vehicle."

"If you say so. I won't tell Albanus it might have been you who drove him to it."

"It wasn't! Would you run away because I shouted at you?"

Valens slid down from the table. "Ah, but I would know you didn't mean it."

19

THE CHILLY EASTERN breeze that had blown the rain away was now plucking at the tents and flapping the bedraggled standards. The queue had curled itself around the back of the medical tent in search of shelter.

As soon as Ruso arrived, a bandy-legged man stepped out of the line and pushed to the front amidst much complaining. His reply of "I'm not sick!" did nothing to pacify his competitors.

Ruso addressed the rest of the queue. "I'll just have a quick word with . . . ?"

"Lucius, sir."

"With Lucius here. I can see he's keen to get back to work." As the queue avenged itself with jeers and some questioning of whether Lucius knew what work was, he led the man under the shelter of the examination area.

"Two things to tell you, sir. I was supposed to be sharing cook duty with Perky the other night, only he never turned up at the tent and nobody's seen him since."

"Didn't anyone question it?"

"Only me, sir. There's always people coming and going. But nobody can remember seeing him after that, and I heard they've found a body in the wall."

"Take no notice," Ruso assured him. "It's nonsense. I'm only chasing Candidus as a favor because his uncle's a friend of mine. If you see him, tell him to report to me before he gets himself into real trouble. What was the other thing?"

"A mate of mine called Olennius wants to hand something in to you, sir. He's on stone-laying duties up at the wall. Shall I tell him to come and find you tonight?"

"No," said Ruso. "I'll go and see him when I've finished here."

What had been a chilly breeze down in the camp was an icy blast on the crest of the hill. The Legion would not be able to work up here for much longer—not because of the discomfort to the men, which was irrelevant, but because if the wet mortar was not washed out of the joints by the winter rains, then the frost would creep into it and destroy it. Damp, freshly quarried stone would flake. Standing water would freeze, and they would have to find extra wood for fires to melt it before the lime could be mixed. Then there would be the snow. Mud made the transport of materials difficult; snow would make it impossible.

Already vanity had been sacrificed to comfort. Woolen caps were pulled down over ears. Layered tunics and leggings of all colors had taken on matching hues of earth and pale lime. The centurion who was currently shouting at someone to get a move on looked as though he had just waded through a bog.

"That's him there," the man said when Ruso asked for Olennius. They both watched for a moment as a fresh bucket of mortar was delivered. Olennius slapped a trowel-load onto his board, chopped it, formed a sausage, rolled it, and flicked it off the trowel into the space where the next stone would fit. It was like watching a cook at work.

A disgruntled patient who was the son of a stonemason had once told Ruso that the wall was a hasty, messy effort where speed was valued over quality. According to him, an ape could do the straight parts. Skilled men like himself, in constant demand for constructing corners and gateways and arches, were rarely given time to do what he called "a proper job."

Ruso watched as Olennius bedded in a roughly squared stone, tapped it with the end of his trowel, squinted at the line, tapped it again, and reached out for the next chop of mortar. He made it look easy. Perhaps an ape could do it, but it certainly wouldn't want to. Not up here.

The centurion cupped his hands around his mouth and yelled, "Olennius!" into the wind.

The man turned. "Boss?"

"Medic to see you!"

Olennius put the trowel down and gave a quick salute before slapping his gloved hands together to try and warm them. The trowel caught the wind, tumbled off the stonework, and landed at his feet.

"I'm trying to track down the property of a man called Candidus!" shouted Ruso. It was the sort of weather that made every conversation sound like an argument. "Also known as Perky!"

Olennius nodded with the enthusiasm of a man who did not want to be flogged for stealing. "I'm glad you've come, sir! I was going to hand it in tonight!" He removed a glove and reached into a little pouch that hung from his belt. After some fumbling he retrieved a folding knife about the size of Ruso's index finger. The uneven letters CAND were burned into the wooden hilt.

Ruso gripped the blunt side of the blade and pulled it out. It was well oiled and the edge was rough against the tip of his finger. "Where was it?"

The man pointed west to where wooden scaffolding was being erected. "Over there, sir!"

"Show me!"

The man set off with confidence across the flattened grass, but as they approached the scaffold he began to falter, glancing down to his left at a clump of bushes shuddering in the breeze. "It was around here somewhere, sir," he said, pausing in the shelter of the wall to rub his head with a gloved knuckle and turn slowly in a half circle. "I can't say exactly. But about this far out." He measured out five paces away from the stonework. "Lying in the grass."

"Open or shut?"

"Shut, sir. It was a bit stiff and damp, but I got it dried out and oiled it and it was fine." Just in case Ruso should be in any doubt, he said, "I asked around but nobody knew who 'Cand' was, so I've been looking after it."

"How long for?"

"Just since yesterday afternoon, sir."

"Next time," grunted his centurion, "hand it in and let me find the owner."

Ruso reached down and slid the knife into the top of his boot lining. "Thanks. I'll give it back to him when I find him."

Olennius said, "Sir, has this missing man got anything to do with . . ."

Ruso followed his glance toward the wall.

"No," said Ruso and the centurion together.

"He's given himself a holiday." Ruso explained, repeating the line about Candidus's uncle being a friend. "I'm trying to get him back before his uncle turns up." It was the truth, but it sounded like an excuse. Olennius was sent back to work. Ruso gazed down at the track that ran alongside the stream, both of them following the course of a boggy natural dip that passed through the line of the wall. To the south, the stream flowed under the road, skirted Senecio's farm, and went down past the quarry. He pointed north. "What's up there?"

"Camp nine," said the centurion. "After that, just native farms. HQ might have a scout who can tell you more."

Candidus's knife had been found at least a hundred paces away from the track. The lad had not struck him as someone who relished unnecessary fresh air and exercise, and it seemed unlikely that a man absent without leave would break away to scramble up a hill, lose his knife, and come back down again to continue his journey. He—or someone else— could possibly have thrown the knife up here, although it was hard to imagine why. Perhaps someone else had borrowed or stolen it and dropped it. Perhaps Candidus had lost it himself while he was up here earlier for some reason that had nothing to do with his disappearance. Perhaps . . .

Perhaps there were even more obscure possibilities, but eventually Ruso would have to face the thought that Candidus might have been near the wall when he vanished.

His gaze drifted to the scaffolding. The uprights now lashed in place gave some sense of the full height to which the stonework would rise. From where he was standing, anything to the north would soon be invisible. You could not see through a wall. You could not see into it, either.

Leaving the centurion with "Let me know if you hear anything of him, will you?" he made his way swiftly back to where Olennius was slapping down another bed of mortar.

"Sir?"

"The truth," Ruso said. "When did you find it?"

Olennius held on to the trowel this time. "I told people I'd got it, sir. I wasn't stealing."

"I know that. Your centurion may not need to hear the exact truth, but I do."

The man counted on his gloved fingers with the point of the trowel. "About four days ago, sir."

Ignoring the hard stare of the usurped centurion, Ruso headed back down to the road. When he was halfway there he stopped and turned. The teams were back at work, mortaring heavy stones into two parallel faces. The wide unfilled hollow between them reminded him of nothing so much as a vast, elongated stone tomb.

20

TILLA CUPPED HER hands and blew on them to warm them before calling again. Finally a man appeared from behind the house and told her that her patient, the young woman with the week-old baby, was not at home.

"But I have walked here. She knew I would be here today."

The man shrugged. "She must have forgotten."

On the way back, Tilla barely noticed the ivy in bloom, nor the rose hips, nor the puddle until she stepped in it. By the time she was back at Ria's bar, the cold had spread beyond the leaks in her boots, and her damp socks were beginning to rub blisters on her toes.

"Nobody came for you, mistress!" Virana called as Tilla hurried past on the way to the loft in search of fresh footwear.

Wearing dry socks and her indoor shoes—she had indoor and outdoor shoes now: such luxury!—she returned to the bar carrying a scroll and her box of medicines. Then, keeping her shawl on, she sat by the entrance, nursing a warm cup of honeyed milk. She opened the scroll and began to run her forefinger along the letters, mouthing them softly to herself, putting the unfamiliar sequences together until they shaped themselves into words.

"These are necessary observances for the healthy person to take during pestilence."

The best advice was to go abroad. Failing that, it was wise to be carried in a litter. After that there was a long list of instructions that included avoiding fatigue and not getting up early in the morning.

It was ridiculous. What normal person could do more than dream of any of those things? It was very difficult to learn anything from a book when she was constantly wanting to argue with its author.

She looked up hopefully as each customer came into the bar, but only two patients wanted to share her table for a quiet chat. One was a soldier's girl worried about her baby's cough, and the other a slave of a passing jeweler whose injured hand needed a fresh dressing. Neither was really a job for a medicus. Anyone with any common sense could have dealt with them.

She told herself it had been a quiet morning everywhere. Nobody wanted to go out in the cold. The fact that she had seen no local patients might have nothing to do with yesterday afternoon. Surely word could not have got around so quickly. Did everyone know she was the wife of a Roman who had sent men to search and threaten to burn down a house where he had been a guest?

She forced herself to struggle on with the scroll. So far it had been useless but it seemed to impress the patients, and besides, it was the only medical book her husband owned that was not in Greek. But even on a good day, she would have had trouble keeping her mind on this nonsense. Today it was hopeless. The letters kept sliding about in front of her eyes, her finger lost its place, and her careful mouthing of the words died away.

The first thing Enica and Conn and the others would do, she was sure, was to rush and tell all their friends about the outrages the army had caused: the burning of Cata's family farm, which everyone would know about, and then the insult to their own home and family that had followed.

She released the edge of the scroll and let it roll back on itself. Then she tightened the roll, tied it, and slid it back into its case. She was not a Roman: Why try to look like one? She was not a local anymore, either. That had been made clear yesterday. At first she had thought there must be some terrible mistake, but the soldier had insisted that he really had been sent out to search by her husband. There was no point in trying to lie: The family understood enough Latin to know what he had said. She could do nothing but apologize and leave as fast as possible, and she knew they were glad she was gone.

There was a chilly draft here. No longer needing the light to read, she pulled her shawl tighter around her shoulders and carried her milk across to a table by the fire that had just been abandoned by a couple of men who looked like messengers of some sort. Then she sat there wondering what she would do all day now if none of her local patients trusted her anymore.

She would be glad to get back to Deva, where almost everyone was a foreigner and most people were either in the army or there because of it. Living in a place like this was much harder if you did not know exactly who you were any longer. The farmers could blame the army for everything that went wrong. The army could blame the farmers. She was caught in the middle, trying to make her husband understand what a terrible insult it was to mistrust people who had welcomed you to their hearth, and to explain to Senecio . . . Senecio had not wanted to listen to her. "You have made your choice, child," he said. That was what had upset her the most. The old man and his family wanted nothing to do with her now. One of the last links with her parents was gone.

"You look sad, mistress. Shall I bring you some more milk?"

Tilla shook her head.

"I don't suppose there will be a wedding blessing now, will there, mistress?"

"Have you no work to do, Virana?"

"Everybody's served, mistress, and there's nothing to wash yet. Is that why you're sad: because that old man won't give you a wedding blessing? Or is it because nobody wants to see you?"

Tilla put her head into her hands. "Virana, ask Ria to find you something to do. If she can't, go and put your feet up. I have a headache."

"I'm sorry, mistress. Can I help?"

"No, thank you. I'm going upstairs to have a sleep."

Upstairs, Tilla pulled the cover over herself to keep warm in the chilly air of the loft. She lay back and listened to the timbers creaking in the wind.

Virana was right, of course. It was only two nights to Samain and she had to face the fact that there would be no wedding blessing. She needed to send a message to her cousin at Coria withdrawing the invitation. Perhaps she should take the news herself. It would be good to get out of here. It would mean two whole days away, though, unless she could get a fast horse. And there were still a few local patients she had promised to see.

She would stay. It was up to the patients whether they decided to come or not. In a couple of weeks she would be back in Deva. In the meantime she would not have anyone say that she had run away out of shame.

She arched her back and wriggled around a lump in the mattress. She would send the message to Aemilia tomorrow. Meanwhile she would lie here with her pretended headache, trying to stifle the memory of her mother's voice. *Nobody likes a girl who feels sorry for herself, Daughter of Lugh!*

"I am not Daughter of Lugh anymore," she whispered into the empty room. "I am Tilla, Roman citizen, wife of Gaius Petreius Ruso, a man from overseas who is very annoying. And do not tell me what you think of that, Mam, because I can guess."

21

IT HAD NOT been a good day. The tribune thought he was an idiot, and if the natives were to hold a Least Popular Roman competition, he had no doubt he would win it.

Even worse, no matter how much Ruso reassured everyone else, he was convinced that something bad had happened to Candidus.

He had to wait for his eyes to adjust before he could see his way across the gloom of the loft. Downstairs, the clatter from the kitchen died away as somebody closed a door. He pulled off his boots, lowered himself down next to the figure on the bed, and closed his eyes. Then he opened them in alarm as something cold flopped onto his head. He retrieved what seemed to be a wet sock and let it fall to the floor, suddenly reminded of the medic from the Second who used to take hot stones from beside the hearth and wrap his dirty socks around them to steam them dry overnight. The man had been dead for a couple of years now—not suffocated by the smell but speared through the throat when he had ridden out with a rescue party to help the victims of a native ambush. There was a lot of sense to building a wall.

A voice beside him said, "I am not asleep."

He rolled over and kissed her gently on the tip of the nose. "Hello."

"Why are you not under the covers? You will get cold out there."

He removed the other wet sock from the pillow. "I didn't want to disturb you."

"But I am not sleeping."

He unbuckled his belt and joined her. "Virana said you had a headache."

"I said that to stop her talking."

"She can talk as much as she likes." Her thigh was warm and smooth under his hand. "As long as she stays out of here for a while."

She drew away.

"Uh?"

"Not now."

"Surely it's not time for—"

"I don't want to."

"Oh." He withdrew the hand. It was going to be one of those you-ought-to-know-what-I'm-thinking moments.

There was a time when he had unjustly assumed these moments were peculiar to his first wife. Or even that it was his own fault—that he had missed a crucial link in the chain of reasoning that would explain how a perfectly normal conversation had suddenly arrived at a place where he knew only two things: firstly, that he had no idea why Claudia had taken offense; and secondly, that whatever it was, she was not going to tell him.

"I've been to see Senecio," he said, guessing.

"I do not suppose either of you spoke of the wedding blessing."

"No."

She sighed.

Ah. The wedding blessing. It would be a while before he was forgiven for that one. If only she had never gotten involved with those people.

Her hair was tickling his nose. He pulled away and lay facing the faint lattice of the rafters and the dark bulge where he had hung Candidus's kit bag, and thought of the time when those blond curls had been gray with grime and so hopelessly matted that he had threatened to cut them off. Then, months later, when she had become much more than an unwanted slave, there had been that peculiar conversation in the middle of the night. She had wriggled about for the umpteenth time and muttered something, and he had tried to hide his irritation with "Can't you sleep?"

Afterward he had lain pondering her reply, wondering what British concept she had intended the Latin words to convey. In the end he had said, "You just told me your hair wakes you up."

"Yes."

"Your *hair?*"

"I forget to tie it back. When I turn over, the hair is caught under my shoulder. Or yours. I must wake up to move the hair so I can move my head."

"I knew you should have let me cut it off."

He was glad she hadn't.

It was raining again. He could hear it dripping off the thatch. "I'm sorry about the wedding blessing."

"I do not think so."

"Well, I'm sorry for you."

No reply. He wondered whether it was worth trying again, or whether that would just make things worse. "It must be lonely for you sometimes, trailing around after me."

She said, "Yes."

"I'm glad you do."

It was too much to hope that she might say she was glad too, but after a pause he felt a hand groping for his own. She said, "I'm hungry."

He drew the hand up to his lips and kissed it. "Can you wait?"

"How long?"

"Half an hour?"

Afterward, when they were dozing in each other's arms amidst a tangle of bedclothes, he heard, "That was not half an hour."

"Are you complaining?"

She giggled. "No."

They lay listening to the world outside, in no hurry to join it. Feet scurried across the room below them. Conversation rose and faded as the bar door was opened and closed. There was more dripping. Boots marched down the street. Someone whistled for a dog.

She said dreamily, "Can you stay here tonight?"

"I wish I could," he said, guiltily remembering that he was supposed to be asking her about the body-in-the-wall rumor, and then remembering Candidus's knife. "Night duty."

"You are always on night duty!"

"Not the night we went to Senecio," he pointed out. "Although I might as well have been."

She sighed. "I know. 'It is a small hospital. There is only one doctor.'"

"It's the truth."

"They should give you a proper clerk."

"Not after we carelessly lost the last one."

"He has caused a lot of trouble." She nuzzled his ear. "Tell Albanus he must look for him himself."

"I'd rather Albanus didn't find out. I don't want to upset him even more after Grata."

She propped herself up on one elbow. "What about Grata?"

"He and Grata have fallen out. No marriage."

"When did you hear this? Why did you not tell me?"

"I forgot," he admitted.

"What happened?"

"I don't know. I'm more worried about his nephew."

"You are hopeless," she told him. "And I am still hungry. At least stay to eat."

As they groped for their clothes she said, "It is Albanus's own fault. He should never have told you that such a silly boy was a good clerk."

"I'm not sure that he did," Ruso admitted. "He was just doing his best to look after him."

"Albanus knows nothing of people," she told him, pointing one slender foot in the air and hiding it inside a sock. "He spends too long with words and writing. He thinks I am bad for you."

"I'm sure he's never said that."

"He thinks I lead you into trouble."

"You do."

By way of reply, Tilla dragged a shawl off the end of the bed and gave it a vigorous shake.

He said, "Have you heard any rumors about the wall?"

"Which rumor would you like?" she offered, flinging the shawl around herself and ramming in the pin. "It will fall down when the snow comes. It will be fifty feet high. People on opposite sides will have to pay money to visit their families. It is an abomination and the gods will have revenge. They have already started in the quarry."

"About a dead person."

She thought for a moment. "Was there not a man over near Banna whose friend fell off the scaffolding and landed on top of him and killed him?" she said. "Then there was a carter bringing supplies who was trampled by his own oxen, and in the summer a man fishing in the dark river found a body that was so rotted away that only the hair told them it was a woman." She pulled her skirts straight. "Are you trying to find out something for the army?"

"There's a new rumor about a body and they want to know how it got started."

"Who is it?"

"I don't know."

"A Roman or one of the people?"

"I don't even know that," he admitted. "Nor where's it's supposed to be."

"Are you sure it is dead?"

"It might not exist at all. It's rather like one of our centurion's ailments." She shook her head. "That is a rumor with no legs or wings, husband."

He said, "I'm not supposed to spread it."

"Ah, a secret rumor." When he did not tell her more, she said, "I do not care. This time I cannot do any spying for the Legion even if I want to. Because of you, nobody will talk to me."

"That's more or less what I told Accius."

There was a creak on the ladder. An unsteady glow rising from the square of the hatch signaled a lamp being carried up toward them.

"Tell me something sensible and I will see what I can find out," Tilla said as Virana's head appeared at floor level. "And then I will decide whether to tell you."

Virana heaved herself up through the opening. "Is that you, master?"

"It is," agreed Ruso, wondering who else she thought it might be.

"There are still seventeen sausages and eight tarts left because of the bad weather and the curfew. Ria has gone to visit her brother, so her husband says you can have some half price as long as nobody tells her. What will you find out, mistress? Can I help?"

"You already help us by working," Ruso assured her.

"I like working." Virana grinned. "You find out all sorts of things in a snack bar. Did you know there is a dead body buried in the emperor's wall?"

Husband and wife exchanged a glance. He said, "It's just a wild rumor, Virana. It isn't true."

"But it must be!" she exclaimed. "If Branan over at the farm will still talk to you, you can ask him yourself. He saw a man put it there."

22

R USO SHED HIS cloak and shook off the worst of the water outside the hospital entrance. He hung it on a nail and went to find Gallus just as the curfew sounded.

The evening ward round was quiet, and he had more time than he wanted to think. The rumor of the body was surely no more than an attempt at sabotage: a tale spread in anger and guaranteed to feed on existing fears, especially with Samain coming up. It was certainly feeding on plenty of fears of his own. What was Candidus's knife doing up at the wall?

Meanwhile, while he was worrying instead of concentrating on dietary advice to combat chronic wind, Candidus might have spent the day relaxing in a warm bathhouse, eating honey cakes, glad he had escaped Nisus's terrifying threats to murder him and wishing he had brought his loaded dice.

If only he had known earlier that Senecio's youngest son had been spreading the rumor. He could have confronted the old man about it this morning. As it was, Tilla had agreed to try and talk to the family tomorrow. They were unlikely to tell her anything, let alone the truth. But she had a better chance than anyone else he could think of, and until he knew the tale about the body was a lie or until Candidus turned up, he knew he would be uneasy. She would go there on the pretext of warning them to prepare for another visit from the soldiers, who would soon be there demanding to know what Branan had seen. After that . . . "If you're going to say or do anything you shouldn't," he told her, "then don't tell me about it."

She had said, "You know I will not," and kissed him.

He had no idea whether she had meant she would not do anything untoward or that she would do whatever she thought was necessary but not tell him about it. It was true that a man had to be master in his own house, but there were times when it was best not to know.

He had deliberately left Pertinax until the end of his round. The man continued to make remarkable progress. It was a shame he did not appreciate it. Despite being trapped in a hospital bed, he seemed to consider himself still on duty and obliged to keep up standards by pointing out any shortcomings that came to his attention. Or, as Valens would have put it, he was well enough to grumble. Ruso resisted the temptation to try and cheer him up by telling him his daughter was on the way. It was anyone's guess what state the roads were in, and in his experience, no matter how skilled they were at terrifying grown men, fathers always worried about their daughters.

He was concentrating on examining the wound, making the usual checks for inflammation and hemorrhage, when he became aware that Pertinax's complaints had turned to ". . . this half-baked nonsense about a body in the wall. I suppose you've heard?"

"Yes, sir."

"The centurions need to work them harder," said Pertinax. "If they want something to be frightened of, they can be frightened of us."

Ruso said, "Can I ask who told you, sir?" Whoever it was, the man clearly needed a good fright himself. Ruso was looking forward to administering it until Pertinax said, "That tribune with the bad smell under his nose. What do they call him?"

"Accius," supplied Ruso. It was not like Pertinax to forget a name.

"Him," Pertinax agreed. "Came in here this morning. I told him you need a better clerk straightaway."

Ruso felt his mouth fall open and closed it again. After repeating the words to himself to check that he had understood correctly, he said, "Thank you, sir."

"Don't thank me," growled Pertinax, swiftly closing the chink of generosity as if he were embarrassed by it. "The place is a shambles. I can tell that even from here. How many times have I got to ask before I get a pair of crutches?"

23

RUSO PLACED THE lamp on the table in the doctor-on-duty room and flipped open the writing tablet he had chosen from the vast selection of used items in the office. Someone had already tried to obliterate what appeared to be a shopping list from the surface of the wax, so he had decided to wipe it clean and put it to better use.

If Albanus did not manage to call in here on the way over to Arbeia, he would arrive at his new job completely unaware that the nephew was missing.

To—Albanus, Tutor at the House of the Prefect, Arbeia

In the absence of the prefect's name or unit, he would have to entrust this to somebody with some common sense and hope for the best.

From—G Petreius Ruso, Medical Officer, XXVV, Parva.
Ruso to Albanus.
I hope you have arrived safely in Arbeia.

He tapped the stylus on the casing of the tablet for a moment, then began:

I am writing to you about your nephew Candidus. He worked here at the hospital for three days but I am sorry to say that we have not seen him since the ninth day before the kalends of November. He left no message and we have been unable to trace him. I am hoping you may have heard from him.

As soon as he turns up I will write again. Meanwhile if you have any idea where he might be please put my mind at rest.

Tilla and I are well and she sends her good wishes.

She didn't, but it would do no harm to pretend. Not knowing what to say about Grata, he ended with:

Go well, old friend.

Then he slapped the tablet shut, put the stylus down, and pinched out the lamp. His eyes felt gritty even when he closed them. He felt better for having written the letter, even though he was not going to send it yet. There was always the chance that when the pharmacist returned from leave—which must be soon—he would know exactly where Candidus was, and they could all stop worrying. If he didn't, the letter would be sent, and the worrying would carry on.

24

"WHERE IS BRANAN?"

This seemed an odd thing for Enica to be asking her. Tilla waited outside the gate, still unsure of her welcome, and said, "I have come to speak with him."

"Did you leave him with Conn?"

Tilla was even more puzzled. "I have not seen either of them."

The color drained from the woman's face. Then she ran back toward the house shouting, "Husband! He is not with her! She is here and the boy is not with her!"

Tilla let herself in and dropped the frayed rope back over the gatepost. When she turned, Senecio was limping toward her. Despite the early-morning frost on the ground, he had not bothered with a cloak. His first words were "Did you not send for my boy yesterday?"

Tilla felt her stomach tighten. "I did not. I have not seen Branan since I was here when the soldiers came."

Enica grabbed her by the shoulders. "Do not lie to me! Where is my son? What have you done with him?"

"I have done nothing!" Tilla cried, trying to raise her hands to defend her face. Enica was powerfully built, and Tilla did not want to fight.

The old man was shouting, "Stop! Stop, wife!"

"Where is my son?"

"I do not know!"

"Stop, wife!"

Enica loosened her grip as she was dragged away by her husband.

"Wife, leave her. She may be speaking the truth."

Safely out of reach, Tilla massaged her shoulders. Enica was breathing heavily, rubbing her own arm and glaring at her husband.

"I have not seen Branan," Tilla repeated. "People are saying he spread a bad story. I came to warn you that there may be trouble."

Senecio frowned. "What story?"

She told them.

Enica said, "We know nothing of this. Where is my son?"

"I don't know."

"The army are blaming him for something so they can take him!"

Tilla said, "Someone told Virana it was him spreading the story. I do not know who."

"It is a lie!"

Senecio rested both hands on his stick and bowed his head.

Tilla said, "When did you last see him?"

Slowly, as if the words did not want to be spoken, the man said, "He was out with the neighbor's boy yesterday. Inam. He did not come back. We thought he must be with the neighbors. When the light was dying, his mother went to fetch him, but Inam had gone home alone. He told her . . ." His voice cracked. He tried again. "He told her you had sent a soldier to fetch Branan."

"But I would have come to the house!"

"We thought perhaps . . ." He paused.

"We thought you were too embarrassed," said Enica, clutching at a fist-ful of her shawl. "I knew we should have gone straight to the fort!"

The other adults were beginning to gather around them now. The skinny man, the man with one eye, and his wife. Cata and her mother and sister were there too. As each one arrived the bad news was passed on: "He is not with her." "She has not seen him." "She says she did not send for him."

"Conn went out last night to fetch him back," Senecio continued. "The patrol would not let him pass on the road because of the curfew."

"He should have gone by the field paths!" Enica said. "I told him."

"Then he would have been arrested when he got there." Senecio looked at Tilla as if hoping for reassurance. "The patrol said they would look out for a lost boy."

"That was a lie too," put in Enica. "I asked a patrol this morning and they had been told nothing of him."

Senecio was looking frail. "Conn has gone to find you. We thought perhaps Branan had stayed with you because of the curfew."

Enica said, "I have been awake all night worrying."

"We must talk to the neighbor's boy again," said Tilla.

Enica glanced at her husband. "How do we know she is speaking the truth? Her man is the cause of all this. Ever since they came here—"

"She would not lie to us," he said. "She is Mara's child."

"Hah! And was not Mara the best liar of them all?"

He raised his stick. "You never met her!"

Enica stepped back. "I am just saying—"

"Daughter of Lugh knows the soldiers," he said. "She can help us."

Enica gave Tilla a look that said she had better not take advantage of the old man's desperation.

When they found Inam, it was obvious he could not describe the soldier who had taken Branan. Between his father urging him to make more of an effort and his mother begging the father not to shout, he began to tremble and then burst into tears in the middle of the yard. "I don't know!" he sniffed. "I thought—I thought he must be your medicus!"

"No, the Medicus was with me."

"They do all look alike under those helmets," said his mother.

Inam's round eyes and stuck-out ears reminded Tilla of a weasel. His bare feet reminded her that not everyone could afford boots. She said, "Did Branan know the soldier?"

Inam shook his head. "I don't know. I don't know anything."

"Of course you know something!" thundered his father, smacking one of the weasel ears as if that would shake a memory loose. As he shouted, "Stop sniveling and think!" Inam's mother stepped in between them. "Frightening him will not help!"

Tilla reached for the boy's grimy hand. "Why don't we go for a walk?" she suggested. "Just you and me." Dumb, Inam nodded and followed her without resistance.

As she pushed open the gate she heard Enica say, "Will you let her steal your son too?"

Senecio's reply was short and impossible to make out. When she turned, the men were in earnest conversation. Both mothers were watching her departure, and she had a feeling that wherever she took the boy, they would not be far behind.

Inam shambled along beside her, rubbing his reddened ear. Tilla said, "Can you show me the place where you met the soldier?"

To her surprise he shook his head.

"Why not?"

He said nothing.

"Were you somewhere you were not supposed to be?" she guessed.

He shrugged and carried on gazing at his feet in the mud, which was still crisp with frost.

"I won't tell them," she said. "But we need to find Branan, and you are the only one who can help."

Silently, the boy led her up the track that joined with the one leading to Senecio's farm. On the way Tilla turned to see if anyone was following them, but the women had the sense to keep their distance. She said, "Did Branan tell you about something he'd seen at the wall lately? Something surprising?"

The boy seemed puzzled.

"Something that might be a secret?"

Inam was saying he didn't think so when an approaching figure began to run toward them. It was Conn, and instead of a greeting he was shouting, "What are you doing with that boy?" More time was wasted while he took Inam away to confirm that she was not lying. He did not ask her pardon for the insult, and there was only bad news to exchange. Nobody had seen Branan.

Virana had confirmed to Conn that Branan had not been to the bar. The gate guards at the fort and the camp had been told about a missing boy but nobody had seen him. They said they would give a message to the centurion. Conn had arranged to have the horn sounded to call for help, and the family would organize a search.

He looked down at Inam. "You said it was that medicus who took him."

The boy stammered something.

"He is not sure now," Tilla explained. "And I know it wasn't the Medicus, because he was with me."

Conn eyed Tilla for a moment, then turned aside and spat. "Swear to me you don't know where my brother is."

"I swear," Tilla told him. "I swear by the sky and the earth and the bones of my ancestors that I do not know where Branan is."

"That man of yours owes it to us—"

"I will tell him," she promised. "He will do all he can."

At that moment they all heard the unearthly wail of the horn calling the people together. Inam's eyes widened and his gaze darted around as if he were expecting warriors to come crashing out from between the trees at any moment.

Tilla could remember the excitement of hearing the horn as a child. Men and boys would be running across the fields toward the sound now, clutching whatever tools could be used as weapons. Women free of small children would be setting aside their work and snatching up coats and shawls and knives and fire irons.

The horn sounded again. Conn pointed at Tilla. "You," he said. "Finish with this boy, quickly. I'll be watching."

"If you want to find your brother," Tilla warned him, "you will watch from a long way away and not frighten him."

Conn looked at her as if he were not going to be told what to do, then shrugged and stepped back.

Gathering up her skirts, she crouched down beside the boy. "You are a very important person today, Inam."

He sniffed, not looking very pleased about being important.

"You are not in trouble. None of this is your fault."

"Will Branan be all right?"

"We are doing everything we can to make sure of that," she promised. "Why don't you take me to where you saw him last, and then I can start to think about where he might be?"

25

WHEN THEY REACHED the main road, Inam turned left and led Tilla along the rough grass verge before stopping a couple of paces back from the roadway. The sun was fully up now, and the frost was retreating into the shadows. She heard the muffled hoofbeats of a couple of local riders cantering toward them, perhaps in response to the horn. Conn hailed them from some distance away, and they stopped to speak to him.

She said to Inam, "You were here?"

He nodded.

"And the soldier came along the road?"

He nodded again.

"Which way did he come from?"

The boy pointed past Conn and the riders, in the direction of the little fort and the scattering of buildings where Tilla was lodging.

"Then what happened?"

Inam resumed his interest in his feet. It was so cold, she doubted he could feel them.

"Did he talk to both of you, or just to Branan?"

After a pause, he mumbled, "Branan."

"Can you remember what he said?"

A shake of the head.

"Did he seem friendly?" When he did not reply she tried, "Was he cross?"

A pause, then a shrug.

"Did he have a beard? Or a big nose, or bandy legs, or a limp, or—anything?"

"Don't know."

Tilla took a slow breath and gazed down the road. She could see a carriage approaching in the distance. "When my brothers were your age," she said, "they used to walk along the side of the road with their hands full of pebbles. They would wait till someone rode past, and if nobody was watching, they threw pebbles at the horse's rump to see if they could make it shy."

Inam looked up. "Did they get caught?"

"Once or twice. When they hit the rider by mistake."

"I would never do that."

"I'm sure you wouldn't."

Finally the boy pointed at the opposite verge. "Branan was over there."

"And you were here?"

He started to cry again. "It wasn't my idea!"

She put her arm around him. Everything about this child looked and felt as though it might snap at any moment. "Nobody is blaming you. Your father only got angry because everyone is worried about Branan."

Finally Inam confessed. It had been a simple prank: The boys would crouch in the grass on either side of the road and wait until a rider or vehicle was approaching at speed. At the last minute they would rise up together, reaching out as if each was holding one end of an invisible rope blocking the carriageway. She could imagine the effect it would have on anyone about to rush past them. They were lucky no nervous guard had loosed a javelin at them.

"Branan was over there because he can run faster than me."

If a victim was not amused, the prankster on the farm side would be able to flee into the shelter of the woods. Whoever was on army land would have to dodge his angry pursuers and get back across the road to safety.

"So you couldn't hear what they were saying over there?"

The nod was more enthusiastic this time.

"But somebody told you Branan was going to see me?"

"He said, 'I've got to go: Our Roman lady is looking for me.' And I waited till it was getting dark and he didn't come back and it was cold, so I went home."

"Did he say he would come back?"

The boy thought about it for a moment. "He said, 'See you later.'"

"Can you remember which way they went?"

Again the small hand rose and pointed. Tilla squinted into the low sun. The soldier had gone east in the direction of the little fort. "Did they run or walk?"

"Walk."

"Do you think they were talking to each other?"

Another shrug.

"When they walked away," she said, indicating a vertical space of about a foot with her hands, "was the soldier this much bigger than Branan?" She trebled the gap. "Or more like this much?"

Inam picked a height in between the two. The soldier was from the Twentieth; he was sure of that and she did not doubt him. It was the sort of thing local boys knew. They were seduced by the glamour of banners and weapons and shiny armor, no matter what their families said about the men who bore them. The soldier had worn armor over a red tunic and he had a helmet on. Yes, the lorica, the jointed plates of armor—not chain mail. No, he could remember no crests or decorations. No, the man's legs were not especially fat or thin. He might have had a beard or he might not. Probably . . . not. But he might. Inam began to chew his lower lip. "I couldn't see."

Tilla waited while the carriage rumbled past them. The driver looked down at her and winked. She pretended not to notice, just as she had pretended not to see the flash of blue in the woods that was exactly the shade Inam's mother was wearing. It seemed the women did not trust Conn as a protector. "We'll go back to your house. Your mam will be waiting."

The boy began to sniffle again. "Will you tell my da?"

"I shall tell him," Tilla promised, "that you are a sensible boy and you have been very helpful."

"Will you find Branan now?"

"I will do my best."

Once Inam was safely home, she would go straight to the fort. It was possible that Conn had been fobbed off at the gates and that Branan had indeed been seized for spreading malicious rumors. Yet, why send only one man, and why trick the boys into thinking it was not an arrest? It was not the Legion's way of doing things.

Something about it was very, very wrong.

26

"AH!" EXCLAIMED RUSO, pleased to see the familiar figure getting up from the stool by the pharmacist's table. "It's today you're back."

Nisus, a man who parted with words as if he were obliged to pay a fee for each one used, responded to this statement of the obvious with silence.

"How was leave?"

"Good, sir."

"Sit down, man. I need a word with you."

Nisus perched back on the stool with his body slightly turned toward his table, as if he were waiting for the conversation to end so he could get on with his work.

"Our clerk's gone missing. I'm hoping you know where he is."

"I see, sir."

Remembering Nisus's tendency to answer the question you asked rather than the question you meant, he said, "Any idea where he might have gone?"

"Far away, I hope, sir."

"Any particular reason?"

"Yes, sir."

"Perhaps you could tell me . . ." Ruso paused, then rearranged the sentence. "Why is that, Nisus?"

"He talked too much."

"Did you tell him that?"

"Yes, sir."

"Did you, ah . . . threaten him in any way?"

"No, sir."

"You're quite sure?"

"Yes, sir."

Ruso left it there for now. He needed to know about the supplies that Nisus had agreed to try and pick up while he was over in Coria.

"Did you get hyssop?"

Nisus pointed to the bowl he was weighing on the scale.

"And honey?"

"Yes, sir."

"Rue?"

"Yes, sir."

Fortunately, when not obliged to converse, Nisus was very good at his job. It was not surprising that he had been irritated by Candidus's slapdash attitude and incessant chatter. Ruso said, "Figs?"

"Some, sir."

"Enough?"

"No, sir."

"We'll have to wheedle a few out of somebody's kitchen."

Nisus assumed an expression like a wet winter afternoon. Ruso said hastily, "I'll do it." He had never thought of himself as a man with charm—that was Valens's job—but even he could do better than that.

To his relief, the struggling conversation was put out of its misery by a barrage of noise from behind the office door. It sounded much as Ruso imagined a large bear might sound if it were trying unsuccessfully to dislodge something disgusting stuck in its throat. He peered around the door to see a huge soldier standing by Candidus's rickety stool and trying not to knock over stacks of writing tablets and scrolls arranged in a semi-circular wall around him as he coughed and waved one arm in an attempt at a salute.

When the man had finally regained control and snatched a drink from his waterskin, Ruso asked, "Who are you?"

"I'm your new clerk, sir. Gracilis." The man looked Ruso in the eye as if daring him to laugh. Ruso remained solemn, largely because Gracilis had the sort of physique that would be useful for hiding behind in the event of an oncoming cavalry charge. If his parents had chosen to call him

"Slender," it was none of anybody else's business. "Sorry I didn't notice you before, Gracilis. Welcome. We're not used to having anybody sitting there, as you've probably guessed."

The reply of "Don't worry, sir, I'll sort all this out" was the sweetest sound Ruso had heard in a long time.

It was swiftly followed by another sound, one that made the muscles of his abdomen clench: the distant wail of a native horn summoning reinforcements. He had not heard it for a couple of relatively peaceful years, but it was a sound that no soldier who had served during the last rebellion would ever forget.

Tilla had insisted on going to the farm alone. He should have made her promise to take someone. Anyone. Better still, anyone and a large dog. Relations with the locals had gone seriously downhill, and now it sounded as though they were gathering to make trouble.

"Sir?"

He returned his attention to the clerk. "Sorry. What did you say?"

"Is there anything I shouldn't touch, sir?"

"Very possibly," Ruso told him, "but none of us would know. Just don't go near anything that isn't a document. How long have you had that cough?"

"Four weeks and two days, sir."

Having ascertained that the man had not tried figs boiled in hyssop, Ruso glanced at his pharmacist. "When the cough mixture's made up, let him have some. Gracilis, you're to take one spoonful every morning and one before you lie down at night."

He had expected Nisus to get straight back to his table, but instead of returning his attention to the pale green and mauve of the dried hyssop under the scale, the pharmacist was watching as the new clerk glanced over each document before adding it to the correct pile on the barricades around him. Finally Nisus said, "Better than the last one, sir."

Ruso, taken aback by this unsolicited opinion, ventured, "Can you remember any conversation you had with the last one?

"I told him to stop talking or I would kill somebody."

Behind the flimsy rampart of administration, Gracilis's eyes widened.

"I thought you didn't threaten him?"

"I was measuring out mandrake, sir."

"Ah," said Ruso, explaining for the benefit of the alarmed clerk: "Medicinal in small quantities, dangerous in large ones. And did that stop him?"

"He went away, sir."

Ruso said, "Perhaps he misunderstood."

The pharmacist might have been considering this possibility, or he might have been staring into space and hoping Ruso would go away so he could get on with measuring out the hyssop.

Ruso tried, "Can you remember anything of what he said?"

Nisus pondered his reply and finally offered, "I wasn't listening, sir."

"Well, try to remember what you weren't listening to."

Nisus let a long breath out through his nose. The hyssop stirred gently in the bowl with the movement of air. Nisus looked as though he might be about to open his mouth to speak when Ruso's ears were assaulted with another bout of coughing.

This was how it would be as they went into the winter: sniffly conversations punctuated by involuntary bursts of noise. As if talking to Nisus were not difficult enough. Finally the pharmacist answered, "Something about meeting somebody for a drink."

"On his last day?"

Nisus shrugged. "On my last day, sir."

"Yes, of course. Sorry. Did he say who?" Perhaps he would not send that letter to Albanus just yet.

"A man he'd seen somewhere else, sir."

"Where?"

Nisus did not know.

"Anything else he said that you can remember?"

Nisus paused. "Nothing relevant, sir."

"Tell me anyway."

"'Doctor Ruso is just as miserable as my uncle.'"

"That," Ruso assured him, "is a compliment."

"He wanted a transfer back to Magnis." Nisus gave a sniff of disapproval. "Said Doctor Valens would be more fun."

Ruso said, "Not if you have to work for him."

Nisus, now positively chatty, ventured another unsolicited opinion. "I was expecting better, sir."

"So was I," Ruso agreed. "Anything else?"

"Something about recruitment, sir."

"What, exactly?"

Nisus opened his mouth, thought for a moment, then closed it again. Anything else he might have considered saying was lost beneath the sound of Gracilis coughing, leaving Ruso free to wonder how he was going to trace a drinking companion with no name and no description. Whoever he was, the man hadn't yet come forward despite all the appeals for information. Which might mean that he was no longer here—or, worse, that he was here but he didn't want to be found.

27

THE HYSSOP HAD arrived not a moment too soon. A couple of the gate guards were pink-eyed and sniffing, and the watch captain's voice had slid down several tones to an impressive growl. He too had heard the horn, and Ruso could tell from his expression that he knew what it meant. The guard had been put on alert, and remote work parties had been recalled, but so far nothing seemed to be happening. Certainly nothing that warranted Fabius putting in an appearance.

On the way back to the hospital Ruso reminded himself that there was a vast expanse of countryside out there within range of the horn, and the chances of anyone he knew being in the wrong part of it at the wrong moment were slim. Or they would have been, had the person not been Tilla.

Dodging an orderly carrying a stack of malodorous bedpans, he slipped into Pertinax's room and closed the door behind him.

The prefect lay motionless, facing the wall. Holding his breath, Ruso stepped across to the bed and placed a hand lightly on the prefect's ribs. He was reassured to feel a rise and fall, but it was not the steady rhythm of sleep. He bent closer and saw something glinting in the wrinkled skin around the man's eyes. There was a faint damp patch on the pillow.

The food and drink brought in this morning had not been touched. Leaving the water jug and cup, he put the tray outside to be taken back to the kitchen. When he closed the door again, Pertinax must have thought he had gone. Otherwise there would never have been that low moan from the bed.

Ruso said, "Sorry if I woke you, sir."

"I heard the horn."

"There's nothing much happening out there, sir."

Without moving, Pertinax said, "You should have let me go. No bloody use to anyone now."

Ruso had been expecting something like this. Pertinax had clung desperately to talk of his duties as if nothing had changed. Now the illusion had faded. He had begun the long struggle to adjust to a new reality.

"Are you in pain, sir?"

"No."

"We can help if you are."

"I can put up with a little pain, boy!"

"Can I take a look at the wound, sir?"

Ruso examined the stump. The swelling was no worse. He wondered how best to comfort a man who was no easier to console than the struggling cavalry stallion that had impaled itself on a fencing stake last month. The first vet who went to help had ended up in a hospital bed himself.

At least you could—allegedly—reason with a man. But the rational comfort offered by philosophy never seemed as useful in the face of real suffering as it did when you were reading about it at home after a good dinner. Reminding Pertinax that things could be worse was unlikely to help, and might well earn him a punch on the nose. In the end he said, "This is a very different challenge from anything you've faced before, sir."

"Always thought I'd die with my boots on," mumbled Pertinax. "Can't even stand up to take a pee. And now the natives are playing up again."

Trying to think of something encouraging, Ruso remembered the large newcomer in the office. "The clerk you asked for has arrived, sir. We all appreciate you putting in a word with the tribune."

Pertinax grunted.

There was a soft knock on the door and a bald head appeared. "Visitors, sir," it croaked.

Before the man could reply to Ruso's "Who is it?" Pertinax growled, "Tell 'em to bugger off."

The whisper of "The legate's physician, sir" was not soft enough.

"I'm not bloody deaf," Pertinax told him, "even if you are. I said, tell them to bugger off. All of them. Especially that one."

The orderly shrank behind Ruso and croaked, "And your wife is waiting in the treatment room to speak to you, sir."

"I'll come and talk to them both," Ruso promised, glad to hear that Tilla was safe from whatever was brewing outside, and wondering how she had managed to get past the gates. No doubt she believed that her reason for coming here was urgent enough to justify whatever disturbance she had caused, but he could not deal with civilian matters until he had finished work. He turned to the figure on the bed. "Sir, if you want anything, just ring the bell."

Pertinax stretched out an arm. The bell tinkled. "I want my foot back," he said.

The legate's physician did not look pleased to be refused entry. Ruso considered offering a tactful excuse and then decided he was not going to take the blame for Pertinax's decision, so he told the truth and was accused of being territorial.

"I wasn't," Ruso told him. "But I am now. I'm sorry you've had a wasted trip, but he's my patient and my superior, and I promised him his wishes would be respected."

Something about the physician's nostrils seemed to tighten. "I shall have to report this to the legate."

"Good idea," said Ruso. "He and the prefect can fight it out between them."

He passed several members of staff as he strode down the corridor to the treatment room. There was something unusually respectful in the way they acknowledged him. He squared his shoulders and lifted his head. It was, he decided, good for morale to be heard standing up for one's patients.

Tilla's news was indeed urgent, and deeply worrying. He understood now why the horn had been sounded, and his plans to ignore whatever she said until later had to be set aside. Putting his head round the office door, he asked, "Has anyone heard anything about a native boy being brought in?"

Gracilis's eyes appeared above the wall of writing tablets. Nisus twisted round on his stool. Neither had heard anything. "I want to know straightaway if you do," Ruso told them, aware that he had been asking the same sort of question about Candidus just now. Gracilis must be wondering what sort of outfit he had joined. "If anybody wants me, I'm going to see Fabius."

As he was about to leave, Gracilis said, "We were sorry to hear the news from your wife, sir."

"Yes," said Ruso, surprised that Tilla had told these two strangers about Branan before she spoke to him. It showed just how desperate she was. "It's very worrying."

28

"YOU CAN BE the one to tell him," Ruso told his wife as they approached the little building that served as the fort HQ.

"Me?"

"You're a native. He'll be frightened of you."

Passing the guard, Ruso was surprised to hear, "Sorry about your father, sir."

He stopped. "My father?"

"It is a great shock," said Tilla, seizing him by the arm and moving him on.

When they were in the cramped entrance hall waiting for Fabius, he hissed, "What about my father?"

"I had to get in here to tell you about Branan. His family are desperate. Imagine if it is our son."

It was bad enough to have no son—impossible to make the next leap, and to imagine the pain of losing one. Instead he said, "What's this got to do with my father?"

"I said to the guards, 'I have to see the Medicus. I have bad news. His father is dead.'"

He slumped back against the wall as understanding dawned. Mercifully, no one here was likely to know that his father had died before he and Tilla had even met.

"I did not lie to them," she insisted.

"Oh. Well, that makes everything fine, then."

"Yes," she said. "That is what I think too."

Fabius looked alarmed when he was told that there was another missing person and that a soldier was to blame, but Tilla gave him no time to feel sorry for himself. "I am thinking, sir, that this is a good chance for you to be a friend to the local people."

"A friend?" He looked incredulous. "They are accusing one of our men—"

"That is why they will thank you for making a search," she said, interrupting, "just as you did for your own man who is missing."

Fabius glanced at Ruso as if hoping he would get his wife under control. Ruso remained impassive.

Fabius said, "We get malicious rumors all the time. How do we know this isn't another one?"

"I know the family, sir," Tilla assured him. "And I have spoken to the boy who saw it happen."

Again Fabius looked to his fellow officer. "If your wife has been implicated in this alleged kidnapping, Ruso, she has a good reason to shift the blame onto my men."

"My wife doesn't lie." Too late, he remembered how she had got past the guards.

Tilla straightened her shoulders. "I am here to find the missing boy, sir."

Fabius rubbed the side of his nose. "This so-called soldier was probably some native dressed up, wanting to cause trouble."

"The witness saw a man from this legion, sir," she insisted. "Not a centurion, just an ordinary soldier. If he was a local man, the boys would know him and know it was some sort of trick."

Fabius sighed and muttered, "Why me?" as if he were the one in trouble.

From somewhere outside, Ruso thought he could hear shouting.

"If you send messages to the other forts, sir," said Tilla, "and ask them to question their men and make a search of their buildings and land, and stop all vehicles on the road and look inside, the local people will think you are on their side."

"Why would I want to—"

"Otherwise they will be wanting to come in and search themselves. I am thinking you will say no, which is your right, and then there will be complaints to the tribune and the legate and—"

"I know what will happen," Fabius groaned. "One thing the natives are very good at is complaining."

Someone was knocking on the door. "We do not want another Regulus," put in Tilla, who had no way of knowing that she had already frightened him with the threat of a fresh reprimand from the tribune.

The new arrival brought a message to say there were angry natives gathering outside the south gate, and all the gates had now been barred. Two natives were demanding to speak to the commanding officer. "They say they're the boy's family, sir."

"They'll find a more senior officer over at camp."

Apparently the watch captain had already growled that at them. "They don't want to go to the camp, sir. They want to come in here."

Fabius's head slumped into his hands. "Let them in. Just the two of them. Make sure you search them properly. And fetch Daminius. All this is giving me a headache."

"It is giving everyone a headache, sir," Tilla told him. "The only cure is to find the boy safe and well. Until then, my people cannot trust yours. Any man in the Legion could be the kidnapper."

To Ruso's relief, she decided to stop there and let Fabius mull over her demands. Outside, the shouting resolved itself into a chant.

Fabius's irritable "What's keeping them?" was answered when Senecio and Conn entered very slowly, the older man walking with a stick and leaning on his son's arm.

Afterward Ruso always remembered the start of that meeting with shame. It was not the way father and son looked like cornered animals, caught between defiance and desperation. It was not the way Fabius turned to Tilla and demanded, "What is he saying?" after Senecio had abandoned his principles and asked in thickly accented but clear Latin, "Where is my son?" It was not Fabius's insistence on pointing out that he personally had no idea where Senecio's son was—something that left Conn observing aloud in British, "We are wasting our time with this one." What left him angry and embarrassed was that the only seat in the room was occupied by a Roman centurion while an obviously lame old man who had suffered a terrible loss was left to stand under escort as if he were about to attack his hosts with his bony fists.

Ruso ordered one of the guards to go and fetch a seat and some water for the visitors. Fabius glared at him. Ruso pretended not to notice.

The old man's eyes met his own. "My sons are my life," he whispered.

From outside the gates—at least, he hoped it was outside—Ruso could hear the continued chanting of angry locals.

"Those are our neighbors out there," Conn said. He pointed in turn to

Ruso, Fabius, and the guards. "If you sons of whores will not give my brother back, our people will come in and find him."

"We're as keen to find him as you are," Ruso told him, glancing at the guards, who looked as though they would like to take Conn outside and explain a few things to him.

"I doubt this. You sent one of my brothers to the next world. Now you have the other one."

Tilla leaned close to Conn, lifted the straggly hair with one finger, and whispered fiercely in his ear. Ruso thought he caught the British words for *insult* and *trying to help*.

Conn scowled at her but reserved his contempt for the Romans. "We are not fools. We know how you can tell who my brother is. We know it must be one of the men from in here."

Fabius was still determined to argue. "Your brother's name has been associated with a malicious rumor."

"Yes. You spread a lie about him, then you take him away. Where is he?"

"Are you denying that he claimed to witness an illegal burial?"

Conn hesitated, perhaps making sure he had unraveled the Latin correctly before deciding how to answer. He said, "My father's people know nothing of this. We do not speak of a burial to anyone."

Fabius sat forward. "Then who did?"

Someone knocked on the door as Conn demanded, "Why do you ask me? Look to your own men. Give us Branan back."

The chair and Daminius had arrived at the same time. Instead of sitting, Senecio clung on to Conn's arm and hissed in British, "That is one of them!"

"Are you sure?"

"I know it!"

While Fabius began to explain the situation to Daminius, Conn was whispering urgently to Tilla. Nobody was bothering with the old man. Ruso stepped forward and urged him into the chair before he fell. Senecio clutched his arm, still very agitated, and insisted in British, "He is one of them! He came to the farm!"

"Silence!" ordered Fabius. He sounded more petulant than authoritative. He turned to his deputy. "Optio?"

"I'll have the men account for their movements yesterday, sir," Daminius promised. "And we'll have all the buildings and the quarry searched."

"Wait!" Tilla cried. "Not yet!"

Ruso frowned. This was going too far. He reached for her arm. "A word in private, wife," he urged, excusing them both and propelling her toward the door. Out in the entrance hall he whispered, "You can try telling Fabius what to do when nobody else is listening, but you can't order his optio about in front of everyone. Daminius is a sensible man and he's trying to help. What's all the fuss about?"

"Daminius is the man who searched the farm."

"Gods above, don't your people ever let go of a grudge? He was only obeying orders! Now he's been ordered to help find Branan."

"This is not a grudge! Listen!" Tilla glanced around to make sure they were alone before putting her arms around him. To anyone passing through the hall, they might have been snatching a moment of un-Roman intimacy. Her breath tickled his ear as he heard, "Senecio has been thinking. What soldier will know to say to Branan, 'The Roman lady wants to see you?' He has been asking himself, 'What Roman could know that Branan has met the Daughter of Lugh?' Who has seen me and Branan together?" She paused, letting him think about that for a moment.

"The search party who went to the farm," he said.

"Yes. And Daminius is one of them."

29

ONE OF THE many disadvantages of having a minuscule HQ build-ing was the lack of privacy. A bemused Daminius was sent to wait in the clerk's office and the three Britons were left under guard in Fabius's room while Ruso and Fabius glanced around the corridor, agreed that they might be overheard, and banished themselves to the middle of the street outside to hold a hurried conversation. The air was still pulsating with the angry chant from the Britons beyond the walls. Ruso tried to shut it out of his mind. "We have to take this seriously," he said. "What the old man is saying makes sense."

"This is absurd!" Fabius kept glancing over at the gates as if he was expecting wild natives to burst through them at any moment. "Why would Daminius have anything to do with stealing a child?"

"They're not saying it's him personally," Ruso pointed out. "They're saying he's one of the eight men it could be."

"I should never have left the Sixth," muttered Fabius. "The gods have sent me nothing but bad luck ever since. Terrible weather, bodies in the wall, men kidnapped and tortured, natives complaining. No wonder I'm ill. I should never have listened to you about that missing clerk."

"We need to check up on all the men who've met the boy," said Ruso, wondering if he had been deliberately paired with Fabius by some senior officer whom he had managed to annoy.

The centurion lifted his head. "Can you hear that? Thanks to you, we've become a target for native revenge!"

"If you'd been sober enough to discipline Regulus properly in the first place, none of this would have happened!"

"It was you who prescribed the wine, Doctor!"

They stood glaring at each other in the street. Finally Ruso said, "This is getting us nowhere. We need the names of everyone on that search party straightaway, and we need to check where they were yesterday afternoon."

"This is beyond our level. I'm not doing anything without authorization."

"You don't need authorization to talk to your own men. Get Daminius to give you the names, keep him here, and have the others rounded up."

"But—"

Their conversation was interrupted by the arrival of the watch captain needing further orders on how to deal with the fifty or so Britons making that racket outside the south gate.

Fabius, whose job it was to give those orders, looked at Ruso and the watch captain and the closed gates as if searching for some hint about how to proceed. Ruso hoped he was not going to do something stupid. He wished the Britons would shut up. They were not helping.

Fabius asked if they were armed.

"Just a few farm tools, sir." The watch captain's growl made him sound more authoritative than his centurion. "And they've got women and children and old people out there."

Fabius looked relieved. "Just ignore them unless they attack."

The watch captain, who might have been hoping that his centurion would take charge of the situation, left with the paltry consolation that whatever went wrong from now on, everyone would know it was Fabius's fault.

"Daminius is a decent man," Ruso continued when the watch captain was out of earshot. "He'll want to help you catch a child snatcher."

"If there is one," snapped Fabius. "If this isn't some plot the natives have cooked up between them. Taking revenge on your ill-judged search party. I've had enough of your bright ideas, Ruso. I want some authorization. We'll need to get a message through to the camp."

"I'll do that," Ruso promised, wondering why Fabius was talking as if the fort were under siege. Since the riot outside the south gate could be seen from the main road, it was more likely to be the officers at the camp who were under siege, surrounded by passersby now clamoring to tell them about the excitement. "I'm going across there for a clinic anyway."

Fabius's eyes widened. "If you go out there, I can't promise my men can protect you."

"It's only a rabble of native families," Ruso assured him, wondering as he said it whether people had assumed the same thing about Boudica and her warriors. "If we send the father and brother home with a promise of action, they'll probably disperse."

"And if they don't?"

"They've got children with them," said Ruso, who was not going to encourage any hint of using force. "I doubt they'll want to stay long." He hoped he was right. It made sense to him that any self-respecting mother would want to get her children home for supper and bedtime. The trouble was, women—even self-respecting ones—did not always behave in the way one predicted. "Can you get Daminius's search party assembled for questioning and make sure they don't talk to anybody?"

"You seem to think I'm some sort of incompetent, Ruso."

"Can you?"

"Of course."

"Good. By then I'll have spoken to the tribune and we'll know what he wants us to do."

With luck, it would be something useful.

30

PEERING THROUGH THE gap between the gates, Ruso could see a thin vertical slice of the crowd that had gathered outside. He caught a glimpse of a brightly dressed woman with a toddler and a baby in her arms, and a young man in a muddy farmworker's tunic. The Britons had sat down on the stone surface of the causeway that carried the road across the ditch, perhaps more to keep their backsides dry than to block the access, since they must know they were obstructing only one of the routes into the fort. Shifting sideways to change his angle of vision—which was annoyingly narrow—he saw a small girl sitting cross-legged in front of a toothless creature with straggly white hair. He had to admit that Fabius had been right to ignore them.

He nodded to the guard to lift the bar. The chant disintegrated into yelling as one of the heavy gates swung partly open. A barrage of missiles splattered against it: rotten apples, cabbage stalks, clods of earth.

Senecio limped forward. As he stepped outside something flew past his ear. Behind him, one of the guards swore. Ruso turned to see the remains of an egg sliding down the shoulder plates of the man's armor. The stench made him gasp. Tilla stepped away, holding her nose.

The barrage stopped. Senecio was leaning on his stick and holding up one hand for silence. Then he thanked them for coming. "It is a comfort to have good neighbors at a time like this."

Someone shouted, "Where's Branan?"

Senecio shook his head. "We do not know. The soldiers say they did not—"

His words were lost beneath the protest. He held up his hand again until the outcry of accusation and disbelief died down. "The soldiers will search their forts and land, and will ask questions of the—"

Ruso's concentration stumbled over the unknown word that must mean suspects or culprits, and he lost the thread of what was being said. When he picked it up again Senecio was, as agreed, asking them to go to their homes. "I beg you to think," he said. "Think where a thief might have hidden my son. Ask your neighbors if anyone has seen him. And search. Search your buildings, your fields, the woods and commons . . ." His voice faltered. He gulped a breath, steadied himself and continued. "Search the streams around your land. Ask everyone. Somebody . . . *somebody* must have seen Branan."

Conn stepped forward and took his father's arm. "My brother has been missing since late yesterday afternoon," he said. "You know what he looks like. Nine years old, brown curly hair, front teeth that do not touch each other. He is wearing a green work tunic and brown trousers and boots."

Another voice yelled, "Great Andraste, take revenge on the Romans!"

There were cries of agreement. Others chimed in with "String them all up!" and one with more imagination shouted, "Gut them and feed them to the dogs!"

Conn held up his hand. "That comes later. First, we find my brother."

The crowd, given something to do, began to disperse just as Ruso had hoped. The old man leaned on his stick and surveyed them. "Many good people are searching for my boy," he said. "It is a bitter thing to be too lame to join them."

Ruso said, "Is there anything more we can do to help? Can we take you home?"

"We have our own cart," Conn told him. "They wouldn't let us bring it in." He put his hand on his father's shoulder. "Perhaps there will be news at the house."

Senecio gently lifted his son's hand. "Go," he said. "Enica is waiting at home. Tell her until he is found, my place is here."

Ruso and Tilla exchanged a glance. "Grandfather," she said, "the soldiers will do everything that can be done here. Conn is right: You should be at home."

The old man lifted his head and looked at everyone standing around him. He said to Tilla, "Daughter of Lugh, see to it that nobody harms my wife." Then he turned and limped back inside the fort. Mercifully Fabius had the sense not to object, and the guards, lacking any instructions, stood back to let him pass.

Conn watched him go for a moment, then turned on his heel and strode toward the waiting cart, where the nondescript woman from the farm stood holding the head of the mule. By the time he reached it, he was surrounded by supporters.

Ruso was suddenly aware of his wife standing beside him. She slipped her hand into his and whispered, "I have to go with them. Pray for us all." Then she ran out after the cart.

When she reached it there was some sort of argument, with Conn seemingly trying to turn her away and Tilla insisting. Conn was no match for Tilla, and Ruso was not surprised when she finally clambered onto the cart to join them. He just hoped the rest of the locals would accept her. This could easily turn into the sort of situation where everyone had to be on one side or the other.

Meanwhile, he hoped that wherever Branan was the gods would look kindly upon him, and that Branan would sense the desperation of all the people who were trying to bring him safely home.

31

"YOU CAN'T LEAVE him there, Ruso!"

"I didn't put him there." Ruso had been surprised at the agility with which the aging Senecio had lowered himself onto his blanket. He was now hunched opposite the entrance to the HQ building. It was impossible for anyone to enter or leave without being aware of the old man's gaze upon them.

Fabius said, "He's in the middle of the road."

"Move him, then. I've got to find Accius and I'm late for clinic at the camp."

"But what—"

Whatever complaint Fabius was about to make died in his throat. The gates had screeched open again and a group of riders was making its way in. At the head of them was the distinctively straight-backed and scowling Tribune Accius.

Ruso sighed. He must be almost an hour late by now. There would be a line of disconsolate patients grumbling about him over at the camp, and the staff would be wondering if they had been forgotten. He put down his medical case and saluted. As he did so, someone shouted a warning, and a mule cart changed course to avoid the old man sitting in the street.

The tribune glared at Ruso and Fabius over the ears of his horse and demanded to know what the hell was going on. "I was told you had a hundred natives hammering on the gates and chanting war songs."

"We've managed to disperse them, sir," said Fabius.

"But you did have?"

Ruso said, "About fifty, sir, including women and children."

"Why in the name of Jupiter didn't you send someone to get me out of my meeting?" He sounded disappointed, as if he had missed the excitement. The cavalrymen with him would be annoyed too. They would have been hoping to see some action.

Ruso said, "I was on my way across to tell you, sir."

"Centurion, is that a native sitting in the middle of the *via principalis*?"

Fabius confirmed that it was. "His son is missing, sir."

"How is his getting run over going to help?"

"He's made a vow, sir," Ruso tried to explain. "He will neither leave the fort nor eat nor set foot indoors until his son is found."

Accius stared at Ruso as if he were not sure he had heard correctly, then slid down from his horse. He took his helmet off and handed it to the groom who ran up to take the reins. "You first, Ruso," he said, leading the way to HQ past the watching form of Senecio. "From the beginning."

On the whole, Ruso felt later, Accius took it rather well. He sent urgent messages to the legate and neighboring units, and instantly grasped the importance of getting the search party to account for their movements yesterday. He also arranged for warnings to slave traders and their agents to look out for a stolen child. "Fabius, get those men rounded up. They're not to speak to each other or anyone else until I join you to question them."

Fabius did not look sorry to be sent away.

"Ruso, I want you here for a moment, then go and see to your patients and come straight back. Remind me what the name is again."

"Branan, sir."

"Not the boy: the father. Why haven't I met him? I thought we knew everyone with influence around here?"

"Senecio, sir. He's a farmer. And a poet. My wife knows him. You may have heard about him singing to the trees."

"Ah. The crazy one."

"Not crazy, sir." At least, not before one of his three sons was killed and another stolen. Now, who knew? "He's just very traditional."

Ruso was acutely aware of the average officer's failure to grasp how the locals saw things, which meant they often ended up negotiating with the wrong people. They would not bother with poets. If Rome were under threat, a general might quote a few lines of Virgil to rally the troops, but he was unlikely to rush to the Forum to enlist the help of some modern scribbler reciting his latest composition. "They hold the knowledge of their tribe in their memories," he explained. "And they put together the latest events in verse. They're like sort of . . . announcers and libraries rolled into one. They believe spoken words have great power."

"This is why I want you along, Ruso. Local knowledge. Mixing with the natives."

"Sir, I don't—"

"You wanted to search for somebody. You can search for this one. Get someone to cover your medical duties and I'll ask Pertinax to lend you to me."

Ruso took a deep breath. Despite trying to learn his wife's language, his energies had been concentrated not on understanding British habits but on weaning her away from them. Recent attempts to mix with the natives had been like leaping into a vast pit of ignorance and finding it filled with many more ways of getting things wrong than most of his comrades could possibly imagine. "I don't know a lot, sir. And I'm not popular with them."

"Never mind. You're the only officer we've got with British connections. You speak the language: You'll know what they're really saying. If they want to find the child, they'll deal with you, like you or not."

"There are Britons in the ranks, sir."

"I don't want a Briton. I want one of us. Cheer up. This isn't as bad as Eboracum."

Privately Ruso thought it could turn out to be a lot worse than Eboracum.

"You never did tell me exactly what went on there."

"No, sir," agreed Ruso, who had no intention of telling him.

"Still, with luck this won't spread any further. After we executed the last lot of troublemakers, the tribes went back to loathing each other even more than they loathe us."

Again the failure to understand. "Sir, I think people tend to unite against a child snatcher."

Accius gave a sigh of exasperation. "What's the matter with the man, luring a child away from his family? I mean, if he wants a boy, why can't he damn well pay for one, like a normal person?"

"There is this business of the body in the wall, sir."

Accius raised one eyebrow.

Aware that the tribune was not going to like this, Ruso continued: "Branan's name was mentioned as the person who put the story about. It's an odd coincidence."

"I'll make some inquiries," Accius promised. "But I very much doubt it's anything to do with that. If our people arrest someone to make an example, they don't do it secretly."

"No, sir. What if whoever put the body there found out that Branan had seen it happen?"

Accius made a noise in his throat that suggested impatience. "That would only make sense if there really were a body, Ruso."

Ruso shifted the weight of his medical case, wishing he had sent Gallus over to the camp to act in his place.

"So your theory," continued Accius, "is that one of our men snatched a child because the child had seen him putting a dead body inside the emperor's latest building project?"

Put that way, it sounded ridiculous. And yet . . . "I can't see any other logical conclusion, sir."

"Then keep looking. And don't breathe a word of your pet theory to anyone else."

"Sir, the natives are bound to work it out for themselves."

"Well, don't help them. We have enough troubles with the wall as it is. Now let's see if I can pacify the mad poet."

It was an odd encounter, like one of those triumphant sculptures on war monuments and military tombstones, depicting a Roman soldier looming over a cowering barbarian. Ruso watched it from the corner by the granary, expecting to be called at any moment to translate. Accius stood upright in gleaming armor with a sword slung at his side. At his feet crouched an elderly native with wild white hair, clothed in a muddle of brown and gold wool. The differences went deeper: In Ruso's experience Accius was logical, efficient, and ambitious, and he was tipped for a role in the Senate. Senecio could neither read nor write, believed in the power of poetry, saw a reason to sing to trees, and trusted that obstinacy and public suffering would help to save his son. Whatever appearances might suggest, he was not cowering: He was simply not making the effort to stand up.

Somehow they managed to converse without help. It seemed Senecio could speak enough Latin when he wanted to.

When they had finished, Accius gave orders to one of his men and beckoned Ruso over.

"The old man will be staying here for a while. I've sent for a couple of British recruits to stand there and make sure nobody flattens him."

Leading Ruso away out of earshot, the tribune added, "I'm not giving him the satisfaction of a fight. With luck he'll get cold and bored and go home. But tell your staff to keep an eye on him. If he looks unwell, have him carted off to a hospital bed. I wouldn't put it past the old goat to die on us."

"I'll tell them, sir." Ruso shifted the case back to his other hand. "Will that be all, sir?"

"Go and see your patients and arrange some cover," Accius told him. "Then come straight back here. I shall want you to deal with communications with the natives, so make yourself available. And don't tell them anything unless I've authorized it first."

"Sir, they really don't trust me."

"Stop fussing, Ruso. The priority is to find the boy. You said yourself: Everyone unites against a child snatcher."

"Yes, sir."

"Oh, and, Ruso . . ."

"Sir?"

"Smarten yourself up a bit. You're representing the Legion. We may be surrounded by barbarians, but there's no need to look like one."

32

NEITHER CONN NOR the woman spoke as the cart jolted them all back to the farm. Or perhaps they did, but Tilla did not notice over the voices of fear and reassurance that were chasing each other around inside her mind. As the cart drew up to the gate she realized she was holding her breath, hoping that Branan would scramble down from his favorite tree to greet them.

Enica was crossing the yard, carrying a basket piled with logs. When she saw the cart she dropped the basket and ran forward to haul the gate open. Tilla knew immediately that there was no good news and that the woman's look of disappointment must be mirrored on her own face.

At least he is not dead, she told herself. She had seen the hope flicker and fade in Enica's eyes. *She knows no more than we do.*

Enica clutched at Conn's arm as he climbed down from the cart. "What did they say?"

"They say they know nothing."

"Where is your father? Why is she here?"

"My father has stayed to shame the Romans," he told her. "They say they will question the men her husband sent here."

A few days ago this woman had looked more like Senecio's daughter than his wife. Now she was pale and hollow-eyed. Her hair was lank and disheveled and her tunic was spattered with grease.

"They have sent messengers to all the forts with a description of your son," Tilla said. "Senecio asked me to see that you come to no harm while he is in the fort reminding the soldiers of what they need to do."

"You?"

Before Tilla could answer, several women came out of the house with a gaggle of children tumbling around their skirts. She recognized a couple of the gossips from Ria's bar, along with Cata, whose bruised cheek had turned from blue to purple, and her mother and sister.

Conn called, "No news!" and their faces fell just as Enica's had. They ushered him and the other woman inside, urging them to come and eat and tell everyone what they had heard and seen, even though he had told them the important part already. Cata's mother called to Enica to come and join them, but Enica replied that she wanted to build the fire. If they wanted to help, could they please look after Conn? She would talk with the doctor's wife.

Tilla bent to help collect the scattered firewood. Enica flung a log into the basket. It landed with a thump. "They must know where he is!" she exclaimed. "They are always spying on people. Asking questions. We see the way they look at Conn at market. How can they not know?"

It was a question Tilla could not answer. She tossed another log in on top of the others.

"Why did my husband send you?"

"Perhaps because I was all there was."

"I warned him to stay away from you!" Enica burst out. "Right at the beginning. I knew you would be trouble! The army never bothered us before you and that medicus came here."

"The army took half your farm before we came here," Tilla objected. "And I never meant to be trouble."

Enica snatched up the basket. "He had this foolish idea about making things better between our people and yours."

Tilla followed her across the rough grass at the back of the houses to a blackened bonfire patch where she supposed the family had planned to celebrate Samain tomorrow. She wanted to say, "Those foreigners are not my people." But then, who were?

Enica crouched beside a small pile of kindling that had already been arranged in the middle of the patch. Her skirts trailed in the old soot. "Things had just settled down again after the troubles," she said. "Then he saw you and he had to bring you and the Roman here. All that talk of weddings." She placed a couple of logs on the pile. "'No more killing,' he said. As if it would bring his dead son back. Of course, nobody listened to him except you."

Tilla swallowed. "My husband—"

"Him? I saw the look on his face when the wedding idea came up. I wasn't a bit surprised when he sent men to raid us."

"That was a mistake."

"And now his people have taken my son. And all because of you, and my old fool of a husband, and his stupid—oh!" Enica raised the last log in the air and sent it crashing down onto the pile. The others tumbled and scattered, one or two rolling several feet away. She sat back in the ash and buried her face in her hands and wept. "How can I help him?" she wailed. "If I search in one place, what if he is in another and I am not there?"

"I know—"

"You know nothing! You have no child! Leave me alone!"

Tilla recoiled, telling herself that Enica had only lashed out because she was in pain herself. She had not meant to hurt. "I am sorry."

"It is as though I have a limb torn off," Enica muttered, almost as if she was talking to herself. "No. It is . . . it is beyond words. And you know what is the worst thing? It may never stop. What if we do not find him?"

Watching her, it struck Tilla for the first time that at least the ache of being barren meant that she was spared a horror like this. You brought a child into the world and you gave a hostage to the gods. She tucked up her skirts to keep them out of the muck and crouched beside Enica. "I am not a mother," she said, "But I know what it is to be torn away from your family. I will do everything I can to help you find your boy."

Enica snatched up a fistful of skirt and wiped her eyes. Then she sniffed, looked at the damp wool, and wiped her nose on it too. "I should not have said those things. Take no notice. "

Tilla said softly, "It may all still come right."

"Nothing is right!" The voice became a howl. "I want my son!"

Tilla said, "I will fetch some food and we will think what to do."

"I know what to do." Enica sniffed. "I have to sacrifice the best lamb."

"It is a good offering."

"I cannot remember the words. My husband does that sort of thing."

"The gods understand," Tilla assured her, glad they were not Romans, whose gods demanded that mortals should get all the words right. It struck her that other families would be building their bonfires for tomorrow night's Samain gatherings. This felt more like building a pyre. She put a hand on the woman's shoulder. "Enica, when did you last take food?"

"I am not hungry."

"Offering the lamb can wait. Come with me into the house and take some bread and put on some clean clothes."

"Nobody knows what to say to me. They keep pouring me drinks and telling me to eat."

Tilla said, "Do you want me to get rid of them for you?"

She sighed. "They are very kind. They all brought things they could not afford to give."

"It is your house. You can say who stays here."

Enica wiped her eyes with the back of her fist. "I want them to stay. But do not make me talk to them."

33

JUST AS TILLA approached the house Conn came out, gnawing on a chicken leg and with a jug clutched in his other hand. Two women carrying waterskins and a sack pushed past her and followed him across to the cart. She guessed he was taking supplies out to the search parties.

The faces around the fire seemed to lose interest when they saw her. Nobody moved to let her near the warmth. She hesitated, back to the wall, not wanting to retreat but not sure how to stay. Enica might think these people meant well, but she was not so sure.

She felt a surge of relief when Cata's mother appeared from the shadows. At least she had one ally here. "Daughter of Lugh, you must eat."

"Senecio asked me to look after Enica," she said, wanting everyone to know that she had a right to be here.

"You must eat." The woman pointed to a low table that, even now, after Conn had taken so much away with him, still held bread and cheeses and hard-boiled eggs and ham and jugs of beer and several jars that might contain honey or preserves or salt.

Each of the visitors must have sacrificed at least a week's worth of supplies. Of course. She had forgotten how things were here. Yet there had been a time when she had thought people were the same everywhere. When they had their first civilian lodgings in Deva, she made the mistake of leaving some blackberries outside next door to share. The neighbor called round and offered to pay for them. She refused to accept, and they were both embarrassed.

It was while she was gathering up food for herself and Enica that they started. They might not have known what to say to Enica's face, but they had plenty to say behind her back. Tilla had a feeling they were only saying it because she herself was there. They had had all afternoon to talk about the terrible things that might be happening to Branan: Why go over them all again now? As if she had not thought of them all herself.

The searchers, they said, might be too late. Branan might be dead already, and buried, and would never be found. He might be held captive somewhere, alone and afraid, at the mercy of a madman. He might be sold to a brothel, where shameful things happened. Or he could be on the way to Rome as a slave or even a trainee gladiator. He might have been sold to the Northerners. With the wall being built, he could be lost forever. And on and on.

Tilla wanted to clamp her hands over her ears and scream, "Shut up!" Instead she hacked the knife through ham she did not really want to eat, and piled more onto her wooden platter.

Imagine never finding out, someone said. How terrible would that be for his family? Waiting every day for news. The old man might—they *all* might—die never knowing . . .

Tilla turned away from the table, unable to stand this mischief-making nonsense any longer. "He will not be on the way to Rome," she said. "The soldiers will check with the slave dealers. There must be laws against selling stolen children."

There was a moment of awkward silence before a voice pointed out, "A child stealer will not give a pig's fart what the law says."

Someone else said, "Nor will those sort of buyers, if they smell a bargain."

Tilla bowed her head, feeling her face begin to redden. She had meant that it might be harder than they thought for the kidnapper to sell the boy, but now that she thought about it, what comfort would that be? If he could not be sold, it was more likely that he would be disposed of.

It had been just as foolish as when she told Cata's family to put in a complaint to Regulus's centurion. How Roman she must seem to these people. She wanted to say, *The world is different out there! In other places, you would be the ones who did not fit in!* But they would never understand, and with all her traveling and her Latin and her fancy reading and writing, she knew no more about how to find Branan than they did.

"That is not how things are here, Daughter of Lugh," put in a kinder voice. She looked up to see Cata's mother. "Perhaps they keep all the laws down in Deva, or even across in Coria where you come from, but it is different here."

"We trusted the Romans to deal with that scum who hit our Cata," put in a voice, gesturing toward Cata's injured face and bandaged hand, ignoring her protest of "He is not scum!" to add, "Instead of helping, they came and burned our house down!"

To Tilla's relief Cata's mother took up the fight. "You are leaving out part of the story, girl. You and your brothers were told to leave him alone, and you did not."

"I told you too!" put in Cata. "I begged you all to let him go!"

"He wasn't hurt!" retorted her sister. "And it was the army's fault for doing nothing about him. Then they followed us here and turned this place upside down as well."

The woman with the lisp joined in. "They didn't even apologize after the old man complained. And now they have taken his boy."

"Sh!" hissed the woman beside her, pointing at Tilla.

The woman with the lisp straightened her neck and raised her chin as if to show she was ready to suffer any blow for her honesty. "I do not care if there is a spy here," she said. "I speak my mind. You all know what I'm saying is true."

"Complaining to the army just makes them worse," put in the sister.

"Exactly! Now that Senecio is making a fuss about them taking his son, he had better keep a good watch. You never know what they will do next."

Tilla put the platter down. "Most of the soldiers do not want trouble," she said. "They just want to build a wall and go back to their base."

"That is not what I heard," put in someone else. "I heard that none of the soldiers want the wall, either. They are saying in private that the emperor is weak and it is a sign of defeat."

"If the officers find anyone who says that," said Tilla, knowing it was true and cross with herself for being sucked into this argument, "he will be very sorry. Soldiers are supposed to obey orders, not give opinions."

"Exactly!" said the woman, wagging a forefinger in the air as if Tilla had just proved her point. "Why do you think they started this rumor about the body in the wall? Because they don't want to build it! They want it pulled down! But they cannot say so. This way they can put the blame on us and then they have a good excuse to arrest anyone they want. And they'll get a good price for a strong young lad."

"But they are not saying anything about the rumor!" insisted Tilla, not sure where to start with such nonsense. "They think Branan has been taken by a criminal."

"You see? It is never their fault!"

"I did not say that!"

"Ah, you wait and see what they do to their own men when they question them," said someone. "Wait and see if they flog them, or use the hot irons on them like they do with us."

"Of course they won't!" said Cata's sister. "Look what they did to that Regulus: a nice warm bed and a transfer to another unit."

Somebody said, "If I got my hands on them, they'd be singing like skylarks by now."

"Somebody else should have gone," said the woman with the lisp. "The old man, bless him, he's too trusting. We can't waste time asking nicely. What good will he do, sitting there and starving? Every moment counts!"

Tilla was tempted to demand, *What good will you do, sitting around and complaining?* But Enica was right: They meant well toward Branan and his family. So instead of arguing she filled a cup with beer, picked up the platter, and levered the door open with her foot.

34

ENICA HAD ABANDONED the bonfire and was gazing out over the gate. "I thought I heard horses," she said. "And then I thought, *I'll ask Branan to climb the tree and look.*"

Tilla rested the cup and platter on the gatepost. They watched in silence as a blackbird flew down onto the track and glanced round before stabbing at something in the mud. It flew up again at the sound of Enica saying, "That is a great deal of food."

For the first time Tilla looked at what she had piled onto the platter. Bread and cheese and ham and bean pottage and two chicken wings. Enough for four people. "I wasn't thinking." Back in the house, they would be saying she was greedy. She offered the platter to Enica. The hands that tore at the bread were rough and ingrained with dirt. Senecio was no fool, for all his singing to trees: He had married a hard worker. And perhaps he knew those other women well enough to know that Enica would need Tilla for support. It was good to think that someone, at least, had faith in her.

Enica led her toward the old bench outside the house, the place where, in better weather, women might sit chatting in the sunshine, spinning fleece or preparing supper while they kept an eye on their children playing in the yard. The hens began to strut around them, stabbing at invisible food between the cobbles and watching for tidbits.

Tilla balanced the cup on the bench and placed the food between them to share. "I have been thinking," she said. "I do not know what the soldiers are doing beyond searching the forts and questioning their own men. But I am wondering if there is another way to search that nobody has tried."

Enica put down the slice of ham she was about to place in her mouth.

Tilla hoped she was not about to give her a new threat to worry about. "If the story about the body in the wall is true," she said, wondering how much of this Enica had worked out for herself, "then—"

"Then your husband should look there for his missing soldier."

It was a good point, but not one Tilla wanted to discuss. "If it is true," she continued, "then there is somebody who did it, and that person wants his name kept secret. If he heard that Branan had seen him, perhaps he took Branan to make sure he was not betrayed." She moved swiftly on to the next part, not dwelling on the thought of Branan in the hands of someone who disposed of bodies in secret places. "But when he finds out he has the wrong boy, and that Branan knows nothing, perhaps he will go looking for the person who really did see him."

"What will he do to Branan?"

"If we can find the witness who really did see what happened at the wall," said Tilla, not answering the question, "then perhaps that person will lead us to the man we should look for."

Enica looked up. "Or woman."

"It could be," Tilla agreed, "but there is a man involved somewhere. Your neighbor's boy saw him take Branan."

"How can we find this person? You may as well dig for the roots of a mountain as try to find the source of a rumor. Everyone will say it is the friend of a friend. Or a traveling tinker, or a stranger in an inn whose name they never knew."

"But whoever it is knows the name of your son," put in Tilla, hoping that Branan's name was not a piece of decoration that some gossip had added further down the chain. "We must think about who might want to place him in such a rumor."

Enica picked up the ham again. "Somebody who saw a body being laid where it could not rest."

Tilla said, "Somebody who wanted to tell but did not want to be punished for the telling."

"Somebody who can watch the wall when most of the soldiers are not around."

"Yes!" Tilla agreed. "Nobody could bury a body while the soldiers are working up there."

"Somebody who does not think kindly of my family."

"Or was just choosing a person to blame," said Tilla. "How many people know your son?"

Enica looked at her as if the question did not make sense. "Everyone," she said. "All the neighbors. People at market. The shopkeepers outside the fort where he makes deliveries."

"The soldiers?"

She nodded. "They come here to buy cheese and milk and sheepskins. Then they come here as guards with the tax collectors. Then your husband's men, searching for the missing soldier."

Before Tilla could answer, Enica continued, "Conn thinks the soldiers made up the story and lied about Branan starting it to cause trouble for us. But I have been thinking: Why do that?"

"It does not seem likely," Tilla agreed, glad the women from the house were not here; no doubt they would say that if something bad could be done, the soldiers would do it. "So it is most likely one of our own people who started the rumor. We have a place to start."

"Maybe a hundred places," said Enica, ripping the ham into shreds. "Maybe five hundred."

Put that way, it did not sound so good.

Enica flung the scraps of meat out into the yard and there was a flurry of eager wings and beaks. "I cannot understand why someone would want to blame a child."

"Perhaps they thought a child would come to no harm," Tilla suggested. "Or would never find out."

"Perhaps they chose a name and it happened to be my son's."

Tilla looked up. "Or perhaps because this rumor maker is a child too."

"A child? Another child is behind all this?" Enica sounded horrified. "A child we know?"

"It is just an idea."

"We must get there first," Enica said, getting to her feet, "before whoever who made the burial finds this child for himself. I will talk to the neighbors."

It might not last long, but Tilla was glad to see Enica's renewed energy as she hurried across the yard.

35

IT WAS A mystery to Ruso why his late arrival for a clinic often seemed to be greeted by more patients than usual. Surely some should have given up and gone away? Lately he had come to the conclusion that for every man who decided—or was told by his centurion—that he was not ill after all, there were another two who simply saw a queue and joined it. The longer the queue stood in place, the greater the effect. The wait might also account for the number who presented him with one complaint and then proceeded to offer several others *while I'm here*. By the time he had escaped from the camp and hurried back to the fort, it was well past midday. Remembering the order to smarten up, he straightened his tunic, adjusted his bootlaces so they were even, and ran his fingers through his hair before making his way across to the HQ building. The guard standing in the middle of the road saluted as if he were not aware of the old man huddled on a blanket at his feet or of the voice crying out in Latin, "Where is my son?"

Ruso paused to crouch beside Senecio. Apart from his hair, the man looked smaller and thinner than before. The hair was a cloud of white, as if all his anxiety and alarm had pushed it out farther from his head. Ruso's "How are you, grandfather?" was in British, but the reply came in Latin.

"Where is my son?"

Ruso lifted the cup that someone had placed beside him. "You should at least drink water."

"Where is my son?"

"Everyone's looking for him."

"Where is my son?"

Maybe he was crazy after all. Ruso left him and hurried on into the wrong room.

Fabius's office was warm and stuffy because it was full of men. Most were crammed together at the far end. They were sitting on the floor in their dirty work clothes and harboring expressions that ranged from boredom to resentment. Ruso recognized Mallius, the formerly blond purveyor of hens, and the thickset man who had tied the rope around him during the rescue, and assumed these were the quarrymen who had raided Senecio's farm on the ill-fated search for Candidus. They were under the supervision of three guards. One of the guards stepped forward to impede his progress while the others continued to stare at the prisoners as if they had orders to stab the next man who moved. Ruso was pleased to see that they were enforcing the order that the men should not speak to each other.

Ruso said, "Where's the tribune?"

Without taking his eyes off the prisoners, one of the guards said, "Tribune Accius is in the clerk's office, sir."

Accius was indeed in the clerk's office, as was Fabius—something Ruso could have deduced without being told, from the shout of "You must be able to remember somebody!" Several of the quarrymen looked up. One or two glanced at each another. Ruso was surprised too. He had never considered Fabius to be a man who shouted at people except on the parade ground, where behaving like a real centurion was unavoidable.

Ruso found the two officers seated behind the clerk's desk, which had been pulled into the middle of the room. Judging by their expressions, Optio Daminius—who was standing facing them—had not come up with a satisfactory answer.

"Ruso!" exclaimed Accius, the warmth of his greeting suggesting that he was glad to be interrupted. "Come in. What news?"

"None that I know of, sir," said Ruso, putting his medical case on the floor. While he had been listening to wheezy chests, pulling teeth, and examining an inguinal hernia, he had heard officers barking orders for all tents to be opened up for inspection. The entire camp had been searched. The boy had not been found.

Ruso had not expected that he would be; it was more a case of convincing both the men and the locals that they were taking this business seriously. A stolen child was much more likely to be hidden on a vehicle, or in a remote shelter, or somewhere in the rolling countryside that stretched for miles in every direction. He said, "My replacement's on his way, sir."

To his relief, there had been a message from Valens at the gate. Valens had agreed to leave his own unit in the care of his many underlings and brave the scorn of Pertinax.

Accius said, "Good," and returned his attention to the man in front of them. He folded his arms on the clerk's desk, and leaned forward. Beside him, Fabius was slightly red in the face. Now that the tribune had occupied the desk space, Fabius did not seem to know what to do with his hands. Eventually he put them behind his back.

Daminius carried on staring at a point on the opposite wall just above the officers' heads. The good-luck charm was still strung around his neck, but for once it did not seem to be working. Ruso saw a muscle twitch above his jaw.

"The optio and several of his men had a free afternoon yesterday," Accius explained.

This was not good news. Since the fort had no proper bathhouse, each man was given one afternoon a week to visit one of the bigger bases nearby. No account of movements was normally expected, and if a man chose to do something else, nobody usually cared.

"Optio, tell the doctor where you were."

"I went for a run, sir. On my own."

"Tell him where."

"I went east along the road to Vindolanda. Then north, up across the building line, west past the lakes, and along the bottom of the cliffs and down through the gap by the stream. I got back here not long before curfew when the gates were still open."

"And in all that time you managed to speak to nobody nor see anyone who might be able to remember you?"

"Sorry, sir."

"What about natives?" Fabius prompted, as if they were a species not covered by the tribune's previous question.

"I may have seen some, sir. I can't remember."

Accius said, "And you say you didn't call in at Vindolanda?"

"No, sir."

"Oh, gods above, man!" exclaimed Fabius. "You can do better than that! We've a child to find."

"I'm very willing to help, sir."

"Then tell us something useful!" snapped Fabius. He sounded more desperate to clear Daminius's name than the man was himself. He had come to rely heavily on his optio.

Ruso was puzzled. In other circumstances, if a man had gone for a run preoccupied with some worry or other, the story might have been almost plausible. But the restrictions on lone travel away from the main roads were still in place—something an optio would know very well. Any legionary running across fields on his own would be both conspicuous and cautious. He said, "Tell us what you know about the native family."

"The father and the eldest son are on the list to watch, sir. The father because he used to stand around chanting to stir up his gods while we were working. The son fought with the rebels in the last troubles. He's got a short temper and a big mouth. Also I believe they're connected to the family that kidnapped Regulus." He swallowed. "And they're friends of your wife, sir. I'm sorry about the boy, sir."

"Thank you. What can you tell me about him?"

"I only saw him the once, sir. Eight or nine years old, I should think. Brown hair, gappy front teeth."

"When did you see him?"

"When we searched the house, sir."

"Do you have any personal connection with the family?"

"No, sir."

"You would have no reason to visit them except on official business?"

"No, sir."

"Did you have any official business there yesterday morning?"

The muscle above the jaw twitched again. "No, sir."

"So why were you there?"

Daminius blinked and swallowed. Nobody else moved.

Ruso, who liked Daminius and had very much been hoping that he was wrong, said, "You were aware of orders not to go onto native property unaccompanied?"

"Yes, sir."

"So?"

Daminius looked him in the eye. "I wanted to go and apologize, sir."

"*Apologize?*" demanded Fabius.

"I wasn't happy about the way I'd led the search the day before, sir. Not after I found out what really happened with Regulus."

Ruso said, "But you didn't apologize, did you?"

"I saw you coming, sir. I wasn't supposed to be there and I didn't have time to wait till you'd gone."

Accius said, "Even if you had been allowed there, you had no authority to apologize on behalf of the Legion."

"No, sir. Only on my own behalf."

Fabius sighed. Ruso reflected that if this was true, then Daminius had more courage than he had himself. If less sense.

"May I speak, sirs?"

Accius leaned back against the wall. "Please do."

"I'm sorry to be wasting your time, sirs. I swear I don't know what's happened to the boy. I'd like to help look for him."

Accius glanced at his fellow officers. "Any more questions?" There were none. "Thank you, Optio. That will be all for now."

When the man had been taken back to join the others, Accius said, "Well?"

Ruso said, "The apology story is plausible."

"Well, we know he was hanging about there for some reason. Why didn't you mention that before?"

"It was a lucky guess, sir. I thought I caught a glimpse of someone in the woods when I went to try and smooth over this business of the raid with the old man; I didn't know it was him."

Accius grunted. "What about the run in the countryside?"

Fabius said, "He's very clear about the route."

"He would be," said Ruso. "It's one of the standard circuits for training runs."

Accius shot Fabius a glance. "Is that correct?"

Fabius agreed that it was, although since Daminius dealt with all that, Ruso assumed he was guessing.

Ruso said, "I think the run sounds a bit odd, sir. Especially since nobody's supposed to be wandering about on his own out there. But that doesn't mean he took the boy."

Accius nodded. "I'll see if I can find his old centurion. See what he thinks. Let's look at the others for a moment. Fabius, show him the list. Ruso, I'll need you to help with checking their stories."

"Yes, sir."

Fabius passed a wax tablet to Ruso, who read:

Daminius	*running alone to Vindolanda and back*
Mallius	*to brothel LARENTIA and DELIA then sleeping in barracks.*
Maternus	~~*Vindolanda with H and F and PEREGRINUS*~~ CONFIRMED
Liber	*to snack bar VIRANA then to brothel blonde girl mole on left buttock*
Festus	*To Vindolanda baths with H, P, Mat then woman TOTIA lodges*
	with leatherworkers
Quintus	*on duty*
Habitus	~~*Vindolanda with MAT and F and P*~~ CONFIRMED
Pollio	*on duty*

The others should be easy enough to check, although it was a pity Mallius had decided to sleep off his afternoon's exertions, presumably alone.

"I've sent to Vindolanda for someone to question this Totia woman," Accius said. "With luck we'll be able to cross Festus off the list soon."

"I'll talk to Virana," said Ruso. "She's part of my household."

"Call in at the brothel while you're out there," Accius told him. "Fabius is having Mallius's messmates brought in to see if anyone saw him asleep."

"My clerk is making sure we have no men unaccounted for," said Fabius, "and that anyone off base was where he was supposed to be."

Ruso noted that the presence of the tribune seemed to have cured most of Fabius's ailments, including the inability to do anything.

"Let's hope we get somewhere with one of them," said Accius.

He did not need to say why. If no other obvious culprit came to light, they would very urgently need a better story out of Daminius. Soldiers were supposed to be protected from professional questioners, but if there was any question hanging over the optio, Accius would have to decide whether he was going to uphold the law or get some answers.

The tribune said none of this. Instead he got to his feet and lifted his chair with both hands, placing it carefully back against the wall. "Ruso, when you've spoken to all those women, come and find me and report. Fabius, chase your clerk and see how he's getting on with pinning everyone else down." Perhaps in case they were wondering what he would be doing, Accius added, "I'll be tracing Daminius's history and reporting to the legate. He's asked to be kept informed. Oh, and we've heard back from the slave trader's agent at Vindolanda. Nobody's tried to sell the boy so far."

On the way out, Ruso visited the imprisoned quarrymen. They looked even glummer than before. Daminius was seated facing the wall with his elbows propped on his knees. Ruso asked Liber, the one whose alibi was "to snack bar VIRANA," to make himself known. Ruso was pleased with what he saw. Not because the gods had favored Liber with a muscular build, a polite demeanor, a full complement of black hair, blue eyes, and white teeth, but because if a young man who looked like that had been seated at one of Ria's tables yesterday, Virana would remember.

36

VIRANA GREETED RUSO with the sort of smile that cheered the weary heart and would have made him feel especially welcome if he had not known that she bestowed it on almost any man wearing a military belt. "I need to tell you something, master!" she cried, breaking off from wiping a table not ten feet away and waving the cloth at him in case he had trouble locating her. "Have you found Branan?"

"Not yet."

"I've remembered the soldier!"

Ruso looked at her, wondering how she knew what he was about to ask, and then realized they were thinking of different soldiers. "Candidus?" He fingered the forgotten letter to Albanus, still tucked inside his belt.

"He was here, but they called him Perky. I thought that was his name. That's why I didn't tell you before."

According to Nisus, one of the last things Candidus had said was that he was meeting someone for a drink. *A man he'd seen before . . . he didn't know where.* Now, when Ruso did not have time to deal with it, the search for Candidus might be leading somewhere. He sat at a corner table and ordered a cup of spiced wine, noting the sidelong glance from a middle-aged woman across the room when he invited Virana to join him. "I need to know who Can—who Perky was with," he said.

"He asked me to come and sit beside him but I told him I had to light the lamps."

"Was he on his own?"

"I told him, master, I don't go with just anybody."

"Of course."

Virana shifted one end of a bench to make more space for herself. "I don't know why nobody believes me."

"It must be very annoying," agreed Ruso. "Who called him Perky?"

"Besides, I can't keep getting up and down now unless I have to. Ria says I can sit by the bar as long as I get up when there's serving to be done." Virana collapsed onto the bench with a sigh, then lifted her skirts, stretched out pale bare legs, and circled her feet in midair.

Aware of the woman turning round to stare, Ruso took refuge in his wine.

"See?" Virana demanded. "It works. Not swollen like they were before. Ria says I can keep a stool by the bar."

"Very good," said Ruso, adding with deliberately clarity, "My wife will be very pleased." He lowered his voice to ask, "What about Candidus?"

She pointed toward the woman. "He was sitting over there." She stopped, as if this had answered the question.

"Virana, I'm in a hurry. Could you—"

"With some men from the fort here," she added. "They were playing dice."

This was new. "How many men? Do you know their names?"

She scratched her head, dislodging one of the pins that never held her hair in place for long. "I think there were two of them," she said, shifting sideways and grunting with the effort of bending to pick the pin up. "I'm not sure. Is there one called Gallus with fair hair?"

"Gallus?" This was worrying. His deputy had not mentioned a social evening with Candidus.

"I know he works at the hospital," said Virana, inadvertently confirming his identity. None of the other staff had fair hair. "And the other one was the hospital cook."

This was even more unexpected. "So Candidus, Gallus, and the cook were playing dice," he prompted. "Then what happened?"

"Then they finished the game and the other two went away. Perky wanted to talk to me. But I didn't sit with him, because I don't—" She registered the expression on his face. "Anyway, he carried the oil jar for me when I filled the lamps and we talked for a bit and then he finished his drink and he went back to the camp."

"On his own?"

"I felt sorry for him. He said it was cold at night and his tentmates weren't very nice."

"Do you think he might have gone somewhere else instead?"

Virana frowned. "Where would he go?"

Where indeed? "Did he mention meeting anyone he hadn't seen for a while?"

Virana's face brightened. "When he first saw me he said, 'Haven't I seen you somewhere before?'" She looked puzzled. "But I don't remember him, and he said he's never been to Eboracum."

"He was probably just making conversation," Ruso told her, wondering if Candidus had also invited her to come and help him polish his equipment, or whatever euphemism they used these days. "Can you remember anything else at all? Did anyone follow him?"

Virana pondered this for a moment.

"This is important," he explained. "You may be the last person who saw him before he disappeared."

"Oh, no, master!" Her confidence was unexpected. "I am not the last person who saw him."

It was all Ruso could do not to grab her and shake the rest of the pins out. "Then who is?"

Virana frowned. "I don't know, master. Surely you saw him the next morning when he was working at the hospital?"

"You're talking about . . ." He paused to think. "The day after market day? Not the day he disappeared?"

Virana said, "You didn't say when. You asked if I saw him."

Ruso let out a long breath and managed, "Yes. That's true. Let's see if you can remember somebody else."

"Another soldier?"

"A man called Liber."

Her face lit up. "He was in here yesterday. Did he say something about me?"

"No," said Ruso. "I'm just trying to sort out who was where when Branan went missing. Can you remember when he arrived and when he left?"

"It was after the mistress had the headache," said Virana. "She went upstairs, and then . . ." She thought for a moment. "You must have seen him yourself, master. He was sitting at table three when you came in."

"I didn't notice," Ruso confessed.

"Then he had to go because he was on duty." She pushed her hair back from her face, leaned across the table, and whispered. "I think he likes me!"

"I think he likes quite a few girls," Ruso told her, wishing he did not have to disappoint her and wondering yet again why Virana's experience had failed to conquer her optimism where good-looking young men were concerned. He downed the last of the wine. "I need to go. Thanks for your help."

"I hope you find Branan soon. He's a nice boy. I like him."

He said, "We're getting nearer," because he had to say something, and because it might be true. For all he knew, the lad had turned up by now. In case he hadn't, Ruso was about to visit the local brothel in the hope of meeting Larentia, Delia, and a blonde girl with a mole on her left buttock.

37

THE WOMAN'S HAIR was dyed a harsh, unnatural fox-pelt red. Heavy makeup had collected in her wrinkles so the painted eyes in the artificially whitened face made him think of black beetles in a snow-drift. But she still had most of her own teeth, or someone else's skillfully attached, and the smile that revealed them was professional. So was the disappointment when she realized Ruso had only come for information and was not intending to pay for it.

Yes, she had heard about the boy. It was a terrible thing.

"Do you have many customers who ask for boys?"

"Not often enough to warrant buying one," she said, as if it were a matter of regret. "I send them to Vindolanda."

"Do you know who those customers are?"

"I know who all my customers are."

Ruso waited.

"Discretion, Doctor," she explained. "I'm sure you understand."

"And I'm sure you understand how urgently we need to know."

The muscles holding the cheeks into a half smile relaxed, and the skin around her mouth fell to a slackness that betrayed her age. Ruso looked her in the eye until she pulled the smile back into place.

She remembered a tall gentleman with only one leg, and one who was short and stout and wheezy. She could hardly have invented anyone less like the man who had taken Branan.

"If you see either of them," he said, "ask them to look out for him on their, ah . . . on their travels."

"I'm sure they will," she said, not in a way he liked. "Now. Who else can we offer you, Doctor?"

38

PERTINAX OPENED HIS eyes. "You."

Still clutching the medical case, which was unlikely to have shielded his reputation when he was seen entering the brothel, Ruso said, "Good afternoon, sir."

"I don't know what's bloody good about it. When am I going to get my crutches?"

Ruso restrained a smile of relief. He pulled up the stool and sat beside the bed. The room smelled normal and Pertinax's grumbling was lucid, all of which was good news. He explained again about the dangers of post-operative bleeding as everything inside the wound grew back together and the stitches no longer held things shut. "So far it's all healing up very nicely," he said, having learned long ago not to say *better than I'd expected*, because the patient then concluded that his earlier words of encouragement had been a lie. "If you move about too much now, you'll delay the recovery and you may end up a lot worse. Especially if you fall, which you will until you get used to a new way of walking."

Pertinax closed his eyes and said, "Hmph," but Ruso was not fooled. The man's brow had smoothed, as if he were secretly glad to have the challenge taken away from him. Then Pertinax sniffed and his brow creased again. "Are there women around here somewhere?"

"Not that I know of, sir."

"Then what's that smell?" The eyes opened. "Not you, is it?"

Ruso plucked the shoulder of his tunic and sniffed. There was a faint whiff of Larentia, who had conveniently turned out to be a blonde girl with a mole in the right place; he had declined her invitation to inspect it. She could vouch for Mallius being fully occupied in the early afternoon and for Liber being in the brothel at the time when he had told Virana he was on duty. He cleared his throat. "I think it might be me, sir."

"You smell like a cheap whore."

It was too complicated to explain. "I must have picked up some woman's scent in passing, sir."

"Hmph. My late wife never fell for that one."

Ruso, who was supposed to be reporting back to Accius, opened his mouth to say what he had come to say, which was that Valens was taking over, but Pertinax said suddenly, "Women. Don't suppose you could have one sent in?"

"I don't think that would be a good idea, sir."

Pertinax grunted. "Shut away in here all day. No idea what's going on. Half-baked stories about bodies in the wall. Some idiot came in here earlier and told me your father's just died. I told him your father's been dead for years. Left you with a lot of debts, didn't he?"

"There's been a misunderstanding, sir."

"What was all that shouting after the horn? Sounded like natives."

"Nothing to worry about, sir."

Pertinax's eyes snapped open and glared at Ruso as if he had been watching him through his eyelids. "I'll decide what I want to worry about."

"Yes, sir."

"You're just like the rest of them: looking at me lying here and thinking, *Poor old boy. He's finished. No foot, no sense.* Is that what you think?"

"No, sir," Ruso assured him.

"Accius wants to take you away for special duties. What for?"

"That's what I came to tell you, sir. I won't be around for a while, but—"

"I know that! I'm asking what for?"

It was some measure of Pertinax's current ambiguous status that the tribune had paid him the courtesy of asking before taking one of his men, but had not thought it necessary to tell him why. It was a sign of how ill Pertinax was that he had not insisted on knowing at the time. "The locals have lost a child, sir. It looks as if one of our men's taken him. They're demanding him back. I'm needed to help with the search because I have native contacts."

The lines on the prefect's forehead deepened. "One of our men?"

"We're questioning some suspects now, sir."

"Good. Don't pussyfoot about."

"No, sir," said Ruso. "Doctor Valens has offered to come and take over here."

"Offered? My son-in-law never volunteers for anything."

"He really did, sir," Ruso insisted. "He's a good doctor: you'll be in safe hands."

For once Pertinax did not argue. Instead he asked how long the child had been missing. When he was told, he shook his head. "All that work we did getting the Brits settled down," he said. "Good men were lost. When I think of some of those lads . . . I can still see their faces."

"Yes, sir," said Ruso, who for months afterward had suffered bad dreams about the men he had failed to save. The natives had raised a much more spirited rebellion than anyone could have expected, and the casualty list had been horrendous.

"And now some twisted fool's gone and stirred them up again," said Pertinax. He lay back on his pillows and gave a graphic description of what he would do to the twisted fool when he was caught. "Very slowly," he added. "In front of the natives."

"I think that would be a popular move, sir," said Ruso, wondering how many of the audience would faint.

"Hmph. But they're not going to ask me what I think, are they?" He gestured toward the end of the bed. "No foot, no sense. Why haven't we caught him yet?"

"We're looking at several men, sir."

"Who?"

At the sound of the first name Pertinax gestured toward his missing foot. "Anybody tell you why I was over at the quarry?"

"No, sir." Ruso suspected he was not the only person who had wondered.

"Good. You're not supposed to know."

There seemed to be no answer to that.

"Don't pass it on. I wanted to watch Daminius at work without that idiot Fabius getting in the way. He's up for centurion. Or was."

"Do you think he could have taken the boy?"

Pertinax grunted. "If he did, my judgment must be going. Who else?"

Pertinax did not recognize the other names whose movements were being checked. "Whoever it is, he'll make a mistake before long," he said. "He's scared. Must be. Have they checked the rolls to see who's missing?"

"It's being done, sir. There are search parties and roadblocks, and local forts and slave traders have been notified. Nothing's come up so far."

The eyes closed, and Pertinax let out a long sigh. "And I'm lying in bed."

Ruso watched him for a moment, then picked up his case and tiptoed toward the door. His hand was on the latch when he heard a voice behind him. "I'm not asleep," it said. "Tell them to find that boy. They must find that boy, alive and well, or everything our lads fought and died for will be thrown away."

39

THE SACRIFICE WAS done, perhaps with the right words and perhaps not, but the smell of roasting lamb drifted off into the woods and the neighbor's dog was hanging around, looking hopeful. Most of the visitors were long gone, promising to search and offer prayers for Branan and to visit their neighbors and try to track down the real source of the body-in-the-wall rumor. They had seemed quietly relieved to go home. There were cows and goats to be milked, hens to be shut away before the fox came, and husbands and children to be fed. They had been given a good excuse to go and do all those things without looking as though they were abandoning Enica with neither husband nor son.

Enica had gathered names of rumor-mongers, promising everyone that whatever came to light would be kept secret from the soldiers: *Nobody will be punished*. Tilla had kept silent. The soldiers had been accused of child stealing. They would do their best to find out everything, and when they did, there was no telling what they would do. You couldn't blame them. They had put a lot of work into that wall only to find themselves with enemies on both sides of it.

Tomorrow they would chase the rumor. Tonight, the day was coming to a close with Branan still not found. The remaining women stood around the fire: Enica with the dried blood of the slaughtered lamb dark on her forehead. Cata with her bruised face and bandaged fingers. Even the woman with the lisp had nothing to say. There was no sound around the fire but the crackling of the wood and the odd hiss as the lamb's fat dripped into the flames. Somewhere beyond the gate, a blackbird was singing his close-of-day song. Tilla felt as though she could reach out and touch the absence of people who should have been there. Branan, of course. Senecio. The dead brother she had never met. Conn and the other men who were out searching.

She pulled her shawl tighter around her shoulders and repinned it. She felt guilty about leaving Enica but she too had something to do. "I will speak to Virana," she promised. "She will know if there are any fresh stories about the body in the wall. If there is any news—" She broke off. Everyone was looking toward the road. The blackbird had sounded the *chack-chack* of a warning cry, and almost straightaway the soldiers appeared.

It seemed Tribune Accius had ridden his gray stallion down the long track to the farm with only four guards in attendance. Beside him, on a bay horse whose coat needed brushing, was Tilla's husband. The horses stopped outside the gate. Enica hurried forward to greet them.

Tilla did not need to see the men's faces under the helmets. She could tell from the way they moved as they swung down from the horses that there was no good news.

A mule cart drew up on the track behind the riders: Conn and the other searchers from the house. They too looked weary. She guessed both groups had already spoken on the way here.

Her husband unfastened his sword, then murmured something to Accius. They seemed to be arguing. Finally Accius handed over his weapon. Leaving the cart to his companions, Conn slung both swords over his shoulder and went into the house without a second glance, as if he disarmed legionary tribunes every day. Tilla wondered what role he had played in the troubles.

Enica stood back, allowing the soldiers to enter. Leaving the guards outside, the officers walked into the yard. The tribune's gaze darted about as if he were assessing the location and looking out for threats and escape routes. Tilla wondered if he had ever been to a native farm before.

She stood back as her husband introduced the tribune and Enica to each other. After a quiet conversation the two men walked up to the fire, bowed, and threw herbs into the flames as a mark of respect. Then they stepped back and waited as the scent of rosemary and bay wafted into the air. Enica went to fetch Conn and the others. They emerged from the house, several of them carrying drinks. Conn wrapped a cloth around his hand and hacked some untidy slices from the outside of what remained of the lamb now that the proper portions had been burned for the gods. None was offered to the soldiers.

Accius was still glancing around, taking it all in. Tilla guessed he would rather have spoken privately with the man in charge than face a group of locals whose language he neither spoke nor understood. But the man in charge would have been Senecio, who was not here, and even if Romans had been good at negotiating with women—which they were not—Enica was in no fit state to deal with him. She had wisely called everyone together, and he was outnumbered.

In spite of all the Army's weapons and armor and discipline and shouting, and despite the Great Wall that would help them to control everybody's movements, they had been unable to stop one of their own people committing a terrible wrong. Yet, the disgrace of having a child snatcher in the ranks did not seem to have taught Accius humility. Tilla listened as he introduced himself, and then to her husband's translation of it. Accius regretted that he had brought no news. He had just spoken to Senecio, who was well, and he had come to say personally how sorry he was that the boy was missing.

Tilla felt they could have worked out for themselves that he had come personally. He could only be speaking of it because he wanted to make sure that they understood what an honor it was. Then he told them that the army was taking "this allegation" very seriously indeed.

Her husband did not translate it as she would have done. *Allegation* was a cautious word but not a good one. It suggested that the tribune thought somebody here might be lying. Her husband translated it as "bad news." Either he did not know the word, or he knew the offense it would cause. She wondered how many of the Britons had noticed.

After that, the tribune told Enica that the army was doing everything in its power to find her boy alive and well. He seemed annoyed when, instead of falling at his feet and thanking him, Enica interrupted.

"She says," Tilla interpreted before her husband had the chance, "the boy has no coat with him."

Accius replied that they knew what the boy was wearing.

That was not what Enica had meant, though. She was worrying about her son out there, enduring a second night with no warm covering.

"The description of the boy has been sent out with despatches to all military establishments in the province together with official posting stations," the tribune announced, "and the legate has ordered a reward to be offered for his safe return."

Tilla left her husband to translate that into British.

The Britons looked unimpressed. Conn was more interested in what had happened to the soldiers who had come to search the farm.

Accius told him they were now under arrest.

"Then why are you here?" Enica demanded. "Why are you not making them tell you where my son is?"

"Let us have them!" put in Conn. "We'll find out." There was a chorus of agreement.

When he could make himself heard, Accius explained that the men had been questioned and their stories were being checked. Meanwhile other searches would continue. "We need to coordinate our efforts." He placed a hand on her husband's arm as if to introduce him. "All messages will go through Medical Officer Ruso. He will keep you informed. If you have anything to tell us, speak to him."

When her husband announced, "From tomorrow morning I will be based at Ria's snack bar," the tribune looked at him in surprise, as if this was something they had not talked about.

Conn wanted to know why, if the army was serious about the search, everyone was being forced to give up for the night because of the curfew.

"Our patrols will be looking throughout the night," Accius told him.

Conn said, "But you don't trust us near you in the dark."

"See?" put in Cata's sister, taking Enica's arm. "They say they care about Branan, but they care more about themselves."

This time, to her husband's credit, he translated every word back to the tribune. Accius tried to wriggle out of it by saying the local searchers needed to sleep, whereas the soldiers had plenty of men and were used to patrolling through the night watches. Conn asked how he thought the farmers managed at lambing time, then.

It was Enica who told him to be quiet. Accius looked relieved and suggested that searchers might go out together.

"No, thanks," said Conn in Latin.

Tilla watched confusion spread as the conversation rolled by too fast for her husband to catch it and clothe it in a different tongue. Accius's scowl deepened. He repeated that they wanted to find the boy. Then, glancing at each of the faces around the fire and lingering on Conn, he added that

nobody should hinder the army's search parties. Otherwise they might not
be able to continue.

Conn said in swift British, "They're threatening to call off the search if
our people don't let them do anything they want."

"That is not what he meant at all!" Tilla burst out. "What he is saying
is—"

"Tilla, I can't translate if you interrupt!"

"But Conn is telling them all wrong!"

"Stop!" The Medicus held up both hands and waited for silence. In slow
and clear British—even to Tilla it sounded odd to hear a Roman with her
own accent—he said, "What the tribune says is that if there is trouble
between the local people and the army, both sides will be too busy defend-
ing themselves to look for the boy."

"Exactly!" said Accius in the same tongue.

There was a moment's stunned silence. It was hard to tell in the poor
light, but Tilla was fairly sure that Accius's fierce features had turned pink
under the helmet.

Conn said, "Where did that come from?"

Accius did not reply.

"I told you!" Conn exclaimed. "You can't trust them. He knows our
tongue. He's been listening."

"Then he knows you mean no harm," said Tilla.

"How do we know they're helping to find my brother? They might be
hiding him."

"You do not know," said Tilla. She looked at the two Roman officers
standing unarmed in Senecio's yard. At the old man's one remaining son.
At his pale wife. At the women who had been burned out of their home.
Then she glanced back at the guards by the gate. "You do not know
whether they can be trusted," she said. "And nothing good that I can tell
you about my husband will change what he did. But Enica's son is missing, and Senecio has vowed not to touch food until he is returned. I have
said this before. Only a fool will waste time fighting with men who have
offered to help. I know you are bitter and ill-mannered, Conn, but I did
not take you for a fool."

Afterward, when the Romans had gone to mount the horses and a thun-
der-faced Conn was fetching their swords, Tilla turned to Enica. "You
must try to sleep tonight. Leave someone else to tend the fire and turn the
lamb. Tomorrow will be a busy day."

"I pray he will be found before then."

"I will be here in the morning and together we will find the person who started that story."

"What if the man who hid the body gets there first?" There was no need to explain. Tilla had offered a possible story and Enica had believed it: There was a body in the wall, and whoever had buried it had stolen her son.

"How can he get there first?" she asked. "He does not have all of us women on his side."

The smile was weak, but it was there. Tilla clasped the rough hand in her own.

Enica said, "I said harsh things to you before."

"They are forgotten," Tilla told her. "Tomorrow we will find the person who told that lie about your son. And if the gods are willing, we will bring Branan home."

40

Ruso would have offered to escort Tilla back from the farm to her lodgings, but his duty lay with the tribune. He was not worried: Most of the trip was on the main road, and his wife was used to fending for herself. So both he and she were surprised when Accius announced that she should walk back with them.

Moments later Accius was calling out, "Not in between the guards! Walk on one side. You're being escorted, not arrested!"

Ruso stifled a smile. As he suspected, the offer was less for his wife's protection than for the goodwill Accius might accrue by being seen to protect a native in public. Accius was no fool. He had not served in Britannia during the rebellion but he must know as well as Pertinax that this business of the kidnapped boy could very easily slip out of control. Especially since their inquiries into yesterday's whereabouts of each member of the search team had gotten them nowhere: Everyone except the supposedly trustworthy optio had a firm alibi. He must also be aware that when news of any trouble was reported back in Rome, the unlucky name that would be associated with it was not that of the legate but of the man whom the legate had assigned to deal with it: Publius Valerius Accius. No wonder he had called Ruso in to help. Accius could do little about what they would say in Rome, but at least he could try to ensure that the name everyone in the Legion here would associate with failure would be somebody else's.

When they turned onto the main road, the stone walls of the fort and the thatched jumble of civilian buildings they could see beyond it were vanishing into the gloom of an early-autumn evening. A few lamps began to glimmer behind the translucent luxury of windows. A native cantered past on a shaggy pony, yelled, "Where's the boy, you thieving bastards?" and did not wait for an answer. They were overtaken by a couple of mule carts whose drivers were hurrying to get in before the gates closed. Just a few moments away from the home of a family paralyzed with fear, others were coming to the end of an ordinary day and looking forward to supper.

Accius insisted on escorting Tilla to the entrance of the snack bar. As she stumbled through the gap left by the one shutter that remained open, Ruso promised to join her later.

The men turned and made their way back toward the fort. Now that Tilla was gone, Ruso could ask the question that had been troubling him for a while. "Sir, is there still any chance it might be an official arrest? Some undercover security unit that nobody knows about?" He hoped that *nobody knows* sounded better than *you aren't important enough to be told about.*

"The legate's looking into that," Accius confirmed, implying that there might be units of which even the legate knew nothing, although Ruso found it hard to imagine why they would arrest a nine-year-old. "What I'm still wondering is whether the Britons have done it themselves."

This was even more provocative from a senior officer than it had been from Fabius. "Sir, the family are genuinely—"

"I didn't say the family are in on it. It would only take two or three mischief-makers to set it up and then sit back and watch the fun."

"But why—"

"They don't like the wall?" Accius suggested. "They don't like the old man? They like causing trouble? I don't know. We don't need to know why, we just need to put a stop to it."

It was becoming apparent to Ruso that if they could not put a stop to it and Branan was not rescued, then whatever the truth, the story would be put out that he had been kidnapped by his own people and the Army were the innocent victims of slander. He could imagine only too well the outrage that would cause among the locals.

"Sir?" It was one of the guards. "Sir, I think I hear something."

Accius raised a hand and the group drew the horses to a halt. There was indeed some sort of disturbance going on. Abandoning the gate in front of them, they turned left, then right, skirting around the corner of the fort between the outer ditch and the wall. There was a confusion of people and vehicles gathered around the south gate. Accius said, "Your Britons are back."

"Not as many this time," said Ruso.

There were eight or ten of them: both men and women as far as he could make out, clustered around the second of the two drivers who were still waiting to take their vehicles in. This time there was no chanting. Instead some sort of argument was going on in British. Accius shook his head. "I can't follow it."

Ruso listened for a moment.

"I think the locals are trying to persuade the driver not to deliver," he said. "They want him to join them instead." He paused. "'You are bringing food to the soldiers,'" he translated, glad Tilla was safely behind the shutters of the snack bar. "He's saying he has hungry children to feed. They're calling him a traitor."

Suddenly the Britons noticed Accius and his men, and the complaints switched to Latin.

"Give us Regulus!"

"We want the child stealer!"

The yells coalesced into a chant of "Regulus! Regulus! Regulus!"

Accius rode forward a few paces and listened for a while as if he were accepting a hymn of praise. Then he raised one hand to call for silence, and to Ruso's surprise it worked.

"Regulus has been transferred elsewhere for punishment," Accius announced. "He could not have taken the boy."

As he spoke, the cart jerked into motion, the driver perhaps hoping to take advantage of the distraction. One of the protesters shouted and they all abandoned Accius and rushed toward it.

There was a brief scuffle around the head of the mule, with the driver lashing at his fellow Britons with his whip and yelling at them to let go. The cart lurched as the mule tried to back away.

Behind him, Ruso heard the bark of an order and a swish of blades against leather as Accius's men drew their swords. Half a dozen gate guards stepped out, shields up and spears raised. Caught between the two, the Britons abandoned the cart and scattered, yelling "Traitor!" and "Friend of the child snatchers!"

Accius ordered his men not to give chase. Under the protection of the guards, they put away their swords and followed the cart under the archway. Once they were inside, the guards lowered their spears and put their shoulders to the gates. The sound of British jeering was overwhelmed by the screech of hinges.

"Marvelous," observed Ruso, temporarily forgetting that he was in the presence of a senior officer. "Now we're protecting a wife beater."

"Yes," said Accius. "But unfortunately he's *our* wife beater." He swung down from his horse. "If this goes on, we'll have to clamp down on movement and gatherings and cancel market day."

Ruso handed the bay's reins to the waiting groom. "It's the Samain festival tomorrow, sir."

"Then they'd better start behaving themselves," said Accius, just as a trumpet blast announced the curfew, "or they'll find that canceled too." He pulled off his helmet and tucked it under one arm. "Right. I hope my cook's made it down here with my dinner. Go and get something to eat and then come over to HQ. We'll work out where we are and decide on our next move." He peered ahead to where a lone legionary stood in the street over what looked like a pile of rags. "What's that noise?"

They stopped to listen. Weaving its way through the usual clump of boots and shouts of orders, the distant clatter of spoons in mess tins and a sudden burst of laughter, came a thin, reedy voice that rose and fell in what Ruso recognized as one of Tilla's tunes. Senecio was singing.

"Doctor," ordered Accius, "get that old fool under cover before he freezes to death."

41

TILLA'S THOUGHTS WERE heavy with sorrow and her stomach weighed down with unwanted food. Enica was not hungry, so she had forced down most of what she had mistakenly piled on the platter and then realized she could not refuse some lamb from the sacrifice. Straightaway, instead of a quiet stroll back to her lodgings, she had been forced to hurry to keep pace with the horses. She stumbled as she made her way past the one open door shutter, entering the bar with more of a fall than a step. An elderly couple looked up from a corner table. They pushed their empty bowls away and got up to leave. The woman was frail and struggled to stand, clutching at her husband's arm, while he stood patiently until she got up on the third attempt. Tilla, unable to tell them she was no more drunk than they were, straightened her skirts, squared her shoulders, and walked past them with as much dignity as she could manage.

Ria came out to clear the bowls. The bar was empty apart from the two of them. "Hardly spent a thing," Ria observed to the empty corner where the couple had sat. "What with the curfew and that missing boy, trade's collapsed." She clapped the empty bowls down on her tray and leaned across to wipe the table. "No news, I suppose?"

Tilla shook her head and slumped down on a bench. She wanted peace and quiet, a cool beer, and then a warm bed. But first she needed to talk to Ria and to Virana.

"At this rate we might as well not have had the new tables made. And if anybody asks me again if I've seen that boy . . ." Ria paused. "Well, they might have the decency to buy something while they're in here."

Tilla cleared her throat and said, "You may have a lot more people coming in about the boy."

Ria took the news surprisingly well, which was explained when she continued, "Tell him I'll want the cash up front. I've had promises from the army before."

"Cash?"

"Well, there's got to be a fee for him using the premises, girl! I'm running a business here, not a message service. It was bad enough before with all your patients coming in here, wanting to tell me about their aches and pains."

"Have there been any patients?" Tilla realized with a jolt that she had forgotten to check.

She was torn between relief and disappointment when Ria said, "Not one. Oh, and your girl's gone off in a huff. I told her, 'Girl, this is a bar, you get called all sorts, take no notice,' but in her condition it doesn't take much."

"I need to talk to her."

"I have to say, I had my doubts about her from the start. But she's a hard worker, and the customers like her, so I let it pass."

"Is she here?" Tilla asked, hoping she did not have a missing girl to worry about now as well.

"I can't give credit against the rent for a girl who doesn't work, you know. Especially not now. I spent half the morning making a new savory cheesecake and I've still got most of it left over. I hope you're hungry."

"No."

Ria rolled her eyes. "Another one!"

"Perhaps just a little," Tilla offered. "Where did Virana go?"

The woman carried the tray of empty bowls to the back of the bar and swung one hip against the door to open it. "You can come out now!" she announced into the gap. "They've all gone and your mistress wants her dinner."

From somewhere behind it a voice called, "I am not coming out!"

Ria let the door swing shut again and joined Tilla on the bench. "I'll tell you what happened," she said. "I doubt Madam will."

Tilla, too tired to argue, sat and waited.

"Some locals came in and got mouthy with a few lads from the camp," Ria explained. "The soldiers had orders to walk away from bother, so they got up and left without buying a thing. I wasn't best pleased. Then the locals picked on your girl instead. Nasty bunch. Most of them from somewhere across the wall. When I told them to clear off home they said they were looking for the stolen boy. I said, 'You won't find him by sitting in a bar insulting people, will you?'"

"Is she hurt?"

"Only her pride." The woman lowered her voice further. "They were making donkey noises, saying every man in the Legion's ridden her. There was talk of shaving her hair off. You know the sort of thing. She ran into the back and she's been there ever since."

Tilla pulled herself to her feet. She had tried many times to explain to Virana that there was a difference between how to get a baby and how to get a husband. Perhaps at last she understood. "I'll talk to her."

The only light in the back room came from a small window paned with thick green glass that opened onto an alley between two buildings. Virana's bed was in the shadows beyond the ladder. Even so, Tilla could see the girl's swollen eyes and disheveled hair. In a voice that was blurred by tears Virana said, "I am not going out there again. You can't make me."

"You do not have to," Tilla assured her, moving across to sit beside her. "I am sorry the men were rude to you."

"Not just men. Girls too." Virana pulled a strand of hair forward, twisting it around her fingers. "They said horrible things."

Tilla doubted anyone had called her any worse names than her own brothers had used back at her family's farm, but the insults of strangers would be far more painful. "They are angry with the army and they think it is clever to hurt anyone who is friends with the soldiers."

Virana sniffed and blew her nose on a cloth. "Conn was there."

"Conn was a part of this?" Tilla felt her blood rise. "He has no right to insult you! I will make sure he apologizes." She would work out how later.

"It was not him who said those . . . things. He came in at the end."

"But did he tell the others to stop?"

Virana shook her head. "He just looked at me."

Tilla said, "This is very wrong. I will speak to him."

"I know it is terrible about his little brother," Virana said, "but it's not my fault. Is it?"

"Of course not. He has no reason to hurt you."

"Anyway, he was nasty before that."

He had never been anything but gruff to Tilla, either. She had seen a different side of him during the search—hardworking, determined—but he was still stubborn and rude. No wonder Enica's friends thought her stepson was a miserable offering.

Virana gave another sniff and scrubbed the cloth across her mouth as if she were trying to scrape away the humiliation. "I am not surprised nobody will marry him. Branan was much nicer. I liked Branan. I used to look forward to seeing him." She looked up. "Is there any—"

"No," said Tilla. "No news at all. But Enica needs to know who started the story about the body in the wall. Can you remember who brought it to the bar?"

42

GETTING THE OLD man under cover was not easy, but Ruso finally managed to persuade Senecio that nobody would see his protest in the dark. The deep arch of the east gateway was not exactly indoors, so he could honorably shelter there from the rain and wind. This led in turn to an argument with the watch captain, who was afraid the old man might open the gates to hordes of murderous tribesmen under the cover of darkness.

Ruso's "Not unless your lads go to sleep" did not go down well.

With Senecio installed under the glare of the torches and of the watch captain, Ruso went to raid the hospital stores.

It seemed Doctor Valens had arrived earlier, dealt with a couple of casualties, and headed over to the centurion's house to introduce himself. Ruso went down to the office to get the key to the bedding store and check for messages, took one look at Nisus still stoically pounding leaves into green pulp by lamplight, and remembered, "Figs!"

"Figs, sir," agreed Nisus in a tone that suggested he might as well have asked for the golden apples of the Hesperides, because he would have stood about as much chance of getting them.

"I'll go for them in a minute," Ruso promised. He needed to try Fabius's kitchen anyway. The hospital cook, having been told that Doctor Ruso was no longer on duty, had fed his dinner to a friend's dog.

Nisus went back to pounding.

Ruso was less of a disappointment to the new clerk. Gracilis looked pleased to be complimented on the reduction of the former shambles to two small piles of documents on the desk and one large one propped against the wall behind Pandora's cupboard. Observing that the door handles were no longer tied shut, Ruso wondered if the man had removed half the contents and burned them, and noted with mild interest that he no longer cared.

"If you have a moment, sir? Just one or two queries."

"I'm not really on duty here now," Ruso told him, reaching up to where the key hung on a nail. "You need to ask Doctor Valens."

Gracilis, a man who could wrestle order out of chaos, was not going to be put off that easily. "He won't know the answers, sir."

"I'm on the way to see the tribune," Ruso explained. "But I'll have a quick look."

Gracilis's one or two queries turned out to be only a fraction of the large *Ask the Doctor* pile behind him. Apart from the usual difficulty in deciphering handwriting, he needed advice on how to deal with one man who seemed to have three different names, three men with the same name but different conditions, and several conditions with no name at all or some tantalizingly useless piece of information such as *Bed XI*. Had they not been in his own handwriting, Ruso would have sworn he had never seen most of them before. Some wax tablets contained two sets of records: the top one apparently created by Candidus and below it the remains of the one he had half obliterated in order to have something to write on. If any of them held the name of the mystery man Candidus had set out to meet, it was impossible to know which. Ruso set aside four difficult questions, resolved three easy ones, deduced that *Bed IV Wobbly Legs* was carpentry rather than medicine, and promised to take a proper look before long.

His raid on the hospital stores produced a couple of clean blankets and a reasonably clean straw mattress, which he lugged over to the east gate. "You gave me hospitality," he explained. "Now it is my turn."

Senecio made no attempt to take them. "Why should I have a comfortable bed when my son has none?"

"Because," Ruso said, his patience giving way, "if you do not stay warm, your son will have no father, either. Use the mattress and put those blankets around you. We have enough to worry about already."

*

Accius need not have worried about his dinner: His cook was indeed at the fort and was now in Fabius's kitchen, poking at something that crackled and spat back at him over the hot coals. Meanwhile Fabius's cook had his back to him and was hacking up carrots with a force that suggested they had just insulted his mother. Both glanced up to see who had come in, ascertained that it was nobody important, and went back to the tasks of sharing a kitchen and ignoring one another. Ruso was put in mind of two cats pretending not to notice each other rather than fight. He was wondering how best to scrounge both figs and dinner when he heard a familiar voice saying, "Allow me!" To his left, the door swung open and revealed a beaming Valens. Tottering in beneath his outstretched arm was Fabius's kitchen maid clutching a tray of dirty crockery.

"Lovely girl," Valens observed as the crockery was placed on the table. "Just served me the most marvelous spiced pork. I had no idea you lived so well over here."

"We manage," Ruso told him, wishing he had arrived earlier.

"Any news about the boy?"

"None."

"Your centurion's offered me a very decent room. Come and see."

The reason Valens wanted to show him a very plain bedroom with a damp stain under the window and a dead wasp on the sill only became clear when they were alone. Valens heaved one of his bags of luggage off the bed and indicated a trunk for Ruso to sit on. "I saw the father out there. I'd say his mind's going."

"He's desperate."

"If somebody took one of my boys . . ."

"He's too lame to go out searching," Ruso explained. "He's exercising the last freedom left to him: the freedom to be bloody awkward. Have someone keep an eye on him overnight, will you?"

Valens nodded. "You need to make sure somebody knows about the patients I saw just now. One's a Ninth Batavian with a broken nose and bruising. He's gone back to his quarters."

Ruso waited to be told why anyone should care about a Ninth Batavian's nose.

"He was taking a shortcut to join up with the Epiacum road and got stopped by a bunch of natives who wanted to search his vehicle in case he had the missing boy in there."

"Why didn't he just let them?"

"Some of the load was his own. He thought they were thieves."

Ruso sighed.

"I've also admitted a blow to the left temple who started vomiting. That was a Briton-on-Briton fight. Somebody looked at somebody's wife the wrong way over a water fountain."

"They're fighting each other?"

"Different tribes," Valens explained. "Three locals against a lad from somewhere in the south who's serving with the Legion. From what I can gather, the Southerners hold the view that the tribes here are like herds of wild animals."

"I believe so."

"The locals accused him of being soft and collaborating with child stealers. I'm told the locals are going around armed with sticks, allegedly for beating down vegetation while they search for the boy they think we've stolen."

Ruso shook his head. How had things got so out of control so quickly? It was like the landslide: The underlying situation must have been far more unstable than anyone suspected.

"Oh, and your centurion wanted to tell me about his palpitations."

Ruso looked at him blankly. Palpitations were one of the few symptoms he could not recall Fabius ever mentioning.

"He also said that you don't listen and just tell him there's nothing wrong with him."

"What's wrong with him," Ruso explained, "is that he reads medical books."

"I thought so."

"So what did you tell him?"

"I gave him an examination that left no possibility unexplored."

"I'm sure that pleased him."

"Then I told him he was a fascinating case and in the circumstances he's lucky to be alive at all."

Ruso said, "Considering the amount of medicinal wine he's drunk, that's true."

"He thinks I'm marvelous."

"You won't feel so marvelous when he drops in for a diagnosis in the middle of the night. Why do you think I refused to share this place with him?"

"Ah, but he won't. I've told him that the latest thinking is completely different to anything he's heard before. His only hope is to build himself up with lots of fresh air and exercise during daylight and rest in his bed throughout the hours of darkness. For a man like him, indoor air during the day is poison."

"What did he say?"

"He did look a bit stunned," Valens confessed. "But he said he was very grateful and he wished he'd consulted me before."

"If that fails, try putting him in a room with your father-in-law. That should buck him up."

Valens grimaced at the mention of Pertinax. "I'll go and see him in a minute," he promised. "Incidentally, in between symptoms, Fabius told me how difficult it was to find out where all his men were yesterday now that some chap called Daminius has been confined to working in the quarry."

"He's Fabius's optio," Ruso explained, "and he's confined for his own protection, in case the natives get hold of him. He's a useful man. That's how Fabius has got away with doing next to nothing for so long."

"The optio's fallen out with the natives?"

Ruso explained about the search party and the list of alibis.

"It must be this Daminius. You've discounted everybody else."

Ruso scratched one ear with his forefinger. "If I were intending to commit a crime, I'd make sure I could prove I wasn't there at the time."

"Perhaps he did it on the spur of the moment."

"Perhaps it isn't him. And perhaps he genuinely didn't stop to talk to anyone."

"So if it's not him, who is it?"

"If I knew that," said Ruso, getting to his feet and feeling a sudden pang of hunger, "I wouldn't be here. In fact, I shouldn't be here anyway." He paused in the doorway. "It's good of you to come over. I appreciate it."

Valens grinned. "Just occasionally, I like to confound the wife's low opinion of me. Meanwhile, if there's anything else I can do, just say."

The loss of the boy seemed to have brought out a sudden generosity in Valens. Perhaps the impending arrival of his wife had helped. It occurred to Ruso that he might as well benefit from this magnanimous mood while it lasted. "Our pharmacist's running short on figs for cough mixture," he said. "And I haven't had any dinner. Do you think you could charm something out of the kitchen?"

43

A EDIC HAD EATEN everything Petta had offered him for supper and the hunger had almost gone away for a while. Now she wanted the unbrother in bed and out from under her feet. For once, Aedic carried him behind the partition without arguing. He took the unbrother's boots off and slid below the blankets with him. Petta wanted to know why Aedic didn't do it like that every night. See? There was no need to make a fuss about it, was there? Aedic, who was not the one making a fuss, took no notice. He cuddled the wriggly unbrother in the darkness, even though everything was mostly the unbrother's fault for making too much noise and getting on Matto's nerves and scaring away the fish so there was a fight.

In the end the wriggling stopped and the soft breathing told him the unbrother was asleep.

Aedic did not sleep. Instead he curled up tight and poked his fingers into his ears, trying to shut out the sound of the unbrother snuffling and the adults talking about the boy who had been kidnapped. But it was hard to keep his fingers rammed far enough into his ears all the time, and when the sounds drifted back he could hear his aunts still going on about how terrible it was. Who would do such a thing? And he thought, *I know who would do it. I said he would come and get Branan, and he did. I made it happen.*

It was not really the fault of the unbrother. Aedic himself was the one who had told them Branan's name, even though he knew Matto would never keep it quiet. When the man found out that Branan knew nothing after all, he would cut Branan's throat and bury him in the wall too, and then start hunting for the one who really had seen what happened.

Aedic.

He pulled up the blankets where the unbrother had thrown them off, and put a hand on one warm chubby leg. The unbrother was all right when he was asleep. Sometimes even when he was awake. When he laughed, it made you want to laugh too. He was all right when Aedic threw him up in the air and he shouted, "Again! Do it again!"

Aedic wished he was still two winters old like the unbrother. The unbrother didn't have to know anything about dead bodies and keeping secrets and telling lies and getting other people into terrible trouble. He didn't know about the man who would murder Branan and find Matto and then come after Aedic and bury him in the wall. All he had to do was run about and shout and try not to fall in the fire or break things.

If only Mam were here. He could have told her all about it, and she would have known what to do. He might as well tell the dog as tell Da. He could hear Da now, over by the hearth, saying the things everyone had heard a hundred times before. You couldn't trust the Romans and you couldn't trust your own people, either. One of the uncles told Da to give it a rest: This wasn't about him, it was about a missing kid, and why didn't he think of somebody else for a change? And Da said, "It's all right for you! They didn't steal your farm!"

Aedic stuffed his fingers tighter into his ears and put his head down under the blankets until he could hardly breathe.

By the time he came up for air, the argument had stopped. He could hear the scrape of the fire being banked up, and the musical trickle of wee into the night bucket. One of the aunts said something about an early start, and the uncle said they would be searching over by Broken Crags in the morning, and the aunt said again that it was a terrible thing, and how must that poor family be feeling, going to bed knowing their boy was out somewhere in the cold?

Aedic wished everybody would stop talking about it. It was as if they had heard about something exciting and they all wanted to be part of it.

It wasn't exciting. It was a snake that writhed inside your stomach and hissed that something very, very bad had happened, it was going to get worse, and it was all your fault.

44

"I CAN'T MAKE HIM go indoors, Tilla!"

"You are the army!" She leaned forward in the bed and retrieved the pillow from behind her. "It is your job to make people do things they do not want to do!" As if to illustrate how this was done, she gave the pillow a couple of hefty punches. "Why else are you here?"

Ruso's left boot landed with a clump on the floorboards. "You complain when we don't respect local wishes." He tugged at the laces of the right boot and dropped it beside its partner. "And then you don't like it when we do." He aimed his socks into the dark beyond-the-lamp oblivion of the corner where he had stowed Candidus's shield.

"But he is an old man!" She dropped the pillow back into place. "It is cold even in here. He will be dead by morning!"

"Perhaps." It was not his fault that Senecio was a stubborn old goat.

Tilla looked as though she were about to raise another objection, so he said, "The sky's clouded over now. It's not as cold as it could be. Valens will make sure the night staff keep an eye on him."

Tilla gave the sort of exaggerated sigh that said this would never have been allowed if somebody sensible had been in charge, then asked, "Do you think the army would lend us horses tomorrow?"

"'Us'?"

"Me and Enica. We need to talk to the man who told Virana about the body. We have other names to follow too. We may have to go a long way to find these people."

He pulled back the covers and slid in beside her. "I'll ask," he promised, doubting their efforts would lead to much, but having no better ideas to offer. "Light out?"

Instead of answering the question she said, "It has been a bad day. Did Virana tell you she was insulted?"

"Ah. She was looking a bit weepy when she let me in. She said she was upset about Branan."

"That too. She said she used to look forward to seeing him."

"Gods above. *Branan*?"

"Not like that, husband."

From somewhere downstairs came the sound of raised voices. Female first, then the rumbling of male resentment. Tilla said, "Ria wants to pack up and move to Deva for the winter when the Legion goes. He wants to stay here where they have always lived."

More argument from downstairs, the tone clear but the words indistinct. Ruso, who had hurried past Ria with a promise that he would talk about a fee for using the bar in the morning, was not sorry to know she was fully occupied.

"A man and a woman," Tilla murmured. "It is not easy."

"Mm," he said. It seemed the safest thing. "Who insulted Virana?"

"Some local people. That is nothing new. But Conn let it happen."

He said, "When this is over, we ought to make him apologize."

In the silence that followed perhaps she too was thinking that if Branan was not found, there would never be a time when this was over.

"If I didn't think he was fond of his father," he said, "I'd have Conn first on the list of suspects. Hiding his brother somewhere just to cause trouble."

Tilla rolled over to face him. "I have wondered this. Whether he is jealous of Branan."

"The doted-on younger son, clever and popular, and the bitter older half brother . . ."

"His girl snatched away by the army."

"What girl?"

She said, "Did you not know?" and proceeded to relay what she admitted was gossip about the girl's rape by a soldier during the troubles, her refusal to have the baby taken away, and a broken betrothal. "They say that is why he is so angry."

"Even so, why would he do this to his father?"

She said, "For liking Branan better."

The reasoning made sense. The practicalities did not. "Branan was taken by a soldier."

"Soldiers can be bribed," she pointed out. "Or imitated. Perhaps there may be some captured equipment still hidden in secret places after the troubles."

"Really?"

She said lightly, "Who knows?"

"Well, you do, clearly."

"Not near here," she assured him.

He let it pass. "If the soldier wasn't really a soldier . . ."

"I am just thinking aloud."

"We've got half the Legion chasing around searching, everybody suspecting everybody else, and the officers busy trying to work out where several thousand men were yesterday afternoon. I'd imagine if anything could make a man like Conn happy, that would be it. I'll see what I can find out."

"How will you do that?"

He had never told her that Conn was under surveillance, for the very good reason that she was not supposed to know. "Sorry. It's been a difficult day. I mean, we both need to be aware of it."

He wondered who was paid to inform on Conn, and whether the security people would be prepared to tell him. Suddenly Tilla said, "There is still no word of Candidus?"

"There's some hint of him arranging to meet a man he'd seen before, but that could be anybody."

"What if the same man stole both of them?"

He frowned. "We've gone from Conn being jealous to some villain who's going around, abducting random people."

She sighed. "Fear is a short rope. Every time I set off toward where Branan might be, I am pulled back by the feeling that I might have just turned my back on him."

He remembered something else. "We're checking everyone's movements, so I suppose I need to confirm that my pharmacist really did go away on leave."

"Did he know Branan?"

"I don't think so."

"Is he the one who said he would kill Candidus?"

"That was a misunderstanding."

The argument downstairs seemed to have ended. She said, "I keep thinking about Branan."

"Me too. It's the not knowing."

"And the fear that the knowing might be worse," she said. "I feel as though I am swimming in a soup made of confusion. What does a child stealer look like?"

"If you could tell by looking, we'd have caught him already."

He pictured Senecio lying out in the cold, worrying about his son. He tried to picture Branan but could not. He saw only the dark shape of the farm dog on the night they had first met, and heard the voice that had greeted him with, *Are you the doctor?* and then said with relief, *Now I can go in out of the rain.*

He rolled across to her, wrapping himself around the warmth of her body. "I am sorry things went so wrong with the old man's family."

"So am I."

He was drifting off to sleep when she wriggled.

"The lamp," she explained, waving an arm across him and trying to reach it.

"I'll do it."

He was almost asleep when a thought drifted across the distant horizon of his mind. It vanished as he tried to focus on it, but to his annoyance he found himself awake and alert, convinced it was something important. If only . . . What had he been thinking about just a moment ago?

He didn't know.

Beside him, his wife stirred and murmured something in her sleep.

It was definitely important. Something he should have queried earlier. If only he could get back to that state of half awareness . . .

By the time he woke, the gray morning light was filtering round the shutter that covered the excuse for a window. His wife was sitting up beside him. She crossed her arms and lifted off her night tunic, shuddering with the cold as she did so. He paused to enjoy the view. Then, when the most interesting parts had vanished under the wrapping of her breast binding, he said, "Tell me again what Virana said about Branan."

45

THE LEGATE'S ATTEMPTS to reassure his centurions at the morning briefing were overridden by the alarming fact of his presence. Usually he was based elsewhere and was only ever seen at the various camps under his command later in the day. He invited Accius to outline the plan for the day's search, then stepped up again and emphasized the importance of not being provoked by the locals. He had spoken with their leaders, who had agreed to ask the people to stay calm. Since Ruso had never heard the locals so much as mention any leaders, he doubted that would have much effect. He listened with interest as the legate dodged the question everyone wanted answered—what would happen if the boy was not found?—and went on to announce that the curfew would remain in place tonight but that Samain celebrations would be permitted as long as the locals stayed on their own property after dark.

It must have been a difficult decision to make. There would be no celebration in Branan's home, but if he was not found, the Samain gatherings elsewhere would provide the ideal breeding ground for trouble. Especially once the fear of meeting the dead in the dark had been overcome by beer and bravado. On the other hand, banning them would stoke more resentment: It would be tantamount to punishing the locals for having one of their children stolen by the army.

Ruso was glad he was only responsible for the life of one man at a time.

Some of the other officers paused to offer a polite "Sorry about your father" to Ruso before leaving with their comrades to relay the day's orders to the men. He waited until they had gone before he made his own contribution.

When they heard what he had to say, the three officers who were still there looked as though they wished he had kept it to himself.

"Why didn't you say this before, man?" demanded the legate, who had the sort of rolling, fruity voice that only authority and an expensive education could bestow.

"I only found out late last night, sir." The thing that had floated over the horizon of his mind was his wife's statement that Virana looked forward to Branan's visits.

"So what you're saying," said Accius, "is that any man who happened to have been in the bar when the boy delivered the eggs could have learned his name and made the link between him and your wife?"

"The barmaid remembers mentioning family matters to him, sir." It was hard to imagine a nine-year-old boy being interested in a wedding blessing, but that would not have stopped Virana from chattering about it.

"Any man at all?" echoed Fabius, dismayed.

The legate said, "Why didn't we think of this earlier?"

Fabius looked at Ruso, who in turn looked at Accius and said, "We relied too much on speculation from the natives, sir."

Accius said, "We're already getting every man to account for his movements, sir."

"I'll talk to the commanders of the other units," the legate said. "The witness might have been mistaken about the kidnapper's outfit. I'll also put the word out amongst our own people that any man behaving suspiciously is to be reported to his centurion. Tribune, you can coordinate the lists of names."

A list of names was necessary and it was sensible, and Ruso knew it. He also knew he didn't like the sound of it. Tilla had once been put on a list of suspects, and it had proved almost impossible to get her name off it until the Emperor himself had intervened to wipe it clean. Who was to say what constituted "suspicious" behavior? What if the accuser was simply settling an old score? Once you started along that route, there was no telling what betrayals and jealousies it would let loose—as several deeply unpopular emperors and their terrified subjects had discovered.

Accius was speaking to him.

"Sorry, sir?"

"Pay attention, Ruso. See what more you can get out of the bar staff."

"I've already checked with them this morning, sir. They're trying to remember who was there when the boy came in." He hoped Ria was trying harder than she had been earlier. She did not seem to mind being woken before dawn with a peculiar question about egg deliveries, but she did object to not yet having an offer of compensation for filling her bar with time wasters.

Despite being wrapped in a blanket, Ria had stepped into her house shoes and pushed her tousled hair back as if she were preparing for battle. "They'll come in here trailing wet mud across my swept floor and smelling of sheep. They'll take up space at my tables and buy nothing."

"I'll see what I can do," he had promised. Now he ventured, "Sirs, we need to pay a fee for the use of the bar."

"Then find somewhere else," said Accius. "Who do these people think they are? You'd think they'd be glad to help."

Ruso had more success with a request for permission to seek out the latest intelligence on Conn, in case there was some native involvement.

"Exactly as I suggested yesterday," put in Fabius.

Accius had the grace not to point out that he had said so too. "They may know something at Vindolanda."

"So," the legate continued, "yesterday we had eight suspects. Now we have several hundred. Is there any good news?"

"The old man's still alive, sir," put in Fabius. "We allowed him to sleep under the gate arch and gave him bedding, and Doctor Valens persuaded him to take some water."

"Well done, man," said the legate. "We don't want him to die on us."

Ruso fought down a childish demand for a share of the credit. "Are we confident the boy's not in our custody, sir?"

"Our people assure me they haven't got him," said the legate. "Security are chasing up their informers."

Ruso was not optimistic. Informers were mostly recruited for their ability to inform on the natives, not on the military.

Setting off across the duckboards to return to the fort, he found himself recalling the prospect of a native wedding, once so embarrassing, with a fond sense of innocence lost.

His nostalgia was pushed aside by a scrape of boots heralding the company of Fabius. He had expected conversation, but it seemed all

Fabius wanted was not to be outside a set of ramparts on his own. They marched together in silence toward another day of searching for a stolen boy.

Already forty or fifty natives had gathered to protest. This time they were outside the east gate, and they were trying different tactics. There was no more chanting. Instead of harassing drivers or sitting down to block the road, they had lined up on either side of it like a ragged parody of a guard of honor. Nearly all seemed to be elderly or lame. There were a couple of women with small babies. Several had even brought rough stools and boxes to sit on.

As the two officers approached, one of the gates opened and a squad of men marched out. After yesterday's barrage of rotten missiles, someone had sensibly ordered them to wear helmets, but nothing was thrown. The natives yelled, "Where is Branan?" and "Child stealers!" and "Give the boy back!"

The legionaries strode on past them without a glance. Fortunately none of the natives seemed to know that Daminius and his men were back at work in the quarry.

"A bunch like that wouldn't frighten anybody," Fabius observed.

Trying to decide from a distance whether one of the protesters had a goiter or just a double chin, Ruso said, "The others will be searching," and only as he said it did he realize what it meant. This was no spontaneous outburst of anger and concern. This was organized. The people who could do little but shout had been sent to protest. The fit and healthy would be working or searching. If the boy was not found, then whoever had arranged this would be considering the next move. Once you started to think of this whole business as a native setup, it changed everything.

His thoughts were distracted by the solitary figure of Tilla clutching a bag that he knew held a day's supply of food and waiting to be let in. "My wife needs to borrow a couple of horses for the search."

"Why don't you try asking at the stables?" suggested Fabius, as if he were not in a position to give the order, or as if Ruso might not know where to look for a horse. "I expect they'll have something."

Ruso wondered whether Daminius ever felt the same desire he was feeling now: the urge to sharpen Fabius up by poking him in the eye with his own vine stick.

He escorted Tilla across to where Senecio had now resumed his position beside the guard in front of the HQ hall. The old man's singing had lost much of its vigor this morning. He looked pale and weary, but if he would not eat, there was little Ruso could do about it. He left Tilla crouching beside him while he went to organize some horses. Perhaps she would get some sense into him. Better still, some food.

He was relieved to see that of the dozen or so animals usually available, four were still in their stalls munching idly on their hay nets. They might as well not have been, though, because, according to the man in charge, "I can't let no military property out to no civilians without no written authorization, sir." Not, it seemed, even if Centurion Fabius already knew about it. "You never know with them natives, sir. 'Specially not the women . . ."

At that point he noticed the look in Ruso's eye and kept the rest of his views on natives, civilians, and women to himself.

Ruso was not going to go running back to Fabius to ask for written permission . . . Finally he managed to get two animals released by pointing out that one of 'them native civilian women' was a Roman citizen, promising that he would pay for any loss or injury, and agreeing that the military property would be escorted by an armed guard.

His negotiations failed to impress Tilla, who could not see why she and Enica needed a guard at all. "Nobody travels with me when I go to help women have babies."

"If you want the horse," he told her, "you have to have the escort."

"He is only there to stop us from stealing your horses." Tilla gave a delicate sniff of disdain. "Tell them we will take an unarmed man. And he must do what he is told and stay at a distance when we go to the houses. Otherwise nobody will talk to us."

In the end they agreed on a dour-faced stable slave with greasy hair. Ruso watched his wife and the slave ride out to collect Enica with a piebald horse trotting beside them on the leading rein. Some men might have relished the prospect of a day's ride in the countryside with two attractive women, but clearly Tilla's escort was not one of them.

Ruso went to offer a pouring of wine and a swift prayer at the altar of Fortuna. Then he made his way across to the hospital. Before he returned to face Ria and her escalating demands for compensation, he needed to make sure Gallus was checking on everyone's movements for the day before yesterday. After that he needed to clear his mind. It seemed now that practically any man who could not account for his movements might be guilty. Just like his wife, Ruso was swimming in a soup made of confusion.

46

RUSO HAD NOT been greeted with such enthusiasm since the time he had performed a free clinic for any local who cared to drop in at the bathhouse over at Coria. Half a dozen people who could not find space on or around the table outside Ria's bar were clustered about the entrance in no discernible order. As he tried to get inside, hands snatched at his tunic. Voices in Latin cried out, "Doctor!" and "Sir!" and in British, "Out of the way! Other people were here before you!"

Inside, all the seats were taken and Ria had been right: There was a distinct tang of sheep. There had to be at least twenty people in there. He was pleased to note that everyone seemed to have bought drinks. That should satisfy Ria's demands for compensation. Virana, edging her way between two tables with a tray held above her head at a precarious angle, paused to beam at him. "We've never been so busy, master!"

"Any more thoughts about who was in the bar when Branan came?"

Her face fell. "I'm sorry, master. There was only me serving and I know there were some customers but I can't remember who."

He told her not to worry. He was fresh from an awkward encounter with Nisus, who had no way of proving that he had been fishing in Coria for the whole of his leave and plainly thought it was ridiculous to try.

He had a point. People might have noticed a hunched figure staring at the water, but it was the nature of fishermen not to want to be disturbed, and Nisus would never have sought anyone out for conversation. He had correctly answered Ruso's trick question of "Did you stay at Susanna's?" by pointing out that Susanna did not rent out rooms. He had stayed at the Phoenix. The name meant nothing to Ruso, who had not been to Coria for a while. New businesses had popped up like mushrooms all along the border. He made a mental note to think about contacting the owner, and moved on.

By contrast, everyone in Ria's bar was eager to help.

"One at a time!" he called over the hubbub, placing himself in the only available space, which was behind the counter. Catching a glimpse of Ria loading pastries onto a platter in the back room, he asked Virana to bring him a spiced wine. "Now, who was first?"

It was exhausting and time-consuming no matter how quickly he tried to process each statement, and he had to cram his notes into smaller and smaller handwriting to fit in the available space on the tablet. Several of the informers could not understand why he was making notes at all, since they expected him to immediately summon troops and rush off to investigate their sightings. Unfortunately there were confident sightings of Branan at roughly the same time in five or six different places. "You may be right," he explained to each one, "but I need to hear everyone." The description of the soldier varied from the hopelessly vague to the startlingly implausible, in which the kidnapper was hiding his features behind a full-face cavalry parade helmet. He tried to push aside the suspicion that this was all part of a native plot to hide the truth.

One account of a boy walking east along the road at about the time Branan vanished sounded promising, but the observer, a thatcher, could not remember whether there was one soldier with him or two. It was supported by a woman who had recognized Branan hurrying along in the company of a single legionary. Since the boy seemed to be going quite willingly, she had assumed it was the Medicus and that "things had been patched up." Closing her eyes, she added, "He might have had . . ." Ruso did not understand the word. Something to do with his legs. "Stocky," translated someone who was listening from the next table in these less-than ideal conditions. "Muscular." That might point to the thickset quarryman, whose name was Festus, but they had confirmed his alibi, and besides, after all the training runs, there were very few men in the Legion who did not have noticeably muscular legs. Ruso wrote it down, took her details, and said someone might be in touch.

"But I've told you everything I know. I don't want you people coming round pestering. I haven't got him, poor lad."

"I know," said Ruso. "Neither have we."

The next report came from north of the wall and might be something, or it might be a man quarreling with his son. The boy had not been restrained in any way and had stayed to argue.

To the woman who complained that this was a waste of time if he wasn't going to do anything about it, he explained again that search parties were already out there and every sighting would be followed up. Finally he confided that he was as frustrated as she was, and moments later heard her telling someone that the Roman was useless. He had no more idea of what to do than anybody else did.

To the man who told him that Branan was on a wagon headed for Pons Aelius and now had dyed red hair and new trousers, while the soldier had changed into civilian clothes, he said, "Did the boy have a gap between his teeth?"

"I couldn't see his teeth."

"How did you know it was him?"

"There was something about the man. I didn't like the look of him."

Ruso hoped Tilla was making better progress than this. He wrote it all down, because these people had had the decency to give up part of their morning to try and help. At least it was better than the last time he had helped to find a missing person. The man had been not only an adult but a tax collector, and he and Albanus had been reduced to knocking on doors and promising rewards to persuade anyone but the man's wife to care.

While Ria served pastries that were still warm from the oven, the witness who had seen someone he didn't like the look of was followed by a woman with a sagging face and burrs stuck in her hair. These were presumably there by accident rather than design. A smell of stale sweat wafted across the counter as she whispered in Latin with the accent of somewhere warmer, "It is not me, Doctor. It is a friend."

"That's fine," he assured her. "Thank you for coming. Just tell me your friend's name and what she saw."

"No names."

"Just what she saw, then."

"It is the spirits," the woman whispered. "They speak to her."

"Spirits?"

"Of the departed."

No wonder there were no names. She was not going to risk an accusation of illegally summoning the dead. "What do—what did they say?"

"They see a boy like him you seek. He is lost."

He supposed even spirits sometimes stated the obvious. "Do they know where he is?"

"Ah, not in this world."

He made a shooing motion to Virana, who had edged toward him clutching a carrot she was supposed to be scraping and was pretending not to listen. When she was gone he said softly, "The spirits think he is dead?"

"He is all alone." The woman clutched at her chest and put her head on one side. "He cries out, 'Mother! Mother!'"

Conversation around them had stilled. People were turning round to watch. It was hard to know what to say next, except to tell her to go away and stop wasting his time with frightening nonsense. "How did he get to the next world?"

The woman placed her forefinger at an angle across her left eyebrow. "A terrible blow, Doctor. Even you could not save him. He fell crying out, 'Mother! Mother!'"

"And when you heard him cry out—"

"My friend heard it," she corrected him. "A friend who does not want to call up spirits. But for the sake of this boy and to help the Legion, she has bravely sacrificed a good black lamb and opened herself to their presence."

"That's very decent of her," said Ruso. "Is there anything else she can tell you? Where the body is? Who did it?"

"Why do you not write this down?"

"I'll remember it," he promised.

The woman informed him very seriously that the culprit was a gray-haired centurion with the Sixth Legion and that the body lay under some trees on a hillside overlooking a beautiful river. No, the spirits knew neither what sort of trees nor which river. But the sun was shining.

He thanked her and proffered a final question. "When the spirits heard the boy calling out," he said, "what were his exact words?"

The woman frowned. "'Mother! Mother!'"

"I see. Thank you very much. That's been very . . . interesting." Especially the part about a native boy calling for his mother in Latin.

"The lamb was very costly."

"Then it's especially generous of your friend," he said, drawing back and slapping his writing tablet shut. "Give her our thanks."

"She has no money left."

"She has our gratitude."

"Hah!" The woman withdrew and spat on the floor. Someone at the next table called, "Never mind, missus. At least you got a free drink."

The show was over. People were standing now, gathering up coats and bags and beginning to make their way out. Ria was grinning at him from the far corner. It was a grin that said she would not be asking for compensation, because if he wished to retain his wife's lodgings, he would be paying for all the drinks and pastries.

He did not have long to dwell on this. On turning to pick up his notes, he was greeted by the sight of a large hand covering them. "My brother is still missing," said Conn in his own tongue. He leaned across the counter, picked up Ruso's cup, and sniffed the dregs.

Ruso felt his fists tighten.

"Are you going to look for him or sit here drinking fancy wine all day?"

He fought down the temptation to rearrange Conn's nose. As calmly as he could manage, he said, "I have a list of ideas to follow up. Can your people deal with some of them?"

"We can deal with all of them."

"I'll pass them on in just a moment," he said. "First we need to talk about my wife's friend. The girl from Eboracum who works here."

"What about her?"

"She's been insulted."

"Not by me."

"You were there."

Conn shrugged. "She's a whore. We need to talk about my brother."

"She's been doing her best to help find your brother. You should go and thank her."

Conn opened his mouth, failed to think of a response, and gave a derisive bark of laughter. It was not very convincing.

"When you've thanked her, we'll talk about where he might be."

The Briton's eyes narrowed. "Your fancy officer said you had to help us."

"She's in the back room. Make it sincere."

Conn lifted his hand and glanced down at the notes he could not read. Then he turned on his heel and strode toward the back of the bar.

47

TILLA WISHED SHE had brought a second writing tablet. Her letters were always larger than she would like, and she struggled to keep them in line at the best of times. Now the wax of the tablet that had caused such amazement at the farm—a local-born woman who could write!—was scarred with stabs at names that she would have trouble reading back later. There were large smoothed patches too. One had been the name of the man who passed the rumor on to Virana, but who turned out to have heard it from his wife, who had already been named as a source by two of Enica's friends—and so it went on, the story of the story looping round and tailing back and blundering into dead ends where the person they needed to see was somewhere else: visiting relatives, trading, or out helping with the search.

It took several tries before they realized they must explain at the beginning that Enica was not there to blame or accuse. She was offering concerned neighbors a chance to help by tracing the real source of the rumor before the child snatcher did. But the rumor had begun its journey several days ahead of them. It had already passed around hearths and over bar tables and market stalls and across boundary walls and even—how things had changed since her parents' day!—between locals lazing in the bathhouses at forts farther along the wall.

The slave followed them around with no sign of cheering up or of understanding anything that was said in British, so they called him by his real name to his face and Dismal to each other. Tilla had tried explaining to him that if he heard a horn he was to say so, because it might be the signal that Branan had come home. "Or it might be a war horn," added Tilla, irritated by his glum face and sullen speech. "The signal for our warriors to rise up and throw your masters back into the sea where they came from." Even then there was no reaction. Perhaps he believed her.

Some of the people they met were suspicious of the military brands on the horses' shoulders. For the same reason they were twice stopped and questioned by army patrols and had to appeal to Dismal to confirm that the horses were not stolen.

Enica said little as they rode along the lanes and down the narrow twisting tracks, except to call out for her son. Tilla doubted he was close enough to hear. While every stone wall, every wooded valley, every ditch or patch of reeds, could be concealing him, any thief with any common sense would have got him well clear of here long ago, knowing people would be searching. Still, Enica looked more alive now that she had gained some sort of purpose.

They left the shelter of the trees and turned left onto the main road with Tilla urging her horse on in front and the slave bringing up the rear. The wind was gusting in from the west, cooling their faces with a light drizzle. They cantered as far as the shortcut by the burned ash tree, where they had to slow again for the horses to pick their way along the stony ground. In the distance Tilla could make out the overgrown ruins of a farm that might have been abandoned by choice, or more likely during the troubles. She thought again about the conversation with Senecio at the fort earlier this morning.

The tune he had been singing was one she had learned from her mother: a very old song about the offering of one man in order to save a people. Not a murder, but a human life sacrificed in the way it had always been done: through the threefold death. She had crouched down beside him and joined in, very softly, with one hand on his arm. When it was over he murmured, "I am lacking in courage, child."

"I do not think so."

He shook his head. "My two older boys believed the gods were with us," he said. "My boys believed it was the time to rise up. I told them yes, this is the time. Because that was what we wanted to believe."

"Your boys were heroes."

His laugh was bitter. "No matter how many you kill, the Romans still have more soldiers to send."

"They have an empire. We are a scattering of tribes."

"We showed them, though. For a while."

"We did," she agreed, wondering if he really believed the price had been worth it.

He said, "I will not lose another son to them."

"Everyone is helping, Grandfather. Today I am taking Enica out looking." She sensed he did not want a complicated explanation about rumors and sources.

He nodded slowly. "You have grown up well, Daughter of Lugh. Your mother would be proud."

The words warmed her inside, even if she could not imagine Mam ever approving of her marrying a Roman. She wanted to hear them again, but a group of soldiers was marching past, and then while she was still repeating them in her mind she heard Senecio say, "It may be the only way to find Branan."

The sky-blue eyes looked into her own. The warm feeling faded as quickly as it had come, replaced by a stillness, as if the gods had stopped their business to listen.

Tilla said, "The threefold death?"

"We must try everything else first," he said. "But I will not lose another son to them."

Senecio, who had wanted no more killing.

Tilla urged her shambling mount into a livelier walk. Surely the old man had not meant it? The threefold death was a thing of the past: something to sing about, not to do. Besides, how would he find a victim? Perhaps he had not thought of that. Worse, perhaps he had. Perhaps he already had someone in mind.

Holy Christos, she prayed, because Christos was one of the gods who could listen anywhere, *let it not come to that. Help us find Branan before it comes to that.*

"They are searching the hill," Enica said, pointing.

A few hundred paces to the east, Tilla could make out eight or nine of their own people strung out across a slope of common land, forcing their way through tall bracken that nobody had harvested. Through the veil of drizzle she could see distant arms rise and fall as they beat a path. From time to time one of them would stop and crouch down for a better look at something. Tilla found she was holding her breath with each pause. *Find him. Find him now. Do not let the old man do something that will never be forgiven.* But every time, the searcher straightened up and moved ahead to keep in line with the others.

Tilla glanced across at Enica, who was no longer watching. Instead she cupped a hand around her mouth and shouted, "Branan! Branan, where are you? It's Mam come for you!"

The piebald horse tossed its head at the sound, and the dying hedge brambles swayed in the breeze. The women rode on.

Of the few children they saw in the lanes and the fields, none were alone and several were seized by their mothers at the approach of strangers, the women showing everyone how fiercely they would defend their young if anyone came too close. A couple of children were armed with sticks.

Tilla had given up trying to argue with the people who told them the army had hidden Branan themselves as revenge for that wife beater being dangled upside down. Nobody suggested what Tilla privately thought more likely: that the boy's disappearance might have something to do with a jealous older brother. When she asked whether it was possible that Branan might have been taken by a local person, Enica was both shocked and dismissive. Every parent they met was warning children to keep away from strangers. Especially soldiers.

Several people complained that children were no longer available to run errands or fetch water on their own. One father even wanted to know if he could claim compensation from the army if he had to put his sheep onto winter feed this early in the season. Watching far too many ewes trying to nibble the last blades of grass in a bare paddock, Tilla protested, "But there is grass still up on the common land. I have seen it."

"Exactly!" exclaimed the father, as if she had just proved his point. "It's no use to me up there, is it? Not if I can't send the children out to shepherd. You go and ask your husband: Whose fault is that? The army's!"

So far no one they spoke to had been approached by anyone else trying to track down the source of the rumor. Tilla was not sure whether this silence was good news or just a sign that they were on the wrong trail altogether. She said nothing of this to Enica, who seemed to be clinging as tightly to the hope of this search as she was to the saddle of the piebald horse every time it went faster than a walk. Tilla had wondered out loud if she should have asked for a cart instead, but Enica insisted she was fine: just a little out of practice. Indeed after a while she did seem to remember how not to bounce about uncontrollably during the trot.

By the end of the morning more names had been flattened back into the wax and others had been added. Three had lines drawn underneath them as well, to show they were boys of about Branan's age. Two of them were brothers, so it made sense to visit them first.

According to Enica, the family of Lucano and Matto had lost their farm when the line for the wall was laid out. The army had moved them all to an abandoned homestead on poor land farther north. They were on the way there now, easing their way down a steep shortcut across a rocky stream. Tilla, riding in front, urged her horse to jump the tumbling water and scramble up the opposite bank between the trees. Dismal's horse followed her own, leaping up the steep slope.

At the top, where the shortcut met the lane, she circled back to wait for Enica and more directions.

The piebald horse reached the stream. Enica let go of the saddle one hand at a time, leaning forward and grabbing two fistfuls of mane. The horse's head jerked up as it leapt, narrowly missing her nose. It bounded up through the trees with Enica's head down alongside its neck. She clung onto the mane while her body bounced farther and farther to one side. She was almost out of the saddle by the time she reached the top.

Tilla seized one flapping rein and drew the horse up beside her own. "Are you all right?"

Enica grasped one of the front pillars of the saddle and heaved herself back up. "I am sorry."

"How long is it since you last rode?"

"I think I was ten winters old. And then only a few times."

Tilla, who had grown up riding her father's horses, stared at her. "Why did you not say this?"

"You did not ask. Anyway, I thought, it is only sitting." She tried to shift positions and winced. "Just at this terrible angle, and being shaken about . . . And wearing my stepson's trousers."

"We will stop and eat," Tilla declared. "You can rest."

Enica shook her head. "If I get down now, I will never get back up. Turn left here. It is no more than a mile. I want to talk to those boys."

48

"RUN ALL DAY, this one will, sir," said the man, whacking the nose of the only remaining animal in the stable as it attempted to bite him. "He's a good horse."

Ruso watched as the leggy bay was led out into the yard. Its ears were flattened back against its head and the whites of its eyes were showing.

"I'll be honest, sir, I wouldn't have gave him to your wife, but you won't have no bother with him. Not once you're up. You're further from his teeth back there."

It was this horse or no horse, and at least when he turned it east toward Vindolanda and urged it forward, it sprang into a willing canter. He wondered whether Tilla and Enica had managed to track down the source of the rumors. He would never have spoken it out loud, but he hoped they were wasting their time. He didn't want there to be a body in the wall. He didn't want to have to worry about whether it was Candidus, and besides, Branan had been missing for two nights now. A boy who had been kidnapped in order to be silenced was not likely to be found alive after that long. And they very much needed to find Branan alive. Not only because he was innocent and friendly and nine years old, and because his family—well, his father—had tried to make strangers welcome, but because Pertinax was right: If they didn't, the fragile peace with the locals would break down again. *Everything our lads fought for will be thrown away.* And Senecio, who wanted no more killing, would see his people swept up into fury and bloodshed once more.

He had done his best to keep the peace by sharing information with Conn. The Britons were following up the sightings however they thought best, with the promise that if help was needed, they were to ask. The army was investigating the whereabouts of every single man on the afternoon that Branan had disappeared.

What he had not told Conn was that he was going to Vindolanda to find out what information Security had on Conn himself. Ruso still had a nagging suspicion that the elder brother might have set this whole thing in motion. Clearly the irony of the army turning itself inside out on behalf of a native family was not lost on him. "We'll help you round up all your men and beat them," Conn had suggested, with a bitterness that belied any suggestion of humor. "You always think it works on us."

Vindolanda's well-worn main street was busy, as usual, and Ruso had to steer the horse between groups of pedestrians who would have moved out of the way a lot faster if they had considered the size of its teeth. The wooden fort at the end of the street was currently housing three times the number of men it was built for, and the cavalrymen queuing outside the stables glared at him before parting to let this unknown officer forward to hand over his horse. When he was finally inside the inconspicuous corner of the HQ building occupied by Security, Ruso showed the permit Accius had signed.

The clerk squinted at it, turned it upside down, held it level to examine it for something or other, and finally agreed to let him pass.

The security officer placed a stack of five or six writing tablets on the desk and kept hold of them. "Give me the name again."

"Conn," Ruso said. "Son of Senecio."

"Interesting. I think we had a question about Senecio the other day."

Ruso, whose enquiries about Senecio had been strictly unofficial, said nothing.

The tablets were parceled up with twine. The officer pulled the strand to one side and bent his head to reveal thinning hair combed across a bald patch. "Conn, son of Senecio, resident on a farm with three buildings seven hundred and fifty paces southwest of the fort known as Parva."

"That's him."

The officer picked at the knot in the twine. Finally he opened the top document and read, giving the occasional "Hm" as he reached an interesting point. Ruso said, "I don't want to waste your time. I can look for myself and let you know when I've finished."

The man shook his head and said, "If only it were that easy."

Ruso refrained from pointing out that it would be that easy if he handed them over.

"Facts are not intelligence, Doctor. Intelligence is what we sift from the random facts that accumulate in our reports."

Ruso waited. Finally he was rewarded with "'Conn. Served as a leader in the troubles. Younger brother Dubnus killed in a skirmish with a unit from the Twentieth.'"

There was not time to dwell on the news that the men who had killed Senecio's second son were from his own legion.

"'Father still alive, mother dead, father remarried, one half brother, Branan.'"

"Branan is the one who's missing," said Ruso, hoping to speed things up.

"No wife or children listed. 'Other occupants of the farm . . .'" He paused, "There are cross-references. Do you want me to look them up?"

"Stay with Conn for now."

"'Thought to retain contact with remaining rebels . . . mostly social . . . Suspicious activities much curtailed since executions of ringleaders after the troubles . . . No associates currently known in other tribes . . .' Some trouble with one of our men over a woman now married to another cross-reference . . . 'Tendency to speak before he thinks . . .'" Ruso could vouch for that.

"Ah. There's a new female associate called . . . holy gods, these people's names . . . Dar—"

"Darlughdacha?"

"Could be."

"It means Daughter of the God Lugh. Also known as Tilla."

The man's eyes widened. "'Married to an officer of whom he doesn't approve.'"

"That's me."

The security officer glanced at the permit again and looked up. "Are you sure you're supposed to have access to this?"

"Absolutely. I'm here because I'm the link. I need to know if he's got any other contacts within the army or if he knows anyone who can impersonate a legionary."

"The former, not that we know of. The latter . . . perhaps. If they got hold of the kit."

"Plus I'd like to know where he was two days ago, between the sixth and twelfth hours."

The security officer sighed. "We use local informers, Doctor. We don't send men to follow 'persons of interest' about all day. Nobody's that interesting."

"Who's our informer?"

The man pursed his lips and indicated the permit. "You'd need more than that. Especially since you're personally involved."

"I need a clear picture of who knows what about the family."

"The man who took the child wasn't our informer, if that's what you're thinking. I can tell you that for certain."

"How do you know?"

The officer sighed. "Listen to me, Doctor. The man who took the child wasn't our informer."

Ruso said, "Ah."

"I shouldn't even have said that much."

"That's not to say your informer didn't pass something on to him. Is this woman reliable?"

"We deal in a world of shadows and tricks of the light," the officer said, "but mostly hard cash. They get paid, or we have some way of pressuring them."

"And can Conn exert counterpressure on her to keep her mouth shut?"

"He doesn't know it's open."

It was about midday when Ruso rescued the Vindolanda stable lads from the horse, which the groom described as a vicious bugger. Feeling oddly protective toward it, Ruso observed that it was temperamentally unsuited to being with the Legion and would probably be happier in a permanent home.

"That's what I tell my centurion, sir," observed the groom. "But I get no sympathy."

Away from the busy streets, Ruso turned the horse's head back toward the west. He felt no better informed now than he had been when he set out. It was still possible that Conn was implicated in the disappearance of his brother but the security report confirmed what, at heart, he had suspected: that Conn was angry rather than vicious. It did not suggest a man who would mastermind a kidnap—and besides, what would he do with the boy afterward?

What would anyone do with the boy?

The horse tossed its head and Ruso was brought back to the present. He wasn't going to answer that question no matter how long and hard he stared at it. Instead he would leave the main road and head up the farm track that was part of the short training run, the route Daminius said he had followed on the afternoon Branan went missing. The route on which Daminius could not remember seeing anyone at all.

He turned off the track onto a flattish expanse of rough grazing, following a broad muddy swath that indicated the passage of many studded boots. A couple of sheep lifted their heads and stopped chewing to stare at him as he passed. On a whim, he aimed the horse at a clump of nettles. It leapt over them without objection.

The route was a favorite because it ran through striking scenery. Long, narrow lakes and reed beds shivered at the base of spectacular cliffs, whose natural defenses would soon be crowned with a long line of wall. Waving cheerfully up to a clutch of small figures waving at him from the top, it occurred to him that they were probably trying to tell him that the north side of the wall was not the most sensible place for a lone man to go for a ride. Luckily he was too far away to be identified. As he left the water behind, the track was less clear and it occurred to him that Daminius could have taken a different path, closer to the wall line or farther north, and that anything he saw now might not be relevant. But when he turned left to follow the stream, he was confident that he was on the right route. It was the only crossing from north to south of the wall here.

That was unfortunate, because instead of facing a clear passage he found himself riding toward a mass of yellowed greenery dangling from branches that stuck upward at the wrong angle. Several Britons were clambering in amongst the branches and he heard the rasp of saws punctuated by the thud of an axe. Someone was looping chains around a broad trunk. It was an old ash, and no doubt as soon as the locals had done the work, the army would commandeer the wood for making weapons to keep them in order. But for now it was an obstruction, and beyond it a team of oxen was stationed, ready to drag it out of the way.

The man setting the chains paused to usher him around to the left. Ruso coaxed the horse through the narrow gap. There was a tangle of black roots grasping at the air on one side, and on the other the deep hollow in the bank that they had failed to cling on to. He nodded his thanks and asked in Latin, "When did this fall?"

"It will be gone very soon."

"But how long has it been here?"

Instead of answering, the man called to a companion in a brown woolen hat and repeated the question in British, prefaced by "The officer wants to know . . ."

To Ruso's surprise the companion was a woman. "Tell him yesterday!"

He looked at the drooping leaves, yellow rather than autumn gold, and the way the rain had washed the mud off the roots, and observed in British, "It looks like longer."

The woman put down the axe and scrambled between the branches until she was close enough to sit on the trunk, level with Ruso. "We had to get a team together," she said. "There is only me and my son to work the land here. And then your people told us to go and look for a lost boy."

"It may help me to find the lost boy if you think very hard about when this tree fell."

She scratched her head through the wool and then carefully straightened the hat. "Now that I have thought," she declared, "It was market day. Then it rained the next day when we started cutting it, then we had to search for the boy. Does this matter?"

"It might," Ruso told her. "Thank you."

He rode on. He doubted the business of the tree would help find Branan but at least it might help consolidate Daminius's alibi so that he could be restored back to his full duties.

And if it wasn't Daminius and it wasn't Conn, who had taken the boy? Now that Virana had unwittingly extended the suspicion to the entire Legion, he had no idea how anyone was going to find out fast enough. The task of examining every possible suspect was overwhelming.

He would have to begin with the small things he could do, and then think about the rest later. He would ask at the bar for messages. He would make sure Senecio was all right. He would tell Accius about the fallen tree on Daminius's route, and while Accius dealt with that, he would think how to check the alibi of the one suspect for whom he was responsible, even if it did seem ridiculous that Nisus might have moved far or fast enough to kidnap anybody. Or wanted to. Ruso would do it because nobody knew what a child snatcher looked like.

49

SEVERAL MILES FARTHER north, another axe swung down and landed with a thunk. Two halves of log flew apart and tumbled onto the yard. The young man retrieved one and tried to balance it back on the tree stump. It fell sideways. He upended it, and this time it stayed. The axe swung again; the process was repeated.

It was only when the dog started barking that he noticed the approaching riders. Axe still in hand, he shouted, "Mam! People!" Then he recognized Enica and opened the gate. "Is it about Branan?"

"We have looked but found nothing," Enica told him. "Now we are looking in a new way. We need to find out who saw the body being put in the emperor's wall."

Lucano, whose upper lip was only faintly fluffy despite his muscular build, looked puzzled. "But I thought—"

"Branan saw nothing."

The youth considered this for a moment. Then he turned round, propped the axe against the stump, and cupped his mouth with his hands to bellow, "Worm! Where are you?"

A couple of chickens sidestepped away from the sound. A goat paused in its efforts to reach under the hurdles that fenced off the vegetable patch. "Worm! Come out, you're wanted!"

A woman appeared in the doorway of the nearest house, wiping her hands on her skirts. "If you tried calling your brother by his name, boy— Enica! Is there news?"

Enica shook her head.

"We searched everywhere here. We are all very sorry."

"He was here just now," Lucano was saying. "Where is he?"

The woman's cry of "Matto! Where are you?" was sharp and fearful.

"Don't worry," called the brother, heading round behind the house toward a wooded area. "I'll find him."

They waited. The piebald horse shambled over to crop a tuft of grass sprouting at the foot of one of the houses. He seemed not to notice Enica tugging on his reins.

Dismal approached, smacked the piebald on the rump with his stick, and led it back.

The mother said, "You must come and sit by the hearth. There is not much, but what we have—"

Enica thanked her but explained that she could not dismount. The woman managed a smile but instantly glanced away, looking for her boy.

A shriek from the woods alarmed the guests and their horses more than the mother. It was followed by a shout of "Let go! Let me go! Mam, he's hurting me!"

"Come when you're called, Worm! Think I don't know where you hide?"

"I never heard you!"

"Liar!"

With that Lucano reappeared, dragging a younger boy by the ear. "See? You've worried Mam now!"

Matto had contorted his body to follow the twist in his ear. "I didn't do anything!"

"You got us into trouble, you little liar. You know who this is?"

Unable to lift his head, Matto circled round crabwise until he could see the visitors through the tangled hair that had fallen over his face. "I didn't do anything!"

"Liar!" Lucano gave the ear an extra twist to make his point. Matto's shrieks drowned his mother's protests. Just as Tilla swung down from her horse to intervene, the older brother let go. The younger one dropped into a crouch with both hands clamped over his ear. Lucano seized the back of his brother's tunic as if he were holding the collar of a dog. "You said," he said, bending down, "that Branan saw somebody hiding a body in the emperor's wall."

"He did!"

"Now he's gone missing and his mam wants to know why you were telling lies about him!"

"I didn't lie!"

Tilla stepped forward and touched Lucano on the arm. "May I speak to him?"

Lucano looked at Enica for guidance, then shrugged and stepped back.

Tilla crouched beside the boy and spoke into his good ear, which was no cleaner than the rest of him. "We are not cross with you," she explained. "We just need to know what happened because we think it might help us find Branan."

Matto sniffed and wiped tears away with a grimy fist. He said, "It's not my fault. I thought it was true."

"Who told you?"

"Aedic started it. He was the one who told everybody."

"Do you know who told Aedic?"

"He said it was Branan. He said nobody was supposed to know."

"Why was that?"

Matto hesitated for a moment, then said, "Dunno."

"Did anybody ask Branan if it was true?"

Matto paused to sniff again. "I was going to. When I saw him. But now the man's got him."

"Which man?"

Matto looked at her as if it was a silly question. "The man who put the body in the wall. He came and got Branan, like Aedic said he would."

"Do you know who this man is?"

Matto shook his head. "Will he get me now?"

"You must stay at home with your family so you'll be safe," Tilla told him. "I will warn your mother and brother. Now tell me about Aedic."

50

"FACE IT, RUSO," Valens said, checking the apple for maggot holes before chopping it in two on the scarred surface of the operating table and handing half of it over. "You're not thinking straight. I grant you he's not the friendliest of characters, but it's a bit much to imagine he spent his leave abducting and murdering people."

"I'm not imagining anything," Ruso told him. "The orders are to pin everyone down. Nisus left on the day that Candidus disappeared, and he came back the day after Branan vanished. I've already sent a message to the Phoenix. I'm just asking you to keep an eye on him."

Valens flicked an apple seed onto the floor. "There must be a quicker way to do this than eliminating several thousand men one by one. Gallus has already wasted half the morning asking all the staff where they were the day before yesterday and then checking it. Besides, what if the chap who took the boy has deserted? It's not much use knowing his name if we don't know where he is."

"There would be a quicker way," Ruso told him, "if Virana could remember who was in the bar when Branan delivered the eggs."

"Will it help if I ask her?"

"No, thanks. I've just come from there and she's upset enough as it is." Although she had been pleasantly surprised by Conn's visit to thank her for her help. "He's not nasty, really," she explained while marveling at his change of heart. "It's just that nobody understands him."

"I have to say," Valens observed, leaning back on the sill of the window, "that it's lucky I was over at the baths with about forty people when the boy went. I'm not sure how well I could account for my movements most of the time. Could you?"

Ruso, his mouth full of apple, was chewing his way through to stating, "I'm never alone!" when it occurred to him that this was not true. Most of the time he felt besieged by patients and staff and rarely escaped except to fall asleep or spend time with his wife—often both at the same time. But he frequently traveled alone from one place of work to another. Although his time, like that of everyone else, was marked by the trumpet calls, anything between them was guesswork. How could he prove that he had gone straight from one location to another? Conversely, if he chose to "lose" some time in between two of them, who would notice?

"It's a messy business," he observed. "And all the time we're looking, the boy could be getting further away."

"Do you remember playing that game with the blindfold?" Valens asked. "You know, the one where you blindfold someone and tell him to find certain people in the room, but everybody keeps tiptoeing about from place to place, so that no matter how hard he tries, he never finds them unless they want him to?"

"No," said Ruso, trying to picture Valens as a child.

"Really?" His friend sounded genuinely surprised. "Of course, it was much more fun when there were girls playing."

"I can imagine."

"And plenty of wine."

"Is this happy memory supposed to help?"

"I thought it might help to express the situation you find yourself in."

"Not just me," Ruso pointed out. "All of us. Except that one of us is only pretending to wear the blindfold."

Ruso stood in the street outside the hospital and realized he had done everything he could think of. There had been no new messages at the bar to follow up on. No wife, either, but waiting for him instead was a very large bill that he promised to deal with later. *Deal with*. Not *pay*. Ria could make of that what she would.

He had spoken briefly with Senecio and told him that there was no news, which was at least better than bad news, but not by much. It was surprising how easily everyone seemed to have grown used to the sight of the old man sitting there. He had noticed the guard twitching the toes of one foot at regular intervals, as if he were singing a song in his head to relieve the boredom. Beside him, Senecio might as well have been a broken-down vehicle awaiting repair or removal.

Ruso had filled a whole morning with activities that were supposed to help rescue Branan, and none of them seemed to have achieved anything. Valens was right: This one-at-a-time thing was hopeless. He straightened his belt and his tunic, checked his bootlaces, ran both hands through his hair, and went to see if Accius had any better ideas. Or any ideas at all.

Inside the HQ, Accius was gathering up his cloak. With him was a man whom Ruso had seen before but never spoken to. He had a thick neck and cropped iron-gray hair. There was something vaguely bovine about his slow, deliberate movements and the way he breathed heavily through his nose. He looked like a man not easily distracted from his task. With a neck like that, he was probably also a man who snored, although Ruso never knew how men like that managed to sleep at all. Were their dreams haunted by the screams of their victims?

Accius caught sight of him. "Any news, Doctor?"

"No, sir."

"Go and find out how the natives are getting on. Come and find me in a couple of hours and we'll see where we've got to." Accius turned to the questioner. "Do you know where you're going?"

"Yes, sir."

"Lead the way, then." The tribune's expression was set in a manner that suggested he was about to face an unpleasant task.

Ruso asked, "Is Optio Daminius in the clear now, sir?"

Accius looked him in the eye. "No. Thanks to you, we now know the optio is lying about where he went that afternoon. Go away, Ruso."

They made an odd couple as they turned immediately right outside the HQ building: the heavy questioner and the upright aristocrat who might one day be a highly respectable senator charged with approving legislation. Ruso, watching from beneath the covered walkway of the barrack block, knew he should stay out of this. He should let whatever was going to happen happen. He had no authority to question it, and besides, Accius had probably wrestled with his own conscience anyway—not about the pain, but about the illegality.

The men turned right again almost immediately before the granary.
Ruso reached the corner of the granary just in time to see them turn in at
the entrance to the workshops. He knew exactly why he had been sent
away. Accius was trying to make sure none of his officers could be accused
of being complicit in the application of torture to a serving soldier.

It was a peculiar form of decency. Sacrificing one's principles for the
sake of the child. If only Ruso could convince himself that the result
would be worth it.

A voice in his head said, *So, can you think of anything else to try?*

He couldn't. Daminius had lied. He was a responsible and ambitious
young officer, he knew how important this was, and he had lied.

A dozen or so men in rough working tunics came out of the mainte-
nance yard. They formed up and marched off in the direction of the
barracks. So the workshops had been emptied of their regular occupants.
Ruso could smell the furnace.

Ruso flattened himself against the wall of the wheelwright's store,
feeling the waft of warm air on his skin. In the gloom of the smithy, the
glow of the burning charcoal picked out dark stripes and curves against
the far wall. He understood now why the questioner seemed to have
brought no equipment. Hanging there were all the implements anyone
could possibly need to loosen a man's tongue. He felt his own tunic
prickle with sweat.

A confused shuffle of footsteps was coming toward him down the street.
He stepped back into the wheelwright's shop until the footsteps had
passed. When he looked again, a barefoot and gagged figure was standing
in the yard, surrounded by four men. Ruso did not recognize the guards.
They were certainly not from the Twentieth. Accius was not going to risk
a mutiny by putting Daminius in the custody of his own messmates.

The Tribune stepped forward and spoke to the prisoner. "Optio
Daminius, none of us want this, but a child is missing and I will do whatever is necessary to find him. Do you understand?"

Daminius nodded.

"Do you have a fresh account of your movements two days ago?"

Daminius shook his head.

Accius stepped back. There was a moment's silence, then he said, "Carry
on."

The questioner spoke to the guards. One of them entered the workshop, squinted up into the rafters, and then slung a rope up over something
and caught the other end. The others stripped a struggling Daminius of his

clothes and prodded him forward. Meanwhile someone pumped the bellows and a roar of white flame shot up from the charcoal.

Ruso caught a glimpse of something hanging beside the identity tag around Daminius's neck. *My lucky charm, sir. Never fails. If you're in trouble, just shout.*

Ruso turned and ran.

51

THERE MUST BE someone in: Why was nobody answering the door? Ruso pulled out his knife, used the hilt to rap on the wood, and yelled, "Fabius!"

He must calm down. He must steady his breathing and try to think logically. He was not the first medic to be put in this position. He had more than once had to tidy victims up after torture, but he had never been present at the time. Several of his unluckier colleagues had been ordered to keep prisoners conscious during the process. Afterward, they had not wanted to talk about it and he had not wanted to ask.

He saw now how sheltered he had been. By Fortune, and by a law to which he'd barely given a thought. Regulations stated that a soldier, being neither a slave, an enemy prisoner, nor a barbarian, was not to be condemned to the mines or to torture.

But . . . what if Daminius was guilty? What if he was a convincing liar, and it was Daminius whom Candidus had gone to meet for a drink? What if Candidus had cheated at dice, and there had been a fight, and Candidus had ended up dead and hidden in the wall, and then Daminius had found out there was a witness, and wanted to silence him, and . . .

Ruso shook his head violently, dislodging the elaborate fantasy that had sprung from a man's simple refusal to reveal where he was on one particular afternoon.

He banged on the door again. "Fabius!"

A voice over his shoulder said, "Everything all right, sir?"

It was Fabius's clerk. "Fine," Ruso assured him. "I just need to talk to the centurion."

The man said, "Very good, sir," and carried on past.

From somewhere inside the house he heard the approach of footsteps. A female voice said, "The centurion is unwell, sir. Please come back later."

"I need to see him now. Open the door."

"Sir, I can't—"

"He knows what this is about. Tell him if he doesn't let me in, I'll stand outside his room and yell through the window."

"Sir, please—"

More footsteps. A male voice. "It's all right, girl. Ruso, have they found the child?"

"No."

"Then I'll deal with whatever it is tomorrow. Go away."

"I meant it. I'll shout outside your window."

The locks rattled. Finally the door was wrenched open, juddering with the force needed to get the damp wood free. Fabius appeared, with the face of the little kitchen girl pale behind him. Fabius dismissed her, and she scuttled away down the corridor.

Ruso shouldered his way in, closed the door, and leaned back against it. For once Fabius looked genuinely ill. His breath smelled of wine and vomit. "Doctor."

Ruso said, "You know what's happening."

"No."

"Is that no, you don't know, or no, you've been told to stay out of it, or no, you're too drunk to know anything?"

"There's no need to be rude. I'm not feeling well."

"What did you say to the tribune about Daminius?"

"Nothing."

"You didn't attempt to defend your own man?"

Fabius winced. "Don't shout, Ruso. My head is aching."

Ruso restrained an urge to punch him and lowered his voice. "How are you hoping to get better, Fabius, knowing they're out there interrogating him?"

"We need to find the boy."

"He's your man. He's loyal, he's hardworking, and the men like him. *I* like him."

"That's not the point." Fabius might have been drinking, but he was sober enough to argue cogently.

"Do you have any idea of how much you owe that man?"

Fabius raised a forefinger. "That, Doctor, is why I am not involved. Nor you."

Ruso dropped his voice to a whisper. "We're not involved because this is illegal, and you know it."

"You think I'm callous, don't you?"

"It doesn't matter what I think."

"I'm not callous. Do you know why I'm not lying in bed? Because until they tell me it's over, I shall be standing in there"—he wheeled round and pointed back toward the corridor—"in there, in front of the shrine, asking the gods to make Daminius tell the truth."

Ruso turned and lifted the door latch. He had no idea how to deal with a man whose response to the torture of his deputy was to drink wine and stand around praying. Fabius even seemed to think that staying out of bed was heroic.

"Where are you going?"

"I'm his doctor. I should be there."

"To do what?"

"Oh, don't waste my time!" Ruso strode away without looking back, but the question still echoed around his mind. *To do what?*

"I don't bloody know," he muttered, not sure whether he was more angry with Fabius for being weak, or Accius for sanctioning torture, or Daminius for telling stupid lies, or Tilla for getting him involved in all this in the first place. As for that unspeakable brute who had lured the boy away . . .

That was the problem. None of them knew who he was, so none of them knew where to place their anger. Instead they were fighting with each other.

Daminius had been strung up by his wrists with his toes barely touching the ground. The glow of the fire in the gloomy workshop lit up his naked flesh and shaded his eyes into deep hollows. The gag had been taken off and his lips were moving, but no sound came out. The little winged phallus hung uselessly around his neck. Perhaps he was reciting a prayer. Ruso remembered that face grinning at him through the muck of the quarry. *That's the spirit, sir.*

Nobody seemed to notice Ruso. He moved closer and felt a waft of warmth from the furnace. So far Daminius appeared to be unhurt. The questioner was taking his time setting up: allowing his victim's fear to build. That was how they worked.

Daminius tensed as the questioner approached. The man stood there for a while looking him up and down. Breathing steadily. Like a purchaser assessing livestock. Finally he said, "Where is the boy?"

Daminius looked him in the eye. "I don't know." He spoke louder, struggling to turn and face the onlookers. "I don't know! I'll swear on anything you want. You need to look for someone else. You're wasting time."

The questioner moved around to pump the bellows. Daminius's eyes glittered in the flames. "Where were you on the afternoon before yesterday?"

"Just say where you were!" urged Ruso, not sure whether he wanted this to stop for the optio's sake or for his own.

Accius spun round. "What are you doing here?"

Ruso, who did not know himself, said nothing.

"This isn't some sort of party, Ruso."

Ruso realized Fabius had thrown on a cloak and followed him. He was looking just past Daminius, using the old trick of concentrating his attention just beyond the thing he did not want to have to see. His face was haggard.

Inside the workshop, the questioner had paused, waiting to know whether to proceed in the presence of witnesses. When all was quiet and no order had come to stop, he repeated, "Where were you on the afternoon of the day before yesterday?"

"I went for a run, sir."

The questioner looked at Accius, who nodded. He reached for a pale rag and began to wrap it around his right hand.

"Tell him!" Ruso begged.

"I'm surprised at you, Ruso," said Accius. "I wouldn't have thought a surgeon would be squeamish." He glanced at the guards. "If the doctor interferes again, take him back to his quarters."

Ruso swallowed. There were four guards, the questioner, and a tribune. All determined to go through with this. All doing it to find the boy and to keep the peace with the Britons. Fabius was doing nothing to stop them, and perhaps he was right. The usual objections to torture—that people would say anything at all to make it stop, and that it was impossible to tell whether the victim was hiding the truth or didn't know it—did not apply. Everyone knew Daminius had lied. All he had to do was to explain exactly where he had been when someone dressed as a legionary lured Branan away.

The questioner moved across to the furnace and lifted out some implement that had been propped in the flames. The tip glowed white, golden, and then red as he turned back to Daminius. The optio twisted to try and avoid it, but with no foothold he swung helplessly back.

Ruso held his breath.

The red-hot tip had just made contact with the skin when the scream came. Not from Daminius, who grimaced and gasped as the stink of his burning flesh hit Ruso's senses. The screaming came from beyond the yard, and it was getting louder as the footsteps approached.

"Stop! Please, masters, officers, I beg you, stop! He knows nothing about the boy! Daminius, tell them!"

Accius gave an order. The iron was withdrawn.

Daminius twisted himself around, struggling to look at the girl. It was Fabius's kitchen maid. She was trying to reach him and being held back by two guards.

At the sight of her, Fabius seemed to recover his speech. "What are you doing here?"

Daminius said, "I don't know what this woman is talking about, sirs."

"Tell them!"

Daminius still said nothing. Accius glared down at the girl. "Well?"

The girl stopped trying to free herself from the guards. She looked round at the group of men and at the naked figure strung up in the light of the burning coals. "He was with me."

52

"ABSOLUTE WASTE OF time," complained Fabius, and for once Ruso agreed with him. The smithy and the wheelwright's shop were now back in action. Daminius had been sent back to laboring duties in the quarry, where Fabius was probably hoping another landslide would bury him. Meanwhile Fabius had asked Ruso to accompany him on a healthy walk around the perimeter track.

"I shan't cause any disruption to the work here," Fabius continued, "but once we're back in Deva, I shall get rid of him."

Having defied a tribune and trespassed on someone else's human property, Ruso was surprised that Daminius had not already been suspended from his duties. On the other hand, the tribune had sanctioned illegal treatment in front of witnesses. Daminius's future was going to be interesting.

Unabashed by Ruso's silence, Fabius carried on. "I can see it all now, looking back. Always finding excuses to come to the house. Volunteering for things. Asking to take on more responsibilities. I should have guessed."

These were the very qualities which Fabius had prized in him until just now. Ruso could not think of another man who would have covered up for his centurion the way that Daminius had, and he had no doubt that Fabius had taken the credit for most of the work his optio did. It occurred to him that the affair with the kitchen maid might have been the only thing that kept Daminius sane. "What will you do with the girl?"

"She'll go back to the dealer." They both stepped across a broad puddle. "I can't have a deceitful little trollop like that in the house. I have a wife back in Deva to consider."

Ruso supposed Fabius would buy himself a new maid to chase.

"I need to write to the dealer straightaway. I may need you as a witness."

"To say she's not satisfactory?" This would hardly get Fabius a better price. It would certainly wreck the girl's chances of being bought by a good family. "Why not just sell her locally?"

"I want my money back. She's still within the six-month guarantee period."

"Ah." If the lovestruck Daminius had thought about buying the girl for himself, he would have to beat the original price.

"I'll have her confined to the kitchen until we get back to Deva. Although why the cook didn't tell me there was something going on, I don't know." He answered his own question with "I suppose she was sleeping with him too. The only place who might pay decent money for her here is the brothel, and it's too much bother selling to them since the law changed."

Considering the fate of slaves in brothels, Ruso took the view that the more bother involved in consigning them there, the better.

"Anyway," Fabius continued, "with all this to deal with, it's just as well my headache has cleared. Doctor Valens was right: I should be staying out in the fresh air during the hours of daylight."

"He's a good doctor."

"You need to get up-to-date with the latest treatments, Ruso. The Greeks don't know everything. You should read about what Doctor Spiculus and his people are doing in Alexandria."

"Really?"

"I've asked Doctor Valens to find me a copy."

"I'd like to see it." Ruso had never heard of a Doctor Spiculus in Alexandria, but he could recall a bartender of that name not fifty paces from where Valens used to live in Londinium.

"Anyway, I've told the tribune that the doctor and I can keep everything going here between us while you search for the boy. A huge quantity of routine work goes into keeping a century running smoothly, you know. People don't appreciate it."

"It's the same with hospitals."

"But you don't have quotas and targets in hospitals," Fabius pointed out. "Obviously it's a pity about the boy, but Second Augusta are already on the march back to Isca. My old comrades in the Sixth expect to finish tomorrow and head south the day after, whereas our men have a turret and another hundred feet of wall to complete before we can all go home. I've explained that we've had a landslide and trouble with the natives and I've practically lost my optio, but it makes no difference. Everyone still expects the stone to arrive on-site as if nothing had happened. Even if they send us more men—which they won't—Daminius says we'll need at least a week."

Daminius says. Daminius was not suspended from duty any more than was the kitchen maid, because Fabius could not manage without them.

53

"LEAVE THAT ALONE!" The young woman let go of the handle in the top grinding stone, grabbed the toddler, and lifted him away. Over his howls of outrage, she shouted, "Do you want to get your fingers mashed?"

The toddler wailed louder. Still squatting, she held him at arm's length, turning toward the unkempt man who had just let Tilla and Enica into the yard. "What's that boy of yours done now?"

"I don't know!" The man glanced around and yelled, "Aedic? Aedic! Get here now!" There was no response. "Where is he?"

"How should I know?" The woman ignored the toddler's frenzied struggles to free himself from her grasp. "He's *your* son!"

Tilla glanced at Enica, who was looking exhausted. The harassed mother thrust the toddler toward the man. "You take this one. I'll see to them."

"I'm busy."

"Oh, and I have nothing to do?"

The woman won. The man tucked the toddler under his arm as if he were a stray and very unruly lamb, and the sound of protest was muffled by the walls as they went indoors.

The woman scrambled to her feet, slapping away the pale drifts of flour on her skirts. A couple of older women came out of the better-kept house across the yard. They recognized Enica, and Tilla heard yet again the conversation that had been repeated at every home they had visited. The sympathy. The hope of good news. The promise of prayers and offerings. And behind it all, unspoken, the fear that Enica's bad luck might rub off on them.

Duty done, the women retreated and stood with their arms folded, as if they were waiting to say, *I told you so,* about something.

Enica said, "We must speak with Aedic, Petta. We think he can help."

But Petta did not know where Aedic was. "He wanders off," she said. "I tell him not to, but he never listens to me and his father does nothing about it."

"When did you last see him?"

The woman scratched the back of her neck. "He brought in the firewood," she said, trying to remember. Then she appealed to her neighbors. "Did anybody see where Aedic went?"

One of them said, "Sometimes he runs errands for the soldiers."

Enica gave a gasp of concern as Tilla asked, "Do you know which ones?"

Nobody did. As if to excuse herself, Petta added, "I have enough to do without worrying about a boy who never does what I tell him."

Tilla wondered whether, if this Aedic had been kidnapped, anyone here would notice. "Has there been anyone here asking for him?"

There had not. Without much hope, she said, "Did he ever talk about seeing something at the wall one day?"

The question reminded one of the neighbors of something. "My son says Aedic sometimes hangs around near the old farm." Seeing Tilla did not understand, she said, "Where he was brought up."

"Our farm?" demanded the husband, who had reappeared in the doorway. The toddler, damp hair still stuck to his forehead, was cramming bread into his mouth. The man turned to his wife. "Nobody told me."

Petta said, "Did you ever ask?"

"What does he go there for? There's nothing left." He turned to Tilla. "They took our land for building on," he said, "turned us off good grazing, burned down the houses and—"

"Oh, stop!" Petta cried. "Nobody cares about your land. A boy has been stolen, and your son knows something about it."

Tilla raised her voice to step in before the argument grew worse. "When you find Aedic, Branan's family need to talk to him straightaway. We need to know what he saw at the wall."

The father said, "I'll tell him."

"It is not safe to send him on his own," Tilla told him, afraid he might be thinking of doing just that. "Do you know where to bring him?"

"We know," growled the father, perhaps annoyed at being told what to do.

They were on the way out when Tilla said, "Do you know where their old farm was?"

Enica, busy dragging her horse's head round so it would carry her back to the road, did not seem to hear. Tilla said, "You need to go home. I will take you back now and find some salve for your tired muscles. Then I will take Dismal and go and look for Aedic."

Enica was too weary to argue. Tilla took hold of the piebald's reins and led it beside her own horse, hoping the other searchers had been more successful and feeling guilty for dragging this poor woman about on horseback for hours, finding nothing, and making her suffering even worse than before. Now she was plagued with a new fear. What if Aedic had disappeared too?

Her thoughts were interrupted by "That is the first time I have spoken with Petta since the business with Conn."

Tilla twisted round to face her companion. "The business with Conn?"

"Petta and Conn were almost betrothed, did you not know?"

"I heard there was a girl," said Tilla, struggling to fit the woman she had just met with the picture of Conn's lost love that she had formed after listening to the gossip at Ria's.

"She left Conn for a soldier. He got her pregnant and then he was posted somewhere else. Conn refused to take her back if she kept the child. So Petta needed a father for the child, Aedic's father was widowed and needed a wife, and you see how it has turned out."

Tilla said, "I heard the soldier forced her."

"That is what she told Conn to start with, but it was a lie."

The story was more complicated than the gossips had thought. "Conn should not be losing sleep over her."

Enica said, "That is what we all told him. But Conn likes to be angry. So my husband still has no grandchildren."

Tilla wondered why people who did not deserve children had no difficulty producing them, and then remembered to tell herself that, compared with many women, she had very little to complain about.

54

A T FIRST RUSO did not recognize the brothel keeper. The fox-pelt color was gone: Today her hair was a startling jet-black to match the makeup around her eyes, but the professional smile was the same. "What's your pleasure, Doctor?"

"A word in private," he suggested.

She led him into a little room that smelled as though the brightly colored rugs and cushions were concealing a bad damp problem.

"I'm told it's harder to buy staff these days," he said, lowering himself onto the little couch as instructed. "Since the change in the law."

"I hope you're not going to make me an offer, sir. We run a respectable house here."

"I'm still looking for the boy. I need to know how your business works. You can't just buy from anybody? What's changed?"

"It's the emperor, sir. May the gods bless him. He's a great improver, isn't he?"

"Undoubtedly," said Ruso, aware that not everyone wanted to be improved.

"Says nobody can sell to us or the gladiator boys unless he can show a good cause in law."

Ruso wondered what would constitute a good cause, and whether it would involve the bad behavior of the slave or the financial desperation of the owner. "What do you think of that?"

"Very commendable, sir."

"And does everyone share that view?"

She tilted her head to one side. "I have heard it suggested, sir, that a business with standards can't run on everybody else's cast-off staff. These days lot of the better houses have taken to breeding their own workers. If you want happy customers, you can't offer them riffraff."

Ruso nodded. "Are there other sources?"

The lips pursed. "All my girls are legal, sir. You can check."

"I'm not here to cause trouble," he reminded her. "If some other owner wanted to buy a stolen boy, where would he—or she—go?"

She glanced at the door. "I have to do business with these people, sir. I can't afford to have it said—"

"Branan is nine years old."

She sighed. "I had a boy once. He died of a fever."

"I'm sorry."

"You won't say who told you?"

"Not a word."

She leaned closer. He had grown used to the damp, but now he was assailed by a sudden waft of garlic. "I hear things," she whispered, "about Lupus over in Coria. Nothing definite, mind. Just rumors. Back-door deals."

"Is Lupus the dealer who has an agent in Vindolanda?"

"That's the one. Down the main street in Vindolanda, turn left just past the butcher's shop and it's the third door on the right. Ask for Piso."

The stable hand had tied the bay up with a very short rope in order to brush him. "Vindolanda again already, sir?"

"I forgot something." Ruso stepped back as the horse shifted sideways and nearly knocked the groom over. He had a feeling that he was going around in circles, but he didn't know what else to try, and nobody else seemed to know, either.

The horse was happy to canter much of the way to Vindolanda: good, not only because Ruso was in a hurry, but also because he could speed past what was obviously turning into a major argument over a pile of broken red crockery at the side of the road. A driver was waving his arms about and shouting at a group of natives. Ruso overheard something about "I've been bloody searched twice already!" He urged the horse on before anyone might imagine he would like to get involved.

Most of Vindolanda's shoppers had gone home now. A few off-duty soldiers were lounging outside the bars. He went down to the fort gate and reported the roadside fracas before heading off in search of Piso.

The dealer's agent was down a side street, exactly where he had been told. He tethered the horse on a short rein, warning the small boys who offered to "watch him for you, mister" not to get too close.

But whatever he might have hoped to learn from Piso, he was out of luck. According to the hulking house slave, the agent had gone away on business. The slave either did not know where or had been instructed not to say. He was not allowed to let anyone in. There was no stock there. The master had taken all of them with him.

"Never mind," Ruso assured him. "Perhaps you can get a message to him." He leaned closer. "I don't want to say this out in the street," he explained, "but there's a bit of a problem over the boy one of our men sold him the other day."

"Yes, sir."

Ruso was aware of trying to steady his voice. *Yes, sir* could mean anything. "I wanted to make sure your master knew about it."

The slave eyed him for a moment, then said, "I think everyone knows, sir."

Now it was the tremble in his hands he needed to steady as well. He waited until a gaggle of children had led a puppy down the street on a length of twine before he leaned forward again. "Your master's problem isn't the boy so much as the seller. He's claiming your master arranged the deal in the first place, and all he did was deliver."

"The seller's been caught, sir?"

"He's singing like a bird in a cage," Ruso told him. "But nobody knows how much of it is true."

The slave's eyes narrowed. "Why should you want to help my master, sir?"

Indeed, why would he? "I can't explain it on the doorstep," said Ruso, truthfully.

He dropped the latch as requested, aware that the slave was at least half a hand taller than he was, and wide enough to block the hallway. The exit was behind him, but he would have to lift the latch and pull the door inward. Before he reached the street the slave would have plenty of time to haul him back. He swallowed. "The seller has been under suspicion for some time, but we have no proof."

" 'We,' sir?"

"The Legion," Ruso explained, deciding to stick to the truth as far as possible. "I'm helping Tribune Accius sort this out."

There was a sound behind the slave. Another figure was moving toward them. "Who's there?" demanded a woman who sounded as though she was not expecting to like the answer. At that point it seemed to dawn on the slave that he had not asked.

"Medical Officer Ruso from Parva," Ruso explained, rescuing him.

"He's come to see the master," the slave told her, shifting to one side in the gloom of the corridor to reveal a short woman with her hair pulled back from her forehead as if it were a nuisance.

She looked Ruso up and down. "The master's not here."

Ruso, wishing she would go back to wherever she had come from, carried on talking to the man. "We realize this puts your master in an awkward position, but if he's willing to testify, we're prepared to accept that he didn't know he was receiving stolen goods."

"The master doesn't receive stolen goods!" exclaimed the woman. "Who's been telling you that? This is an honest business."

"We know," said Ruso. "But anyone can be deceived. So the sooner he brings the boy back, the better."

The woman said, "What boy?" at exactly the same moment as the man said, "I'll tell the master when he comes home, sir."

"Will that be today?"

"Probably not, sir."

"When?"

"We don't know," said the woman.

"What do you do if anyone arrives to conduct business?"

"This great oaf takes messages," the woman said, prodding the man in the ribs.

"Tell me how to find your master," he said, "and I'll go and sort things out with him before he gets into worse trouble."

The man looked at the woman, who said, "We don't know where he is."

Ruso was losing patience. "Then how do you get messages to him?"

"He'll send someone," said the woman primly. "When he's ready."

Ruso wondered if it would be possible to get the official questioner back from wherever he had gone. This dancing around the truth was a waste of time. The gods alone knew where Branan would end up unless they got hold of him fast. Recalling the name mentioned by the brothel keeper, Ruso asked, "Has he gone to Coria to see Lupus?"

Again the man looked at the woman, and that told Ruso what he needed to know. He put one hand on the latch. "Tell him he needs to hand the boy in at the nearest army base straightaway and have them send a message back to the fort at Parva. The longer the boy is away, the worse it gets for your master."

He stopped himself just in time from saying, *Everyone will be looking out for the boy, so he can't be sold.* If that were the case, their master might think his safest course was to do away with Branan, deny all knowledge of everything, and blame his slave for talking nonsense. Instead Ruso thanked them for their help and stressed the urgency of the message.

He was at the end of the street, searching his purse for small coins for small boys, when he heard the man's voice behind him requesting, "A quick word, sir."

His spirits rose as the slave looked round to make sure the woman had not followed him. They sank again when he heard, "I wanted to ask about joining the Legion, sir."

Ruso looked at him. "I'm sorry," he said. "Only free citizens can enroll."

"I'm hoping to be freed shortly," the man explained. "Freedmen can join now."

"Are you sure?" Ruso had heard this somewhere before. It seemed to be a common misconception.

"Your man who sold the boy. He's a freedman. I recognized him."

Ruso was about to respond when he heard the woman shout, "What are you doing out there?"

"You must be mistaken," Ruso told him, willing the woman to go away. "What did you think his name was?"

The slave shook his head. "I'm no good with names, sir. And it was some years back, but I remember that face. We were sold by the same dealer. I think he went to a family down south."

The woman was hurrying toward them. "What are you telling him?" she called. "You keep your mouth shut!"

"Describe the man you remember," Ruso urged.

The slave looked nonplussed. "But you've got him locked up. You said."

"I'm just trying to compare . . ." But Ruso was floundering, and the slave knew it. Ruso backed toward the horse and freed the reins.

"Where's he going?" demanded the woman. "What have you said to him, you great lump?"

Ruso grabbed the saddle and vaulted up, but the slave had seized the horse by the bridle. He was saying, "Sir, my master—agh! Get off!"

Smacked on the nose, the horse unclamped its teeth from the man's arm and danced sideways. Ruso kicked it into motion, not caring which way it went as long as it was out of there. By the time he managed to catch hold of the reins and regain some sort of control, he was careering up Vindolanda's main street and terrified pedestrians were darting for cover. Glancing back, he saw people running after him. The slave was clutching the bitten arm, but whatever he was yelling was lost beneath the clatter of hooves on stone.

"Good horse!" Ruso told it as it swerved to avoid a pack mule and an old man with a sack over one shoulder. When he reached the road he turned east, speeding toward Coria.

55

H E TRIED TO hail a couple of official dispatch riders on the way to
Coria, but both deliberately rode straight toward him, so he had to
dodge as they thundered past in a blur of flying manes and hooves. He
should have paused to ask Accius for a permit, although how they would
see him waving it at that speed, he did not know. Instead he pulled in
down by the river at Cilurnum to give the horse a brief rest and send
identical messages to Accius and Tilla:

On the way to question slave trader in Coria. Hopeful.

Coria was a busy little town on a crossroads, and like Vindolanda, it had
grown up under emperors who did not dream of Great Walls. Its lush
meadows and broad river valley made it a favorite leave destination, but
by the time Ruso reached it he was too weary to appreciate it. Even the
horse was too tired to bite anyone as it was led into the stables at the fort.
There were dark patches of sweat on its coat and its mouth was flecked
with foam. Ruso's suspicion that he did not look a great deal better was
confirmed when the groom directed him to the bathhouse without being
asked. Instead, he left a message for the commanding officer and then
hurried through the streets to the Phoenix Inn.

Nisus had stayed there for the whole of his leave, as Ruso had expected. The owner knew of the slave trader called Lupus, who was often in town, but did not know where he might be found at the moment. Since it was close, he tried the *mansio* next. The manager seemed to think his arrival was some kind of test and assured him that an establishment funded by taxpayers did not accommodate that sort of person. Ruso was willing to bet that it would accommodate almost any sort of person if there were no official visitors in residence and the guest was willing to pay, but he did not bother to argue. He and Tilla had spent some time in Coria a few years ago, and he knew someone who would be far more helpful in the hunt for the slave trader.

"Doctor!" cried Susanna. Her tone of surprise caused several of her customers to look up from their food. "What are you doing here?"

"I'm trying to find someone."

She looked perplexed for a moment, then held out both arms, offering a public embrace he wasn't expecting. "It is good to see you! How long has it been?"

"Too long," he said, glancing around the brightly decorated snack shop and comparing it favorably with Ria's. He could not imagine Ria hugging anyone. Or paying anyone to paint scenery on the walls.

Susanna's necklace sparkled and her hair was more subtly colored than before. He said, "You look well."

"Hard work and the goodness of God, Doctor. Sit down. You look worn-out. What can I get you?"

He had intended to rush, but she was right: He was tired, and he needed to eat. He sat, leaning back against a wall on which peacocks and doves strutted in a rather blotchy garden. Before he could order anything, Susanna had joined him and dispatched one of her girls—not one he remembered—to bring them both drinks and him a bowl of pancakes with honey. "You'll like them," she promised. "Now, let's see, what's happened to everybody since you were here? I hear you and Tilla are married and having a blessing!"

"We married in Gaul," he told her. Her face fell when he explained who he was looking for. "We heard. That poor family. Such a terrible thing, and in daylight too! They're lucky they have you there to help."

It was not a popular view, but he enjoyed hearing it anyway. Conscious of the couple on the next table now straining to catch every word, he leaned closer to ask a delicate question.

"Lupus?" Susanna considered her answer for a moment. Then she said, "Yes. Yes, I'd say he might. It's a pity you weren't here yesterday. He was sitting at that table over there."

He blinked. Surely it couldn't be that easy?

It wasn't. "But he was leaving town today."

"I need to know whether he sold the boy on while he was here," he said. "If he didn't, I need to find him."

A soft hand closed over his. "You leave the locals to me, Doctor. If that little boy's here, I'll find out."

After a faintly embarrassing pause while she gazed deep into his eyes, Susanna let go. "Aemilia will be sorry to have missed you," she said. "They're out of town."

"That's a shame," he said, relieved. Tilla's cousin Aemilia meant well, but today he did not have time to listen to her.

"In fact, I thought . . ." She stopped. "Well, I must have misunderstood." She patted him on the hand. "You enjoy your meal while I just pop out and ask where Lupus went. I'll get the girls to pack you up some food to take with you."

Ruso allowed himself to relax back against the doves and peacocks. Finally, somebody was pleased to see him. Better still, she seemed to know what to do.

The pancakes arrived, generously dolloped with honey, and as he sliced each golden surface and rolled it onto his spoon, he began to word his next message to Tilla. He would tell Accius as well, of course, but he wanted to imagine Tilla crouching beside the old man and saying, "Good news! Your boy is on the way home!" He could imagine the welcome as he rode back to the farm with the boy seated—no, two on a horse would never work over that distance. He would get a pony assigned to the boy. Or maybe they would arrive in style, in an official vehicle supplied by the local commandant. The news would have run ahead of them. Neighbors, weary with searching but elated, would be lining the road, cheering and waving. Locals and foreigners together, differences forgotten in the joy of knowing that a missing child was safe and well. Ruso would sit back in the carriage and smile the satisfied smile of a man whose efforts had been justly rewarded, and modestly tell everyone that Fortune had been kind to him and that he was glad to have been able to help.

The elation did not last.

56

R USO HAD ARRIVED at the wrong time of day for a man who wanted a fresh horse. Everything was either out or worn out. Finally he was granted the reserve mount: a mare with a peculiarly uncomfortable gait and reins repaired with twine.

Luckily, Lupus's cartload of caged stock trundled along no faster than the couple of dozen slaves chained behind it could walk. Three men with clubs were assigned to encourage them, but even so, the assembly was only a couple of miles out of town and heading east when Ruso found it. That was when his vision of triumph began to fade.

He surveyed the lines of chained slaves as he passed, but there was no sign of Branan. The cage held only a nursing mother and a couple of small children. There were two men at the front of the vehicle: one who was driving the mules and another whose skinny neck poking out from a mound of furs reminded Ruso of an ostrich. "Lupus?"

It was, but Lupus did not recall any native boy sold to his agent in Vindolanda.

"We know he bought him," insisted Ruso, struck by a sudden fear that the agent might have got rid of the boy privately rather than deliver him to Lupus. "There are witnesses."

The neck sank into the furs as if fearing attack.

"If we don't find him, the family can still prosecute your agent for receiving stolen goods." It ought to be true, although he had no idea whether it was.

The neck twisted round. "Piso!"

Lupus signaled Ruso away with one skinny arm while a bald-headed man with muscular shoulders and a club in one hand strode forward to speak to him. So this was the man Ruso had failed to find in Vindolanda. He guessed the big slave who had said too much would be meeting the blunt end of that club when his master got home.

After a moment's consultation the bald man retreated and Ruso was summoned back.

"My man in Vindolanda bought the boy in good faith. The seller said the family had handed him over to pay off a debt."

"Did he ask the boy if that was true?"

"The families don't usually tell them. Otherwise they run away before we collect."

"Where is he now?"

The vehicle jolted in and out of a large pothole, which gave Lupus's "I don't know" a kind of hiccup in the middle.

Ruso held the mare back until Lupus drew level with him again. "What happened to the boy?"

Lupus poked his index finger into his mouth and retrieved something from between his teeth. He looked at it, wiped it off on the furs, and said, "The boy escaped before they got to Coria."

"That's a twenty-mile trip. Where exactly did they lose him?"

"I'm very annoyed about it. Piso should have had more sense."

Ruso said, "If any harm has come to that boy, the family will hold you responsible."

"But the family handed him over. The loss is mine."

"No they didn't," said Ruso, eyeing the scrawny neck and wondering whether he could lean across and wring it. "Haven't you heard there's a child been stolen?"

Lupus sighed. "Every time someone goes missing, traders like me are the first to get the blame. But the moment they want staff, it's a different story."

Ruso reined in the mare and let the cart go on ahead. Eventually the chained slaves were shuffling past. Ruso caught Piso's eye and said, "Where did you lose the boy?"

Piso frowned. "The old crow's blaming me, is he?"

"We can talk about blame later. Where's the boy?"

"How should I know?" He stepped closer. "When we found out half the army was looking for him, I wanted to hand him in. It was the boss's idea to let him go."

So Branan had not run away at all. "When was that?"

"Last night. Back in Coria."

"You turned a child loose on his own in a town miles from home? At night?"

The man shrugged. "He'll be all right. He's a local."

Ruso leaned sideways and grabbed Piso's club with one hand and the back of his tunic with the other, pulling it up so the front rose tight under his chin. The mare, taken by surprise, sidestepped away from the disturbance and Ruso would have been unseated but for one thigh hooked under the horn of the saddle. "He's nine years old!" Ruso hissed, aware of the other guards coming back to intervene. Trying to lever himself back up without letting go, he said, "Do you know how much trouble you're in? The Legate of the Twentieth has ordered this search. The governor himself has asked to be kept informed."

"It wasn't my idea to let him go!"

"You bought him. You knew who he was and you didn't bring him back. You'd better help us find him. And catch the seller. If you're lucky, the governor just might not throw you to the Britons."

With that, Ruso dropped the club and pushed himself back up into the middle of the saddle. It was hard to make a credible threat if you fell off your horse while doing it.

Several natives who had paused to watch returned to clearing the roadside ditch when he glared at them. Piso retrieved his club and straightened his tunic before saying that he had no idea where Branan had gone last night. Yes, it was after dark. Down by the bridge. No, he had not been given any supplies or warm clothing. The boss had said the natives would take him in.

"In the middle of the night?" Ruso demanded. "What was he supposed to do, knock on doors?"

Piso shrugged, as if these things were no concern of his. "Ask the boss."

"How do I know you didn't just kill him and dump him?"

"A body is hard to get rid of. It was easier if he wandered off."

Ruso shook his head. "You people."

"I was just doing what I was told."

"Tell me something useful. Tell me who sold him to you."

"A legionary called Marcus."

"Marcus what?"

But of course the man did not know, and since there were probably several hundred Marcuses serving with the Twentieth alone, it was a fine name to pick if someone wanted to stay anonymous. "Had you seen him before?"

"Maybe. I see a lot of people."

"Try harder. What did he look like?"

"Sort of . . . brown hair. Not tall, not short. Not fat, not thin."

"Of course not." This was hopeless. Ruso was gathering his thoughts, ready to head back into town, when Piso said, "He had one pale arm."

"He had what?" asked Ruso, wondering if he had heard correctly.

"One arm. It was paler than the other one. You didn't notice until you saw the two together, but it was. The left, I think."

Ruso eyed the bald head for a moment, wondering whether there was any point in persisting or whether already Piso was starting to make things up. Finally he said, "All this is going in my report. If you've lied to me—"

"If I'd lied, I'd have come up with something better."

57

HE WENT TO Susanna's first, because that was the place to get things done. Susanna herself was out looking for anyone who had just bought a boy slave, but one of the girls promised to pass on the news. They were now looking for a child on his own who had been down by the bridge late last night. Then he went over to the fort, where a glum clerk in the CO's office arranged to send an urgent warning downriver to the port. As the man observed, if anyone picked up the boy and put him on a ship, he would be lost forever.

Ruso needed to start where the boy had started, so he walked the familiar road down to the bridge. Back at Deva, he would have nailed up notices or scrawled on prominent walls: *MISSING—Branan, nine years old, last seen on the third day before the kalends of November. Any information to . . .* He could have put up signs at milestones and crossroads and public latrines. Whereas for the illiterate Britons the only way to find out something was to have someone tell you. News grew wings on market days, but the rest of the time word of mouth was hopelessly inefficient.

While Susanna spread the word around the civilians of Coria, and the local CO sent the message down to his men through his centurions, someone was going to have to ride around to every farm for miles, asking if a lone boy had been seen—especially one traveling west. And that someone would have to hope that the locals would tell him the truth. Much as the Britons complained about foreigners, they were not above using each other as slaves when it suited them. He wondered briefly whether to send an update back to everyone at Parva, then decided to wait. There was nothing they could do tonight, and with luck the boy would be found by morning.

He leaned back against the parapet of the bridge and tried to think where a boy would have gone from here in the dark. Not uphill to the town, surely. He would want to put as much distance as possible between himself and his captors. But which way? Would he stick to the roads for speed or the field paths for safety? Ruso tried to remember whether it had been cloudy last night. He had paid very little attention, but it would have mattered to Branan. During the day he would have known from the sun that he had traveled east; at night he would need the stars to find his way home. If there were no stars . . . Ruso turned to face the road that led south out of the valley, away from town. It was the main route to the rest of the province. It would have taken Branan in the wrong direction, but it was the quickest way away from here, and when the sun rose there would be plenty of farm carts that might give him a lift.

Ruso folded his arms and closed his eyes. *Think.*

This had been the problem all along. Not knowing which way to turn. But it was no good circling in one place and trampling it bare like a tethered goat. Sooner or later Branan would head for home. Ruso would leave Coria to Susanna and the local force and spread the word at the farms and roadside stations on the way back to Parva.

He opened his eyes and saw his own folded arms. How could a man end up with his left arm paler than his right? Nobody carried a shield for that long. But . . . there had been that time when he had an injured leg strapped up for weeks, and when the dressings had come off . . .

He was almost back up at the west gate when a dispatch rider came out at a canter. Ruso held up both hands, waving wildly as he stepped into the road, shouting, "Stop, I need to send a message!"

This rider was better-mannered than the others. Instead of running Ruso down, he swerved, waving cheerily back. If he heard Ruso yelling, "Tell the tribune at Parva to look again at Mallius!" he showed no sign of it.

Mallius, the sometime-blond soldier who had passed the water up to the stranded prefect in the quarry. Mallius, the supplier of a dead hen of unknown provenance. Mallius, who had been part of the search party that had seen Branan and Tilla together at the farm. Mallius, whose wrist and forearm must have been bandaged for at least a month and which, even in this climate, would have emerged more sun-starved than the rest of him.

The same Mallius who had been fully occupied at the brothel, and then certifiably asleep, on the afternoon of the kidnap, and who had no reason that Ruso knew of to steal and sell a child.

Ruso shook his head. Accius, if he got the message, would have to puzzle that one out for himself. Ruso had a boy to find.

He was halfway to Susanna's when he saw her careering down the street, waving one hand in the air and holding her skirts out of the mud with the other. There was news! He ran to meet her, feeling a smile escaping his caution.

And then it froze.

Gasping for breath, Susanna managed to get the story out. "He was seen! Lupus's man met some fur traders. On the bridge. They took the boy north. I think he's been sold."

58

A T LAST TILLA had some use for her escort. With Dismal following her, and the military brands on the horses, nobody dared to question her right to ride down the track that crossed the line of wall where the soldiers were working. The weary Enica pointed toward the rough slopes where Aedic's family had lived. At the top, Tilla could see the builders tidying up, ready for the end of the day's work. They were leaning out from the scaffold to throw covers over the freshly laid stones and gathering their equipment together, ready to carry it back down to the camp. Tilla swallowed. This looked very much like the place where her husband had described Candidus's knife being found. But there was no sign of a boy, and no one answered their cries of "Aedic!"

There was little news to exchange on either side when they delivered Enica home. Dismal had clearly been hoping the search would be abandoned for the day, and his face fell even further when Tilla explained that they were now going to retrace their steps to the wall and carry on hunting for Aedic. Instead of following her, he turned his horse the other way and peered across the fields below the house to where the trees marked the passage of the stream.

"What is it?"

"Be quicker down that way and through the quarry, miss."

Tilla let him lead her down past a half-ruined farm building. After some exploring, during which Dismal appeared to be lost but was not going to admit it, they found a place where they could jump the horses over a tumbled section of wall. They scrambled down a bank and cantered north, following a broad track that was in unusually good repair along the course of the stream. After a couple of hundred paces it curved into a large cleared area where the side of the hill had been hacked away. Part of the cliff had tumbled into a steep slide of loose earth and rock. She held the horse back, gazing up at it. This must be what her husband had climbed across to rescue Valens's father-in-law.

How simple everything had seemed just a few days ago, when the biggest problem of her afternoon had been the thought that her husband would be late for supper. Now they were both out hunting for other people's missing children and she had no idea where he was or whether anything would ever be quite the same again.

"Miss!"

The voice made her jump. She recognized the man who had led the search party: What was his name? Daminius. But instead of telling her to clear off out of the quarry, he was slipping his work hammer into a loop on his belt and asking, "Any news about the boy, miss?"

"They would have sounded the horn," she told him. Since he was free, she supposed they must have decided he had nothing to do with Branan's disappearance. "Have you seen my husband?"

"I heard he was going to Vindolanda." There was something about the man's expression that said there was more, but all he said was "Keep well clear of the landslide, miss. Just in case."

She explained about the search for Aedic, and he nodded. "There's a big clump of bushes up toward the wall where they've got the scaffolding. About a hundred paces east of the stream. He sometimes hides there."

"You know him?"

"Warn him to watch out. Most of the lads know he's harmless, but my replacement might think he's a spy."

"Your replacement? Are you being sent away?"

The optio shrugged, and she thought there was a slight flinch, as if he had disturbed a forgotten injury. "This is the Legion, miss. You never know."

"I wish you well," she said, and meant it. She was about to ride on when she noticed what was hanging around his neck. "Did you lend that to my husband?"

He picked up the little winged phallus and grimaced. "I don't know what he did to it," he said. "I've had nothing but bad luck ever since he got his hands on it. Miss, are you the one who helped Fabius's kitchen maid?"

He was a man full of surprises. How did he know that? She wondered whether he knew about the girl's plea for a charm against pregnancy. "I have met her. Why do you ask?"

From across by the little hut, a voice shouted, "Hey! Are you working or talking?"

"You might not see her again," he said. "Her master might send her away. I thought I should tell you she was very grateful."

Then, before Tilla could ask what was going on, he said, "I hope you find both those boys soon, miss," and went back to work, twisting the hammer out of his belt as he walked.

59

TILLA CROUCHED DOWN in front of the bushes, which stank of urine. "I know you're there," she said gently. "I can see your foot." The foot was snatched back out of sight.

"I just want to talk to you," she said.

There was a scuffling from somewhere amongst the leaves. Dismal shouted a warning and she sprang to her feet, catching sight of a small figure scrambling away from her up the hill, then veering to the left as if he were trying to get down to the stream. She grabbed fistfuls of skirt and ran after him. Dismal rode round to cut him off. The boy realized the danger and changed course like a startled animal, running back across the slope, trying not to get trapped against the wall. Tilla managed to intercept him and there was one of those silly dodging games with him feinting to one side and then trying to run in the opposite direction. Dismal closed in. Finally she flung herself at the boy and they ended up rolling down the damp hillside in a flurry of arms and legs and skirts.

When they had disentangled themselves Tilla said, "Your knee is bleeding. Let me look."

The boy did not even spare a glance at the hole in his trousers. He was keeping a wary eye on Dismal. He whispered, "Is that him?"

"Who?"

The boy did not answer.

"You must be Aedic. I am Darlughdacha. Tilla for short."

Again, no answer.

She said, "That man is with me. Does he look like someone you're afraid of?"

The boy nodded. That was progress.

"You are safe with me," she assured him, but he was still watching Dismal's every move and bracing himself, ready to run. Tilla called to Dismal not to come any closer. "You see?" she told Aedic. "He won't hurt you while I'm here."

"I didn't do anything."

"I know," she told him. "Is the man you are afraid of one of the soldiers?"

For a moment she thought he was refusing to answer again. Then she heard, "He got Branan. Now he'll come for me."

"Who is coming for you? That man there, or someone like him?"

He said, "He put a body inside the wall."

"You saw him do it?"

"I didn't mean to! It wasn't my fault!"

"I know," said Tilla, placing one hand over his. "Tell me about the man."

"I can't," the boy mumbled. "I don't know anything. I don't know what he looks like. It was too dark."

Tilla felt her shoulders slump. She had spent a whole day tracing the source of the rumor, and now she had found him, he knew nothing that was of any use at all. "Why did you say it was Branan who saw him?"

The boy became agitated. "I didn't mean to do it! I didn't mean any harm! He was hurting me!"

"The man?"

The boy shook his head violently. "Matto."

"So you told Matto something to make him stop hurting you?"

"Mam said you shouldn't tell lies. But Mam's in the next world and there's only Petta, and Petta doesn't like me."

"I don't think it's just you," said Tilla, who had the impression that Petta didn't like anyone.

He said, "Is it true people can pass through from the next world at Samain?"

"I have never seen it," Tilla confessed. The meeting she longed for with her own family had never happened. No one could tell her how to find the hills that opened at Samain to let the living go inside. All she could truthfully say was, "I think they can see us and they watch over us."

"Do you think Mam can see me?"

"I'm sure she can," Tilla assured him. "My family are all gone to the next world too. Perhaps they have met."

He said, "I thought she might come tonight."

"And so you wait for her here, where you used to live."

He nodded.

"I think she will know where to find you wherever you are," she told him, pushing away the fear that she had deserted her own ghosts by following the army. There was no time to dwell on that now. "But she may not be able to come to you. Were you here waiting for your Mam when you saw the man with the body?"

He shrugged. "I s'pose." He looked at her. "All of your family?"

"All of them. The Northerners came raiding."

There was no need to explain further: Even a child of this age had heard the stories. He said, "Are you still sad?"

"It is an ache that I carry inside me wherever I go," she told him. "But I am still glad I have my life here. I do not want to join them before my time comes."

He nodded thoughtfully. They sat in silence for a while. Dismal, still keeping his distance, allowed the horses to graze. The sun was sinking in a clear sky and a chilly breeze rattled the bushes.

"We must go," said Tilla, getting to her feet. "I should have taken you back to your family before. They will worry about you, out alone tonight."

"No they won't," he said, and she was afraid it was true.

"I will get someone to take you back." She was sure the Legion would help. She had visited Aedic's family on a military-branded horse, with an escort from the fort, and the last thing the army wanted was any whiff of their being involved in the disappearance of another boy. "Do you want to ride my horse?"

He nodded, eager. "I've never been on a horse before."

She gave him a leg up into the saddle, ignoring Dismal's obvious disapproval, and led the animal down toward the little fort. Halfway there the boy interrupted her gloomy thoughts about being no closer to finding Branan with "Tilla can't be short for Darlughdacha."

"It's a long story," she told him.

60

THE FUR TRADERS had apparently left Coria at midday, heading
north on their mountain ponies. There was very little daylight left
now. No time to round up helpers. No time to leave messages with anyone
except Susanna, whose warnings to be careful were barely necessary. Ruso
suspected he was about to do one of the stupidest things he had ever done
in his life, so he was definitely going to do it as carefully as possible.

Turning the mare's head north, he urged her into a canter up the long
gradient. He wished he still had the bay. Biting was a minor problem. This
one's gait was like riding a cart down a flight of steps. The bay would have
been less conspicuous too. The gray would be highly visible against everything except fog, and to his left the sun was drifting downward in a clear
sky. Under tonight's full moon, she would shine like a beacon.

He pressed on, because there was nothing else to do but sit easy and try
not to bounce as the mare carried him past the first milestone. He let her
relax into a trot for a while as he passed the second. Many of the names
engraved on the stones were of places much farther north: destinations no
Roman was ever likely to see again. He had met veterans who could
remember tramping south down this road, part of a disgruntled with-
drawal of troops that left the northern tribes rejoicing as they settled down
into their old domestic rivalries. Still, there were some scattered military

outposts up here, left behind to keep an eye on the border tribes whose territories straddled the wall. With luck, he would run into one of the patrols from Habitancum or Bremenium on the way up. If he did not, and the traders got the boy beyond the reach of Rome, he had no idea what he would do. He urged the mare back into a canter.

He saw no patrols: just locals, some carrying piles of firewood. People joining their neighbors for tonight's celebrations, untroubled by any curfew beyond the one they imposed upon themselves because their heads were full of ghost stories. Occasionally a group contained an elderly person clinging on to a donkey or wrapped in blankets and being jolted along in a cart.

Four milestones. The road was rougher up here, although the potholes had been filled with rubble and it was flanked with wide grass verges, a comforting reminder that he was not yet completely out of civilization. He tried to keep an eye on his surroundings, but the sun was sliding down behind the western hills, and every time he looked to the left he was dazzled. Soon it would be dark. If Susanna had managed to let the CO at Coria know that Ruso had rushed off alone in pursuit of the missing boy, it seemed no support had been arranged. There was no sign of any cavalry galloping north to join him, and he doubted they would signal ahead. He would be alone on the road with no protection beyond his weapons and his armor, which were already attracting the wrong sort of attention. He had seen the looks on the faces of other travelers and the way men in the fields stopped work to stare as he passed. He wondered about pausing to hide his kit and picking it up on the way back, but he knew that, close up, he could no more pass for a native than the horse could. He would just look like a deserter, despised by both sides.

And then he reached the fork in the road. He slowed the mare to a walk and stopped to ask a couple of small girls lugging a bucket of water whether they had seen the Northerners go past on their ponies. They stared up at him, openmouthed. One of them let go of the handle and fled as the water sloshed all over the remaining child's feet. She stood as if paralyzed, her eyes wide with shock. Ruso backed the horse away from her. When the scream finally came, she flung the bucket toward him and ran. Struggling to steady the frightened horse, Ruso debated briefly whether to stay and explain or get away. The sounds of angry voices and footsteps crashing through the woods told him that he and the horse were of one mind. Behind him, the shouts of "Leave our kids alone!" died away and then there were only the hoofbeats and the voice in his head asking, *What if the traders went the other way?* And even if they had not, the question remained: *What are you going to do when you find them? Reason with them? Appeal to their sense of natural justice? Offer them money?* He had very little with him, but if they agreed to come to the nearest army base (how likely was that?), he might be able to talk his way into borrowing some. On the other hand, since they had just sold their furs, they might not be interested in money. After all, they had just given some of it away to buy a slave.

His courage was fading with the light. What had he been thinking, back there on the bridge in Coria? That he could tackle half a dozen tribesmen by himself? That the fur traders would be businessmen like Lupus, pretending to respect the law and eager to retain a little goodwill in exchange for the army's protection? That he could catch up with them and say, *Can we have our boy back, please?*

Ahead of him, a figure was pulling up the staked chain of a pony that had been grazing on the grass verge. Keeping his distance this time, Ruso asked his question. He was in luck. The old man looked him up and down for a moment as if deciding whether it was wise to speak, and then admitted that he had seen the fur traders pass by some time ago. They might have had a boy with them. No, he did not know what sort of boy. He had not taken much notice. It was best not to have anything to do with the fur traders if you could help it.

When asked why, the old man told him that they lived in the wild and hunted things for a living and were half bear themselves. They had a manner of speaking amongst themselves that nobody understood. Now that they had been to town and traded furs for their winter supplies, they would go back into the mountains and not be seen for months.

Ruso tried to ignore the shriveling sensation inside his stomach. When he asked how long ago they had passed, the man looked blank. Presumably it was not the sort of question he was used to answering. This was a world with no clocks, where an often invisible sun was the only way to judge the passing of time.

Finally the man said, "They may be at the Three Oaks Inn. That is where they leave the road and go toward the hills."

"How far is that?"

"Two more of your miles."

Ruso, thoroughly unsettled, thanked him and rode on, partly because of a foolish desire not to look like a coward in front of a native, but mostly because the five or six miles of lonely road behind him were just as nerve-racking as the two in front.

Once the old man and his pony had faded into the gloom, Ruso's doubts returned. It seemed Branan's captors would turn off the road well short of Habitancum, where he had been hoping he might muster some help. He was heading alone into unknown territory where he knew none of the natives. He did not have the authority of the Legion, nor the support from Tilla, Valens, or Albanus that he had enjoyed in past crises. He did not even have the slim protection of being able to prove he was a healer: He had brought no instruments or medicines with him that would mark him out from any other Roman officer.

He dug the fingers of one hand into a fistful of coarse gray mane and glanced at the looming shapes of the trees on either side of the road. This was madness. He should turn back. There was no shame in admitting he had made a mistake. He should go back and fetch help now, while he still could.

Except . . . Branan was somewhere ahead of him, and if he did not find those men before they headed off into the hills, he never would. How could he face Senecio and Enica, knowing he had abandoned their child? What would he say to Tilla? He thought of her, back in the relative safety of Parva, hunting for the rumormonger and trying to comfort the family she had so wanted to be a part of. She too had been stolen from her people and taken north. She had spent long months waiting for rescuers who never came.

He was not going to let that happen to Branan. However things turned out tonight, he would do his best to let the boy know he was not forgotten. Someone had come. Someone wanted to take him home.

61

THE GATE GUARDS were unusually welcoming, although they were disappointed when Tilla told them the nervous-looking boy she had brought in on an army horse was not the one who had been stolen. The watch captain had a message to show her: It seemed Branan had been taken to Coria by a slave trader, and her husband had gone to get him back. In the light of this the tribune had called off the local search and he was now relying on Tilla to persuade the father to stop hanging around the fort and go home.

"Has the old man been told this?"

"We tried, miss, but he won't believe us."

Senecio wept with relief when she told him the news was true: She had read the words for herself in her husband's own writing. Branan was alive, and the army was on the trail of the slave trader. Aedic stood pink-faced and staring at the ground as she knelt beside the old man and assured him that slave traders looked after their stock and that none of them wanted to be seen dealing in stolen children. Grasping Senecio's cold hand, she reminded him that her husband was a man of authority. Such an officer had only to say that Branan had been snatched from his family and the trader would have to hand him over.

Finally, the old man agreed to go home. The watch captain was so relieved to be rid of him that he did not even bother to object when Tilla asked to have Aedic safely delivered home too.

On the short walk back to Ria's bar she was stopped two or three times by people wanting to know the latest news. She told them and tried to share their delight. Only now that there was hope for Branan was it dawning on her that she had traveled many miles today and barely eaten. She needed to sit down quietly in the company of a good dinner. A rich tasty soup with fresh bread to dunk in it, or . . .

She stopped on the threshold of Ria's, her hands raised to her face in dismay. There were three people sharing a jug of something at the table beside the counter, and until this moment she had forgotten about all of them. Somewhere the goddess must be laughing. Here was her prayed-for Samain meeting with her family. Her cousin Aemilia and Aemilia's husband Rianorix had traveled all the way from Coria expecting to celebrate a wedding blessing that was not happening. If that were not bad enough, sitting on the stool next to them was the thin form of Albanus, who had arrived to visit his nephew.

"Cousin!" cried Aemilia. "At last! Where have you been?"

"Don't worry, mistress!" Virana called from behind the bar. "I've told everybody everything!"

Everything? That the wedding blessing was withdrawn, that Albanus's nephew had disappeared days ago, and that a child had been stolen? No wonder nobody was looking happy.

Aemilia's artificial curls flopped around her ears as she made a great deal of fuss about the wasted journey, using the fluent Latin that her father had insisted she learn. "We would never have gone to find you at the old man's farm if we had known, cousin. It was so embarrassing! Thank goodness we brought our own cart for the luggage and we left the children at home." They had even brought a gift: a pair of fine linen sheets that she managed to mention several times while her husband poured himself another beer and drank it. He looked away when Tilla caught him sneaking a glance at her.

She was glad she was not alone with him. It must be at least three—no, four years. He was little changed. Perhaps a little heavier. No doubt Aemilia would make sure he came home every night for dinner. If the northern raiders had not come and snatched Tilla away, this was the man she would have married. What was that expression Senecio had used

about her mother? *We were very close at one time.* Had her mother and
Senecio expected to marry too? And if the pair of them had met again in
later years, after they had both grown into different lives, would Senecio
have hidden behind his beer and left his wife to do all the talking, as
Rianorix was now?

Albanus was clutching his wine cup with both hands and looking
intently at Aemilia as if he were waiting for a sign that she might stop
talking. "I can only say I am sorry," Tilla said when she could get a
word in.

"We heard about the stolen boy all the way over in Coria," Aemilia
continued, "but of course we didn't know you had anything to do with
it. What a dreadful thing, to lose a child! We left strict instructions with
the staff, didn't we?" She did not wait for her husband to respond. "The
children are to be watched at all times. The nursery slave is to watch the
children and the housekeeper is to watch the nursery slave and make sure
she does what she's told. You can't be too careful."

Tilla said, "Branan is with a—" as Albanus said, "I hear your husband
is searching for the boy." But before Tilla could explain, Aemilia
exclaimed, "We did our best to help, you know. I got the staff to search
the whole of the brewery and the yard and check the malting house in
case that poor boy was in there, although I don't know why he would be
unless he escaped and tried to hide. Of course, if we'd known it was his
father doing your wedding blessing, we would never have set out. Oh,
and, cousin, do you remember Susanna in the snack bar? She said to wish
you well and if she hears anything about the boy she'll be in touch
straightaway."

Albanus took a quick breath, but he was not fast enough.

"She'll be so disappointed when I tell her there's no blessing. Perhaps
you could get someone else to do it. Have you thought of that? Now that
we've come all this way, I'm sure we could find somebody you haven't
upset. Don't you think so?" She twisted round to survey the other occupants of the bar. "Perhaps the owner here could suggest someone."

Tilla put a hand on Albanus's arm. "I am sorry you had a wasted trip
too," she told him. "My husband is away searching for the stolen boy and
nobody is here to see you."

Aemilia turned her attention to Albanus. "It's such a shame," she
agreed. "Fancy your nephew not being here after you've come all that
way! You poor man! You'd think somebody would know where he was,
wouldn't you?"

Albanus glanced across to where Virana was lighting the lamp in the bracket above the counter. "Nobody was available to talk to me at the fort," he said to Tilla. "The young lady here did try to explain, but I don't think I quite understand. Could you please tell me exactly what has happened to my nephew?"

62

RIA'S DIMLY LIT storeroom smelled of beer and onions, but it was the only respectable place Tilla could think of to hold a private conversation. Wishing her husband were here to explain all this himself, she fetched down what was left of Candidus's kit. While Albanus exclaimed softly over it, lifting the shield and trying the helmet on for size, she put the lamp in the bracket, brushed the dust off the third step of the loft ladder, and sat down.

Albanus put the kit to one side and perched himself on top of a barrel. He placed his hands on his bony knees and leaned forward as if he were anxious not to miss anything.

Still trying to think how to smooth the path of the bad news, Tilla cleared her throat. "Your nephew was here until a few days ago," she said. "He worked in the hospital for my husband."

When she hesitated, Albanus prompted, "And then?"

"Then one day he did not come. My husband waited, but he did not turn up."

"Did he send a message?"

"No. So my husband spoke to lots of people and sent letters asking for him and found some of his things still in his tent, but nobody knew where he was. Then he arranged for the army to search all the local farms, but Candidus was not there, either."

"I see." Albanus pressed his hands between his knees. "Everyone's gone to a great deal of trouble."

She would not tell him that the search had wrecked her own chances of a wedding blessing. "The officers think he has run away."

"I see. Oh, dear. I had so hoped that joining the Legion . . ." His voice trailed away into a disappointed silence.

Tilla shifted uneasily on the ladder and wondered if it would be kinder to stop there. Albanus seemed to have no trouble believing that his nephew had run off. But then he looked up. "You said that the officers think he deserted his post. Is that what you think too?"

She blinked. She had expected Albanus to ask her what her husband thought. This was a much harder question to dodge. She said, "I think it is possible that he has run away, yes."

Albanus said nothing for a moment. Tilla thought she heard the curfew being sounded. Out in the bar, Ria was shouting that it was closing time. Then he said, "Please do me the honor of being completely honest with me. Is there reason to think that something worse has happened to him?"

"That is possible too," Tilla confessed, wondering how to explain. "It is all very complicated."

To her surprise, this seemed to bring Albanus to himself. He delved into the folds of his tunic and pulled out a writing tablet, followed by a stylus. "Perhaps I can help," he said, flipping the tablet open and sitting poised for dictation like the clerk he had once been. "Please. Tell me everything."

When she had finished he spent a moment rereading his notes, tapping the blunt end of the stylus on the edge of the tablet. Finally he said, "This is all very worrying."

"It may not be Candidus," she said, carefully avoiding saying the word *body*.

Albanus tucked the tablet into his belt and propped the stylus behind one ear. "It may not," he agreed, "but his knife was found near the right place at the wall, and you have not mentioned anyone else who was missing at the time."

"It could be someone that nobody knows." She tried to make that sound more likely by adding, "From a long way away."

"Perhaps it is," he agreed, getting to his feet. "Yes. Of course. Thank you for explaining. Thank you for everything you and your husband did to help find my nephew. I'm so sorry to have caused everyone all this bother."

Her "Where are you going?" came out harsher than she had intended, and Albanus looked startled. He began to apologize again.

"Don't you want to look for him?"

He scratched his thinning hair. "I shall have to think what to do. This has all been rather a shock."

She said, "Sit down, Albanus!" and to her surprise he did exactly that. "I know you would rather deal with my husband," she told him, "but he is not here, and you only have me, and if we do not work together, he will be very cross with us both."

Was that relief on his face?

"Tonight I am tired from trying to find missing boys," she said, "but my husband is dealing with all that now. In the morning we must think of a new way to look for Candidus. Something the tribune will not find out about."

Albanus's eyes widened. "You think a tribune is involved in this?"

"Accius is a good officer," she explained, "but his orders are to get the wall built. He is never going to agree that there may be someone buried inside it, even though I have met the person who saw it happen. He will want to cover up anything he finds out, so that the season's work is finished and the Legion can go home. If your nephew is inside the wall and we leave everything to the soldiers, you will never know."

Albanus shuddered, and Tilla knew he was thinking of Candidus's spirit, condemned to wander these windswept hills without the proper rites that would send him on his way to the next world, or whatever it was that Romans thought was on the other side of their gloomy River Styx. Then he straightened his shoulders and drew himself up to his full height so that his gaze met her chin. "I promised my sister I would look after her son," he said. "I will be grateful for any help you can offer."

"Good," said Tilla, stifling a yawn and feeling her stiffening muscles protest as she rose from the step. She was too tired to feel hungry now. She led him out into the bar, where Virana was sweeping up and Ria was setting out clean cups for tomorrow morning. Her cousin and Rianorix had gone, and she had failed to wish them good night or even find out where they were staying. "I have kept you past the curfew."

Virana said, "He's staying here," just as they were all startled by a bang on the shutters.

They exchanged glances. Ria shouted, "Too late, we're closed!"

"Open up!" came the voice. "News from Coria!"

63

A NATIVE YOUTH WITH wild hair and bleary eyes stumbled over the threshold and looked at the three women. "Which one of you is the Medicus's wife?"

Tilla stepped forward. "Is the boy found?"

The lad sniffed and wiped his nose with the back of his hand. "Message from Susanna. She says to tell you the boy's been taken north by some fur traders. The Medicus has gone after him, and he wants you to tell the tribune to look again at Mallius."

"North?" Tilla put a hand to her mouth. She remembered being taken away by strangers from another tribe. The thought of something like that happening to a child made her shudder. "Who went with the Medicus?"

The youth shrugged. "That's all I know. I came as fast as I could. Thought I'd never get here. There's patrols out."

"You are very brave, coming all that way," Virana told him. "Especially tonight."

"And now you'll be wanting a drink and some supper," put in Ria, as if he had arrived specially to inconvenience her.

The youth grinned. "Thanks, missus. And the horse too."

Virana pointed out that he would need a bed for the night as well, but the youth said he would be happy to sleep in the stable. Ria told Virana to bring food and went to rouse her husband to deal with the horse. When she was gone, Virana said, "Are you all right, mistress? You look very tired."

"You should rest," Albanus agreed. "There is nothing we can do tonight."

Tilla stared at them both. "Rest?" she demanded. "My husband will be murdered by foreigners, and Branan will be taken up into the mountains and never seen again! How can I rest?"

Albanus gulped. "Are you quite sure?"

She subsided onto a bench. "No. Of course not. I am sorry." She pressed her eyelids with her fingertips to relieve the tiredness.

"Why has the tribune got to look at Mallius?" asked Virana.

"I don't know." Tilla opened her eyes and blinked the dryness away. "Don't tell anyone."

"Has he done something bad?"

"I am not even sure who he is," she admitted.

"Oh, you know!" Virana insisted. "The one who used to make his hair lighter. The one who hurt his wrist. He likes wine and not beer."

None of those things was a reason for the tribune to take an interest in him.

"You must have seen him," Virana continued. "He was one of the ones who went to search the farm and they upset everybody looking for Candidus, and then people thought one of them might have stolen Branan and then they didn't."

The youth had gone to see to the horse, Virana was in the kitchen fetching his food, and Tilla was alone with Albanus in the bar. He looked as downcast as she felt. She tried to think of something hopeful to say but could not. Finally he said, "Your husband is a good man."

"I know," she said, ashamed of wishing that sometimes he would be a little less good and a little more safe. She had no idea how she would sleep tonight after hearing Susanna's message. She must try to think about something else. "We should look at this Mallius ourselves," she said. "He might know what happened to Candidus."

Albanus interlaced his fingers around his wine cup. "It is kind of you to suggest it, but is he not safely inside a barracks somewhere?"

"I mean it," she insisted. "Before the tribune gets the message in the morning and has a chance to cover anything up."

Albanus stared into the dregs of his wine. "Even if we are able to speak with him, we have no power to investigate, and he has no incentive to tell us anything."

It was true. Whoever had caused Candidus's disappearance must have lied repeatedly since then: Why would he stop now? They did not even know what they were accusing him of. They could hardly stand in front of the man like angry parents, demanding, "Is there something you would like to tell us?"

They could not speak to him at all if he was on one side of a military wall tonight and they were on the other. "We have Candidus's kit," she said, thinking aloud. "Are you about the same size?"

Albanus shook his head. "Much of what is here used to be mine," he admitted, "but I'm afraid nobody is likely to mistake me for a legionary with no armor or belt or weapons. And there is the matter of the password."

The ladder creaked as Tilla got to her feet. "I am going outside to make an offering to the goddess," she told him. "Perhaps she will help."

She bought three perfect white eggs from Ria, who was busy making sure all the slops were cleared out of the kitchen and the hearth fire was raked. Even in town it was wise to follow the Samain customs.

The yard was almost dark but she felt oddly safe kneeling under the apple tree, hearing the horse shifting about in the stable and surrounded by the high fence with the gate barred against thieves. The gods were listening tonight, she was sure of it. They had already answered one prayer, even if it was not in the way that she had wanted. She had asked to see her family; she had been shown Aemilia.

Scraping a little hole between the roots of the tree, she said the new prayer and then poured out the contents of the eggs one by one. As the glistening liquid sank away into the earth, the idea came to her.

Back in the privacy of the storeroom, with the youth gulping down a late supper in the bar, Albanus was not impressed with what he heard. It was not, he felt, an approach that her husband would recommend.

"Perhaps not," Tilla agreed. "But my husband is not here. Do you want the man who killed Candidus to be punished or not?"

Albanus shifted his position on the lid of the barrel. "That apparently simple question is rather difficult to answer," he said. "You see, those are not valid alternatives." He raised and lowered his hands in parallel, as if he were shaping the argument he was about to present to her. "The premise behind your question is that my misgivings about your plan indicate an unwillingness to pursue the disappearance of my nephew. Whereas what I am questioning is—"

"If you have a better plan, I will be glad to hear it."

The hands dropped. "No."

"So," she continued, wondering if Albanus's nitpicking was one of the reasons Grata had called off their betrothal, "we know that we cannot make this man confess anything. We know we may never find out the truth. But if this works and he is guilty, the memory of tonight will haunt his waking fears and punish him in his nightmares. If he is innocent, we will all go home to bed and it will be just another strange story of Samain."

Albanus, as she expected, raised objections, but he could come up with nothing better.

"So," she said, "will you help me or not?"

64

GETTING PAST THE curfew was simple enough: All Tilla had to do was to wait until the patrol had passed the bar and count very slowly to twenty. The soldiers were not her main concern tonight. She pulled the hood forward to hide her hair and slunk down the deserted street in the moonlight, clutching her bag against her chest and with her fist closed around the little pouch of snakeskin she had hung around her neck for protection. She did not want to be noticed, and thus have to risk replying to a greeting. This was not, as far as she knew, one of the places where those who had left this world could pass back into it. But everyone knew about the dead pretending to befriend the living, and few of the stories ended well. That was why, when she offered up her regular Samain prayer for a sight of her family, she had always added, "And let us know each other." Then tonight the goddess had shown her Aemilia, which was not what she had wanted at all.

She tried to tread lightly, but as she passed the gloom of a doorway a burst of ferocious barking spurred her to run, hugging the bag tighter to stop the bottles clinking.

It was a relief to reach the solid gates of the fort. The gods were kind: One of the guards from earlier was still on duty and it was surprisingly easy to get in, even at this hour and without the password. With the bag of medicines, nobody questioned her story that she had been asked to visit a patient.

She understood why when she finally found herself in the comfortable warmth of Fabius's kitchen. She did not need her carefully prepared excuse for a private word with the kitchen maid: Even in the dim lamplight she took one look and simply told the cook she needed to inspect the girl's injuries. When she saw the bruises hidden beneath the drab tunic, she wanted to get hold of Fabius's vine stick and beat him with it until he looked even worse than his victim. Instead all she could do was offer salve and sympathy as the girl gave a broken account of what had happened. Now she understood why Daminius had hinted that he would be leaving.

"Where can I find him tonight?"

The girl blinked at her through eyes swollen with crying. "I am not allowed to go near him. I should not speak or even think of him."

"Just tell me where he might be," said Tilla. "I think he can help me find out who stole the boy."

"But he knows nothing! Why does nobody believe him? He was with me!"

Tilla put her hand over the girl's. "I believe you both," she said, "but I need to talk to him. Someone has come who will help us, and if this works, it could make things better for him."

And if it didn't, he would be in worse trouble. All of which made her feel doubly anxious as she strode down the paved street in the moonlight, carrying her bag at her side and following the girl's directions to the black hulk of the barrack block. *The last door on the left. Do not look nervous. Act as if knocking on the doors of soldiers' quarters at night is a perfectly respectable thing for a married woman to do. If it goes wrong, you can always scream.*

She did not get as far as the doors, because the steady tramp of boots and the jingle of metal strap ends on a military belt grew louder and a voice said, "Are you lost, miss? That's the barracks."

Do not sound anxious. Or friendly.

"I need to speak with Optio Daminius." The effort of holding her voice down from a squeak made it oddly gruff, as if she were trying to talk like a man.

Whoever this was let out a long breath. There was a scrape of gravel as his feet shifted. She mouthed a silent prayer to Christos and any other god that might be listening and lifted her bag, hoping the man could see what it was in the stark light. "I am the wife of your medicus. I need to ask Daminius for an escort to visit a patient."

He said, "Is it true the boy's been taken to Coria, miss?"

"It is," she said, not wanting to share the bad news about the fur traders. "My husband has gone to look for him."

"That's good," he said, probably wondering whether her absent husband knew what she was up to. "Wait there, miss."

Moments later she overheard, "You got Daminius there, mate? Tell him it's his lucky night."

65

THE MOON HAD turned the world into silver with inky shadows. Ruso could make out the road stretching ahead, but the only things he could confidently identify in front of him were the pale peaks of the mare's ears. On either side, beyond the skeletons of trees, orange pinpoints of Samain bonfires appeared and vanished again as he passed the hills.

With luck, the fur traders would have stopped for the night. He would still be gaining on them even though he needed to let his tired mount slow to a walk for a while. He peered at the verges, searching for the next milestone and hoping he had not missed it. In this light it might be hard to tell the Three Oaks from any other building.

A couple of hundred paces farther on, he urged the mare back into a trot, but only for a few strides. He knew what to expect from this horse now, and this wasn't it. He tried again. The mare responded, but the regular lurch was still there, and he saw her head dip each time the offside front leg went forward.

Ruso swore under his breath.

He was in the dark, miles from anywhere, on a lone hunt for men who killed for a living, and now he had a lame horse.

There was nothing for it but to get down and walk. Catching himself thinking that at least it wasn't raining—gods above, he was starting to think like a Briton—he loosened the girth and ran one hand down the mare's nearside leg, but he could neither see in the dark nor feel through the muck of the road. He wiped his fingers in the mare's mane and began to lead her up the road.

He need not have worried about seeing the Three Oaks: If he had not spotted the sparks rising into the sky from the bonfire, he would have heard the wailing pipes and the shouts of people cheering on the dancers. Of course. They would be celebrating Samain here too, rejoicing in being alive as they frightened each other with stories about the dead walking.

The Three Oaks was set well back from the road. Its land was surrounded by a ditch, with a bank of earth on the far side and a fence on top. The gates were shut and nobody seemed to be about, so he scrambled across the ditch. Through a gap in the fence, he could see a crowd circling the flames more or less in time to the music, yelling one of those British chants that he never associated with anything good. Beyond the fire, leaning against the side of the building, was a knot of men with dark shapes over their shoulders that could be animal skins.

The racket the dog made at his arrival must have been heard, but it was a while before anyone made a response. He had to bang on the gate three times before a voice cried out in British, wanting to know who was there.

"I am a stranger in need of water and rest!" he replied in the same tongue, hoping his grasp of the traditional request for hospitality might earn him some native respect. "My horse went lame."

In response he heard only the chanting and the music. Then it struck him that he had chosen the worst possible way to approach a lone gate slave on the one night of the year when the Britons' heads were full of tales about dangerous strangers prowling around after dark. It was just as well he had not announced that he was looking for a boy. Switching to Latin, he shouted, "Medical Officer Gaius Petreius Ruso, Twentieth Valeria Victrix! Open up!"

The gate creaked open an inch, then another inch, and then far enough for him to get his boot in the gap. The slave stammered in rough but comprehensible Latin that Sir could come in, but he would have to share a bed, and there was no food except what was being roasted.

"Better than being on the road," said Ruso as the gate was slammed shut behind him and the bar scraped into place.

He surrendered his sword and led the limping mare across the cobbles. The ostler did not look pleased to see him: Ruso seemed to have interrupted the after-dark guided tour of the stables that he was giving to a very giggly girl.

He was too late for the baths, which was just as well, as he had no intention of wasting time in them—although what he was going to do instead, he did not know. Glancing across to confirm that the men in animal skins were still lounging against the wall, he went to join the crowd.

The fur traders were still keeping to themselves on the edge of the celebrations, clutching drinks and watching the dancers. He could not see a boy with them. His gaze followed the track of one small figure after another, but he recognized no one.

There was no reason for the men to suspect he was pursuing them, so he had no hesitation in working his way around the edge of the dance to stand nearby. It was not difficult: nobody here seemed keen to stand next to a soldier, especially one who had been on the road without bathing for as long as Ruso had. Finally he was no more than five paces away.

There were half a dozen of them: big men with shaggy hair and thick animal pelts around their necks that made their shoulders look even bigger. But it was the shape he now saw on the ground at their feet that caught his attention. The light from the fire came and went but finally he made out the figure of a boy, curled up asleep like a puppy. Ruso took a sharp breath.

He had found Branan.

He could not remember any other evening taking so long to pass. Alone in the dark amongst a strange tribe, his previous confidence that everyone was united against a child snatcher had waned. He was hungry, exhausted, and sore from riding, and not sure he could trust his own judgment. There seemed to be no other Roman guests, and no obvious surveillance, either. Did that mean that these people could be trusted, or that the local commander did not want to pick a fight? This was not a *mansio*, a safe haven for traveling Romans. If he told the staff who that slave boy was, would they back him up? Or would they bundle him aside, not wanting trouble with their customers? If he got it wrong, and Branan was lost tonight, he could be lost forever.

While Ruso argued with himself, the fur traders' capacity for drink seemed to be enormous and they clearly had no intention of going to sleep until it was filled. A couple of them went forward to join the dance, but the one with the boy at his feet stayed propped against the wall, talking to his companions, sometimes cupping one hand around his mouth to shout over the pipes and the chanting.

After the dancing the storytellers got to work while everyone else sat around the fire and ate. Ruso crouched down and accepted a share of the roast meat. These days he could understand much of what was being said, which made the storytelling marginally less tedious than it had been in the past, but tonight he was not interested in the tangled and strangely inconclusive affairs of the British dead. Just a few paces away, Branan still seemed to be asleep. He hoped they had not drugged him. The gods alone knew what had happened to the boy over the last three days, and his trials were not over yet. Even if Ruso managed to creep up and rescue him while the men were asleep—so far he had no better plan—they would have to escape on foot.

He was pinching himself to stay awake when something scratchy and malodorous pushed up against his neck from behind. He shifted away but someone seized his arm and a gruff voice spoke in his ear. It took him a moment to disentangle the accent. "You speak our tongue, Roman?"

"Some."

"My brother wants to know if you like small boys." The man's other hand pointed directly at Branan.

Ruso swallowed. "I might be interested."

"We know. You keep looking at him. How much will you offer?"

He could hardly believe his luck. "Let me have a look at him first."

The blow knocked him sideways. It was a moment before he could lift himself above the fuzziness and work out that the shrieking and slapping were coming from a woman in whose lap he had landed. Apologizing, he got up and staggered, stumbling over several more people and rubbing his ear. All the fur traders were gathered together now, shouting at him and pointing. He remembered what he had heard just before the blow. "Child snatcher! Leave his son alone!"

Others voices had taken up the cry: "Child-snatcher!"

"Get him!"

"Trying to steal that man's son!"

"It's the child snatcher!"

Somewhere a voice was shouting for calm but hands were pulling at him, hauling at his armor and his tunic and grabbing his hair. Someone punched him in the head and he stumbled, lunging for something to grab onto to keep his balance. If he went down now he would not get up.

"Branan!" he yelled. "Branan, wake up, it's the Medicus!"

"Ask him what he did with the boy!" shouted someone.

"There he is!" he yelled, wrenching an arm loose and struggling to climb over his tormentors. "That boy is stolen! Branan, wake up! It's the Medicus, come to take you home!"

"Child snatcher!"

"Liar!"

Then it was all fists and boots and elbows and yelling and pain, the stink of sweat and the tang of blood in his mouth. When he fell, he was still shouting Branan's name, and he barely saw the flash of firelight on the blade.

66

TILLA LENGTHENED HER stride to stay between the two soldiers, who were keeping up a smart military pace along the moonlit road. The breeze snatched at her clothes and sent cold fingers down her neck. There must be Samain bonfires all around, but they were hidden on the left by the whispering black woods, and on the right by the rise of the land and the half-built wall that ran in silhouette along its crest.

She had guessed well: She had been able to persuade a bitter Daminius to help her, and to her relief he still had enough influence to bring Mallius with him, which was the whole point of asking. So here she was, a healer with two legionaries kindly guarding her as she answered a nighttime call to a patient who did not exist. At the time it had seemed like a clever plan. But now wandering spirits sighed in the trees with every gust of wind. All of Albanus's objections made sense, and she wished she was back by the fire at Ria's.

Seeing her glance at the woods, Daminius said, "All right, miss?"

"I thought I heard something."

"A fox or a badger, miss," he said, loud enough for Mallius to hear. He chuckled. "Or one of your ghosts."

"You should not show disrespect. You do not know who is listening."

"Sorry, miss."

She was slightly breathless with the effort of keeping up, but her escort did not offer to slow the pace. She guessed they too would be glad when this was over. "We should be safe," she said. "I made an offering before I came out."

"We'll look after you, miss," Mallius assured her, adjusting his grip on his shield. She frowned. She did not want this man to think about helping her. She wanted him to be more nervous than she was herself, otherwise this trip would be a waste of time.

Where was Albanus? Scanning ahead, she said, "My husband says I am foolish to be afraid of the man in the wall."

"Don't you worry, miss," Daminius told her. "All the officers say it's nonsense."

There he was! Albanus. Crossing the road about fifty paces in front of them. He was wearing Candidus's helmet, just as they had agreed. The big rectangular shield covered most of his body. That and the dark cloak he had borrowed hid the absence of armor, a sword, and a proper military belt. "Your patient is a lucky woman, miss," Daminius continued, pretending he had seen nothing. "A lot of healers wouldn't go out tonight."

Daminius was a good actor. She had guessed that he would be: How else had he managed to deceive his centurion about the kitchen maid?

The figure of Albanus dipped as it stepped down to cross the ditch. By the time they were level with it, it was walking away from them over the grass.

"What do you think, Mallius?" Tilla asked, forcing herself not to watch as Albanus approached the woods. "Is there a man in the wall?"

No reply.

"Answer the lady, soldier!" ordered Daminius. "Well? Is there a dead man inside the wall?"

Mallius, who had turned to stare at the departing Albanus, returned his gaze to the front and mumbled that he didn't know.

"Of course you know!" snapped Daminius. "There's nothing up there. It's official. The lady's husband is quite right."

Mallius said, "Yes, sir," and glanced behind him again.

"People are still saying things," Tilla observed as the road climbed the slope. "Only today I spoke to someone who swears he saw the body being hidden. He even says he saw who did it."

"He's lying," Daminius said.

"Perhaps," said Tilla. "But I think in the morning I will take this person to the tribune. Then they can go and open the wall in the place he shows them, and everybody will see if there is anything there."

"I'd pay to join that work party," said Daminius.

"It will be good to know the truth," Tilla continued. "People are afraid. They are saying the man's spirit walks at night, searching for someone to give him the proper burial rites."

She risked a glance and caught Mallius staring at her. She hoped she had not said too much. It had been a long day, and she was not at her best. "Anyway," she said briskly, "it is good news about the boy. My husband will bring him back safe tomorrow and we will find out who stole him. Then perhaps this curfew will be—"

She stopped. They all saw it at the same time: something moving on the road far ahead. The sound of hoofbeats came toward them on the wind. For once Tilla was relieved to catch the glint of moonlight on armor. Moments later they were surrounded by four riders on stamping horses, and Daminius was explaining who his small party were and what they were doing out here. She dared not look to see where Albanus was, but she saw that Mallius was glancing round as if he were wondering the same thing. That was good.

Satisfied, the cavalry patrol cantered off into the night. Mallius propped his spear against his shield and loosened his chinstrap with one finger, gazing after the riders as if wishing he could join them.

Fifty paces farther on he glanced back again. Tilla turned. The sight of the soldier striding along behind them made her jump even though she was half expecting it. Albanus was too far away for his features to be visible in the poor light, but close enough for his slight frame to recall that of his nephew.

Mallius said, "We're being followed."

They stopped. Gazing at Albanus, who now stood like a statue in the road, Daminius said, "Where?"

"Did you see someone?" asked Tilla. She watched Mallius narrow his eyes to squint at Albanus in the stark pallor of the moon.

"Description?" Daminius prompted.

"I thought . . . one of our men."

"Moonlight," said Daminius, as if that explained everything. "But I wouldn't put it past the natives to creep around in the dark. Keep your eyes open."

Mallius hissed, "Look again, sir." He had his spear raised now. Tilla hoped he was not going to fling it to see if the ghost was solid.

Daminius turned to Tilla. "Can you see anything, miss?"

"I see the road," she said. "And the trees, and the moon."

Mallius looked from one to other of them, then back at the statuelike figure on the road. His voice had an oddly strangled quality, as if all the muscles in his throat had tightened up. "There's nothing there, is there?"

"I can see there's nothing there," Daminius retorted. "You're worse than a bloody native. Sorry, miss. No offense. How far now?"

"The next turn on the left." Tilla tried to signal *Go away* behind her back. The ghost had done his job. She wanted to get back to the warmth and safety of Ria's.

"Isn't this where the missing boy lives?" Now Daminius was sounding nervous too.

"We are going to their neighbors," said Tilla. Branan's household was the last one she would want to disturb tonight. "It is about a hundred paces," she said, taking the left fork onto the track and stepping into an empty blackness where the overhanging trees blocked out the moonlight and it was impossible to see their footing. She remembered to add, for the sake of the pretense, "I thought they would send someone to meet us at the corner."

"Should have brought a torch and a flint," Daminius muttered. "I'll go in front. Miss, you walk behind me. Watch the rear, mate. Don't talk to any ghosts."

The trees bent and shuffled above them. Tilla stumbled forward, keen not to lose touch with her escort in the dark. She had chosen somewhere she would be recognized: They were on the way to the house of Inam, the boy who had last seen Branan, but she had never been down this track at night. She flinched as something snatched at her skirts and was glad to feel the scrape of a bramble as she brushed it away. "I am glad I have you with me," she said truthfully.

There was an orange glow ahead. As they drew closer she could make out a gate silhouetted against a small bonfire in the paddock by the house. The flames had died to embers, and nobody seemed to be around to tend it. Tilla pursed her lips. This was going to be awkward. She had not expected the family to be in bed.

Behind her, Daminius muttered, "I thought this was party night?"

"They are showing respect for their neighbors and the missing boy," Tilla guessed. She was going to have to disturb them now; she could hardly admit to her escort that she had invented this call to lure one of them out at night. "Hello!" she cried in British, realizing she would have to go through the whole pretense in case Mallius understood. "It is the Daughter of Lugh, the healer!"

When there was no other response, Daminius said, "Is this the right house, miss?"

Since she was not expected anywhere, it was as right as any other. "Hello?" she cried again. "It is the healer!"

A voice she recognized as Inam's father shouted, "The fire is raked and there is no water in the house! There is nothing for you here! Go away!"

Daminius said, "What's he saying?"

She could have translated the words, but he would never have understood about the creatures who came out of the burial mounds searching for homes where there was warmth and something to drink.

"It is not a spirit!" she cried, not wanting to leave the family in a state of fear. "It is me, Daughter of Lugh, friend of your neighbors. You son Inam helped me to look for Branan. I will come to the house so you can see it is me!"

She left the soldiers at the gate and carried on the rest of the conversation through the closed door, sheltering under the dark of the porch and explaining that she had been sent an urgent plea to call here. She could hear a whispered argument going on inside the house, but still there was no welcome. Finally she suggested that somebody must have played a joke on her, and they sounded relieved when she said she was sorry to disturb them and would go away.

She picked her way back across the yard to the gate, wondering if she would have a chance to explain in daylight, or whether this time next year people would be telling a fresh story of a family who had barred the door against a ghost that was trying to trick its way into the house using a false voice. Perhaps she would keep quiet. Otherwise the family would have to admit that they had sent away a lone woman in the dark after she had come to help them.

Her escort had moved away from the gate, perhaps suspecting the sight of them would frighten the family even more. Unable to see them in the inky blackness under the trees, she said softly in Latin, "I am very sorry. This was a wasted journey. Somebody got the message wrong."

Nobody answered. A fresh gust of wind sent the trees dancing and whispering. Tilla felt her stomach muscles tighten. She pushed her hood back and something brushed against her face. Only a falling leaf, surely. She drew her knife. "Daminius?" she called. "Mallius? Where are you?"

Was that a muffled cry? Then movement in the woods that was not the wind: another cry and the sound of clumsy creatures crashing through undergrowth. She tried to go toward it, but the brambles clawed her back and the sounds were getting fainter. "Daminius!"

She dragged herself out of the thorns and retreated to the gate. Clutching her bag with one hand and the knife with the other, straining to see around her in the dark, she shouted, "Daminius, where are you? It is time to leave! Come back!"

But nobody came.

67

TILLA CREPT BACK along the track toward the road, her mind racing to make some sense of what was happening. Perhaps Mallius had panicked and run away, and Daminius had given chase. If only one of them had at least shouted back. They must have heard her: The movement in the woods had sounded close by. Now she was alone here with the echoes of the old stories: the hanged man who came to life and killed the family who gave him water, the women and cattle who were stolen away into the burial mounds, and those captured alive who were sent back with impossible gifts from the rulers of the dead—buttercups and primroses in November—along with warnings of bad things to come.

She pushed the Samain tales away and moved on, reminding herself that morning was drawing closer. Something good might be revealed by the rising sun. With luck, Mallius would be caught and confess, and Albanus would find out the truth about his nephew, and all this would have been—

She stifled a scream.

"Umph!" gasped the thing she had walked into. Then it stepped back and demanded, "Who goes there?"

"Albanus!" She put away the knife and groped for an arm to cling to. Judging by the way he returned her grasp, he was as relieved as she was.

"It worked!" she whispered. "I think he has run away in fright. He will never be at peace now."

But Albanus was too agitated to listen. He was pulling her along, gabbling about getting help. "Please hurry, madam! We must get to the fort!"

She wished he would slow down. This was a bumpy farm track, not an army road, and besides, who was he to drag her about in the dark? She wrenched her arm out of his grip and stopped, her own fears fading now that she was with somebody more nervous than herself. "There is nothing we can do now," she told him. "The soldiers will find him and—"

"Madam, they are captured!"

"Captured?" She could barely see him, but she had the impression that Albanus was hopping from foot to foot in agitation.

"By natives!" He grabbed her arm again, hauling her toward the road. He was surprisingly strong for a small man who spent most of his life sitting at a desk.

"What natives? Where did they go?"

But instead of answering, Albanus gave a sudden cry and fell, almost pulling her over with him. He seemed to be writhing about on the ground, muttering words that she only heard her husband use when he thought she wasn't listening.

Tilla grabbed for her knife and crouched to make herself a smaller target, hissing, "What is it?"

"Nothing!" he gasped, not troubling to keep quiet. "It is nothing. Sorry. It will be all right in a—oh, dear!"

He had turned his foot on a stone in the track. She groped inside her bag for cooling medicines and a bandage.

"No need," he insisted. "I can get up if you give me your arm. Epictetus teaches that pain is—agh!"

Whatever Epictetus said, it was soon clear that Albanus could barely stand, let alone walk. Clinging to her arm, he gasped, "Madam, I am sorry not to be able to protect you, but someone must go and fetch help for the two men."

"Fetch help to where?" she demanded, appalled at the thought of rousing soldiers to go crashing about the local farms yet again. "Who took them?" She sat Albanus down again inside the smooth dry curve of the shield. "Tell me what you saw."

Albanus had not seen very much. Following at a suitably ghostly distance, he had heard movement in the woods and hidden himself inside the borrowed cloak. He heard people creeping past him and a soft whisper of British. Too late, he realized he should have shouted a warning to the soldiers. There was a scuffle, muffled cries, and then he thought he saw struggling figures being dragged away into the woods. The next thing he heard was Tilla calling for her escort.

"Are you sure you saw them struggling?"

"We must have the woods searched with torches in case they lie injured."

"Let me go to Senecio," said Tilla, trying not to put pressure on the damaged ankle as she unrolled the bandage around it.

"We must raise the alarm!" he insisted. "We—ow!"

"Sorry."

"We need search parties out here immediately. Before the natives get away."

"The soldiers will start a riot." She paused with the roll of bandage under his heel. "There will be fighting in every house they enter."

"Madam, please! We gain nothing by arguing. Let me finish the dressing. I am sure your husband would want us to fetch help."

He was right, of course. That was exactly what her husband would want to do, and with good reason. But if her fears were correct, then it would be the end for Senecio and his family, whether or not Branan turned up. "Albanus, if we fetch the soldiers, they will find out that Daminius was helping us, and he will be in terrible trouble even if he is rescued. Is that what you want?"

Albanus gave a shuddering sigh. "If I believed the gods cared, I would believe they are punishing me for taking part in this foolish plan."

Tilla, suspected he would have liked to add *with this foolish woman.* "We were trying to give justice for your nephew."

Albanus groaned. "I should never have—"

"Well, you did." He gasped as she tightened the knot. "Sorry. Now put your hand in mine and try to stand."

He managed to stand on one leg but insisted on leaning on the shield. He did not want her to help him walk. He wanted her to hurry away and fetch the legionaries, and when she said she would only do that when she had spoken to Senecio, he gave an "Oh!" of exasperation and took a hop away from her, using the shield in place of a stick.

"Where are you going?"

"You must do what you think is your duty, madam." There was a grunt of sudden effort, as if he were hauling the shield out of the mud, then a crunch as he placed it back down again. "I shall do mine. I have been part of a—" Here there was a splash and a muttering of "Oh, dear!" before "I have been part of a rash venture that has left two of our men in enemy hands." Another grunt. Another crunch. Another splash. "No matter that I believe one of them has done something terrible to my nephew." His voice was fainter as he hobbled away. "I must do my—agh!—my utmost to save them."

"I am trying to save them too!" she called after him. It was true, but she had an uncomfortable feeling that her husband would say she was putting Roman lives in greater danger just to save a few Britons from their own folly.

"Regardless of the consequences to myself," Albanus added, as if he were making a speech.

"Then you need to go the other way," she told him. "Turn around. The fort is north of here."

The movement stopped. When he asked if she was sure, there was suspicion in his voice.

"I will not come with you," she told him, "But you are a good friend to my husband and I would not lie to you." Skirting the barely visible puddle, she put a hand on his skinny shoulder. "May the gods protect you this night, Albanus. I will come and find you as soon as I can."

"May the gods protect us all, madam." His shoulder moved under her touch. The shield thumped down into the mud once more, and she felt water splatter over her boots as he hopped back through the puddle.

68

THERE WAS A tiger on his face. It was digging its claws into his forehead, and it had mauled him all over. Everything ached and throbbed, except the parts that stabbed instead. He should do something to make it stop. What did you do against a tiger? Nothing people tried in the arena worked for long.

Jupiter's holy bollocks, that hurt. Like having liquid fire poured over his forehead.

Play dead. Don't flinch. Don't moan. Don't . . .

Too late.

. . . flap one hand about, vaguely hoping to frighten it off.

A voice said, "He's reacting to pain, sir."

An older voice said, "Good."

Ruso wondered what was good about it. He decided to go back to sleep. Then he decided not to when the tiger gripped both sides of his head and tried to gnaw his eye out. "Get off!" came out slurred.

One eye was blinded, but the other opened to reveal a huge bloodstained shape moving about just above his nose. "No!" He tried to beat away the shape and spring up, but his body refused to listen.

"Speak to him," the older voice suggested.

"It's all right," somebody said, even though it wasn't. "We're just cleaning you up and putting a few stitches in."

A few stitches in what? "Where am I?"

"This is the treatment room," said his informer unhelpfully.

"Sick bay, Habitancum," put in the older voice. "Under the excellent care of a trainee medic of the Fourth Gauls."

Holy gods. They were letting a trainee loose on him. Perhaps they thought he was beyond saving. "Have I lost the eye?"

To his further alarm, the trainee who had been stabbing a needle through his skin said, "Has he, sir?"

"No."

Ruso thought it was the best word he had ever heard.

"You were lucky," continued the senior man. "You'll find it when the swelling goes down. We're just putting your eyebrow back together."

"Just one more," said the trainee, sounding nervous now that he was treating a patient who talked back. Then he added, as he had no doubt been trained to, "This will sting a bit."

Ruso chose a cobweb wafting in a draft above him to concentrate on and clenched his teeth. Instantly a bolt of lightning shot through his jaw and into his neck. He did not feel the needle going in.

"Oh, and we think we may need to pull a tooth," added the trainee.

Ruso was in too much pain to tell him he needn't sound so cheerful about it.

"Done!" The trainee sounded relieved.

Giant metal blades filled Ruso's vision. There was a final tug as the thread was snipped. He gave up trying to work out why he was here, and asked.

"You went to a party that got a bit out of control," answered the senior man.

That was when it came back. The bonfire. The fur traders. The crowd turning on him. He felt suddenly short of breath. "Where's the boy?"

The man said, "You can see him when we've tidied you up."

"Is he all right?"

The man said, "Tell him."

The trainee took a breath. "Bruising to the arms and face," he said. "Some rope burn around the neck and wrists. No broken bones that we can detect, and nothing life threatening."

Ruso tried to steady his breathing. Tried to think. This was something he knew about. "Did you check him all over?"

"Of course."

"Head injuries?"

"None. And he's eating everything he's given."

Ruso made an effort to relax. "I feel as though I've been kicked by a horse."

"They slashed through the ties on your lorica," said the senior man. "Then they unpeeled you like a prawn."

It was not a pleasant image, picturing the iron plates of the lorica wrenched apart to reveal the vulnerable torso inside. He said, "What have you put on the boy's rope burn?"

There was silence for a moment. Then the trainee said, "D'you think he might be a medic, sir?"

"I doubt it," the other one said. "What would a medic be doing on his own late at night at the Three Oaks?"

Ruso clutched at the side of the table and tried to pull himself up. "I need transport. I need to get the boy back to Parva."

They both laughed at that. "You're not going anywhere, my friend," said the senior of the two. "Doctor's orders."

69

TILLA TOOK A couple of deep breaths and the cold air sliced down her throat. She felt slightly calmer now that she was doing something. Walk. Keep walking. Put your mind on one thing. Do not, however much you want to, scream. By the time she reached the place where the track divided, Albanus was far behind and the twisting feeling in her stomach had become nausea. *Sacred goddess, holy mothers, great Lord Christos, let those two soldiers be safe . . .* Not only because one of them was definitely innocent and had tried to help her, but because she could not bear the thought of the consequences for everyone else if the thing she feared was really happening.

The track to the farm was invisible in the shadow of the trees. Unable to see what was beneath her, she slid in soft mud and cold water seeped over the tops of her boots. It was no worse than she deserved.

It had not been up to her to do anything about Mallius. That part of the message had been for the tribune. Yesterday her husband had told her very clearly that she could not tell Daminius what to do, but she had thought she knew better. Now she had not only shamed her husband, she had put his comrades in danger too.

"It will all be all right when the sun rises," she whispered, as if speaking it aloud would make it true. "Perhaps in the morning my husband will come back with Branan and everything will be all right again."

They might even have the wedding blessing. That would please Aemilia.

Aemilia. How could she have forgotten to tell her cousin the blessing was withdrawn? Was there anything she had not made a mess of lately?

You should not have used Daminius.

"Oh, shut up!"

There was no sign of the dog as she pushed open the gate, which was not good. *Holy Christos, mothers and goddess, let them all be asleep in bed. Let them not be a part of whatever is happening. Then I can run to the fort for help.* Tapping a knuckle on the door, she said, "It is the Daughter of Lugh. Is anyone awake?"

To her surprise the creak of someone getting out of a chair was immediate. A quiet female voice that she recognized as Cata's mother came from the other side of the door. "Go away, Daughter of Lugh. It is not safe for you here."

"I need to talk to Senecio and Conn!"

"They are not here. Nobody is here. Only me and Cata, looking after the children."

"Where did they all go?"

Silence.

"Are you still there?"

"Go!" the woman insisted. "They do not trust you. They know Branan has been taken north into the high mountains. Somebody spoke to a messenger from Coria."

"What have they done with the soldiers?"

Silence.

"Are they here?"

"You can do nothing for them. Go a long way away. Go back to Deva with your Roman before Conn takes you too. He does not listen to the old man anymore."

"Are the soldiers still alive?"

The woman hesitated for a moment. "They said if we did not want to watch, we should mind the children."

Tilla swallowed. She felt shaky with exhaustion and fear. "Just tell me where they went."

There was another pause before, "The old hut down toward the stream. But you cannot get there. They will have lookouts."

She had passed that old hut this afternoon with Dismal. It was two or three hundred paces down through the pasture. The sensible thing would be to hurry back to the fort now and summon help. But if she did that, even if the family escaped, they would be hunted down and executed. Besides, even if Daminius survived, when the officers found out that he had helped her to betray one of his own men he would be in just as much danger from his own people as he had been from the Britons. "I thank you," she said, and set off to pick her way across the rough pasture alone.

The lookout had not thought to hide. He was standing by the gate, stamping his feet and blowing on his cold hands. It was a simple matter to creep along by the wall and throw a stone so she could slip past while he looked the wrong way. She was almost annoyed. If this was how her people fought, no wonder they lost.

She bent to summon the dog as she arrived. It ran up to her, pushing its nose into her hand and circling around her, its tail thumping against her skirts. The simplicity of its welcome made her eyes well with tears. Dogs knew nothing of guilt.

Once she could make out the wall at the lower end of the pasture, she heard voices raised in argument. The breeze carried the smell of baking bread. It was not a pleasure. There could be only one reason to bake bread down here and at this hour.

She had never seen the threefold death take place, but everyone knew about it. It was something that parents rarely spoke of until their children were old enough to know, but by then it was only one of the many frightening things that the children had already learned about from their older brothers and sisters. *That's what will happen to you if you tell on us!*

When older people spoke of the threefold death, they did so with respect, but with no sign of intent. It was a thing for others. The ancestors. The elders. The chosen. The seers. The courageous and the powerful. She had never dreamed that anyone she knew would dare make it happen. But Senecio was a man who sang to dying trees and shouted at the thunder. She had no doubt that Senecio was serious.

Now that she had moved closer, she could hear that they were arguing over whether to kill both of the prisoners or just Mallius the child stealer. Conn, of course, wanted to do away with both. Senecio and Enica thought the life of the child stealer would be enough.

"And we leave the other one around to betray us?"

She had to stop this before it was too late, and before Albanus reached the fort and brought help. It would not take long to feed the sacred bread and mistletoe to the victims. They would be stripped naked and told to kneel. First came the blow to the head, always hard enough to stun. This was not an especially cruel death. It was not about causing pain to the victim. It was a sacred, awe-inspiring gift of a human life to the gods. Second, the offering of breath as the twisted sinew tightened around the neck. Then the offering of the blood as the throat was slit and the head was held down over the bowl.

If a prophecy was needed, the victim's entrails would be examined for omens. Finally, his body would be offered to the earth: firmly staked down in the wettest patch of ground the gift givers could find. Ideally, where water met land in a bog that never went dry. After a summer like this, there would be no shortage of gift-giving places.

She crept around the outside of the building, testing each step as she picked her way over a jumble of loose stone. The building was ramshackle—she had seen that in daylight—but she could not find any gaps large enough to peer through.

She thought again about running for help. Conn was too bright to leave witnesses alive. Once she was inside, she was a prisoner too, and who would show Albanus's rescue party where to go? Then she had what she hoped was a better idea.

She took a series of short, shallow breaths and thumped on the door with both fists. "Run!" she gasped. "The soldiers are coming!"

The dog, excited, started to bark.

A voice shouted, "Who is that?"

"Darlughdacha, wife of the doctor! I have seen men from the fort! Get out before they catch you!"

A sliver of orange light appeared, widening as the door was dragged open across the dirt floor. The crowded gloom of the hut smelled of fresh bread, old animal droppings, and fear. People parted to let her approach the fire.

"You must get away!" she cried, glancing from face to face and trying to make each person think she was talking especially to them. On one side stood men she guessed were Conn's friends. On the other, familiar faces from the farm. "I have seen them on the road! They will be here at any moment!"

There was a murmur of anxiety, people looking to each other, to Conn, to the old man.

Senecio was in his chair, and Conn had moved forward to take charge. Now he nodded to one of the men, who got up and left. Enica glanced up from where she was crouched over the bread on the griddle. She did not meet Tilla's gaze. Tilla noticed that the dog had followed her into the warmth.

She saw Daminius and Mallius now, lying on the far side of the fire.

Their arms were tied. Their eyes looked blank. She supposed they were drugged. She stepped up to Conn. "While your man goes to look, the soldiers are getting closer!"

He pushed her aside and turned to address the men. "Take no notice!" he ordered. "This woman is a liar like her mother before her. She says whatever suits her at the time. She is trying to stop the offering."

Tilla said, "If you kill these men, even if you escape, the army will hunt you and your families down and crucify you all."

"She told me my brother was with a slave trader!" Conn too was trying to convince the onlookers. "She said he would be brought back soon. It was a lie. She is working for the Romans."

"I was told—"

"How will any of us get Branan back from the far mountains? We have no peace with those tribes and the soldiers dare not go up there."

She said, "My husband has gone after him."

Nobody looked impressed. Daminius was looking around as if he were trying to make sense of what was happening. A streak of dribble glistened at the side of his mouth. Either he was drooling or he had spat something out.

"I was taken to the far mountains," Tilla reminded them. "I came back."

"You were not nine winters old," Conn pointed out, and there was a murmur of agreement.

She needed to keep him talking. She could do nothing more. Soon they would know for certain that she had lied about the soldiers. Albanus could not possibly have hobbled as far as the fort yet. She said, "You will not get Branan back if you are all sent to die in the arena for murdering two of the emperor's men."

"So the soldiers are not at the door, then?" Conn smirked at his audience. "She thinks we are as stupid as the people she works for." He ordered the men to wake the prisoners up. "We will take the officer first," he said. "The child stealer can watch and see what awaits him."

People craned to see what was happening on the far side of the fire. Some of the men began to kick and slap the prisoners to rouse them, and she saw Cata's sister trying to force Daminius's mouth open while somebody tipped up a jug and water splattered over his face. Someone struck up a chant of "*Wake them up! Wake them up!*"

All this time Senecio had not spoken. She shouted over the chant, "You cannot let this happen!"

He shook his head, and when she leaned closer he told her, "I am an old

man, Daughter of Lugh. I do not have much longer. This offering is the
only thing I can do for my son. If the gods are pleased, they will show us
where he can be found."

So it would be the entrails, then. Or he might prefer to read death
throes. There were many ways of interpreting the threefold death.

Daminius was squirming and gasping for breath. She heard Mallius cry
out in pain.

From somewhere deep in her memory came her husband's voice telling
someone that he could never reason with Tilla because reason was a blunt
weapon in the face of belief.

"Is this why my mam left you?" she shouted. "Because she would not
be a part of things like this? You said, 'No more killing'!"

The chant faltered, as if people had dropped out to listen.

"A life for a life!" Senecio's cry cut through the last of the voices. "I will
have my son back!"

That was when she said it. The thing she had not even been aware of
thinking. "Will you not listen to your own daughter?"

It had been a guess. A tiny suspicion that had taken root. He did not
deny it. He did not even seem surprised. All he said was "This is not the
time, child."

And that was how she knew it was true. On this strange and terrible
night, her Samain prayer had been answered.

"This is the only time!" she urged. "There will be no other time after
this. The gods will turn their backs on you when they see you murder this
man Daminius who was sent to help you. Conn will have to kill me too,
because I will not keep silent. Then my husband and his men will hunt
you all down."

"If it will bring my son back," Senecio said, "I will do this thing. And
you, child—you must decide whether you are with your father and your
brothers, or with your Roman husband."

"For what? Is this what you want Branan to come home to? Burned
houses and memories and ghosts?" She knelt beside his chair. "Am I worth
less to you because I was not raised in your home? Or because I am a
woman? Will you lose your only daughter too?"

"Enough!" Conn roared, seizing Tilla by the arm and dragging her away
from Senecio's chair. "You talk too much."

"I am trying to help!"

Conn shoved her so hard she stumbled and fell. He told Enica to get the
bread ready and his men to strip the victims.

"You call yourselves heroes and warriors?" Tilla shouted from the shadows by the hut wall, seeing a dark stain of urine spreading on the front of Mallius's tunic as they cut his bonds ready to drag off his clothes. "You cowards torment two helpless men while a real warrior has gone to rescue Branan! Why are you not riding to join him? Why—"

But nobody was listening to her, because the door had crashed open and a voice was yelling in British with a Roman accent, "Nobody is to move!"

70

TOO LATE, RUSO realized he had just scooped up somebody else's son in an enormous hug. He was not given to displays of affection; the closest physical contact he usually had with children was when his nieces and nephews leapt on him uninvited. And now here he was, with a boy helpless in his arms. How long should one hold on before letting go? Branan was surprisingly heavy and beginning to slide out of his grasp. Ruso lowered him to the floor, aware that various parts of himself that had stopped hurting were now starting again. He patted the boy on the shoulder, cleared his throat, and said, "I'm glad you're safe."

Branan retreated to a safe distance and peered at Ruso's battered face in the lamplight with unashamed curiosity. Then the boy said, "Are you not going to thank me for rescuing you?"

Ruso sat down on the bed, hoping the room would stop dancing around him. "Did you?"

"I shouted at them not to hurt you," Branan explained. "I kept on shouting, 'Help me, I've been stolen!' and the horrible man with the furs round his neck said he would slit my tongue if I didn't shut up. And then a lady said, 'Are you the missing boy?' and I said, 'I'm Branan,' so she started telling everybody who I was. And then most of them stopped hitting you."

"Then I thank you very much," he said, trying to focus on the boy's face and remind himself that his jaw was not broken: It was only tooth-ache. "Very much indeed."

Branan bowed his head graciously. At that moment an orderly poked his head around the door and asked if he could come in. He turned out to be the advance guard for a squad of hospital staff who all wanted to see the famous Branan. "Everybody knows about you," they told him. A couple of them pressed small gifts into his hand. One was a honey cake.

The boy grinned, showing the gap in his teeth. Ruso thought he had never seen such a fine sight.

"Shall we go home now?"

"I'll see to it," Ruso promised.

Ruso was aware that he was behaving just like his most annoying patients: the sort who had no time for doctors, always wanted to do too much too soon, and refused to listen to advice. At last, he felt, Pertinax had a reason to be proud of him. The man himself could not have done a better job of complaining about his confinement. Finally the local doctor agreed to let him leave on the first carriage that would take him tomorrow morning, but only after Ruso had promised that nobody here would be blamed if he dropped dead on the road. "The only other problem is," Ruso confessed, "I've got no money."

"We'll club together," the medic assured him. "It'll be worth it to get rid of you."

Ruso attempted a smile and wished he hadn't. He suspected it came out as more of a lopsided leer. Then, remembering, he said, "I left a lame horse at the inn."

"They'll sort it out. It's a decent place. They would have helped you get the boy back if you'd asked."

"I didn't know who to trust."

"No?" The medic grinned. "Welcome to the border, soldier."

71

THERE WAS A collective gasp and a shuffle of confusion as people fell over each other in their haste to get away from the door. Tilla heard the word "Traitor!" breathed in her ear.

"Nobody move!" yelled the soldier again. "Give us our men!"

Tilla heard the swish of swords being drawn, and Conn's command of "No weapons!"

Her opinion of him rose. In a confined space like this, weapons were useless. They might hold the soldiers at bay, but he would know that none of his people could escape even if they broke the walls down. The soldiers were not fools. They would have the place surrounded. The doorway was wide enough only to show a couple of iron helmets in silhouette, but there were torches blazing outside in other hands. The dim-witted look-out and the man sent after the soldiers must have been captured.

"Give us our men! Now!"

Daminius and Mallius were staggering to their feet, Mallius pulling down the tunic Conn's people had tried to tear off him.

Tilla did not recognize the voice of the soldier. She had no idea what he knew or how they had found this place so soon. But she knew that if she did not think of something quickly, then everything she had feared would come to pass. Mallius would tell them he had been lured into a trap and leave out the reason why. Daminius would be punished for his part in it, Senecio's family would be executed, and her husband would be disgraced by the shame of a treacherous wife.

Daminius was wiping his mouth and straightening his damp clothing. Pushing a couple of Conn's men aside, she moved into the firelight and took him by the arm. "Let me help you, sir," she suggested. "The Samain beer was stronger than you thought. My brother should have warned you."

Mallius stumbled across to the doorway, flailing his arms about like a drowning man trying to reach land. He was crying out about prisoners and ghosts and murder and cannibals.

"Too much beer," said Tilla for the soldiers' benefit. "He can hardly speak."

She spoke to Conn in British. She dared not say anything secret: Some of the legionaries were Britons and would understand. "I told you not to let them drink so much, brother," she said. "Now look. One of them has wet himself and they are both in trouble with their officers, and it is all your fault."

To Daminius she said, "I am sorry, sir. I should not have invited you. I did not know your friends would be worried about you."

"Shouldn't have accepted," Daminius told her, his voice slurred. "Big mistake. Big, big—"

"Out!" came the order from the door.

"Yes, sir," Daminius agreed, but instead of stepping forward he tottered sideways and put his arm around Conn's neck. "Can you tell'im from me," he said to Tilla, "we mus' do this again sometime. I'll 'range the same sort of thing f'r'im at my place." Then he lifted up the little phallus from around his neck and kissed it before shambling toward his rescuers with the words, "Sorry, sir. Bit of a night out. Lovely people."

72

FIRST THE SHRIEK. Then: "Oh, my boy! My precious, precious boy!"

Tilla slapped down the bowl of cream that was halfway to butter and leapt up from the bench.

Enica was crouching in the gateway, rocking a small figure in her arms. Senecio was lurching toward them, the tip of his stick clacking and sliding on the cobbles.

"I saved the doctor, Mam!" Branan cried from the safety of his mother's embrace. "I saved him and I'm famous and they gave me presents!"

"My son!" Senecio threw his stick aside. Together he and Enica engulfed the boy.

"Did you miss me?" came a muffled voice from within the huddle. "Is the dog here?"

Tilla closed her eyes. She had thought she would dance with joy when—if—the good news came. Instead she found she was trembling. She was relieved. But oh, so very tired. All the lost sleep drifted toward her and bade her welcome, and she had to force her eyes open so as not to topple over.

There were other figures in the yard now. Shouts of delight. Weeping. Children leaping about and two of them spinning each other round in dizzying circles. The dog barking and jumping up at the growing family group and finally being dragged into it by a small arm.

Beyond them she saw a man who seemed to be moving with extreme care, as if his limbs might detach themselves at any moment. She recognized the figure and the hair, but neither the gait nor the face was right. He paused to watch the ecstatic crowd in the gateway. Then he turned and started back the way he had come.

"Husband!" she cried, edging round the family and lifting her skirts to step over the wagging tail of the dog. "Husband! It is me!"

Ruso wanted to walk back to the fort, but Tilla persuaded him to stop at Ria's, where she and Albanus helped him up to the loft bedroom. Albanus gallantly retreated, murmuring that the doctor did not need to hear any bad news at the moment, and left her to tend his injuries and administer poppy tears to ease the pain. Virana was keen to assist, but crying, "Oh, don't hurt him!" every time the patient winced was not the kind of help Tilla needed. Instead Virana was sent to the fort to let Centurion Fabius know that the boy was safe and that if they wanted the Medicus, they would have to send a vehicle and some of the hospital staff to fetch him. When the girl had gone, Tilla tried to tell her husband the new story of her life: that Senecio was her real father. It was thrilling and frightening at the same time, as if the ground of her past had shifted underneath her. He mumbled vaguely, "That's nice," and drifted off to sleep. She tried not to feel disappointed.

A while later Virana brought a reply. Centurion Fabius was delighted that the boy was found and he hoped the doctor would feel better soon. Meanwhile, what was the best cure for white spots on the tongue?

Valens arrived and woke Tilla's patient with a jug of very expensive wine which he had managed to smuggle past Ria. He brought good wishes from the hospital, said that the stitching wasn't too bad for a first attempt, and wanted to know when Ruso would be back at work. It seemed Valens's father-in-law was convinced that Valens was withholding crutches as part of a personal quarrel. The pharmacist had fallen out with the new clerk, the assistant said the carpenter was useless, and Fabius had got his hands on a scroll full of new diseases.

To which her husband replied, "I think I'll be sick for a very long time."

He wanted to talk to Albanus. She tried to suggest that he had some sleep first, but he insisted. So she had to tell him about Mallius being afraid of the pretend ghost of Candidus. When she had finished, he looked exhausted. All the joy at finding Branan seemed to have drained away. "I will send Albanus up," she promised, "but not for long."

She found Albanus seated at a corner table with Virana. The girl had placed a plump hand over his skinny one and was gazing deep into his eyes.

"What a shame!" Virana said as they watched him climb up into the loft. "He's such a kind man, even if he is too thin and not very handsome. I told him his nephew helped me light the lamps and I thought he was going to cry."

Anything else she might have said was cut short by Ria wanting to know whether the vegetables were going to chop themselves or whether Virana might like to join in. Tilla, aware that she had taken the girl away from her duties, offered to help. That was how she was in the back room wielding a knife when Ria strode in to announce that now a tribune had arrived wanting to visit the Medicus, and how many more soldiers were going to be tramping their muddy boots through her back room?

Tilla tipped a pile of shredded cabbage into the pot. "Did he buy a drink?"

Ria had to admit that he had.

Tilla put the knife down and wiped her hands. "I'll see to him."

Virana said, "Has that nice Albanus come down yet?"

"Is that nice Albanus any good at chopping onions?" demanded Ria.

Virana said she did not expect so.

"Then he's no concern of yours, girl."

Tilla was glad Accius had come. It would remind her husband of the good thing he had done, and take his mind off his failure to protect Candidus. She told Accius that her husband was not well enough to answer questions, then waited in the background, rolling laundered bandages along her lap and folding clothes that did not need folding. Finally she had a chance to offer the version of last night's events that she wanted the tribune to hear. In return he told her he was arranging for Branan to take a look at Mallius and see if he was the kidnapper. He said nothing at all about the wall or what might be hidden inside it.

Only when they were alone again did her husband give Tilla a look whose meaning she recognized in spite of the black eye and the swelling.

"I am not sure the tribune believed Mallius saw a ghost," she admitted.

"I'm not sure he believed any of it," Ruso said, his voice still sounding odd because he was trying not to move his jaw.

She leaned over and kissed his forehead.

"Ow."

"I may have left a few things out," she admitted. "But he does not need to know them. Two soldiers went out with me last night to visit a patient, one of them thought he saw a ghost on the way, and then I invited them to the Samain celebration at the farm."

"You expect Accius to believe that you invited a murder suspect to a party? And that party was being given by a family whose son was missing?"

She shrugged. "Accius expects me to believe there is no body in the emperor's wall."

Instead of replying, Ruso reached for the cup of water beside the bed, then eased himself down and closed his good eye. "I'm going to sleep," he told her. "Don't wake me up until somebody else has sorted out this mess."

Moments later she heard, "Did I dream it, or did you tell me that you think the old man is your father?"

"It seems there was much my mother did not tell me."

"So Branan is your brother?"

"As is Conn."

He gave a grunt that might have been amazement, or disbelief, or simple exhaustion. "I think I'm glad for you."

She said, "I think I am glad too. But it feels very strange."

In reply there was only a soft snore.

She went down to the bar to tell Ria that she and her husband both needed to sleep and they could not accept any more visitors, but another one arrived while she was there.

Aemilia.

Aemilia and her husband were not offended. Not at all. She had not complained about coming all this way for a wedding that nobody had told them was canceled, because everybody had been very busy and she could see that sending a message to a long-lost cousin was not very important. Now they had come across from their lodgings to see that lovely husband of hers and tell him he was a hero but they could not see him because everyone else had already visited and worn him out. Which was a shame, but just another one of those things.

"No it's not," put in her husband, not bothering to look up from his beer. "It's bloody annoying."

Aemilia told him he needn't be so grumpy just because Ria's beer wasn't as good as their own.

"The brewery is doing very well," she told Tilla. "We're expanding. We've left one of our freedmen in charge, but we really can't stay away any longer if there isn't a wedding."

"So tell me," said Aemilia's husband, looking at Tilla over his cup, "is there a body in the wall or not?"

Their eyes met. He was still handsome, if a little more creased around the eyes and thicker around the waist. Tilla wondered briefly what would have happened if she had married him and not the man lying in the bed upstairs. It had been possible, before the Northerners' raid on her family's farm had changed her life forever. Now she could not even answer his simple question truthfully. But neither could she bring herself to lie to him. Instead she offered the biggest distraction she could think of.

"You have not come all this way for nothing," she said. "There will be a wedding. I will ask my father."

Rianorix frowned. "Your what?"

"Senecio," she explained, then paused. These people knew the ages of her brothers. To tell this story was to betray her mother. But then, had her mother not betrayed the man she had married—the man everyone had thought was Tilla's father? But before she could say more, Aemilia asked, "You know, I'm sure Daddy once said something about your mam and a stranger from over in the hills."

"People knew?" Tilla sank back against the wall, feeling the ground of her childhood slip beneath her once more. "What did he say?"

But Aemilia could not remember the details. "It was a long time ago," she said, waving it off with a flick of the hand. "I never thought anything of it."

Tilla looked from one to the other of them. "Why did nobody ever tell me?"

Aemilia's husband poked his forefinger into his beer and hooked something out. "Perhaps the same reason you won't tell me there's a body in the wall," he said.

73

THE REST OF the day of Ruso's return had passed between sleep and pain and, blurring the two, regular doses of poppy tears administered by Tilla. Several times she tried to ask him questions, but when he tried to grasp them they slid away, so he decided to answer, "Yes," to everything and sort it out later. The tribune came back. He wanted to talk about Mallius and Daminius, Tilla and Conn. Ruso could not remember what he was supposed to say, or even exactly what he knew, so he pretended to be more ill than he felt. It was surprisingly easy once you started to pay attention to every little twinge and gurgle. He even began to convince himself until he realized this was probably how Fabius started. At other times he lay alone, hearing distant voices and the clatter of crockery from Ria's kitchen, thinking about what had happened and deciding he must get up. But not just yet. He would just lie here for a moment longer, letting his tongue explore the tender gap where his tooth used to be.

He did not wake until well past dawn.

"Sit down, man. You look as though you should be in your own hospital."

Ruso gratefully lowered the salute and persuaded the muscles that had stiffened up overnight to let him sink back onto Ria's bench. He hoped the legate and the tribune would go away soon so he could tackle the bowl of honeyed porridge that steamed in front of him. He had woken very hungry but unable to chew anything.

The legate said, "I hear you saved the boy single-handed."

"Not really, sir," he confessed. "I had quite a lot of help."

"Well, well done anyway."

"Thank you, sir."

"You'll be pleased to hear that the boy's identified Mallius as the kidnapper. We've got him locked up and the natives seem to have calmed down at last."

"That's good, sir." Did senior officers tire of the bland statements they heard in response to their speeches? Or did they simply ignore them, like the bleating of sheep? At least the man had taken the trouble to visit and congratulate him. It was an honor, and one Ruso wished he felt well enough to appreciate.

Moments later the legate had swept out of Ria's bar on his way to deal with the next crisis. Ruso forced himself not to look longingly at the porridge. The legate had gone, but he had left the tribune behind.

"A word in private, Ruso," said Accius, swinging a leg over the nearest bench and resting his elbows on the table. "This Mallius chap. It's not as straightforward as it might be. He says it wasn't him, he doesn't know anything about anything, the boy has identified the wrong man, he was asleep when the boy was taken, and all he did the other night was mistake a patch of moonlight for a ghost."

"Well, he would, sir."

"The sleep thing isn't a problem. I've reinterviewed everyone and it seems our witness didn't see the face of whoever it was in the bed. There are other candidates."

"And the boy identified him?"

"Oh, that's conclusive. We'll try him for kidnap. But whatever antics your wife got up to the other night didn't really give us any answers about Candidus, and frankly it would be useful to get this thing settled. Nobody wants it coming back to bite us later on. I was wondering if you had any thoughts."

So the legate was pretending to know nothing while his junior dealt with the problem. It seemed Accius was reluctant to risk using torture again, especially now that there was no life at stake. That was something to be glad about. There were men who got a taste for it.

"He'll be executed anyway for the boy."

Ruso shook his head, trying to clear the drowsiness of the poppy, and wished he had not. Then he said, "Do we have the men's records here, sir?"

"They're all back at Deva as far as I know. Why?"

"Just a thought. Can I talk to Mallius?"

"Go to the east gatehouse at Parva. Tell them I sent you."

74

W ARNED BY VALENS that nobody had been allowed in to clean the
prisoner up, Ruso arrived at the gatehouse with his medical case and
a jug of water. Mallius looked as though someone had picked him up by his
chains and swung him round and round the cubicle, crashing him into the
stone walls as he spun. Ruso's own bruising and stitching and black eye—
which he could now open, thank the gods—felt trivial in comparison. At
least the first half hour of his visit was spent washing and examining and
applying salve and bandaging, and in between, Mallius wept and groaned
and insisted that he had nothing to do with anything, nobody believed him,
the boy was lying, they were going to kill him for thinking he'd seen a
ghost, and was there anything the doctor could do to convince them?

"Perhaps," mused Ruso, wiping salve off his fingers and dropping the
cloth back into his case, "it would help if we send for your family."

Mallius's eyes widened. "No! They mustn't know, sir. They would be
heartbroken. It would kill my mother."

"We should contact them before the trial, though," Ruso insisted. "You
should have someone there."

"Please don't, sir. Please."

Ruso sighed and shut the case. "Let's save them the trouble, then. They
won't recognize you anyway, will they?"

"Sir?"

Mallius's apparent innocence was impressive. But then, he'd had plenty of practice. "What's your real name?"

"Real name, sir?"

"It definitely isn't Mallius. His family wouldn't have known you even before you were beaten up, would they?"

The red-rimmed eyes stared into his own for a moment. Then the man slumped back against the wall, all sign of weeping suddenly gone. "I never thought it would do any harm."

Ruso waited.

"It was the slave at the dealer's, right?"

"He recognized you," Ruso told him. "You should never have stopped bleaching your hair."

"I thought he did." He sighed. "I never wanted to hurt anybody. Seven years of no bother, then just when I stop looking over my shoulder, two people turn up out of the past."

"The Legion wasn't the best choice you could have made."

"I was hoping to get a transfer overseas, sir."

"You couldn't join in the first place," Ruso pointed out. "You were a slave. Were you ever freed?"

"I wasn't far off," said the man who was not Mallius. "I had plenty saved up to make a good start in business. And then the new wife came."

The story came out slowly and in a confusing order, but what Ruso managed to piece together was that Mallius had been a trusted slave in a wealthy household until the owner remarried. The new wife took a fancy to him, which left him in the extremely awkward position of having to disobey either master or mistress. He turned the woman down, and she accused him of rape. The new husband, still dazzled by love, believed her. Mallius—whose real name was Agelastus—fled. By some kindness of the gods he happened to be passing a bar when the young man really called Mallius was killed in a knife fight.

"You just happened to be passing?"

"It was a miracle, sir."

Agelastus helped the anxious and illiterate bar owner by writing to the family, explaining that young Mallius had died of a fever and been cremated far from home. In exchange, he was allowed to keep the recruitment letter that was in Mallius's pack. So Agelastus the runaway slave did his best to turn blond to match the description on the recruitment records and became Mallius of the Twentieth Legion.

"And then?"

"It was all fine until Candidus turned up, sir. He remembered seeing me at my master's house. I tried to explain to him why he had to shut up but he thought it was funny."

"Funny?"

"That I'd got away with it for so long." Mallius's hand trembled as he reached for the cup of water Ruso had brought him. "I could just see him telling all his cronies over a game of dice. It was all right for him, but I'd have been executed. All because of an idle little blabbermouth who thought he was clever."

Ruso took a breath. "Is he in the wall?"

Mallius tried to straighten his shoulders. "There is no body in the wall, sir. The legate says so."

"Don't play games with me."

The man slumped again. "I didn't know the kid was watching. When I found out, I had to do something. But I didn't hurt him, sir. I sold him to somebody who promised he would feed him."

"Branan didn't see you hide the body," Ruso told him. "Somebody else did."

Mallius let out a long breath.

"He must have told you that he didn't see anything. Why didn't you just make up some excuse and release him?"

"He was acting scared, sir. He was acting like he was lying."

"He thought he was in trouble for playing a prank on the road," Ruso told him. "What did you do to him?"

The man who was not Mallius was talking to his chained hands now and mumbling. It seemed that even he could feel shame. "I didn't hurt him, sir, I swear. I just told him his house would be burned like that other one if he didn't do what he was told." He looked up. "I was going to let the family know where he was as soon as we were on the way back to Deva. He would have been found."

"He was found," Ruso told him. "No thanks to you."

Mallius sighed and closed his eyes. "Then the trader's slave remembered seeing me before. It was like the revenge of the gods. They give and then they take away again, sir."

Ruso hoped Mallius's philosophy would comfort him where he was going, because if the army did not behead him, then he could well be sold for the entertainment of the crowds at the amphitheater. He might not die straightaway. He might languish in captivity for as long as a year, all the

time building up pictures in his mind of how his death would be
delivered.

"I never hurt him, sir. I wouldn't do that."

It sounded oddly plaintive, as if the man had committed some act of
special kindness. Perhaps, in his own mind, he had. The story of the false
rape accusation was plausible. On the other hand, it sounded suspiciously
like an old Jewish tale Ruso had once heard, and it was just the sort of
story a slave would invent to justify running away. The convenient death
of the real Mallius was either a very lucky coincidence or the cover story
for another murder.

Whatever the truth of this man's tale, it was going to end only one way.

"Sir, can I have something to ease the pain?"

Ruso considered this for a moment.

"I know I don't deserve it, sir."

Ruso opened his case and brought out the poppy, suspecting he was
doing this largely because the effects of his own dose this morning had not
yet worn off. "That's for getting the water up to Pertinax," he said, using
the rounded end of a bronze probe to measure a drop into the cup. A
second drop trembled at the base of the probe and he stirred it in. "And
this is for not hurting Branan."

By the time Ruso got back to Ria's, he was exhausted and the aches had
returned to gnaw at his bones. Tilla was not there. Virana looked up from
serving a jug of wine to Albanus, and Daminius said she had gone out,
which he could have deduced for himself. He blinked at Daminius and
said, "Shouldn't you be on duty?"

"I just dropped by to thank you, sir. It was very good of you."

"Ah," said Ruso, guessing that sooner or later he would remember what
Daminius was grateful for. "It was nothing."

"It's not nothing to us, sir."

Ruso, none the wiser, said, "Good. I'm pleased."

"I promise I'll repay you as soon as we get to Deva, sir. I've got enough
in my savings."

"Good," said Ruso again, with less confidence. The broad smile of
approval from Virana did nothing to restore it.

He promised to join Albanus for lunch just as soon as he had had a nap,
but lunch was long gone by the time he woke up again, and it was halfway
through the afternoon. Tilla arrived carrying a bowl of warm water and a
towel and announced that everything was ready. She told him that all he

had to do was wash, get dressed, and turn up. By way of encouragement, she whipped off all the bedclothes and began rummaging about in a trunk for clean clothes.

He had a worrying suspicion that he knew what she was talking about and that he had agreed to it yesterday under the cheering influence of the poppy. Rather than risk a direct question, he tried, "Remind me of what I did for Daminius."

She pulled his best cream tunic out of the trunk and flapped it vigorously to get rid of the creases. "You have kindly lent him the money to buy Fabius's kitchen maid. It is very good of you."

"But I haven't got any money! If I had, I'd spend it on a kitchen maid of my own."

She eyed him over the top of the tunic.

"That didn't sound quite how I intended."

"You do not have money, but Serena has arrived to visit her father and she always has plenty of money because her father says she does not deserve to live like a doctor's wife."

"So, in effect, Valens's wife has lent money to a man she doesn't know in order for him to buy the slave he was having an affair with?"

"No. She has lent it to you to buy a horse. You have lent it to Daminius."

Ruso groaned. "Is there anything else I've done that I should know about?"

"I did ask you," she said. "You said yes."

"Was I full of poppy?"

"You do remember that we are to have the wedding blessing this afternoon?"

He rolled over to put his feet on the floor so she could not see his face. "Of course. But I don't feel up to a big fuss."

"Just the family and a few friends. I shall be there waiting for you. I will ask Conn to fetch you in the cart."

He did not want to spend time with Conn. "I'll walk."

"It's raining."

"I know."

Ruso suspected he and Albanus made a comical pairing as they limped down the farm track in the rain, one leaning on a stick to support a bandaged ankle and the other shuffling along as if he had aged forty years in the last couple of days. Still, he was glad of the opportunity for an uninterrupted conversation about Albanus's lost nephew, who had failed to realize the danger he was in once he had recognized a runaway slave who did not want to be caught.

When he had finished, Albanus was silent. They separated to skirt around opposite sides of a puddle. Albanus said, "All this has caused you a great deal of trouble, sir."

Ruso opened his mouth to assure him it was no trouble at all, but the words would not make their way past the dull ache in his jaw. Instead he said, "If he were my nephew, I'm sure you'd have done the same." Albanus, without the distraction of Tilla, would probably have dealt with it in a much more professional manner. He said, "I'm sorry it ended the way it did."

"Thank you, sir." But Albanus had further apologies to make. He seemed to think he was entirely responsible for the ghost escapade, since he had failed to strangle the plan at birth, and when it all went wrong—as he had anticipated—he had then sat nursing a sprained ankle and sent Tilla off into the night alone.

"I thought it was a bad idea from the start, sir, but your wife was very keen, and I thought I'd better try and help. But I didn't."

"Don't worry," Ruso assured him. "I know how persuasive my wife can be." He squinted through the drizzle, assessing how much farther they had to walk. "I hope you don't mind coming to a thing like this when you've just had bad news."

"That's quite all right, sir. I'm glad to be asked. Weddings are always cheerful."

Something else occurred to Ruso as they passed the leaf-spattered fork in the track and turned in amongst the trees. "You never did tell me what happened to—"

"Hah!" interrupted Albanus, as if he did not want Grata's name mentioned. "A fat old merchant flaunted his moneybags in front of her, sir."

"Oh. I'm sorry."

"She seemed to think he wouldn't last long. She promised to marry me next, but I wasn't sure I liked the sound of that."

Ruso doubted that the fat old merchant would have liked it much, either. He said, "I'm glad you're here."

"I wish I had come sooner, sir."

From up in the oak tree there was a cry of "There you are!" and Branan scrambled down to where the dog was waiting for him.

Ruso glanced across the yard and saw Enica watching her son from the porch. "Your eye looks even worse today!" Branan exclaimed. "Come and show everybody."

75

JUST A SMALL affair, Tilla had said. Just the family and a few friends. The roar that went up as he arrived made him wonder if he had come to the wrong place. Perhaps there was a cockfight going on in there somewhere. Branan gave him a push and whispered, "Go on!"

The air inside the house was vibrant with cheering and heavy with the smell of smoke and wet wool and beer and pork crackling. There were people sitting on skins around the hearth with their knees jammed into other people's backs, and human shapes filled all the space back into the darkness behind the wicker screens.

Ruso was led forward to sit next to Tilla on the bench with the tickly fur, which had been moved nearer to Senecio's chair. Tilla was pink-faced with the heat and unusually demure in a pale green dress he was fairly sure he hadn't seen before. Her hair was swept up into some sort of complicated knot and adorned with what he at first thought were large spiders but turned out to be flowers. Maybe the poppy was still affecting him.

"Mostly family," she whispered, in answer to his question. "Just a few neighbors."

Ruso gazed round at the unfamiliar faces and foresaw a lot of *You must remember them: You met them at our wedding* conversations.

"The friends are yours," she added.

Someone handed him a brimming cup of beer and said, "Pass it on." As his eyes adjusted to the poor light he could make out Aemilia and her husband. Conn and the other people from the farm. Virana sitting awkwardly next to Ria. Enica by the door, where she could see if Branan tried to leave. He thought he recognized the baker from outside the fort, and then, over by the wall, behind all these natives, he found himself looking at Accius and Daminius with Gallus from the hospital, standing upright in full parade kit and looking deeply uncomfortable. Daminius in particular looked as though he would rather be almost anywhere else. Ruso assumed Tilla had invited him by way of apology for whatever had happened last night, but it might have been kinder to leave him alone. Fabius, he supposed, was too ill to leave the fort.

Senecio heaved himself to his feet almost unnoticed and said, "Friends!" This brought on a chorus of "Shh!" and "Stop shushing, we can't hear!"

"Friends," he said, indicating the bride, "this is my precious daughter, Darlughdacha, whom the gods have sent home to me at last. She is even more beautiful and brave than her mother, so already we have enjoyed several arguments." He paused to let the laughter die away. "This is Gaius Petreius Ruso, a man of great courage who brought our son back to us. His people and his farm are far across the sea in the south of Gaul. We welcome him into our family."

There was movement over by the door, with more people crowding in and a loud whisper in Latin: "Sorry we're late. You know how long women take to get ready."

Ruso, spying a true friend, stood and beckoned Valens over. Serena, stouter than Ruso remembered, picked her way between the seated guests with obvious distaste. She accepted a beer cup from a grinning native with buckteeth and wild hair and passed it straight on. Ruso wondered if he should thank her for the money.

The next part was as long and tedious as only a Briton—or a politician—could have made it. As Senecio sang the history of Tilla's people from the time they had descended from the gods, Ruso found himself watching the progress of the beer and willing it to come round again. Even Serena relented and took a sip before passing it on. While the locals cheered at the mention of each familiar character, he felt himself starting to nod off.

He was woken by a painful elbow in the ribs. "It is your turn!" Tilla hissed.

"What?"

"Thank him for the beautiful verse about us and tell the story of your people and how we met."

Everyone was looking at him. "Me?" he whispered. "Why didn't you warn me?"

"I did! You said yes!"

It was Tilla who spoke up. "His people do not sing their story," she explained. "They write things down instead."

"Perhaps he will read it to us," suggested Senecio.

Bride and groom exchanged glances. She said, "He has not brought the writing with him."

There was a faint murmur of disapproval.

"That is the problem with writing." The old man shook his head, apparently in pity for the simpletons who had to rely upon the work of pens and styluses. "It has to be carried, and is very easily left behind."

Ruso cast around frantically for something suitable to say. Surely there was some poem that mentioned Britannia without saying how remote it was and how brave the emperor was to go there?

And then he remembered. Of course: Tell the story of your people. He eased himself to his feet, glad his jaw had almost stopped aching. "'I sing,'" he declared, although he was not singing at all, "'of arms, and of the man fated to be an exile . . .'"

The first few lines of the *Aeneid* were schoolboy stuff, but by the time he reached the part about the famously pious man driven to suffering, he was already beginning to falter. With some prompting from Valens, he got as far as bemoaning the heaviness of the cost of founding the Roman race before he ground to a halt. Then he remembered he was supposed to be adding a verse about Tilla, and could not think how to start again.

"'The Trojans were barely out of sight of Sicily,'" continued a voice beside him, "'in deeper water, merrily spreading sail . . .'"

Albanus, the son of a teacher. Albanus, the loyal friend who with luck would know enough of the poem to give him time to think of something to say about his wife.

Albanus was enjoying himself now. The Trojans' merriment had been swept away and they were in the middle of a shipwreck. The Romans present were listening and nodding at the familiar passages. Most of the Britons were listening politely, even if they understood very little of it. Only Virana was fidgeting and shifting about, disturbing her neighbors. Ruso frowned at her, but she was too busy whispering to Ria to notice.

Ruso decided to let the story run until Neptune calmed the storm. That would be a good place to end. He definitely needed to stop Albanus before it became clear that the *Aeneid* was the story of a man who had fallen in love with a foreign woman and then abandoned her to grief and suicide while he sailed away to Italy because he had more important things to do.

The Trojans were still floundering in heavy seas when there was a shriek from the other side of the hearth. Virana was bent over, clutching the sides of her vast belly. "It's coming!"

Albanus faltered for a moment, then pressed on, not wanting to abandon the Trojan sailors in mid-shipwreck.

"It's coming!" Virana cried again. "It's coming now!"

Albanus stopped.

"And then," Ruso declared, placing a hand on his clerk's shoulder, "by a miracle of the gods, one of them found himself on the shores of Britannia! And there he met a beautiful British woman and he—"

"Ohhh! I'm going to die!"

People were shuffling out of the way to let Tilla through. "You are not going to die," she told Virana. "Be quiet. I never liked this poem, either, but it is nearly over."

"And he married her," Ruso continued. "Then the Daughter of Lugh took the new name of Tilla and they traveled together and had many adventures and now here they are."

It was not a grand ending, but the fact that it had ended at all seemed to merit applause and the passing of more beer.

Senecio raised one hand in blessing toward the groom and one to the bride, who was now well out of reach of either of them, helping Virana toward one of the wicker partitions and whispering to the women about lights and water and a birthing stool. "Daughter of Lugh and Gaius Ruso, son of Petreius, may our mighty Brigantia and her land and her trees and her waters look kindly upon you. May there always be warmth at your hearth and plenty at your harvests. May you bring honor to our people and live to see many grandchildren."

The words were kindly meant, and who knew? Perhaps now that they had a local blessing, the British gods would indeed grant them children.

It seemed to be all over. Senecio was leaning back in his chair and smiling fondly at his youngest son, while Virana was wailing and Tilla was calling sharply for more lights.

Ruso leaned close to Albanus and murmured, "Thank you. I didn't know it as well as I thought."

"Nor me," said Valens. "I don't remember some of those lines at all."

"I'm not surprised, sirs," Albanus said. "I had to make quite a few of them up."

Ruso was saying, "But we got away with it," when he heard Conn's voice in British booming above the chatter. "Welcome to the family, Roman!"

"It is an honor," Ruso told him in the same tongue.

"Now you can tell us what we all want to know!" After another shriek from Virana, Conn looked round to make sure his audience was still with him. "Is there a body in the emperor's wall or not?"

Ruso looked at Accius and knew from the expression on his face that he had understood the question.

"Never mind the wall," put in Senecio. "Why did that man steal my son?"

"Breathe with me," came a soft voice from behind the partition. "Breathe with me. You are not going to die. Enica, we need more light here!"

Ruso began, "My wife was right," and from behind the partition came "Thank you!"

There was a ripple of laughter, but Ruso knew that if he got this answer wrong, then he, Gaius Petreius Ruso, would become the man who had undermined the emperor's great project for the province of Britannia. He caught Accius's eye. The scowl was fiercer than usual and Accius mouthed, "No."

"My wife was right to say that Branan was taken because of the rumor of a body in the wall," he continued. "Legionary Mallius murdered one of his own comrades, and when he heard that a boy was claiming to have seen someone hiding a body, he panicked."

"It was hidden in the wall," put in Conn. "You left that part out."

"The rumor said it was in the wall," Ruso agreed. "The rumor also said Branan saw it happen."

"That was a lie."

"Exactly. And now we know where listening to gossip leads."

Albanus was glancing from one to the other of them as though he knew something important was going on but didn't know what. From behind the partition Ruso heard Tilla asking for a knife. There was something in her voice he did not like. Besides, the knife should sever the cord after the baby was delivered, but there was no sound of a newborn cry: just Virana's wailing that she was dying, and sobbing and begging someone to make it stop. Several of the women exchanged glances.

Conn said, "So, is it—"

Ruso placed a hand on Albanus's skinny shoulder. "My friend came many miles to see his nephew being properly and decently laid to rest."

"So is the body in the wall, or not?"

"Conn, stop it!" Enica emerged from behind the partition. She lowered her voice. "Stop all this talk of death: The child has the cord around its neck!"

"Push!" cried Tilla from behind the screen. "Push again now!" and Virana began to make a ghastly groaning, straining noise something like a cow while Tilla assured her she was doing well and to keep going. Finally their voices died away. There was a long and dreadful silence. Some people looked at the floor. Others looked at Conn. There were whispers from behind the partition. People began to stir and mutter to each other. Senecio had both hands clutched on top of his stick.

The scratchy, angry wail of a newborn was almost immediately drowned out by cheering. Hardly anyone apart from Ruso heard Conn say to his father, "We should have killed that bastard Mallius when we had the chance," or Senecio's reply of "The man is hated by them as well as us. One day our people will rise again. Until then we wait. Let them do the dirty work."

76

IT WAS STILL dark when Tilla woke him and said Albanus was waiting. Ruso mumbled, "What for?"

"You must go up to the wall."

Even as he said, "Uh?" he remembered. Albanus had bowed to pressure.
The Legion had decided they could get away with it, and he was too
gentle to insist.

By the time the three of them reached the wall, the night was giving way
to a gray morning of murky drizzle. As Ruso hauled himself up the last few
paces of the slope, Tilla took him by the arm. He did not have the energy
to object. He was surprised and embarrassed by how exhausted he was.

There were two shadowy figures moving about up there. Albanus had
told him to expect the tribune. He assumed the other was a guard, but the
voice that murmured a quiet greeting was that of Daminius.

Accius handed his cloak to Daminius, dug into a bag Ruso had not
noticed resting by the wall, and draped a white toga over his military kit
with practiced efficiency. He pulled up a fold to cover his head and shook
the metal rattle to frighten away any evil spirits.

It was not the usual sort of funeral speech, but this was no ordinary
funeral. It began by swearing all those present to silence in the name of
Jupiter, Best and Greatest. Then it continued:

"In light of the fact that, firstly, there is no visible evidence for the location of Candidus, who is presumed dead, and, secondly, the exact spot under suspicion can no longer be identified, it has been decided to hold this ceremony here this morning in the sight of the gods." He gestured toward the anonymous rows of squared stones. "By tomorrow engraved lettering resembling a centurial building marker will have been created at an appropriate point."

At least Albanus had got some sort of marker out of them.

"Those of us who can interpret the meaning of the engraving will understand its significance."

"Those of us who understand it, sir," put in Albanus, "can be proud that my nephew has the biggest memorial in the empire."

Accius, not looking pleased, cleared his throat, shook the rattle again, and got on with the official rites.

Afterward the toga vanished back into the bag. Albanus asked to be left alone there for a few moments. The others walked down through the wet grass in silence, only Accius pausing to accept the salute of the men trudging up the hill to start the day's work.

77

THE TWENTIETH LEGION finally left for Deva on a blustery day in mid-November. While her husband was busy getting his patients loaded onto transport for the journey, Tilla ran down to the farm to say a last good-bye. When she started to cry, Senecio told her she must go with her husband: What was the point of all that effort to bless their marriage otherwise? But his words were blurred: He was weeping too.

She found Conn down in the bottom field checking on the sheep. "Twenty-three?" he said, asking her to confirm.

She counted, trying to mark their positions as they shifted about. "No . . . yes." They both tried again to make sure. Then she said, "I want you to know something. It was not me who called the army when you took the soldiers to the hut, nor that skinny one who hurt his ankle."

Instead of arguing, Conn said, "I know. Cata's mother said you wouldn't have had time."

"Perhaps they were just passing."

He shook his head. "I think we have an informer. I don't know who it is, but that is not the first time the soldiers have known things they shouldn't."

She started to ask, "But who—" and then realized she did not want to know.

"I'll find out," he promised. "Somebody will be sorry."

"You could try not doing anything worth the telling."

The smile transformed his face.

She said, "And you could try smiling more often."

"You should have met my brother Dubnus. You'd have liked him better."

She said, "I shall learn to like you well enough. Find a wife, Conn. The old man will not last forever, and he wants grandchildren."

"Any more orders?"

"I will be back with more in the spring," she promised.

Pertinax swung himself toward the hospital wagon on his crutches, telling his anxious helpers to stop circling round him like bloody vultures: He wasn't dead yet.

His daughter turned to Ruso and said, "Valens says you haven't bought a horse with my money."

"I'm still deciding," he told her.

"He says you've never bought a horse in all the years he's known you."

"I'm taking some time to choose," he admitted. "I'll pay you back in Deva if I don't go ahead."

Serena shook her head. "You always were indecisive, Ruso. I don't know how your wife puts up with— Not that way, Pa! Turn around! "

Watching Pertinax pause and then shuffle round in a circle to park his backside on the floor of the wagon, Ruso said, "I'm not quite sure myself."

"I don't know how she puts up with that girl, either."

Ruso glanced across the street to see Virana hurrying toward them. Her baby daughter was swathed in a thick golden blanket that had been a gift from . . . he still found it hard to refer to them as "Tilla's family." He was ashamed to say it, but she had been exclusively his for so long that he was jealous.

"Virana's a friend," he said. "She's not coming back to Deva," he added, with no pleasure. "She's going home." He had insisted they stick to her agreed departure date, but no matter how annoying she could be, he would miss her cheerful smile, her willingness to work, and her unwavering loyalty. And Tilla would miss the baby, because Tilla always found it hard to part with babies. She was, in that respect, the worst possible person to be a midwife. She had tried to channel her efforts into medicine for the sick and injured, but the babies kept coming and somebody had to deliver them.

He had no idea what Virana was doing in the fort, or who she had charmed on the gate to gain access. "Is everything all right?"

"I must talk to you, master."

Ruso turned away from Pertinax, who had managed to bottom-shuffle his way into the wagon and was swearing because he had dropped one of his crutches in the street. Ruso now took little notice of his complaining. He had looked Ruso in the eye after Branan's return and said, "Good man." Ruso had left the room feeling three feet taller.

Virana said, "It's about your wedding present for the mistress."

"I haven't organized one yet," he confessed.

"I know. And I have spoken with Albanus, and we both think it is a good idea. But he says I must ask you first because you might say no, and then the mistress would be upset."

He hoped whatever it was would not be expensive. He still had yet to find a way to recoup the cost of all the drinks and pastries the locals had enjoyed at Ria's.

Virana held up the baby toward him. It was, like most babies, small and round and pink. It had wispy dark hair and a thin red scratch on its nose, probably made with its own fingernails. It smelled of milk and baby and nothing else at the moment, and it seemed to be asleep. It was, in short, as good as a baby was likely to get.

"Very nice," he said, because he never knew what to say about babies.

"Your wife loves her very much already. She is no trouble. And if it was not for you, I don't know where I would be."

Tears welled up in the girl's eyes as she was saying something about Tilla finding a nurse for the journey, and when she stopped talking he had no idea what else she had said or what to say in reply. Then she thrust the baby at him and he had to grab hold and press it against his chest for fear of dropping it, which meant that when she ran for the gates he could not give chase. He could only shout, "Virana, come back!"

She stopped, calling, "Will you look after her?"

"Don't go!"

"Will you?"

"We'll bring her to visit!"

Gods above, what was he saying? A man didn't take on a child like he might a stray dog. He had to give it thought, to consider all the options, to find a suitable baby, to make preparations. To talk to his wife, although he already knew what Tilla would say.

"Virana!"

"Albanus will know where to find me!"

The shouting woke the baby up and it began to cry. He was wondering what to do with it when Serena climbed down from the hospital wagon and said, "Well! And Valens swore it was nothing to do with you! Hold its head, for goodness' sake. Don't you know anything?"

The baby was such a shock that he did not tell his wife about the other thing until the wide expanses of the border country were a distant memory and they were almost within sight of the familiar red walls of Deva. Tilla was sitting in the back of a wagon, cradling the baby, and the wet nurse had gone to see her man, who was an armorer with the first cohort.

Ruso said lightly, "The tribune's being recalled to Rome in the spring."

Tilla's response of "Mm" made it plain she did not much care.

"He says he may need a good man."

She looked up. "A doctor?"

"With some other duties. He'll have a big household. He'll be going into politics . . . or whatever they do after they come out of the army and before they get to be senators."

"I hope he finds the right man, then. Politics is not for you."

"It would be a chance to see Rome."

"I have just found my family! And we have little Mara!"

"I know," he said. "We have all winter to think it over."

She kissed the baby's fuzzy head. "Rome is very hot," she warned, in that way she had of talking to the baby when she wanted to say something her husband might not want to hear. "And noisy, and crowded, and smelly. And full of criminals. Would you like to go there?"

"Or would you like to stay in Britannia in the rain?" Ruso asked her.

"It would be leaving everything I know behind," Tilla said.

"We don't have to go."

"But then," she added, "a lot of what I thought I knew was wrong anyway."

Ruso grinned.

"That missing tooth shows when you smile."

"Are you complaining?"

"Never," said Tilla. "Well . . . only sometimes."

Author's Note

An archaeological theory is a fragile edifice, and some of those now standing tall may have been knocked down and rebuilt into different shapes by the time this book goes to print. Despite the splendid wealth of evidence we have from Hadrian's Wall, much remains to be discovered, and even the basic question of what the wall was actually *for* remains a matter of debate.

The area around the wall was probably cleared of locals like Aedic's family when the building project began. There are ruins of native houses in the so-called military zone, but there must have been families like Senecio's who clung on nearby, farming whatever land remained to them and having to deal with the army and the disruption as best they could. Sadly, their names and stories are lost to us. However, the line of defensive ditches now known as the vallum to the south of the wall was put in after the original plan was laid out, which suggests that the locals inside the border may not have been as reliable as Hadrian might have hoped.

The traces of the little fort I have called Parva (we don't know what the Romans called it) can still be seen on the ground, as can the shapes of many of the temporary camps around it, including the one with a stream running through the middle. The line of the wall just to the north was quarried away in the first half of the twentieth century, leaving a spectacular cliff and lake but a dearth of Roman archaeology. However, the wall still stands several courses high where it runs across Aedic's stolen farmland just to the east, and whatever lies deep within its core remains undisturbed.

The threefold death was inspired by the Iron Age "bog bodies" found in various locations across Europe. As usual, we can deduce what the perpetrators did, but we have no idea why they did it, nor what they called it, so I have filled in a few tempting gaps. Since my aim is to tell a story rather than join an argument, I leave to others such debates as the delightfully named "Tunic Wars" about the likely colors of soldiers' clothing. Those who enjoy details will find them in:

Vindolanda Letters Online at http://vindolanda.csad.ox.ac.uk/ or many are available in book form from http://www.vindolanda.com/books;

An Archaeological Guide to Walking Hadrian's Wall: From Bowness-on-Solway to Wallsend (West to East), an eBook by M. C. Bishop, (details of Mike Bishop's books, and much more, may be found at http://perlineam-valli.org.uk/);

Peter Hill, *The Construction of Hadrian's Wall*;

Graham Sumner, *Roman Military Dress*; and

Miranda Green, *The Gods of the Celts* and *The World of the Druids*.

ACKNOWLEDGMENTS

For advice, encouragement, editing, and sound common sense, I'm grateful to the professionals—Peta Nightingale, Araminta Whitley, George Lucas, Lea Beresford, David Chesanow, Morgan Hedden, and the production team at Bloomsbury.

Any factual errors, inventions, and dubious conclusions in the book are all my own work, but there would have been more of them without Ray and Katy Ashford, Mike Bishop, Peter and Jenni Coats, Vicki and Mike Finnegan, and Ben Kane. Thank you, all!

It's many years since I've seen the cement-mixer driver who told me the legend of the body inside the motorway bridge, but Eric, if you read this, thanks for the inspiration.

Finally, I'm grateful to Andy Downie for heroically reading several drafts when it was hard to tell the difference between them.

A NOTE ON THE AUTHOR

Ruth Downie is the author of the *New York Times* bestselling *Medicus*, as well as *Terra Incognita*, *Persona Non Grata*, *Caveat Emptor*, and *Semper Fidelis*. She is married with two sons and lives in Devon, England.

Don't miss the other riveting novels in the bestselling Medicus series:

MEDICUS

Ruso is caught in the middle of an investigation into the deaths of prostitutes in Deva when he rescues a slave, Tilla, from a brutal beating by her master. As Ruso adjusts to Tilla's presence in his life, he must summon all his forensic knowledge to find a killer who may be after him next.

Paperback ISBN: 978-1-59691-427-8 / eBook ISBN: 978-1-59691-774-3

TERRA INCOGNITA

In Britannia, Ruso must try to prove the former lover of his British slave, Tilla, innocent of the murder of a Roman soldier—and the Army wrong—by finding another suspect. Soon both Ruso's and Tilla's lives are in jeopardy, as is the future of their burgeoning romantic relationship.

Paperback ISBN: 978-1-59691-518-3 / eBook ISBN: 978-1-59691-966-2

PERSONA NON GRATA

Ruso has been called home to Gaul and he brings Tilla to meet his family, who are being sued for bankruptcy. Their icy treatment of Tilla is the least of Ruso's worries, however, when the plaintiff in the bankruptcy suit winds up dead.

Paperback ISBN: 978-1-60819-047-8 / eBook ISBN: 978-1-60819-111-6

CAVEAT EMPTOR

Despite our hero's best efforts to get himself fired from investigating the disappearance of a Roman tax collector in Britannia, he and Tilla find themselves trapped at the heart of an increasingly treacherous conspiracy involving the legacy of Boudica, the rebel queen.

Paperback ISBN: 978-1-60819-707-1 / eBook ISBN: 978-1-60819-592-3

SEMPER FIDELIS

Can the mysterious injuries and even deaths plaguing Ruso's men in the Twentieth Legion really be caused by a curse? When the Emperor Hadrian and his distinctly unimpressed empress, Sabina, finally arrive for a long-awaited visit to Britannia, Tilla begins to find some answers—and is marked as a security risk by the Army.

Paperback ISBN: 978-1-62040-049-4 / eBook ISBN: 978-1-62040-050-0

Available now wherever books are sold
www.bloomsbury.com